Short Stories

1896 – 1904

Anton Chekhov

First Edition, 2013

ISBN: 978-1484183588

CONTENTS

AN ARTIST'S STORY

I

It was six or seven years ago when I was living in one of the districts of the province of T--, on the estate of a young landowner called Byelokurov, who used to get up very early, wear a peasant tunic, drink beer in the evenings, and continually complain to me that he never met with sympathy from any one. He lived in the lodge in the garden, and I in the old seigniorial house, in a big room with columns, where there was no furniture except a wide sofa on which I used to sleep, and a table on which I used to lay out patience. There was always, even in still weather, a droning noise in the old Amos stoves, and in thunder-storms the whole house shook and seemed to be cracking into pieces; and it was rather terrifying, especially at night, when all the ten big windows were suddenly lit up by lightning.

Condemned by destiny to perpetual idleness, I did absolutely nothing. For hours together I gazed out of window at the sky, at the birds, at the avenue, read everything that was brought me by post, slept. Sometimes I went out of the house and wandered about till late in the evening.

One day as I was returning home, I accidentally strayed into a place I did not know. The sun was already sinking, and the shades of evening lay across the flowering rye. Two rows of old, closely planted, very tall fir-trees stood like two dense walls forming a picturesque, gloomy avenue. I easily climbed over the fence and walked along the avenue, slipping over the fir-needles which lay two inches deep on the ground. It was still and dark, and only here and there on the high tree-tops the vivid golden light quivered and made rainbows in the spiders' webs. There was a strong, almost stifling smell of resin. Then I turned into a long avenue of limes. Here, too, all was desolation and age; last year's leaves rusted mournfully under my feet and in the twilight shadows lurked between the trees. From the old orchard on the right came the faint, reluctant note of the golden oriole, who must have been old too. But at last the limes ended. I walked by an old white house of two storeys with a terrace, and there suddenly opened before me a view of a courtyard, a large pond with a bathing-house, a group of green willows, and a village on the further bank, with a high, narrow belfry on which there glittered a cross reflecting the setting sun.

For a moment it breathed upon me the fascination of something near and very familiar, as though I had seen that landscape at some time in my childhood.

At the white stone gates which led from the yard to the fields, old-fashioned solid gates with lions on them, were standing two girls. One of them, the elder, a slim, pale, very handsome girl with a perfect haystack of chestnut hair and a little obstinate mouth, had a severe expression and scarcely took notice of me, while the other, who was still very young, not more than seventeen or eighteen, and was also slim and pale, with a large mouth and large eyes, looked at me with astonishment as I passed by, said something in English, and was overcome with embarrassment. And it seemed to me that these two charming faces, too, had long been familiar to me. And I returned home feeling as though I had had a delightful dream.

One morning soon afterwards, as Byelokurov and I were walking near the house, a carriage drove unexpectedly into the yard, rustling over the grass, and in it was sitting one of those girls. It was the elder one. She had come to ask for subscriptions for some villagers whose cottages had been burnt down. Speaking with great earnestness and precision, and not looking at us, she told us how many houses in the village of Siyanovo had been burnt, how many men, women, and children were left homeless, and what steps were proposed, to begin with, by the Relief Committee, of which she was now a member. After handing us the subscription list for our signatures, she put it away and immediately began to take leave of us.

"You have quite forgotten us, Pyotr Petrovitch," she said to Byelokurov as she shook hands with him. "Do come, and if Monsieur N. (she mentioned my name) cares to make the acquaintance of admirers of his work, and will come and see us, mother and I will be delighted."

I bowed.

When she had gone Pyotr Petrovitch began to tell me about her. The girl was, he said, of good family, and her name was Lidia Voltchaninov, and the estate on which she lived with her mother and sister, like the village on the other side of the pond, was called Shelkovka. Her father had once held an important position in Moscow, and had died with the rank of privy councillor. Although they had ample means, the Voltchaninovs lived on their estate summer and winter without going away. Lidia was a teacher in the Zemstvo school in her own village, and received a salary of twenty-five roubles a month. She spent nothing on herself but her salary, and was proud of earning her own living.

"An interesting family," said Byelokurov. "Let us go over one day. They will be delighted to see you."

One afternoon on a holiday we thought of the Voltchaninovs, and went to Shelkovka to see them. They - the mother and two daughters - were at home. The mother, Ekaterina Pavlovna, who at one time had been handsome, but now, asthmatic, depressed, vague, and over-feeble for her years, tried to entertain me with conversation about painting. Having heard from her daughter that I might come to Shelkovka, she had hurriedly recalled two or three of my landscapes which she had seen in exhibitions in Moscow, and now asked what I meant to express by them. Lidia, or as they called her Lida, talked more to Byelokurov than to me. Earnest and unsmiling, she asked him why he was not on the Zemstvo, and why he had not attended any of its meetings.

"It's not right, Pyotr Petrovitch," she said reproachfully. "It's not right. It's too bad."

"That's true, Lida - that's true," the mother assented. "It isn't right."

"Our whole district is in the hands of Balagin," Lida went on, addressing me. "He is the chairman of the Zemstvo Board, and he has distributed all the posts in the district among his nephews and sons-in-law; and he does as he likes. He ought to be opposed. The young men ought to make a strong party, but you see what the young men among us are like. It's a shame, Pyotr Petrovitch!"

The younger sister, Genya, was silent while they were talking of the Zemstvo. She took no part in serious conversation. She was not looked upon as quite grown up by her family, and, like a child, was always called by the nickname of Misuce, because that was what she had called her English governess when she was a child. She was all the time looking at me with curiosity, and when I glanced at the photographs in the album, she explained to me: "That's uncle . . . that's god-father," moving her finger across the photograph. As she did so she touched me with her shoulder like a child, and I had a close view of her delicate, undeveloped chest, her slender shoulders, her plait, and her thin little body tightly drawn in by her sash.

We played croquet and lawn tennis, we walked about the garden, drank tea, and then sat a long time over supper. After the huge empty room with columns, I felt, as it were, at home in this small snug house where there were no oleographs on the walls and where the servants were spoken to with civility. And everything seemed to me young and pure, thanks to the presence of Lida and Misuce, and there was an atmosphere of refinement over everything. At supper Lida talked to Byelokurov again of the Zemstvo, of Balagin, and of school libraries. She was an energetic, genuine girl, with convictions, and it was interesting to listen to her, though she talked a great deal and in a loud voice - perhaps because she was accustomed to talking at school. On the other hand, Pyotr Petrovitch, who had retained from his student days the habit of turning every conversation into an argument, was tedious, flat, long-winded, and unmistakably anxious to appear clever and advanced. Gesticulating, he upset a sauce-boat with his sleeve, making a huge pool on the tablecloth, but no one except me appeared to notice it.

It was dark and still as we went home.

"Good breeding is shown, not by not upsetting the sauce, but by not noticing it when somebody else does," said Byelokurov, with a sigh. "Yes, a splendid, intellectual family! I've dropped out of all decent society; it's dreadful how I've dropped out of it! It's all through work, work, work!"

He talked of how hard one had to work if one wanted to be a model farmer. And I thought what a heavy, sluggish fellow he was! Whenever he talked of anything serious he articulated "Er-er with intense effort, and worked just as he talked - slowly, always late and behind-hand. I had little faith in his business capacity if only from the fact that when I gave him letters to post he carried them about in his pocket for weeks together.

"The hardest thing of all," he muttered as he walked beside me - "the hardest thing of all is that, work as one may, one meets with no sympathy from any one. No sympathy!"

II

I took to going to see the Voltchaninovs. As a rule I sat on the lower step of the terrace; I was fretted by dissatisfaction with myself; I was sorry at the thought of my life passing so rapidly and uninterestingly, and felt as though I would like to tear out of my breast the heart which had grown so heavy. And meanwhile I heard talk on the terrace, the rustling of dresses, the pages of a book being turned. I soon grew accustomed to the idea that during the day Lida received patients, gave out books, and often went into the village with a parasol and no hat, and in the evening talked aloud of the Zemstvo and schools. This slim, handsome, invariably austere girl, with her small well-cut mouth, always said dryly when the conversation turned on serious subjects:

"That's of no interest to you."

She did not like me. She disliked me because I was a landscape painter and did not in my pictures portray the privations of the peasants, and that, as she fancied, I was indifferent to what she put such faith in. I remember when I was travelling on the banks of Lake Baikal, I met a Buriat girl on horseback, wearing a shirt and trousers of blue Chinese canvas; I asked her if she would sell me her pipe. While we talked she looked contemptuously at my European face and hat, and in a moment she was bored with talking to me; she shouted to her horse and galloped on. And in just the same way Lida despised me as an alien. She never outwardly expressed her dislike for me, but I felt it, and sitting on the lower step of the terrace, I felt irritated, and said that doctoring peasants when one was not a doctor was deceiving them, and that it was easy to be benevolent when one had six thousand acres.

Meanwhile her sister Misuce had no cares, and spent her life in complete idleness just as I did. When she got up in the morning she immediately took up a book and sat down to read on the terrace in a deep arm-chair, with her feet hardly touching the ground, or hid herself with her book in the lime avenue, or walked out into the fields. She spent the whole day reading, poring greedily over her book, and only from the tired, dazed look in her eyes and the extreme paleness of her face one could divine how this continual reading exhausted her brain. When I arrived she would flush a little, leave her book, and looking into my face with her big eyes, would tell me eagerly of anything that had happened - for instance, that the chimney had been on fire in the servants' hall, or that one of the men had caught a huge fish in the pond. On ordinary days she usually went about in a light blouse and a dark blue skirt. We went for walks together, picked cherries for making jam, went out in the boat. When she jumped up to reach a cherry or sculled in the boat, her thin, weak arms showed through her transparent sleeves. Or I painted a sketch, and she stood beside me watching rapturously.

One Sunday at the end of July I came to the Voltchaninovs about nine o clock in the morning. I walked about the park, keeping a good distance from the house, looking for white mushrooms, of which there was a great number that summer, and noting their position so as to come and pick them afterwards with Genya. There was a warm breeze. I saw Genya and her mother both in light holiday dresses coming home from church, Genya holding her hat in the wind. Afterwards I heard them having tea on the terrace.

For a careless person like me, trying to find justification for my perpetual idleness, these holiday mornings in our country-houses in the summer have always had a particular charm. When the green garden, still wet with dew, is all sparkling in the sun and looks radiant with happiness, when there is a scent of mignonette and oleander near the house, when the young people have just come back from church and are having breakfast in the garden, all so charmingly dressed and gay, and one knows that all these healthy, well-fed, handsome people are going to do nothing the whole long day, one wishes that all life were like that. Now, too, I had the same thought, and walked about the garden prepared to walk about like that, aimless and unoccupied, the whole day, the whole summer.

Genya came out with a basket; she had a look in her face as though she knew she would find me in the garden, or had a presentiment of it. We gathered mushrooms and talked, and when she asked a question she walked a little ahead so as to see my face.

"A miracle happened in the village yesterday," she said. "The lame woman Pelagea has been ill the whole year. No doctors or medicines did her any good; but yesterday an old woman came and whispered something over her, and her illness passed away."

"That's nothing much," I said. "You mustn't look for miracles only among sick people and old women. Isn't health a miracle? And life itself? Whatever is beyond understanding is a miracle."

"And aren't you afraid of what is beyond understanding?"

"No. Phenomena I don't understand I face boldly, and am not overwhelmed by them. I am above them. Man ought to recognise himself as superior to lions, tigers, stars, superior to everything in nature, even what seems miraculous and is beyond his understanding, or else he is not a man, but a mouse afraid of everything."

Genya believed that as an artist I knew a very great deal, and could guess correctly what I did not know. She longed for me to initiate her into the domain of the Eternal and the Beautiful - into that higher world in which, as she imagined, I was quite at home. And she talked to me of God, of the eternal life, of the miraculous. And I, who could never admit that my self and my imagination would be lost forever after death, answered: "Yes, men are immortal"; "Yes, there is eternal life in store for us." And she listened, believed, and did not ask for proofs.

As we were going home she stopped suddenly and said:

"Our Lida is a remarkable person - isn't she? I love her very dearly, and would be ready to give my life for her any minute. But tell me" - Genya touched my sleeve with her finger - "tell me, why do you always argue with her? Why are you irritated?"

"Because she is wrong."

Genya shook her head and tears came into her eyes.

"How incomprehensible that is!" she said. At that minute Lida had just returned from somewhere, and standing with a whip in her hand, a slim, beautiful figure in the sunlight, at the steps, she was giving some orders to one of the men. Talking loudly, she hurriedly received two or three sick villagers; then with a busy and anxious face she walked about the rooms, opening one cupboard after another, and went upstairs. It was a long time before they could find her and call her to dinner, and she came in when we had finished our soup. All these tiny details I remember with tenderness, and that whole day I remember vividly, though nothing special happened. After dinner Genya lay in a long arm-chair reading, while I sat upon the bottom step of the terrace. We were silent. The whole sky was overcast with clouds, and it began to spot with fine rain. It was hot; the wind had dropped, and it seemed as though the day would never end. Ekaterina Pavlovna came out on the terrace, looking drowsy and carrying a fan.

"Oh, mother," said Genya, kissing her hand, "it's not good for you to sleep in the day."

They adored each other. When one went into the garden, the other would stand on the terrace, and, looking towards the trees, call "Aa-oo, Genya!" or "Mother, where are you?" They always said their prayers together, and had the same faith; and they understood each other perfectly even when they did not speak. And their attitude to people was the same. Ekaterina Pavlovna, too, grew quickly used to me and fond of me, and when I did not come for two or three days, sent to ask if I were well. She, too, gazed at my sketches with enthusiasm, and with the same openness and readiness to chatter as Misuce, she told me what had happened, and confided to me her domestic secrets.

She had a perfect reverence for her elder daughter. Lida did not care for endearments, she talked only of serious matters; she lived her life apart, and to her mother and sister was as sacred and enigmatic a person as the admiral, always sitting in his cabin, is to the sailors.

"Our Lida is a remarkable person," the mother would often say. "Isn't she?"

Now, too, while it was drizzling with rain, we talked of Lida.

"She is a remarkable girl," said her mother, and added in an undertone, like a conspirator, looking about her timidly: "You wouldn't easily find another like her; only, do you know, I am beginning to be a little uneasy. The school, the dispensary, books - all that's very good, but why go to extremes? She is three-and-twenty, you know; it's time for her to think seriously of herself. With her books and her dispensary she will find life has slipped by without having noticed it. . . . She must be married."

Genya, pale from reading, with her hair disarranged, raised her head and said as it were to herself, looking at her mother:

"Mother, everything is in God's hands."

And again she buried herself in her book.

Byelokurov came in his tunic and embroidered shirt. We played croquet and tennis, then when it got dark, sat a long time over supper and talked again about schools, and about Balagin, who had the whole district under his thumb. As I went away from the Voltchaninovs that evening, I carried away the impression of a long, long idle day, with a melancholy consciousness that everything ends in this world, however long it may be.

Genya saw us out to the gate, and perhaps because she had been with me all day, from morning till night, I felt dull without her, and that all that charming family were near and dear to me, and for the first time that summer I had a yearning to paint.

"Tell me, why do you lead such a dreary, colourless life?" I asked Byelokurov as I went home. "My life is dreary, difficult, and monotonous because I am an artist, a strange person. From my earliest days I've been wrung by envy, self-dissatisfaction, distrust in my work. I'm always poor, I'm a wanderer, but you - you're a healthy, normal man, a landowner, and a gentleman. Why do you live in such an uninteresting way? Why do you get so little out of life? Why haven't you, for instance, fallen in love with Lida or Genya?"

"You forget that I love another woman," answered Byelokurov.

He was referring to Liubov Ivanovna, the lady who shared the lodge with him. Every day I saw this lady, very plump, rotund, and dignified, not unlike a fat goose, walking about the garden, in the Russian national dress and beads, always carrying a parasol; and the servant was continually calling her in to dinner or to tea. Three years before she had taken one of the lodges for a summer holiday, and had settled down at Byelokurov's apparently forever. She was ten years older than he was, and kept a sharp hand over him, so much so that he had to ask her permission when he went out of the house. She often sobbed in a deep masculine note, and then I used to send word to her that if she did not leave off, I should give up my rooms there; and she left off.

When we got home Byelokurov sat down on the sofa and frowned thoughtfully, and I began walking up and down the room, conscious of a soft emotion as though I were in love. I wanted to talk about the Voltchaninovs.

"Lida could only fall in love with a member of the Zemstvo, as devoted to schools and hospitals as she is," I said. "Oh, for the sake of a girl like that one might not only go into the Zemstvo, but even wear out iron shoes, like the girl in the fairy tale. And Misuce? What a sweet creature she is, that Misuce!"

Byelokurov, drawling out "Er-er," began a long-winded disquisition on the malady of the age - pessimism. He talked confidently, in a tone that suggested that I was opposing him. Hundreds of miles of desolate, monotonous, burnt-up steppe cannot induce such deep depression as one man when he sits and talks, and one does not know when he will go.

"It's not a question of pessimism or optimism," I said irritably; "its simply that ninety-nine people out of a hundred have no sense."

Byelokurov took this as aimed at himself, was offended, and went away.

III

"The prince is staying at Malozyomovo, and he asks to be remembered to you," said Lida to her mother. She had just come in, and was taking off her gloves. "He gave me a great deal of interesting news. . . . He promised to raise the question of a medical relief centre at Malozyomovo again at the provincial assembly, but he says there is very little hope of it." And turning to me, she said: "Excuse me, I always forget that this cannot be interesting to you."

I felt irritated.

"Why not interesting to me?" I said, shrugging my shoulders. "You do not care to know my opinion, but I assure you the question has great interest for me."

"Yes?"

"Yes. In my opinion a medical relief centre at Malozyomovo is quite unnecessary."

My irritation infected her; she looked at me, screwing up her eyes, and asked:

"What is necessary? Landscapes?"

"Landscapes are not, either. Nothing is."

She finished taking off her gloves, and opened the newspaper, which had just been brought from the post. A minute later she said quietly, evidently restraining herself:

"Last week Anna died in childbirth, and if there had been a medical relief centre near, she would have lived. And I think even landscape-painters ought to have some opinions on the subject."

"I have a very definite opinion on that subject, I assure you," I answered; and she screened herself with the newspaper, as though unwilling to listen to me. "To my mind, all these schools, dispensaries, libraries, medical relief centres, under present conditions, only serve to aggravate the bondage of the people. The peasants are fettered by a great chain, and you do not break the chain, but only add fresh links to it - that's my view of it."

She raised her eyes to me and smiled ironically, and I went on trying to formulate my leading idea.

"What matters is not that Anna died in childbirth, but that all these Annas, Mavras, Pelageas, toil from early morning till dark, fall ill from working beyond their strength, all their lives tremble for their sick and hungry children, all their lives are being doctored, and in dread of death and disease, fade and grow old early, and die in filth and stench.

Their children begin the same story over again as soon as they grow up, and so it goes on for hundreds of years and milliards of men live worse than beasts - in continual terror, for a mere crust of bread. The whole horror of their position lies in their never having time to think of their souls, of their image and semblance. Cold, hunger, animal terror, a burden of toil, like avalanches of snow, block for them every way to spiritual activity - that is, to what distinguishes man from the brutes and what is the only thing which makes life worth living. You go to their help with hospitals and schools, but you don't free them from their fetters by that; on the contrary, you bind them in closer bonds, as, by introducing new prejudices, you increase the number of their wants, to say nothing of the fact that they've got to pay the Zemstvo for drugs and books, and so toil harder than ever."

"I am not going to argue with you," said Lida, putting down the paper. "I've heard all that before. I will only say one thing: one cannot sit with one's hands in one's lap. It's true that we are not saving humanity, and perhaps we make a great many mistakes; but we do what we can, and we are right. The highest and holiest task for a civilised being is to serve his neighbours, and we try to serve them as best we can. You don't like it, but one can't please everyone."

"That's true, Lida," said her mother - "that's true."

In Lida's presence she was always a little timid, and looked at her nervously as she talked, afraid of saying something superfluous or inopportune. And she never contradicted her, but always assented: "That's true, Lida - that's true."

"Teaching the peasants to read and write, books of wretched precepts and rhymes, and medical relief centres, cannot diminish either ignorance or the death-rate, just as the light from your windows cannot light up this huge garden," said I. "You give nothing. By meddling in these people's lives you only create new wants in them, and new demands on their labour."

"Ach! Good heavens! But one must do something!" said Lida with vexation, and from her tone one could see that she thought my arguments worthless and despised them.

"The people must be freed from hard physical labour," said I. "We must lighten their yoke, let them have time to breathe, that they may not spend all their lives at the stove, at the wash-tub, and in the fields, but may also have time to think of their souls, of God - may have time to develop their spiritual capacities. The highest vocation of man is spiritual activity - the perpetual search for truth and the meaning of life. Make coarse animal labour unnecessary for them, let them feel themselves free, and then you will see what a mockery these dispensaries and books are. Once a man recognises his true vocation, he can only be satisfied by religion, science, and art, and not by these trifles."

"Free them from labour?" laughed Lida. "But is that possible?"

"Yes. Take upon yourself a share of their labour. If all of us, townspeople and country people, all without exception, would agree to divide between us the labour which mankind spends on the satisfaction of their physical needs, each of us would perhaps need to work only for two or three hours a day. Imagine that we all, rich and poor, work only for three hours a day, and the rest of our time is free. Imagine further that in order to depend even less upon our bodies and to labour less, we invent machines to replace our work, we try to cut down our needs to the minimum. We would harden ourselves and our children that they should not be afraid of hunger and cold, and that we shouldn't be continually trembling for their health like Anna, Mavra, and Pelagea. Imagine that we don't doctor ourselves, don't keep dispensaries, tobacco factories, distilleries - what a lot of free time would be left us after all! All of us together would devote our leisure to science and art. Just as the peasants sometimes work, the whole community together mending the roads, so all of us, as a community, would search for truth and the meaning of life, and I am convinced that the truth would be discovered very quickly; man would escape from this continual, agonising, oppressive dread of death, and even from death itself."

"You contradict yourself, though," said Lida. "You talk about science, and are yourself opposed to elementary education."

"Elementary education when a man has nothing to read but the signs on public houses and sometimes books which he cannot understand - such education has existed among us since the times of Rurik; Gogol's

Petrushka has been reading for ever so long, yet as the village was in the days of Rurik so it has remained. What is needed is not elementary education, but freedom for a wide development of spiritual capacities. What are wanted are not schools, but universities."

"You are opposed to medicine, too."

"Yes. It would be necessary only for the study of diseases as natural phenomena, and not for the cure of them. If one must cure, it should not be diseases, but the causes of them. Remove the principal cause - physical labour, and then there will be no disease. I don't believe in a science that cures disease," I went on excitedly. "When science and art are real, they aim not at temporary private ends, but at eternal and universal - they seek for truth and the meaning of life, they seek for God, for the soul, and when they are tied down to the needs and evils of the day, to dispensaries and libraries, they only complicate and hamper life. We have plenty of doctors, chemists, lawyers, plenty of people can read and write, but we are quite without biologists, mathematicians, philosophers, poets. The whole of our intelligence, the whole of our spiritual energy, is spent on satisfying temporary, passing needs. Scientific men, writers, artists, are hard at work; thanks to them, the conveniences of life are multiplied from day to day. Our physical demands increase, yet truth is still a long way off, and man still remains the most rapacious and dirty animal; everything is tending to the degeneration of the majority of mankind, and the loss forever of all fitness for life. In such conditions an artist's work has no meaning, and the more talented he is, the stranger and the more unintelligible is his position, as when one looks into it, it is evident that he is working for the amusement of a rapacious and unclean animal, and is supporting the existing order. And I don't care to work and I won't work. . . . Nothing is any use; let the earth sink to perdition!"

"Misuce, go out of the room!" said Lida to her sister, apparently thinking my words pernicious to the young girl.

Genya looked mournfully at her mother and sister, and went out of the room.

"These are the charming things people say when they want to justify their indifference," said Lida. "It is easier to disapprove of schools and hospitals, than to teach or heal."

"That's true, Lida - that's true," the mother assented.

"You threaten to give up working," said Lida. "You evidently set a high value on your work. Let us give up arguing; we shall never agree, since I put the most imperfect dispensary or library of which you have just spoken so contemptuously on a higher level than any landscape." And turning at once to her mother, she began speaking in quite a different tone: "The prince is very much changed, and much thinner than when he was with us last. He is being sent to Vichy."

She told her mother about the prince in order to avoid talking to me. Her face glowed, and to hide her feeling she bent low over the table as though she were short-sighted, and made a show of reading the newspaper. My presence was disagreeable to her. I said good-bye and went home.

IV

It was quite still out of doors; the village on the further side of the pond was already asleep; there was not a light to be seen, and only the stars were faintly reflected in the pond. At the gate with the lions on it Genya was standing motionless, waiting to escort me.

"Everyone is asleep in the village," I said to her, trying to make out her face in the darkness, and I saw her mournful dark eyes fixed upon me. "The publican and the horse-stealers are asleep, while we, well-bred people, argue and irritate each other."

It was a melancholy August night - melancholy because there was already a feeling of autumn; the moon was rising behind a purple cloud, and it shed a faint light upon the road and on the dark fields of winter corn by the sides. From time to time a star fell. Genya walked beside me along the road, and tried not to look at the sky, that she might not see the falling stars, which for some reason frightened her.

"I believe you are right," she said, shivering with the damp night air. "If people, all together, could devote themselves to spiritual ends, they would soon know everything."

"Of course. We are higher beings, and if we were really to recognise the whole force of human genius and lived only for higher ends, we should in the end become like gods. But that will never be - mankind will degenerate till no traces of genius remain."

When the gates were out of sight, Genya stopped and shook hands with me.

"Good-night," she said, shivering; she had nothing but her blouse over her shoulders and was shrinking with cold. "Come to-morrow."

I felt wretched at the thought of being left alone, irritated and dissatisfied with myself and other people; and I, too, tried not to look at the falling stars. "Stay another minute," I said to her, "I entreat you."

I loved Genya. I must have loved her because she met me when I came and saw me off when I went away; because she looked at me tenderly and enthusiastically. How touchingly beautiful were her pale face, slender neck, slender arms, her weakness, her idleness, her reading. And intelligence? I suspected in her intelligence above the average. I was fascinated by the breadth of her views, perhaps because they were different from those of the stern, handsome Lida, who disliked me. Genya liked me, because I was an artist. I had conquered her heart by my talent, and had a passionate desire to paint for her sake alone; and I dreamed of her as of my little queen who with me would possess those trees, those fields, the mists, the dawn, the exquisite and beautiful scenery in the midst of which I had felt myself hopelessly solitary and useless.

"Stay another minute," I begged her. "I beseech you."

I took off my overcoat and put it over her chilly shoulders; afraid of looking ugly and absurd in a man's overcoat, she laughed, threw it off, and at that instant I put my arms round her and covered her face, shoulders, and hands with kisses.

"Till to-morrow," she whispered, and softly, as though afraid of breaking upon the silence of the night, she embraced me. "We have no secrets from one another. I must tell my mother and my sister at once. . . . It's so dreadful! Mother is all right; mother likes you - but Lida!"

She ran to the gates.

"Good-bye!" she called.

And then for two minutes I heard her running. I did not want to go home, and I had nothing to go for. I stood still for a little time hesitating, and made my way slowly back, to look once more at the house in which she lived, the sweet, simple old house, which seemed to be watching me from the windows of its upper storey, and understanding all about it. I walked by the terrace, sat on the seat by the tennis ground, in the dark under the old elm-tree, and looked from there at the house. In the windows of the top storey where Misuce slept there appeared a bright light, which changed to a soft green - they had covered the lamp with the shade. Shadows began to move. . . . I was full of tenderness, peace, and satisfaction with myself - satisfaction at having been able to be carried away by my feelings and having fallen in love, and at the same time I felt uncomfortable at the thought that only a few steps away from me, in one of the rooms of that house there was Lida, who disliked and perhaps hated me. I went on sitting there wondering whether Genya would come out; I listened and fancied I heard voices talking upstairs.

About an hour passed. The green light went out, and the shadows were no longer visible. The moon was standing high above the house, and lighting up the sleeping garden and the paths; the dahlias and the roses in front of the house could be seen distinctly, and looked all the same colour. It began to grow very cold. I went out of the garden, picked up my coat on the road, and slowly sauntered home.

When next day after dinner I went to the Voltchaninovs, the glass door into the garden was wide open. I sat down on the terrace, expecting Genya every minute, to appear from behind the flower-beds on the lawn, or from one of the avenues, or that I should hear her voice from the house. Then I walked into the drawing-room, the dining-room. There was not a soul to be seen. From the dining-room I walked along the long corridor to the hall and back. In this corridor there were several doors, and through one of them I heard the voice of Lida:

" 'God . . . sent . . . a crow,' " she said in a loud, emphatic voice, probably dictating - " 'God sent a crow a piece of cheese. . . . A crow . . . a piece of cheese.' . . . Who's there?" she called suddenly, hearing my steps.

"It's I."

"Ah! Excuse me, I cannot come out to you this minute; I'm giving Dasha her lesson."

"Is Ekaterina Pavlovna in the garden?"

"No, she went away with my sister this morning to our aunt in the province of Penza. And in the winter they will probably go abroad," she added after a pause. " 'God sent . . . the crow . . . a piece . . . of cheese.' . . . Have you written it?"

I went into the hall, and stared vacantly at the pond and the village, and the sound reached me of "A piece of cheese. . . . God sent the crow a piece of cheese."

And I went back by the way I had come here for the first time - first from the yard into the garden past the house, then into the avenue of lime-trees. . . . At this point I was overtaken by a small boy who gave me a note:

"I told my sister everything and she insists on my parting from you," I read. "I could not wound her by disobeying. God will give you happiness. Forgive me. If only you knew how bitterly my mother and I are crying!"

Then there was the dark fir avenue, the broken-down fence. . . . On the field where then the rye was in flower and the corncrakes were calling, now there were cows and hobbled horses. On the slope there were bright green patches of winter corn. A sober workaday feeling came over me and I felt ashamed of all I had said at the Voltchaninovs', and felt bored with life as I had been before. When I got home, I packed and set off that evening for Petersburg.

--

I never saw the Voltchaninovs again. Not long ago, on my way to the Crimea, I met Byelokurov in the train. As before, he was wearing a jerkin and an embroidered shirt, and when I asked how he was, he replied that, God be praised, he was well. We began talking. He had sold his old estate and bought another smaller one, in the name of Liubov Ivanovna. He could tell me little about the Voltchaninovs. Lida, he said, was still living in Shelkovka and teaching in the school; she had by degrees succeeded in gathering round her a circle of people sympathetic to her who made a strong party, and at the last election had turned out Balagin, who had till then had the whole district under his thumb. About Genya he only told me that she did not live at home, and that he did not know where she was.

I am beginning to forget the old house, and only sometimes when I am painting or reading I suddenly, apropos of nothing, remember the green light in the window, the sound of my footsteps as I walked home through the fields in the night, with my heart full of love, rubbing my hands in the cold. And still more rarely, at moments when I am sad and depressed by loneliness, I have dim memories, and little by little I begin to feel that she is thinking of me, too - that she is waiting for me, and that we shall meet. . . .

Misuce, where are you?

MY LIFE

THE STORY OF A PROVINCIAL

I

The Superintendent said to me: "I only keep you out of regard for your worthy father; but for that you would have been sent flying long ago." I replied to him: "You flatter me too much, your Excellency, in assuming that I am capable of flying." And then I heard him say: "Take that gentleman away; he gets upon my nerves."

Two days later I was dismissed. And in this way I have, during the years I have been regarded as grown up, lost nine situations, to the great mortification of my father, the architect of our town. I have served in various departments, but all these nine jobs have been as alike as one drop of water is to another: I had to sit, write, listen to rude or stupid observations, and go on doing so till I was dismissed.

When I came in to my father he was sitting buried in a low arm-chair with his eyes closed. His dry, emaciated face, with a shade of dark blue where it was shaved (he looked like an old Catholic organist), expressed meekness and resignation. Without responding to my greeting or opening his eyes, he said:

"If my dear wife and your mother were living, your life would have been a source of continual distress to her. I see the Divine Providence in her premature death. I beg you, unhappy boy," he continued, opening his eyes, "tell me: what am I to do with you?"

In the past when I was younger my friends and relations had known what to do with me: some of them used to advise me to volunteer for the army, others to get a job in a pharmacy, and others in the telegraph department; now that I am over twenty-five, that grey hairs are beginning to show on my temples, and that I have been already in the army, and in a pharmacy, and in the telegraph department, it would seem that all earthly possibilities have been exhausted, and people have given up advising me, and merely sigh or shake their heads.

"What do you think about yourself?" my father went on. "By the time they are your age, young men have a secure social position, while look at you: you are a proletarian, a beggar, a burden on your father!"

And as usual he proceeded to declare that the young people of to-day were on the road to perdition through infidelity, materialism, and self-conceit, and that amateur theatricals ought to be prohibited, because they seduced young people from religion and their duties.

"To-morrow we shall go together, and you shall apologize to the superintendent, and promise him to work conscientiously," he said in conclusion. "You ought not to remain one single day with no regular position in society."

"I beg you to listen to me," I said sullenly, expecting nothing good from this conversation. "What you call a position in society is the privilege of capital and education. Those who have neither wealth nor education earn their daily bread by manual labour, and I see no grounds for my being an exception."

"When you begin talking about manual labour it is always stupid and vulgar!" said my father with irritation. "Understand, you dense fellow - understand, you addle-pate, that besides coarse physical strength you have the divine spirit, a spark of the holy fire, which distinguishes you in the most striking way from the ass or the reptile, and brings you nearer to the Deity! This fire is the fruit of the efforts of the best of mankind during thousands of years. Your great-grandfather Poloznev, the general, fought at Borodino; your grandfather was a poet, an orator, and a Marshal of Nobility; your uncle is a schoolmaster; and lastly, I, your father, am an architect! All the Poloznevs have guarded the sacred fire for you to put it out!"

"One must be just," I said. "Millions of people put up with manual labour."

"And let them put up with it! They don't know how to do anything else! Anybody, even the most abject fool or criminal, is capable of manual labour; such labour is the distinguishing mark of the slave and the barbarian, while the holy fire is vouchsafed only to a few!"

To continue this conversation was unprofitable. My father worshipped himself, and nothing was convincing to him but what he said himself. Besides, I knew perfectly well that the disdain with which he talked of physical toil was founded not so much on reverence for the sacred fire as on a secret dread that I should become a workman, and should set the whole town talking about me; what was worse, all my contemporaries had long ago taken their degrees and were getting on well, and the son of the manager of the State Bank was already a collegiate assessor, while I, his only son, was nothing! To continue the conversation was unprofitable and unpleasant, but I still sat on and feebly retorted, hoping that I might at last be understood. The whole question, of course, was clear and simple, and only concerned with the means of my earning my living; but the simplicity of it was not seen, and I was talked to in mawkishly rounded phrases of Borodino, of the sacred fire, of my uncle a forgotten poet, who had once written poor and artificial verses; I was rudely called an addlepate and a dense fellow. And how I longed to be understood! In spite of everything, I loved my father and my sister and it had been my habit from childhood to consult them - a habit so deeply rooted that I doubt whether I could ever have got rid of it; whether I were in the right or the wrong, I was in constant dread of wounding them, constantly afraid that my father's thin neck would turn crimson and that he would have a stroke.

"To sit in a stuffy room," I began, "to copy, to compete with a typewriter, is shameful and humiliating for a man of my age. What can the sacred fire have to do with it?"

"It's intellectual work, anyway," said my father. "But that's enough; let us cut short this conversation, and in any case I warn you: if you don't go back to your work again, but follow your contemptible propensities, then my daughter and I will banish you from our hearts. I shall strike you out of my will, I swear by the living God!"

With perfect sincerity to prove the purity of the motives by which I wanted to be guided in all my doings, I said:

"The question of inheritance does not seem very important to me. I shall renounce it all beforehand."

For some reason or other, quite to my surprise, these words were deeply resented by my father. He turned crimson.

"Don't dare to talk to me like that, stupid!" he shouted in a thin, shrill voice. "Wastrel!" and with a rapid, skilful, and habitual movement he slapped me twice in the face. "You are forgetting yourself."

When my father beat me as a child I had to stand up straight, with my hands held stiffly to my trouser seams, and look him straight in the face. And now when he hit me I was utterly overwhelmed, and, as though I were still a child, drew myself up and tried to look him in the face. My father was old and very thin but his delicate muscles must have been as strong as leather, for his blows hurt a good deal.

I staggered back into the passage, and there he snatched up his umbrella, and with it hit me several times on the head and shoulders; at that moment my sister opened the drawing-room door to find out what the noise was, but at once turned away with a look of horror and pity without uttering a word in my defence.

My determination not to return to the Government office, but to begin a new life of toil, was not to be shaken. All that was left for me to do was to fix upon the special employment, and there was no particular difficulty about that, as it seemed to me that I was very strong and fitted for the very heaviest labour. I was faced with a monotonous life of toil in the midst of hunger, coarseness, and stench, continually preoccupied with earning my daily bread. And - who knows? - as I returned from my work along Great Dvoryansky Street, I might very likely envy Dolzhikov the, engineer, who lived by intellectual work, but, at the moment, thinking over all my future hardships made me light-hearted. At times I had dreamed of spiritual activity, imagining myself a teacher, a doctor, or a writer, but these dreams remained dreams. The taste for intellectual pleasures - for the theatre, for instance, and for reading - was a passion with me, but whether I had any ability for intellectual work I don't know. At school I had had an unconquerable aversion for Greek, so that I was only in the fourth class when they had to take me from school. For a long while I had coaches preparing me for the fifth class. Then I served in various Government offices, spending the greater part of the day in complete idleness, and I was told that was intellectual work. My activity in the scholastic and official sphere had required neither mental application nor talent, nor special qualifications, nor creative impulse; it was mechanical. Such intellectual work I put on a lower level than physical toil; I despise it, and I don't think that for one moment it could serve as a justification for an idle, careless life, as it is indeed nothing but a sham, one of the forms of that same idleness. Real intellectual work I have in all probability never known.

Evening came on. We lived in Great Dvoryansky Street; it was the principal street in the town, and in the absence of decent public gardens our *beau monde* used to use it as a promenade in the evenings. This charming street did to some extent take the place of a public garden, as on each side of it there was a row of poplars which smelt sweet, particularly after rain, and acacias, tall bushes of lilac, wild-cherries and apple-trees hung over the fences and palings. The May twilight, the tender young greenery with its shifting shades, the scent of the lilac, the buzzing of the insects, the stillness, the warmth - how fresh and marvellous it all is, though spring is repeated every year! I stood at the garden gate and watched the passers-by. With most of them I had grown up and at one time played pranks; now they might have been disconcerted by my being near them, for I was poorly and unfashionably dressed, and they used to say of my very narrow trousers and huge, clumsy boots that they were like sticks of macaroni stuck in boats. Besides, I had a bad reputation in the town because I had no decent social position, and used often to play billiards in cheap taverns, and also, perhaps, because I had on two occasions been hauled up before an officer of the police, though I had done nothing whatever to account for this.

In the big house opposite someone was playing the piano at Dolzhikov's. It was beginning to get dark, and stars were twinkling in the sky. Here my father, in an old top-hat with wide upturned brim, walked slowly by with my sister on his arm, bowing in response to greetings.

"Look up," he said to my sister, pointing to the sky with the same umbrella with which he had beaten me that afternoon. "Look up at the sky! Even the tiniest stars are all worlds! How insignificant is man in comparison with the universe!"

And he said this in a tone that suggested that it was particularly agreeable and flattering to him that he was so insignificant. How absolutely devoid of talent and imagination he was! Sad to say, he was the only architect in the town, and in the fifteen to twenty years that I could remember not one single decent house had been built in it. When any one asked him to plan a house, he usually drew first the reception hall and drawing-room: just as in old days the boarding-school misses always started from the stove when they danced, so his artistic ideas could only begin and develop from the hall and drawing-room. To them he tacked on a dining-room, a nursery, a study, linking the rooms together with doors, and so they all inevitably turned into passages, and everyone of them had two or even three unnecessary doors. His imagination must have been lacking in clearness, extremely muddled, curtailed. As though feeling that something was lacking, he invariably had recourse to all sorts of outbuildings, planting one beside another; and I can see now the narrow entries, the poky little passages, the crooked staircases leading to half-landings where one could not stand upright, and where, instead of a floor, there were three huge steps like the shelves of a bath-house; and the kitchen was invariably in the basement with a brick floor and vaulted ceilings. The front of the house had a harsh, stubborn expression; the lines of it were stiff and timid; the roof was low-pitched and, as it were, squashed down; and the fat, well-fed-looking chimneys were invariably crowned by wire caps with squeaking black cowls. And for some reason all these houses, built by my father exactly like one another, vaguely reminded me of his top-hat and the back of his head, stiff and stubborn-looking. In the course of years they have grown used in the town to the poverty of my father's imagination. It has taken root and become our local style.

This same style my father had brought into my sister's life also, beginning with christening her Kleopatra (just as he had named me Misail). When she was a little girl he scared her by references to the stars, to the sages of ancient times, to our ancestors, and discoursed at length on the nature of life and duty; and now, when she was twenty-six, he kept up the same habits, allowing her to walk arm in arm with no one but himself, and imagining for some reason that sooner or later a suitable young man would be sure to appear, and to desire to enter into matrimony with her from respect for his personal qualities. She adored my father, feared him, and believed in his exceptional intelligence.

It was quite dark, and gradually the street grew empty. The music had ceased in the house opposite; the gate was thrown wide open, and a team with three horses trotted frolicking along our street with a soft tinkle of little bells. That was the engineer going for a drive with his daughter. It was bedtime.

I had my own room in the house, but I lived in a shed in the yard, under the same roof as a brick barn which had been built some time or other, probably to keep harness in; great hooks were driven into the wall. Now it was not wanted, and for the last thirty years my father had stowed away in it his newspapers, which for some reason he had bound in half-yearly volumes and allowed nobody to touch. Living here, I was less liable to be seen by my father and his visitors, and I fancied that if I did not live in a real room, and did not go into the house every day to dinner, my father's words that I was a burden upon him did not sound so offensive.

My sister was waiting for me. Unseen by my father, she had brought me some supper: not a very large slice of cold veal and a piece of bread. In our house such sayings as: "A penny saved is a penny gained," and" Take care of the pence and the pounds will take care of themselves," and so on, were frequently repeated, and my sister, weighed down by these vulgar maxims, did her utmost to cut down the expenses, and so we fared badly. Putting the plate on the table, she sat down on my bed and began to cry.

"Misail," she said, "what a way to treat us!"

She did not cover her face; her tears dropped on her bosom and hands, and there was a look of distress on her face. She fell back on the pillow, and abandoned herself to her tears, sobbing and quivering all over.

"You have left the service again . . ." she articulated. "Oh, how awful it is!"

"But do understand, sister, do understand . . . ." I said, and I was overcome with despair because she was crying.

As ill-luck would have it, the kerosene in my little lamp was exhausted; it began to smoke, and was on the point of going out, and the old hooks on the walls looked down sullenly, and their shadows flickered.

"Have mercy on us," said my sister, sitting up. "Father is in terrible distress and I am ill; I shall go out of my mind. What will become of you?" she said, sobbing and stretching out her arms to me. "I beg you, I implore you, for our dear mother's sake, I beg you to go back to the office!"

"I can't, Kleopatra!" I said, feeling that a little more and I should give way. "I cannot!"

"Why not?" my sister went on. "Why not? Well, if you can't get on with the Head, look out for another post. Why shouldn't you get a situation on the railway, for instance? I have just been talking to Anyuta Blagovo; she declares they would take you on the railway-line, and even promised to try and get a post for you. For God's sake, Misail, think a little! Think a little, I implore you."

We talked a little longer and I gave way. I said that the thought of a job on the railway that was being constructed had never occurred to me, and that if she liked I was ready to try it.

She smiled joyfully through her tears and squeezed my hand, and then went on crying because she could not stop, while I went to the kitchen for some kerosene.

II

Among the devoted supporters of amateur theatricals, concerts and *tableaux vivants* for charitable objects the Azhogins, who lived in their own house in Great Dvoryansky Street, took a foremost place; they always provided the room, and took upon themselves all the troublesome arrangements and the expenses. They were a family of wealthy landowners who had an estate of some nine thousand acres in the district and a capital house, but they did not care for the country, and lived winter and summer alike in the town. The family consisted of the mother, a tall, spare, refined lady, with short hair, a short jacket, and a flat-looking skirt in the English fashion, and three daughters who, when they were spoken of, were called not by their names but simply: the eldest, the middle, and the youngest. They all had ugly sharp chins, and were short-sighted and round-shouldered. They were dressed like their mother, they lisped disagreeably, and yet, in spite of that, infallibly took part in every performance and were continually doing something with a charitable object - acting, reciting, singing. They were very serious and never smiled, and even in a musical comedy they played without the faintest trace of gaiety, with a businesslike air, as though they were engaged in bookkeeping.

I loved our theatricals, especially the numerous, noisy, and rather incoherent rehearsals, after which they always gave a supper. In the choice of the plays and the distribution of the parts I had no hand at all. The post assigned to me lay behind the scenes. I painted the scenes, copied out the parts, prompted, made up the actors' faces; and I was entrusted, too, with various stage effects such as thunder, the singing of nightingales, and so on. Since I had no proper social position and no decent clothes, at the rehearsals I held aloof from the rest in the shadows of the wings and maintained a shy silence.

I painted the scenes at the Azhogins' either in the barn or in the yard. I was assisted by Andrey Ivanov, a house painter, or, as he called himself, a contractor for all kinds of house decorations, a tall, very thin, pale man of fifty, with a hollow chest, with sunken temples, with blue rings round his eyes, rather terrible to look at in fact. He was afflicted with some internal malady, and every autumn and spring people said that he wouldn't recover, but after being laid up for a while he would get up and say afterwards with surprise: "I have escaped dying again."

In the town he was called Radish, and they declared that this was his real name. He was as fond of the theatre as I was, and as soon as rumours reached him that a performance was being got up he threw aside all his work and went to the Azhogins' to paint scenes.

The day after my talk with my sister, I was working at the Azhogins' from morning till night. The rehearsal was fixed for seven o'clock in the evening, and an hour before it began all the amateurs were gathered together in the hall, and the eldest, the middle, and the youngest Azhogins were pacing about the stage, reading from manuscript books. Radish, in a long rusty-red overcoat and a scarf muffled round his neck, already stood leaning with his head against the wall, gazing with a devout expression at the stage. Madame Azhogin went up first to one and then to another guest, saying something agreeable to each. She had a way of gazing into one's face, and speaking softly as though telling a secret.

"It must be difficult to paint scenery," she said softly, coming up to me. "I was just talking to Madame Mufke about superstitions when I saw you come in. My goodness, my whole life I have been waging war against superstitions! To convince the servants what nonsense all their terrors are, I always light three candles, and begin all my important undertakings on the thirteenth of the month."

Dolzhikov's daughter came in, a plump, fair beauty, dressed, as people said, in everything from Paris. She did not act, but a chair was set for her on the stage at the rehearsals, and the performances never began till she had appeared in the front row, dazzling and astounding everyone with her fine clothes. As a product of the capital she was allowed to make remarks during the rehearsals; and she did so with a sweet indulgent smile, and one could see that she looked upon our performance as a childish amusement. It was said she had studied singing at the Petersburg Conservatoire, and even sang for a whole winter in a private opera. I thought her very charming, and I usually watched her through the rehearsals and performances without taking my eyes off her.

I had just picked up the manuscript book to begin prompting when my sister suddenly made her appearance. Without taking off her cloak or hat, she came up to me and said:

"Come along, I beg you."

I went with her. Anyuta Blagovo, also in her hat and wearing a dark veil, was standing behind the scenes at the door. She was the daughter of the Assistant President of the Court, who had held that office in our town almost ever since the establishment of the circuit court. Since she was tall and had a good figure, her assistance was considered indispensable for *tableaux vivants,* and when she represented a fairy or something like Glory her face burned with shame; but she took no part in dramatic performances, and came to the rehearsals only for a moment on some special errand, and did not go into the hall. Now, too, it was evident that she had only looked in for a minute.

"My father was speaking about you," she said drily, blushing and not looking at me. "Dolzhikov has promised you a post on the railway-line. Apply to him to-morrow; he will be at home."

I bowed and thanked her for the trouble she had taken.

"And you can give up this," she said, indicating the exercise book.

My sister and she went up to Madame Azhogin and for two minutes they were whispering with her looking towards me; they were consulting about something.

"Yes, indeed," said Madame Azhogin, softly coming up to me and looking intently into my face. "Yes, indeed, if this distracts you from serious pursuits" - she took the manuscript book from my hands - "you can hand it over to someone else; don't distress yourself, my friend, go home, and good luck to you."

I said good-bye to her, and went away overcome with confusion. As I went down the stairs I saw my sister and Anyuta Blagovo going away; they were hastening along, talking eagerly about something, probably about my going into the railway service. My sister had never been at a rehearsal before, and now she was most likely conscience-stricken, and afraid her father might find out that, without his permission, she had been to the Azhogins'!

I went to Dolzhikov's next day between twelve and one. The footman conducted me into a very beautiful room, which was the engineer's drawing-room, and, at the same time, his working study. Everything here was soft and elegant, and, for a man so unaccustomed to luxury as I was, it seemed strange. There were costly rugs, huge arm-chairs, bronzes, pictures, gold and plush frames; among the photographs scattered about the walls there were very beautiful women, clever, lovely faces, easy attitudes; from the drawing-room there was a door leading straight into the garden on to a verandah: one could see lilac-trees; one could see a table laid for lunch, a number of bottles, a bouquet of roses; there was a fragrance of spring and expensive cigars, a fragrance of happiness - and everything seemed as though it would say: "Here is a man who has lived and laboured, and has attained at last the happiness possible on earth." The engineer's daughter was sitting at the writing-table, reading a newspaper.

"You have come to see my father?" she asked. "He is having a shower bath; he will be here directly. Please sit down and wait."

I sat down.

"I believe you live opposite?" she questioned me, after a brief silence.

"Yes."

"I am so bored that I watch you every day out of the window; you must excuse me," she went on, looking at the newspaper, "and I often see your sister; she always has such a look of kindness and concentration."

Dolzhikov came in. He was rubbing his neck with a towel.

"Papa, Monsieur Poloznev," said his daughter.

"Yes, yes, Blagovo was telling me," he turned briskly to me without giving me his hand. "But listen, what can I give you? What sort of posts have I got? You are a queer set of people!" he went on aloud in a tone as though he were giving me a lecture. "A score of you keep coming to me every day; you imagine I am the head of a department! I am constructing a railway-line, my friends; I have employment for heavy labour: I need mechanics, smiths, navvies, carpenters, well-sinkers, and none of you can do anything but sit and write! You are all clerks."

And he seemed to me to have the same air of happiness as his rugs and easy chairs. He was stout and healthy, ruddy-cheeked and broad-chested, in a print cotton shirt and full trousers like a toy china sledge-driver. He had a curly, round beard - and not a single grey hair - a hooked nose, and clear, dark, guileless eyes.

"What can you do?" he went on. "There is nothing you can do! I am an engineer. I am a man of an assured position, but before they gave me a railway-line I was for years in harness; I have been a practical mechanic. For two years I worked in Belgium as an oiler. You can judge for yourself, my dear fellow, what kind of work can I offer you?"

"Of course that is so . . ." I muttered in extreme confusion, unable to face his clear, guileless eyes.

"Can you work the telegraph, any way?" he asked, after a moment's thought.

"Yes, I have been a telegraph clerk."

"Hm! Well, we will see then. Meanwhile, go to Dubetchnya. I have got a fellow there, but he is a wretched creature."

"And what will my duties consist of?" I asked.

"We shall see. Go there; meanwhile I will make arrangements. Only please don't get drunk, and don't worry me with requests of any sort, or I shall send you packing."

He turned away from me without even a nod.

I bowed to him and his daughter who was reading a newspaper, and went away. My heart felt so heavy, that when my sister began asking me how the engineer had received me, I could not utter a single word.

I got up early in the morning, at sunrise, to go to Dubetchnya. There was not a soul in our Great Dvoryansky Street; everyone was asleep, and my footsteps rang out with a solitary, hollow sound. The poplars, covered with dew, filled the air with soft fragrance. I was sad, and did not want to go away from the town. I was fond of my native town. It seemed to be so beautiful and so snug! I loved the fresh greenery, the still, sunny morning, the chiming of our bells; but the people with whom I lived in this town were boring, alien to me, sometimes even repulsive. I did not like them nor understand them.

I did not understand what these sixty-five thousand people lived for and by. I knew that Kimry lived by boots, that Tula made samovars and guns, that Odessa was a sea-port, but what our town was, and what it did, I did not know. Great Dvoryansky Street and the two other smartest streets lived on the interest of capital, or on salaries received by officials from the public treasury; but what the other eight streets, which ran parallel for over two miles and vanished beyond the hills, lived upon, was always an insoluble riddle to me. And the way those people lived one is ashamed to describe! No garden, no theatre, no decent band; the public library and the club library were only visited by Jewish youths, so that the magazines and new books lay for months uncut; rich and well-educated people slept in close, stuffy bedrooms, on wooden bedsteads infested with bugs; their children were kept in revoltingly dirty rooms called nurseries, and the servants, even the old and respected ones, slept on the floor in the kitchen, covered with rags. On ordinary days the houses smelt of beetroot soup, and on fast days of sturgeon cooked in sunflower oil. The food was not good, and the drinking water was unwholesome. In the town council, at the governor's, at the head priest's, on all sides in private houses, people had been saying for years and years that our town had not a good and cheap water-supply, and that it was necessary to obtain a loan of two hundred thousand from the Treasury for laying on water; very rich people, of whom three dozen could have been counted up in our town, and who at times lost whole estates at cards, drank the polluted water, too, and talked all their lives with great excitement of a loan for the water-supply - and I did not understand that; it seemed to me it would have been simpler to take the two hundred thousand out of their own pockets and lay it out on that object.

I did not know one honest man in the town. My father took bribes, and imagined that they were given him out of respect for his moral qualities; at the high school, in order to be moved up rapidly from class to class, the boys went to board with their teachers, who charged them exorbitant sums; the wife of the military commander took bribes from the recruits when they were called up before the board and even deigned to accept refreshments from them, and on one occasion could not get up from her knees in church because she was drunk; the doctors took bribes, too, when the recruits came up for examination, and the town doctor and the veterinary surgeon levied a regular tax on the butchers' shops and the restaurants; at the district school they did a trade in certificates, qualifying for partial exemption from military service; the higher clergy took bribes from the humbler priests and from the church elders; at the Municipal, the Artisans', and all the other Boards every petitioner was pursued by a shout: "Don't forget your thanks!" and the petitioner would turn back to give sixpence or a shilling. And those who did not take bribes, such as the higher officials of the Department of Justice, were haughty, offered two fingers instead of shaking hands, were distinguished by the frigidity and narrowness of their judgments, spent a great deal of time over cards, drank to excess, married heiresses, and undoubtedly had a pernicious corrupting influence on those around them. It was only the girls who had still the fresh fragrance of moral purity; most of them had higher impulses, pure and honest hearts; but they had no understanding of life, and believed that bribes were given out of respect for moral qualities, and after they were married grew old quickly, let themselves go completely, and sank hopelessly in the mire of vulgar, petty bourgeois existence.

III

A railway-line was being constructed in our neighbourhood. On the eve of feast days the streets were thronged with ragged fellows whom the townspeople called "navvies," and of whom they were afraid. And more than once I had seen one of these tatterdemalions with a bloodstained countenance being led to the police station, while a samovar or some linen, wet from the wash, was carried behind by way of material evidence. The navvies usually congregated about the taverns and the market-place; they drank, ate, and used bad language, and pursued with shrill whistles every woman of light behaviour who passed by. To entertain this hungry rabble our shopkeepers made cats and dogs drunk with vodka, or tied an old kerosene can to a dog's tail; a hue and cry was raised, and the dog dashed along the street, jingling the can, squealing with terror; it fancied some monster was close upon its heels; it would run far out of the town into the open country and there sink exhausted. There were in the town several dogs who went about trembling with their tails between their legs; and people said this diversion had been too much for them, and had driven them mad.

A station was being built four miles from the town. It was said that the engineers asked for a bribe of fifty thousand roubles for bringing the line right up to the town, but the town council would only consent to give forty thousand; they could not come to an agreement over the difference, and now the townspeople regretted it, as they had to make a road to the station and that, it was reckoned, would cost more. The sleepers and rails had been laid throughout the whole length of the line, and trains ran up and down it, bringing building materials and labourers, and further progress was only delayed on account of the bridges which Dolzhikov was building, and some of the stations were not yet finished.

Dubetchnya, as our first station was called, was a little under twelve miles from the town. I walked. The cornfields, bathed in the morning sunshine, were bright green. It was a flat, cheerful country, and in the distance there were the distinct outlines of the station, of ancient barrows, and far-away homesteads. . . . How nice it was out there in the open! And how I longed to be filled with the sense of freedom, if only for that one morning, that I might not think of what was being done in the town, not think of my needs, not feel hungry! Nothing has so marred my existence as an acute feeling of hunger, which made images of buckwheat porridge, rissoles, and baked fish mingle strangely with my best thoughts. Here I was standing alone in the open country, gazing upward at a lark which hovered in the air at the same spot, trilling as though in hysterics, and meanwhile I was thinking: "How nice it would be to eat a piece of bread and butter!"

Or I would sit down by the roadside to rest, and shut my eyes to listen to the delicious sounds of May, and what haunted me was the smell of hot potatoes. Though I was tall and strongly built, I had as a rule little to eat, and so the predominant sensation throughout the day was hunger, and perhaps that was why I knew so well how it is that such multitudes of people toil merely for their daily bread, and can talk of nothing but things to eat.

At Dubetchnya they were plastering the inside of the station, and building a wooden upper storey to the pumping shed. It was hot; there was a smell of lime, and the workmen sauntered listlessly between the heaps of shavings and mortar rubble. The pointsman lay asleep near his sentry box, and the sun was blazing full on his face. There was not a single tree. The telegraph wire hummed faintly and hawks were perching on it here and there. I, wandering, too, among the heaps of rubbish, and not knowing what to do, recalled how the engineer, in answer to my question what my duties would consist in, had said: "We shall see when you are there"; but what could one see in that wilderness?

The plasterers spoke of the foreman, and of a certain Fyodot Vasilyev. I did not understand, and gradually I was overcome by depression - the physical depression in which one is conscious of one's arms and legs and huge body, and does not know what to do with them or where to put them.

After I had been walking about for at least a couple of hours, I noticed that there were telegraph poles running off to the right from the station, and that they ended a mile or a mile and a half away at a white stone wall. The workmen told me the office was there, and at last I reflected that that was where I ought to go.

It was a very old manor house, deserted long ago. The wall round it, of porous white stone, was mouldering and had fallen away in places, and the lodge, the blank wall of which looked out on the open country, had a rusty roof with patches of tin-plate gleaming here and there on it. Within the gates could be seen a spacious courtyard overgrown with rough weeds, and an old manor house with sunblinds on the windows, and a high roof red with rust. Two lodges, exactly alike, stood one on each side of the house to right and to left: one had its windows nailed up with boards; near the other, of which the windows were open, there was washing on the line, and there were calves moving about. The last of the telegraph poles stood in the courtyard, and the wire from it ran to the window of the lodge, of which the blank wall looked out into the open country. The door stood open; I went in. By the telegraph apparatus a gentleman with a curly dark head, wearing a reefer coat made of sailcloth, was sitting at a table; he glanced at me morosely from under his brows, but immediately smiled and said:

"Hullo, Better-than-nothing!"

It was Ivan Tcheprakov, an old schoolfellow of mine, who had been expelled from the second class for smoking. We used at one time, during autumn, to catch goldfinches, finches, and linnets together, and to sell them in the market early in the morning, while our parents were still in their beds. We watched for flocks of migrating starlings and shot at them with small shot, then we picked up those that were wounded, and some of them died in our hands in terrible agonies (I remember to this day how they moaned in the cage at night); those that recovered we sold, and swore with the utmost effrontery that they were all cocks. On one occasion at the market I had only one starling left, which I had offered to purchasers in vain, till at last I sold it for a farthing.

"Anyway, it's better than nothing," I said to comfort myself, as I put the farthing in my pocket, and from that day the street urchins and the schoolboys called after me: "Better-than-nothing"; and to this day the street boys and the shopkeepers mock at me with the nickname, though no one remembers how it arose.

Tcheprakov was not of robust constitution: he was narrow-chested, round-shouldered, and long-legged. He wore a silk cord for a tie, had no trace of a waistcoat, and his boots were worse than mine, with the heels trodden down on one side. He stared, hardly even blinking, with a strained expression, as though he were just going to catch something, and he was always in a fuss.

"You wait a minute," he would say fussily. "You listen. . . . Whatever was I talking about?"

We got into conversation. I learned that the estate on which I now was had until recently been the property of the Tcheprakovs, and had only the autumn before passed into the possession of Dolzhikov, who considered it more profitable to put his money into land than to keep it in notes, and had already bought up three good-sized mortgaged estates in our neighbourhood. At the sale Tcheprakov's mother had reserved for herself the right to live for the next two years in one of the lodges at the side, and had obtained a post for her son in the office.

"I should think he could buy!" Tcheprakov said of the engineer. "See what he fleeces out of the contractors alone! He fleeces everyone!"

Then he took me to dinner, deciding fussily that I should live with him in the lodge, and have my meals from his mother.

"She is a bit stingy," he said, "but she won't charge you much."

It was very cramped in the little rooms in which his mother lived; they were all, even the passage and the entry, piled up with furniture which had been brought from the big house after the sale; and the furniture was all old-fashioned mahogany. Madame Tcheprakov, a very stout middle-aged lady with slanting Chinese eyes, was sitting in a big arm-chair by the window, knitting a stocking. She received me ceremoniously.

"This is Poloznev, mamma," Tcheprakov introduced me. "He is going to serve here."

"Are you a nobleman?" she asked in a strange, disagreeable voice: it seemed to me to sound as though fat were bubbling in her throat.

"Yes," I answered.

"Sit down."

The dinner was a poor one. Nothing was served but pies filled with bitter curd, and milk soup. Elena Nikiforovna, who presided, kept blinking in a queer way, first with one eye and then with the other. She talked, she ate, but yet there was something deathly about her whole figure, and one almost fancied the faint smell of a corpse. There was only a glimmer of life in her, a glimmer of consciousness that she had been a lady who had once had her own serfs, that she was the widow of a general whom the servants had to address as "your Excellency"; and when these feeble relics of life flickered up in her for an instant she would say to her son:

"Jean, you are not holding your knife properly!"

Or she would say to me, drawing a deep breath, with the mincing air of a hostess trying to entertain a visitor:

"You know we have sold our estate. Of course, it is a pity, we are used to the place, but Dolzhikov has promised to make Jean stationmaster of Dubetchnya, so we shall not have to go away; we shall live here at the station, and that is just the same as being on our own property! The engineer is so nice! Don't you think he is very handsome?"

Until recently the Tcheprakovs had lived in a wealthy style, but since the death of the general everything had been changed. Elena Nikiforovna had taken to quarrelling with the neighbours, to going to law, and to not paying her bailiffs or her labourers; she was in constant terror of being robbed, and in some ten years Dubetchnya had become unrecognizable.

Behind the great house was an old garden which had already run wild, and was overgrown with rough weeds and bushes. I walked up and down the verandah, which was still solid and beautiful; through the glass doors one could see a room with parquetted floor, probably the drawing-room; an old-fashioned piano and pictures in deep mahogany frames - there was nothing else. In the old flower-beds all that remained were peonies and poppies, which lifted their white and bright red heads above the grass. Young maples and elms, already nibbled by the cows, grew beside the paths, drawn up and hindering each other's growth. The garden was thickly overgrown and seemed impassable, but this was only near the house where there stood poplars, fir-trees, and old limetrees, all of the same age, relics of the former avenues. Further on, beyond them the garden had been cleared for the sake of hay, and here it was not moist and stuffy, and there were no spiders' webs in one's mouth and eyes. A light breeze was blowing. The further one went the more open it was, and here in the open space were cherries, plums, and spreading apple-trees, disfigured by props and by canker; and pear-trees so tall that one could not believe they were pear-trees. This part of the garden was let to some shopkeepers of the town, and it was protected from thieves and starlings by a feeble-minded peasant who lived in a shanty in it.

The garden, growing more and more open, till it became definitely a meadow, sloped down to the river, which was overgrown with green weeds and osiers. Near the milldam was the millpond, deep and full of fish; a little mill with a thatched roof was working away with a wrathful sound, and frogs croaked furiously. Circles passed from time to time over the smooth, mirror-like water, and the water-lilies trembled, stirred by the lively fish. On the further side of the river was the little village Dubetchnya. The still, blue millpond was alluring with its promise of coolness and peace. And now all this - the millpond and the mill and the snug-looking banks - belonged to the engineer!

And so my new work began. I received and forwarded telegrams, wrote various reports, and made fair copies of the notes of requirements, the complaints, and the reports sent to the office by the illiterate foremen and workmen. But for the greater part of the day I did nothing but walk about the room waiting for telegrams, or made a boy sit in the lodge while I went for a walk in the garden, until the boy ran to tell me that there was a tapping at the operating machine. I had dinner at Madame Tcheprakov's. Meat we had very rarely: our dishes were all made of milk, and Wednesdays and Fridays were fast days, and on those days we had pink plates which were called Lenten plates. Madame Tcheprakov was continually blinking - it was her invariable habit, and I always felt ill at ease in her presence.

As there was not enough work in the lodge for one, Tcheprakov did nothing, but simply dozed, or went with his gun to shoot ducks on the millpond. In the evenings he drank too much in the village or the station, and before going to bed stared in the looking-glass and said: "Hullo, Ivan Tcheprakov."

When he was drunk he was very pale, and kept rubbing his hands and laughing with a sound like a neigh: "hee-hee-hee!" By way of bravado he used to strip and run about the country naked. He used to eat flies and say they were rather sour.

IV

One day, after dinner, he ran breathless into the lodge and said: "Go along, your sister has come."

I went out, and there I found a hired brake from the town standing before the entrance of the great house. My sister had come in it with Anyuta Blagovo and a gentleman in a military tunic. Going up closer I recognized the latter: it was the brother of Anyuta Blagovo, the army doctor.

"We have come to you for a picnic," he said; "is that all right?"

My sister and Anyuta wanted to ask how I was getting on here, but both were silent, and simply gazed at me. I was silent too. They saw that I did not like the place, and tears came into my sister's eyes, while Anyuta Blagovo turned crimson.

We went into the garden. The doctor walked ahead of us all and said enthusiastically:

"What air! Holy Mother, what air!

In appearance he was still a student. And he walked and talked like a student, and the expression of his grey eyes was as keen, honest, and frank as a nice student's. Beside his tall and handsome sister he looked frail and thin; and his beard was thin too, and his voice, too, was a thin but rather agreeable tenor. He was serving in a regiment somewhere, and had come home to his people for a holiday, and said he was going in the autumn to Petersburg for his examination as a doctor of medicine. He was already a family man, with a wife and three children, he had married very young, in his second year at the University, and now people in the town said he was unhappy in his family life and was not living with his wife.

"What time is it?" my sister asked uneasily. "We must get back in good time. Papa let me come to see my brother on condition I was back at six."

"Oh, bother your papa!" sighed the doctor.

I set the samovar. We put down a carpet before the verandah of the great house and had our tea there, and the doctor knelt down, drank out of his saucer, and declared that he now knew what bliss was. Then Tcheprakov came with the key and opened the glass door, and we all went into the house. There it was half dark and mysterious, and smelt of mushrooms, and our footsteps had a hollow sound as though there were cellars under the floor. The doctor stopped and touched the keys of the piano, and it responded faintly with a husky, quivering, but melodious chord; he tried his voice and sang a song, frowning and tapping impatiently with his foot when some note was mute. My sister did not talk about going home, but walked about the rooms and kept saying:

"How happy I am! How happy I am!"

There was a note of astonishment in her voice, as though it seemed to her incredible that she, too, could feel light-hearted. It was the first time in my life I had seen her so happy. She actually looked prettier. In profile she did not look nice; her nose and mouth seemed to stick out and had an expression as though she were pouting, but she had beautiful dark eyes, a pale, very delicate complexion, and a touching expression of goodness and melancholy, and when she talked she seemed charming and even beautiful. We both, she and I, took after our mother, were broad shouldered, strongly built, and capable of endurance, but her pallor was a sign of ill-health; she often had a cough, and I sometimes caught in her face that look one sees in people who are seriously ill, but for some reason conceal the fact. There was something naïve and childish in her gaiety now, as though the joy that had been suppressed and smothered in our childhood by harsh education had now suddenly awakened in her soul and found a free outlet.

But when evening came on and the horses were brought round, my sister sank into silence and looked thin and shrunken, and she got into the brake as though she were going to the scaffold.

When they had all gone, and the sound had died away . . . I remembered that Anyuta Blagovo had not said a word to me all day.

"She is a wonderful girl!" I thought. "Wonderful girl!"

St. Peter's fast came, and we had nothing but Lenten dishes every day. I was weighed down by physical depression due to idleness and my unsettled position, and dissatisfied with myself. Listless and hungry, I lounged about the garden and only waited for a suitable mood to go away.

Towards evening one day, when Radish was sitting in the lodge, Dolzhikov, very sunburnt and grey with dust, walked in unexpectedly. He had been spending three days on his land, and had come now to Dubetchnya by the steamer, and walked to us from the station. While waiting for the carriage, which was to come for him from the town, he walked round the grounds with his bailiff, giving orders in a loud voice, then sat for a whole hour in our lodge, writing letters. While he was there telegrams came for him, and he himself tapped off the answers. We three stood in silence at attention.

"What a muddle!" he said, glancing contemptuously at a record book. "In a fortnight I am transferring the office to the station, and I don't know what I am to do with you, my friends."

"I do my best, your honour," said Tcheprakov.

"To be sure, I see how you do your best. The only thing you can do is to take your salary," the engineer went on, looking at me; "you keep relying on patronage to *faire le carrière* as quickly and as easily as possible. Well, I don't care for patronage. No one took any trouble on my behalf. Before they gave me a railway contract I went about as a mechanic and worked in Belgium as an oiler. And you, Panteley, what are you doing here?" he asked, turning to Radish. "Drinking with them?"

He, for some reason, always called humble people Panteley, and such as me and Tcheprakov he despised, and called them drunkards, beasts, and rabble to their faces. Altogether he was cruel to humble subordinates, and used to fine them and turn them off coldly without explanations.

At last the horses came for him. As he said good-bye he promised to turn us all off in a fortnight; he called his bailiff a blockhead; and then, lolling at ease in his carriage, drove back to the town.

"Andrey Ivanitch," I said to Radish, "take me on as a workman."

"Oh, all right!"

And we set off together in the direction of the town. When the station and the big house with its buildings were left behind I asked: "Andrey Ivanitch, why did you come to Dubetchnya this evening?"

"In the first place my fellows are working on the line, and in the second place I came to pay the general's lady my interest. Last year I borrowed fifty roubles from her, and I pay her now a rouble a month interest."

The painter stopped and took me by the button.

"Misail Alexeyitch, our angel," he went on. "The way I look at it is that if any man, gentle or simple, takes even the smallest interest, he is doing evil. There cannot be truth and justice in such a man."

Radish, lean, pale, dreadful-looking, shut his eyes, shook his head, and, in the tone of a philosopher, pronounced:

"Lice consume the grass, rust consumes the iron, and lying the soul. Lord, have mercy upon us sinners."

V

Radish was not practical, and was not at all good at forming an estimate; he took more work than he could get through, and when calculating he was agitated, lost his head, and so was almost always out of pocket over his jobs. He undertook painting, glazing, paperhanging, and even tiling roofs, and I can remember his running about for three days to find tilers for the sake of a paltry job. He was a first-rate workman; he sometimes earned as much as ten roubles a day; and if it had not been for the desire at all costs to be a master, and to be called a contractor, he would probably have had plenty of money.

He was paid by the job, but he paid me and the other workmen by the day, from one and twopence to two shillings a day. When it was fine and dry we did all kinds of outside work, chiefly painting roofs. When I was new to the work it made my feet burn as though I were walking on hot bricks, and when I put on felt boots they were hotter than ever. But this was only at first; later on I got used to it, and everything went swimmingly. I was living now among people to whom labour was obligatory, inevitable, and who worked like cart-horses, often with no idea of the moral significance of labour, and, indeed, never using the word "labour" in conversation at all. Beside them I, too, felt like a cart-horse, growing more and more imbued with the feeling of the obligatory and inevitable character of what I was doing, and this made my life easier, setting me free from all doubt and uncertainty.

At first everything interested me, everything was new, as though I had been born again. I could sleep on the ground and go about barefoot, and that was extremely pleasant; I could stand in a crowd of the common people and be no constraint to anyone, and when a cab horse fell down in the street I ran to help it up without being afraid of soiling my clothes. And the best of it all was, I was living on my own account and no burden to anyone!

Painting roofs, especially with our own oil and colours, was regarded as a particularly profitable job, and so this rough, dull work was not disdained, even by such good workmen as Radish. In short breeches, and wasted, purple-looking legs, he used to go about the roofs, looking like a stork, and I used to hear him, as he plied his brush, breathing heavily and saying: "Woe, woe to us sinners!"

He walked about the roofs as freely as though he were upon the ground. In spite of his being ill and pale as a corpse, his agility was extraordinary: he used to paint the domes and cupolas of the churches without scaffolding, like a young man, with only the help of a ladder and a rope, and it was rather horrible when standing on a height far from the earth; he would draw himself up erect, and for some unknown reason pronounce:

"Lice consume grass, rust consumes iron, and lying the soul!"

Or, thinking about something, would answer his thoughts aloud:

"Anything may happen! Anything may happen!"

When I went home from my work, all the people who were sitting on benches by the gates, all the shopmen and boys and their employers, made sneering and spiteful remarks after me, and this upset me at first and seemed to be simply monstrous.

"Better-than-nothing!" I heard on all sides. "House painter! Yellow ochre!"

And none behaved so ungraciously to me as those who had only lately been humble people themselves, and had earned their bread by hard manual labour. In the streets full of shops I was once passing an ironmonger's when water was thrown over me as though by accident, and on one occasion someone darted out with a stick at me, while a fishmonger, a grey-headed old man, barred my way and said, looking at me angrily:

"I am not sorry for you, you fool! It's your father I am sorry for."

And my acquaintances were for some reason overcome with embarrassment when they met me. Some of them looked upon me as a queer fish and a comic fool; others were sorry for me; others did not know what attitude to take up to me, and it was difficult to make them out. One day I met Anyuta Blagovo in a side street near Great Dvoryansky Street. I was going to work, and was carrying two long brushes and a pail of paint. Recognizing me Anyuta flushed crimson.

"Please do not bow to me in the street," she said nervously, harshly, and in a shaking voice, without offering me her hand, and tears suddenly gleamed in her eyes. "If to your mind all this is necessary, so be it . . . so be it, but I beg you not to meet me!"

I no longer lived in Great Dvoryansky Street, but in the suburb with my old nurse Karpovna, a good-natured but gloomy old woman, who always foreboded some harm, was afraid of all dreams, and even in the bees and wasps that flew into her room saw omens of evil, and the fact that I had become a workman, to her thinking, boded nothing good.

"Your life is ruined," she would say, mournfully shaking her head, "ruined."

Her adopted son Prokofy, a huge, uncouth, red-headed fellow of thirty, with bristling moustaches, a butcher by trade, lived in the little house with her. When he met me in the passage he would make way for me in respectful silence, and if he was drunk he would salute me with all five fingers at once. He used to have supper in the evening, and through the partition wall of boards I could hear him clear his throat and sigh as he drank off glass after glass.

"Mamma," he would call in an undertone.

"Well," Karpovna, who was passionately devoted to her adopted son, would respond: "What is it, sonny?"

"I can show you a testimony of my affection, mamma. All this earthly life I will cherish you in your declining years in this vale of tears, and when you die I will bury you at my expense; I have said it, and you can believe it."

I got up every morning before sunrise, and went to bed early. We house painters ate a great deal and slept soundly; the only thing amiss was that my heart used to beat violently at night. I did not quarrel with my mates. Violent abuse, desperate oaths, and wishes such as, "Blast your eyes," or "Cholera take you," never ceased all day, but, nevertheless, we lived on very friendly terms. The other fellows suspected me of being some sort of religious sectary, and made good-natured jokes at my expense, saying that even my own father had disowned me, and thereupon would add that they rarely went into the temple of God themselves, and that many of them had not been to confession for ten years. They justified this laxity on their part by saying that a painter among men was like a jackdaw among birds.

The men had a good opinion of me, and treated me with respect; it was evident that my not drinking, not smoking, but leading a quiet, steady life pleased them very much. It was only an unpleasant shock to them that I took no hand in stealing oil and did not go with them to ask for tips from people on whose property we were working. Stealing oil and paints from those who employed them was a house painter's custom, and was not regarded as theft, and it was remarkable that even so upright a man as Radish would always carry away a little white lead and oil as he went home from work. And even the most respectable old fellows, who owned the houses in which they lived in the suburb, were not ashamed to ask for a tip, and it made me feel vexed and ashamed to see the men go in a body to congratulate some nonentity on the commencement or the completion of the job, and thank him with degrading servility when they had received a few coppers.

With people on whose work they were engaged they behaved like wily courtiers, and almost every day I was reminded of Shakespeare's Polonius.

"I fancy it is going to rain," the man whose house was being painted would say, looking at the sky.

"It is, there is not a doubt it is," the painters would agree.

"I don't think it is a rain-cloud, though. Perhaps it won't rain after all."

"No, it won't, your honour! I am sure it won't."

But their attitude to their patrons behind their backs was usually one of irony, and when they saw, for instance, a gentleman sitting in the verandah reading a newspaper, they would observe:

"He reads the paper, but I daresay he has nothing to eat."

I never went home to see my own people. When I came back from work I often found waiting for me little notes, brief and anxious, in which my sister wrote to me about my father; that he had been particularly preoccupied at dinner and had eaten nothing, or that he had been giddy and staggering, or that he had locked himself in his room and had not come out for a long time. Such items of news troubled me; I could not sleep, and at times even walked up and down Great Dvoryansky Street at night by our house, looking in at the dark windows and trying to guess whether everything was well at home. On Sundays my sister came to see me, but came in secret, as though it were not to see me but our nurse. And if she came in to see me she was very pale, with tear-stained eyes, and she began crying at once.

"Our father will never live through this," she would say. "If anything should happen to him - God grant it may not - your conscience will torment you all your life. It's awful, Misail; for our mother's sake I beseech you: reform your ways."

"My darling sister," I would say, "how can I reform my ways if I am convinced that I am acting in accordance with my conscience? Do understand!"

"I know you are acting on your conscience, but perhaps it could be done differently, somehow, so as not to wound anybody."

"Ah, holy Saints!" the old woman sighed through the door. "Your life is ruined! There will be trouble, my dears, there will be trouble!"

VI

One Sunday Dr. Blagovo turned up unexpectedly. He was wearing a military tunic over a silk shirt and high boots of patent leather.

"I have come to see you, he began, shaking my hand heartily like a student. "I am hearing about you every day, and I have been meaning to come and have a heart-to-heart talk, as they say. The boredom in the town is awful, there is not a living soul, no one to say a word to. It's hot, Holy Mother," he went on, taking off his tunic and sitting in his silk shirt. "My dear fellow, let me talk to you."

I was dull myself, and had for a long time been craving for the society of someone not a house painter. I was genuinely glad to see him.

"I'll begin by saying," he said, sitting down on my bed, "that I sympathize with you from the bottom of my heart, and deeply respect the life you are leading. They don't understand you here in the town, and, indeed, there is no one to understand, seeing that, as you know, they are all, with very few exceptions, regular Gogolesque pig faces here. But I saw what you were at once that time at the picnic. You are a noble soul, an honest, high-minded man! I respect you, and feel it a great honour to shake hands with you!" he went on enthusiastically. "To have made such a complete and violent change of life as you have done, you must have passed through a complicated spiritual crisis, and to continue this manner of life now, and to keep up to the high standard of your convictions continually, must be a strain on your mind and heart from day to day. Now to begin our talk, tell me, don't you consider that if you had spent your strength of will, this strained activity, all these powers on something else, for instance, on gradually becoming a great scientist, or artist, your life would have been broader and deeper and would have been more productive?"

We talked, and when we got upon manual labour I expressed this idea: that what is wanted is that the strong should not enslave the weak, that the minority should not be a parasite on the majority, nor a vampire for ever sucking its vital sap; that is, all, without exception, strong and weak, rich and poor, should take part equally in the struggle for existence, each one on his own account, and that there was no better means for equalizing things in that way than manual labour, in the form of universal service, compulsory for all.

"Then do you think everyone without exception ought to engage in manual labour?" asked the doctor.

"Yes."

"And don't you think that if everyone, including the best men, the thinkers and great scientists, taking part in the struggle for existence, each on his own account, are going to waste their time breaking stones and painting roofs, may not that threaten a grave danger to progress?"

"Where is the danger?" I asked. "Why, progress is in deeds of love, in fulfilling the moral law; if you don't enslave anyone, if you don't oppress anyone, what further progress do you want?"

"But, excuse me," Blagovo suddenly fired up, rising to his feet. "But, excuse me! If a snail in its shell busies itself over perfecting its own personality and muddles about with the moral law, do you call that progress?"

"Why muddles?" I said, offended. "If you don't force your neighbour to feed and clothe you, to transport you from place to place and defend you from your enemies, surely in the midst of a life entirely resting on slavery, that is progress, isn't it? To my mind it is the most important progress, and perhaps the only one possible and necessary for man."

"The limits of universal world progress are in infinity, and to talk of some 'possible' progress limited by our needs and temporary theories is, excuse my saying so, positively strange."

"If the limits of progress are in infinity as you say, it follows that its aims are not definite," I said. "To live without knowing definitely what you are living for!"

"So be it! But that 'not knowing' is not so dull as your 'knowing.' I am going up a ladder which is called progress, civilization, culture; I go on and up without knowing definitely where I am going, but really it is worth living for the sake of that delightful ladder; while you know what you are living for, you live for the sake of some people's not enslaving others, that the artist and the man who rubs his paints may dine equally well. But you know that's the petty, bourgeois, kitchen, grey side of life, and surely it is revolting to live for that alone? If some insects do enslave others, bother them, let them devour each other! We need not think about them. You know they will die and decay just the same, however zealously you rescue them from slavery. We must think of that great millennium which awaits humanity in the remote future."

Blagovo argued warmly with me, but at the same time one could see he was troubled by some irrelevant idea.

"I suppose your sister is not coming?" he said, looking at his watch. "She was at our house yesterday, and said she would be seeing you to-day. You keep saying slavery, slavery . . ." he went on. "But you know that is a special question, and all such questions are solved by humanity gradually."

We began talking of doing things gradually. I said that "the question of doing good or evil everyone settles for himself, without waiting till humanity settles it by the way of gradual development. Moreover, this gradual process has more than one aspect. Side by side with the gradual development of human ideas the gradual growth of ideas of another order is observed. Serfdom is no more, but the capitalist system is growing. And in the very heyday of emancipating ideas, just as in the days of Baty, the majority feeds, clothes, and defends the minority while remaining hungry, inadequately clad, and defenceless. Such an order of things can be made to fit in finely with any tendencies and currents of thought you like, because the art of enslaving is also gradually being cultivated. We no longer flog our servants in the stable, but we give to slavery refined forms, at least, we succeed in finding a justification for it in each particular case. Ideas are ideas with us, but if now, at the end of the nineteenth century, it were possible to lay the burden of the most unpleasant of our physiological functions upon the working class, we should certainly do so, and afterwards, of course, justify ourselves by saying that if the best people, the thinkers and great scientists, were to waste their precious time on these functions, progress might be menaced with great danger."

But at this point my sister arrived. Seeing the doctor she was fluttered and troubled, and began saying immediately that it was time for her to go home to her father.

"Kleopatra Alexyevna," said Blagovo earnestly, pressing both hands to his heart, "what will happen to your father if you spend half an hour or so with your brother and me?"

He was frank, and knew how to communicate his liveliness to others. After a moment's thought, my sister laughed, and all at once became suddenly gay as she had been at the picnic. We went out into the country, and lying in the grass went on with our talk, and looked towards the town where all the windows facing west were like glittering gold because the sun was setting.

After that, whenever my sister was coming to see me Blagovo turned up too, and they always greeted each other as though their meeting in my room was accidental. My sister listened while the doctor and I argued, and at such times her expression was joyfully enthusiastic, full of tenderness and curiosity, and it seemed to me that a new world she had never dreamed of before, and which she was now striving to fathom, was gradually opening before her eyes. When the doctor was not there she was quiet and sad, and now if she sometimes shed tears as she sat on my bed it was for reasons of which she did not speak.

In August Radish ordered us to be ready to go to the railway-line. Two days before we were "banished" from the town my father came to see me. He sat down and in a leisurely way, without looking at me, wiped his red face, then took out of his pocket our town *Messenger*, and deliberately, with emphasis on each word, read out the news that the son of the branch manager of the State Bank, a young man of my age, had been appointed head of a Department in the Exchequer.

"And now look at you," he said, folding up the newspaper, "a beggar, in rags, good for nothing! Even working-class people and peasants obtain education in order to become men, while you, a Poloznev, with ancestors of rank and distinction, aspire to the gutter! But I have not come here to talk to you; I have washed my hands of you -" he added in a stifled voice, getting up. "I have come to find out where your sister is, you worthless fellow. She left home after dinner, and here it is nearly eight and she is not back. She has taken to going out frequently without telling me; she is less dutiful - and I see in it your evil and degrading influence. Where is she?"

In his hand he had the umbrella I knew so well, and I was already flustered and drew myself up like a schoolboy, expecting my father to begin hitting me with it, but he noticed my glance at the umbrella and most likely that restrained him.

"Live as you please!" he said. "I shall not give you my blessing!"

"Holy Saints!" my nurse muttered behind the door. "You poor, unlucky child! Ah, my heart bodes ill!"

I worked on the railway-line. It rained without stopping all August; it was damp and cold; they had not carried the corn in the fields, and on big farms where the wheat had been cut by machines it lay not in sheaves but in heaps, and I remember how those luckless heaps of wheat turned blacker every day and the grain was sprouting in them. It was hard to work; the pouring rain spoiled everything we managed to do. We were not allowed to live or to sleep in the railway buildings, and we took refuge in the damp and filthy mud huts in which the navvies had lived during the summer, and I could not sleep at night for the cold and the woodlice crawling on my face and hands. And when we worked near the bridges the navvies used to come in the evenings in a gang, simply in order to beat the painters - it was a form of sport to them. They used to beat us, to steal our brushes. And to annoy us and rouse us to fight they used to spoil our work; they would, for instance, smear over the signal boxes with green paint. To complete our troubles, Radish took to paying us very irregularly. All the painting work on the line was given out to a contractor; he gave it out to another; and this subcontractor gave it to Radish after subtracting twenty per cent. for himself. The job was not a profitable one in itself, and the rain made it worse; time was wasted; we could not work while Radish was obliged to pay the fellows by the day. The hungry painters almost came to beating him, called him a cheat, a blood-sucker, a Judas, while he, poor fellow, sighed, lifted up his hand to Heaven in despair, and was continually going to Madame Tcheprakov for money.

VII

Autumn came on, rainy, dark, and muddy. The season of unemployment set in, and I used to sit at home out of work for three days at a stretch, or did various little jobs, not in the painting line. For instance, I wheeled earth, earning about fourpence a day by it. Dr. Blagovo had gone away to Petersburg. My sister had given up coming to see me. Radish was laid up at home ill, expecting death from day to day.

And my mood was autumnal too. Perhaps because, having become a workman, I saw our town life only from the seamy side, it was my lot almost every day to make discoveries which reduced me almost to despair. Those of my fellow-citizens, about whom I had no opinion before, or who had externally appeared perfectly decent, turned out now to be base, cruel people, capable of any dirty action. We common people were deceived, cheated, and kept waiting for hours together in the cold entry or the kitchen; we were insulted and treated with the utmost rudeness. In the autumn I papered the reading-room and two other rooms at the club; I was paid a penny three-farthings the piece, but had to sign a receipt at the rate of twopence halfpenny, and when I refused to do so, a gentleman of benevolent appearance in gold-rimmed spectacles, who must have been one of the club committee, said to me:

"If you say much more, you blackguard, I'll pound your face into a jelly!"

And when the flunkey whispered to him what I was, the son of Poloznev the architect, he became embarrassed, turned crimson, but immediately recovered himself and said: "Devil take him."

In the shops they palmed off on us workmen putrid meat, musty flour, and tea that had been used and dried again; the police hustled us in church, the assistants and nurses in the hospital plundered us, and if we were too poor to give them a bribe they revenged themselves by bringing us food in dirty vessels. In the post-office the pettiest official considered he had a right to treat us like animals, and to shout with coarse insolence: "You wait!" "Where are you shoving to?" Even the housedogs were unfriendly to us, and fell upon us with peculiar viciousness. But the thing that struck me most of all in my new position was the complete lack of justice, what is defined by the peasants in the words: "They have forgotten God." Rarely did a day pass without swindling. We were swindled by the merchants who sold us oil, by the contractors and the workmen and the people who employed us. I need not say that there could never be a question of our rights, and we always had to ask for the money we earned as though it were a charity, and to stand waiting for it at the back door, cap in hand.

I was papering a room at the club next to the reading-room; in the evening, when I was just getting ready to go, the daughter of Dolzhikov, the engineer, walked into the room with a bundle of books under her arm.

I bowed to her.

"Oh, how do you do!" she said, recognizing me at once, and holding out her hand. "I'm very glad to see you."

She smiled and looked with curiosity and wonder at my smock, my pail of paste, the paper stretched on the floor; I was embarrassed, and she, too, felt awkward.

"You must excuse my looking at you like this," she said. "I have been told so much about you. Especially by Dr. Blagovo; he is simply in love with you. And I have made the acquaintance of your sister too; a sweet, dear girl, but I can never persuade her that there is nothing awful about your adopting the simple life. On the contrary, you have become the most interesting man in the town."

She looked again at the pail of paste and the wallpaper, and went on:

"I asked Dr. Blagovo to make me better acquainted with you, but apparently he forgot, or had not time. Anyway, we are acquainted all the same, and if you would come and see me quite simply I should be extremely indebted to you. I so long to have a talk. I am a simple person," she added, holding out her hand to me, "and I hope that you will feel no constraint with me. My father is not here, he is in Petersburg."

She went off into the reading-room, rustling her skirts, while I went home, and for a long time could not get to sleep.

That cheerless autumn some kind soul, evidently wishing to alleviate my existence, sent me from time to time tea and lemons, or biscuits, or roast game. Karpovna told me that they were always brought by a soldier, and from whom they came she did not know; and the soldier used to enquire whether I was well, and whether I dined every day, and whether I had warm clothing. When the frosts began I was presented in the same way in my absence with a soft knitted scarf brought by the soldier. There was a faint elusive smell of scent about it, and I guessed who my good fairy was. The scarf smelt of lilies-of-the-valley, the favourite scent of Anyuta Blagovo.

Towards winter there was more work and it was more cheerful. Radish recovered, and we worked together in the cemetery church, where we were putting the ground-work on the ikon-stand before gilding. It was a clean, quiet job, and, as our fellows used to say, profitable. One could get through a lot of work in a day, and the time passed quickly, imperceptibly. There was no swearing, no laughter, no loud talk. The place itself compelled one to quietness and decent behaviour, and disposed one to quiet, serious thoughts. Absorbed in our work we stood or sat motionless like statues; there was a deathly silence in keeping with the cemetery, so that if a tool fell, or a flame spluttered in the lamp, the noise of such sounds rang out abrupt and resonant, and made us look round. After a long silence we would hear a buzzing like the swarming of bees: it was the requiem of a baby being chanted slowly in subdued voices in the porch; or an artist, painting a dove with stars round it on a cupola would begin softly whistling, and recollecting himself with a start would at once relapse into silence; or Radish, answering his thoughts, would say with a sigh: "Anything is possible! Anything is possible!" or a slow disconsolate bell would begin ringing over our heads, and the painters would observe that it must be for the funeral of some wealthy person. . . .

My days I spent in this stillness in the twilight of the church, and in the long evenings I played billiards or went to the theatre in the gallery wearing the new trousers I had bought out of my own earnings. Concerts and performances had already begun at the Azhogins'; Radish used to paint the scenes alone now. He used to tell me the plot of the plays and describe the *tableaux vivants* which he witnessed. I listened to him with envy. I felt greatly drawn to the rehearsals, but I could not bring myself to go to the Azhogins'.

A week before Christmas Dr. Blagovo arrived. And again we argued and played billiards in the evenings. When he played he used to take off his coat and unbutton his shirt over his chest, and for some reason tried altogether to assume the air of a desperate rake. He did not drink much, but made a great uproar about it, and had a special faculty for getting through twenty roubles in an evening at such a poor cheap tavern as the *Volga*.

My sister began coming to see me again; they both expressed surprise every time on seeing each other, but from her joyful, guilty face it was evident that these meetings were not accidental. One evening, when we were playing billiards, the doctor said to me:

"I say, why don't you go and see Miss Dolzhikov? You don't know Mariya Viktorovna; she is a clever creature, a charmer, a simple, good-natured soul."

I described how her father had received me in the spring.

"Nonsense!" laughed the doctor, "the engineer's one thing and she's another. Really, my dear fellow, you mustn't be nasty to her; go and see her sometimes. For instance, let's go and see her tomorrow evening. What do you say?"

He persuaded me. The next evening I put on my new serge trousers, and in some agitation I set off to Miss Dolzhikov's. The footman did not seem so haughty and terrible, nor the furniture so gorgeous, as on that morning when I had come to ask a favour. Mariya Viktorovna was expecting me, and she received me like an old acquaintance, shaking hands with me in a friendly way. She was wearing a grey cloth dress with full sleeves, and had her hair done in the style which we used to call "dogs' ears," when it came into fashion in the town a year before. The hair was combed down over the ears, and this made Mariya Viktorovna's face look broader, and she seemed to me this time very much like her father, whose face was broad and red, with something in its expression like a sledge-driver. She was handsome and elegant, but not youthful looking; she looked thirty, though in reality she was not more than twenty-five.

"Dear Doctor, how grateful I am to you," she said, making me sit down. "If it hadn't been for him you wouldn't have come to see me. I am bored to death! My father has gone away and left me alone, and I don't know what to do with myself in this town."

Then she began asking me where I was working now, how much I earned, where I lived.

"Do you spend on yourself nothing but what you earn?" she asked.

"No."

"Happy man!" she sighed. "All the evil in life, it seems to me, comes from idleness, boredom, and spiritual emptiness, and all this is inevitable when one is accustomed to living at other people's expense. Don't think I am showing off, I tell you truthfully: it is not interesting or pleasant to be rich. 'Make to yourselves friends of the mammon of unrighteousness' is said, because there is not and cannot be a mammon that's righteous."

She looked round at the furniture with a grave, cold expression, as though she wanted to count it over, and went on:

"Comfort and luxury have a magical power; little by little they draw into their clutches even strong-willed people. At one time father and I lived simply, not in a rich style, but now you see how! It is something monstrous," she said, shrugging her shoulders; "we spend up to twenty thousand a year! In the provinces!"

"One comes to look at comfort and luxury as the invariable privilege of capital and education," I said, "and it seems to me that the comforts of life may be combined with any sort of labour, even the hardest and dirtiest. Your father is rich, and yet he says himself that it has been his lot to be a mechanic and an oiler."

She smiled and shook her head doubtfully: "My father sometimes eats bread dipped in kvass," she said. "It's a fancy, a whim!

At that moment there was a ring and she got up.

"The rich and well-educated ought to work like everyone else," she said, "and if there is comfort it ought to be equal for all. There ought not to be any privileges. But that's enough philosophizing. Tell me something amusing. Tell me about the painters. What are they like? Funny?"

The doctor came in; I began telling them about the painters, but, being unaccustomed to talking, I was constrained, and described them like an ethnologist, gravely and tediously. The doctor, too, told us some anecdotes of working men: he staggered about, shed tears, dropped on his knees, and, even, mimicking a drunkard, lay on the floor; it was as good as a play, and Mariya Viktorovna laughed till she cried as she looked at him. Then he played on the piano and sang in his thin, pleasant tenor, while Mariya Viktorovna stood by and picked out what he was to sing, and corrected him when he made a mistake.

"I've heard that you sing, too?" I enquired.

"Sing, too!" cried the doctor in horror. " She sings exquisitely, a perfect artist, and you talk of her 'singing too'! What an idea!"

"I did study in earnest at one time," she said, answering my question, "but now I have given it up."

Sitting on a low stool she told us of her life in Petersburg, and mimicked some celebrated singers, imitating their voice and manner of singing. She made a sketch of the doctor in her album, then of me; she did not draw well, but both the portraits were like us. She laughed, and was full of mischief and charming grimaces, and this suited her better than talking about the mammon of unrighteousness, and it seemed to me that she had been talking just before about wealth and luxury, not in earnest, but in imitation of someone. She was a superb comic actress. I mentally compared her with our young ladies, and even the handsome, dignified Anyuta Blagovo could not stand comparison with her; the difference was immense, like the difference between a beautiful, cultivated rose and a wild briar.

We had supper together, the three of us. The doctor and Mariya Viktorovna drank red wine, champagne, and coffee with brandy in it; they clinked glasses and drank to friendship, to enlightenment, to progress, to liberty, and they did not get drunk but only flushed, and were continually, for no reason, laughing till they cried. So as not to be tiresome I drank claret too.

"Talented, richly endowed natures," said Miss Dolzhikov, "know how to live, and go their own way; mediocre people, like myself for instance, know nothing and can do nothing of themselves; there is nothing left for them but to discern some deep social movement, and to float where they are carried by it."

"How can one discern what doesn't exist?" asked the doctor.

"We think so because we don't see it."

"Is that so? The social movements are the invention of the new literature. There are none among us."

An argument began.

"There are no deep social movements among us and never have been," the doctor declared loudly. "There is no end to what the new literature has invented! It has invented intellectual workers in the country, and you may search through all our villages and find at the most some lout in a reefer jacket or a black frock-coat who will make four mistakes in spelling a word of three letters. Cultured life has not yet begun among us. There's the same savagery, the same uniform boorishness, the same triviality, as five hundred years ago. Movements, currents there have been, but it has all been petty, paltry, bent upon vulgar and mercenary interests - and one cannot see anything important in them. If you think you have discerned a deep social movement, and in following it you devote yourself to tasks in the modern taste, such as the emancipation of insects from slavery or abstinence from beef rissoles, I congratulate you, Madam. We must study, and study, and study and we must wait a bit with our deep social movements; we are not mature enough for them yet; and to tell the truth, we don't know anything about them."

"You don't know anything about them, but I do," said Mariya Viktorovna. "Goodness, how tiresome you are to-day!"

"Our duty is to study and to study, to try to accumulate as much knowledge as possible, for genuine social movements arise where there is knowledge; and the happiness of mankind in the future lies only in knowledge. I drink to science!"

"There is no doubt about one thing: one must organize one's life somehow differently," said Mariya Viktorovna, after a moment's silence and thought. "Life, such as it has been hitherto, is not worth having. Don't let us talk about it."

As we came away from her the cathedral clock struck two.

"Did you like her?" asked the doctor; "she's nice, isn't she?"

On Christmas day we dined with Mariya Viktorovna, and all through the holidays we went to see her almost every day. There was never anyone there but ourselves, and she was right when she said that she had no friends in the town but the doctor and me. We spent our time for the most part in conversation; sometimes the doctor brought some book or magazine and read aloud to us. In reality he was the first well-educated man I had met in my life: I cannot judge whether he knew a great deal, but he always displayed his knowledge as though he wanted other people to share it. When he talked about anything relating to medicine he was not like any one of the doctors in our town, but made a fresh, peculiar impression upon me, and I fancied that if he liked he might have become a real man of science. And he was perhaps the only person who had a real influence upon me at that time. Seeing him, and reading the books he gave me, I began little by little to feel a thirst for the knowledge which would have given significance to my cheerless labour. It seemed strange to me, for instance, that I had not known till then that the whole world was made up of sixty elements, I had not known what oil was, what paints were, and that I could have got on without knowing these things. My acquaintance with the doctor elevated me morally too. I was continually arguing with him and, though I usually remained of my own opinion, yet, thanks to him, I began to perceive that everything was not clear to me, and I began trying to work out as far as I could definite convictions in myself, that the dictates of conscience might be definite, and that there might be nothing vague in my mind. Yet, though he was the most cultivated and best man in the town, he was nevertheless far from perfection. In his manners, in his habit of turning every conversation into an argument, in his pleasant tenor, even in his friendliness, there was something coarse, like a divinity student, and when he took off his coat and sat in his silk shirt, or flung a tip to a waiter in the restaurant, I always fancied that culture might be all very well, but the Tatar was fermenting in him still.

At Epiphany he went back to Petersburg. He went off in the morning, and after dinner my sister came in. Without taking off her fur coat and her cap she sat down in silence, very pale, and kept her eyes fixed on the same spot. She was chilled by the frost and one could see that she was upset by it.

"You must have caught cold," I said.

Her eyes filled with tears; she got up and went out to Karpovna without saying a word to me, as though I had hurt her feelings. And a little later I heard her saying, in a tone of bitter reproach:

"Nurse, what have I been living for till now? What? Tell me, haven't I wasted my youth? All the best years of my life to know nothing but keeping accounts, pouring out tea, counting the halfpence, entertaining visitors, and thinking there was nothing better in the world! Nurse, do understand, I have the cravings of a human being, and I want to live, and they have turned me into something like a housekeeper. It's horrible, horrible!"

She flung her keys towards the door, and they fell with a jingle into my room. They were the keys of the sideboard, of the kitchen cupboard, of the cellar, and of the tea-caddy, the keys which my mother used to carry.

"Oh, merciful heavens!" cried the old woman in horror. "Holy Saints above!"

Before going home my sister came into my room to pick up the keys, and said:

"You must forgive me. Something queer has happened to me lately."

VIII

On returning home late one evening from Mariya Viktorovna's I found waiting in my room a young police inspector in a new uniform; he was sitting at my table, looking through my books.

"At last," he said, getting up and stretching himself. "This is the third time I have been to you. The Governor commands you to present yourself before him at nine o'clock in the morning. Without fail."

He took from me a signed statement that I would act upon his Excellency's command, and went away. This late visit of the police inspector and unexpected invitation to the Governor's had an overwhelmingly oppressive effect upon me. From my earliest childhood I have felt terror-stricken in the presence of gendarmes, policemen, and law court officials, and now I was tormented by uneasiness, as though I were really guilty in some way. And I could not get to sleep. My nurse and Prokofy were also upset and could not sleep. My nurse had earache too; she moaned, and several times began crying with pain. Hearing that I was awake, Prokofy came into my room with a lamp and sat down at the table.

"You ought to have a drink of pepper cordial," he said, after a moment's thought. "If one does have a drink in this vale of tears it does no harm. And if Mamma were to pour a little pepper cordial in her ear it would do her a lot of good."

Between two and three he was going to the slaughter-house for the meat. I knew I should not sleep till morning now, and to get through the time till nine o'clock I went with him. We walked with a lantern, while his boy Nikolka, aged thirteen, with blue patches on his cheeks from frostbites, a regular young brigand to judge by his expression, drove after us in the sledge, urging on the horse in a husky voice.

"I suppose they will punish you at the Governor's," Prokofy said to me on the way. "There are rules of the trade for governors, and rules for the higher clergy, and rules for the officers, and rules for the doctors, and every class has its rules. But you haven't kept to your rules, and you can't be allowed."

The slaughter-house was behind the cemetery, and till then I had only seen it in the distance. It consisted of three gloomy barns, surrounded by a grey fence, and when the wind blew from that quarter on hot days in summer, it brought a stifling stench from them. Now going into the yard in the dark I did not see the barns; I kept coming across horses and sledges, some empty, some loaded up with meat. Men were walking about with lanterns, swearing in a disgusting way. Prokofy and Nikolka swore just as revoltingly, and the air was in a continual uproar with swearing, coughing, and the neighing of horses.

There was a smell of dead bodies and of dung. It was thawing, the snow was changing into mud; and in the darkness it seemed to me that I was walking through pools of blood.

Having piled up the sledges full of meat we set off to the butcher's shop in the market. It began to get light. Cooks with baskets and elderly ladies in mantles came along one after another, Prokofy, with a chopper in his hand, in a white apron spattered with blood, swore fearful oaths, crossed himself at the church, shouted aloud for the whole market to hear, that he was giving away the meat at cost price and even at a loss to himself. He gave short weight and short change, the cooks saw that, but, deafened by his shouts, did not protest, and only called him a hangman. Brandishing and bringing down his terrible chopper he threw himself into picturesque attitudes, and each time uttered the sound "Geck" with a ferocious expression, and I was afraid he really would chop off somebody's head or hand.

I spent all the morning in the butcher's shop, and when at last I went to the Governor's, my overcoat smelt of meat and blood. My state of mind was as though I were being sent spear in hand to meet a bear. I remember the tall staircase with a striped carpet on it, and the young official, with shiny buttons, who mutely motioned me to the door with both hands, and ran to announce me. I went into a hall luxuriously but frigidly and tastelessly furnished, and the high, narrow mirrors in the spaces between the walls, and the bright yellow window curtains, struck the eye particularly unpleasantly. One could see that the governors were changed, but the furniture remained the same. Again the young official motioned me with both hands to the door, and I went up to a big green table at which a military general, with the Order of Vladimir on his breast, was standing.

"Mr. Poloznev, I have asked you to come," he began, holding a letter in his hand, and opening his mouth like a round "o," "I have asked you to come here to inform you of this. Your highly respected father has appealed by letter and by word of mouth to the Marshal of the Nobility begging him to summon you, and to lay before you the inconsistency of your behaviour with the rank of the nobility to which you have the honour to belong. His Excellency Alexandr Pavlovitch, justly supposing that your conduct might serve as a bad example, and considering that mere persuasion on his part would not be sufficient, but that official intervention in earnest was essential, presents me here in this letter with his views in regard to you, which I share."

He said this, quietly, respectfully, standing erect, as though I were his superior officer and looking at me with no trace of severity. His face looked worn and wizened, and was all wrinkles; there were bags under his eyes; his hair was dyed; and it was impossible to tell from his appearance how old he was - forty or sixty.

"I trust," he went on, "that you appreciate the delicacy of our honoured Alexandr Pavlovitch, who has addressed himself to me not officially, but privately. I, too, have asked you to come here unofficially, and I am speaking to you, not as a Governor, but from a sincere regard for your father. And so I beg you either to alter your line of conduct and return to duties in keeping with your rank, or to avoid setting a bad example, remove to another district where you are not known, and where you can follow any occupation you please. In the other case, I shall be forced to take extreme measures."

He stood for half a minute in silence, looking at me with his mouth open.

"Are you a vegetarian?" he asked.

"No, your Excellency, I eat meat."

He sat down and drew some papers towards him. I bowed and went out.

It was not worth while now to go to work before dinner. I went home to sleep, but could not sleep from an unpleasant, sickly feeling, induced by the slaughter house and my conversation with the Governor, and when the evening came I went, gloomy and out of sorts, to Mariya Viktorovna. I told her how I had been at the Governor's, while she stared at me in perplexity as though she did not believe it, then suddenly began laughing gaily, loudly, irrepressibly, as only good-natured laughter-loving people can.

"If only one could tell that in Petersburg!" she brought out, almost falling over with laughter, and propping herself against the table. "If one could tell that in Petersburg!"

IX

Now we used to see each other often, sometimes twice a day. She used to come to the cemetery almost every day after dinner, and read the epitaphs on the crosses and tombstones while she waited for me. Sometimes she would come into the church, and, standing by me, would look on while I worked. The stillness, the naïve work of the painters and gilders, Radish's sage reflections, and the fact that I did not differ externally from the other workmen, and worked just as they did in my waistcoat with no socks on, and that I was addressed familiarly by them - all this was new to her and touched her. One day a workman, who was painting a dove on the ceiling, called out to me in her presence:

"Misail, hand me up the white paint."

I took him the white paint, and afterwards, when I let myself down by the frail scaffolding, she looked at me, touched to tears and smiling.

"What a dear you are!" she said.

I remembered from my childhood how a green parrot, belonging to one of the rich men of the town, had escaped from its cage, and how for quite a month afterwards the beautiful bird had haunted the town, flying from garden to garden, homeless and solitary. Mariya Viktorovna reminded me of that bird.

"There is positively nowhere for me to go now but the cemetery," she said to me with a laugh. "The town has become disgustingly dull. At the Azhogins' they are still reciting, singing, lisping. I have grown to detest them of late; your sister is an unsociable creature; Mademoiselle Blagovo hates me for some reason. I don't care for the theatre. Tell me where am I to go?"

When I went to see her I smelt of paint and turpentine, and my hands were stained - and she liked that; she wanted me to come to her in my ordinary working clothes; but in her drawing-room those clothes made me feel awkward. I felt embarrassed, as though I were in uniform, so I always put on my new serge trousers when I went to her. And she did not like that.

"You must own you are not quite at home in your new character," she said to me one day. "Your workman's dress does not feel natural to you; you are awkward in it. Tell me, isn't that because you haven't a firm conviction, and are not satisfied? The very kind of work you have chosen - your painting - surely it does not satisfy you, does it?" she asked, laughing. "I know paint makes things look nicer and last longer, but those things belong to rich people who live in towns, and after all they are luxuries. Besides, you have often said yourself that everybody ought to get his bread by the work of his own hands, yet you get money and not bread. Why shouldn't you keep to the literal sense of your words? You ought to be getting bread, that is, you ought to be ploughing, sowing, reaping, threshing, or doing something which has a direct connection with agriculture, for instance, looking after cows, digging, building huts of logs. . . ."

She opened a pretty cupboard that stood near her writing-table, and said:

"I am saying all this to you because I want to let you into my secret. *Voilà!* This is my agricultural library. Here I have fields, kitchen garden and orchard, and cattleyard and beehives. I read them greedily, and have already learnt all the theory to the tiniest detail. My dream, my darling wish, is to go to our Dubetchnya as soon as March is here. It's marvellous there, exquisite, isn't it? The first year I shall have a look round and get into things, and the year after I shall begin to work properly myself, putting my back into it as they say. My father has promised to give me Dubetchnya and I shall do exactly what I like with it."

Flushed, excited to tears, and laughing, she dreamed aloud how she would live at Dubetchnya, and what an interesting life it would be! I envied her. March was near, the days were growing longer and longer, and on bright sunny days water dripped from the roofs at midday, and there was a fragrance of spring; I, too, longed for the country.

And when she said that she should move to Dubetchnya, I realized vividly that I should remain in the town alone, and I felt that I envied her with her cupboard of books and her agriculture. I knew nothing of work on the land, and did not like it, and I should have liked to have told her that work on the land was slavish toil, but I remembered that something similar had been said more than once by my father, and I held my tongue.

Lent began. Viktor Ivanitch, whose existence I had begun to forget, arrived from Petersburg. He arrived unexpectedly, without even a telegram to say he was coming. When I went in, as usual in the evening, he was walking about the drawing-room, telling some story with his face freshly washed and shaven, looking ten years younger: his daughter was kneeling on the floor, taking out of his trunks boxes, bottles, and books, and handing them to Pavel the footman. I involuntarily drew back a step when I saw the engineer, but he held out both hands to me and said, smiling, showing his strong white teeth that looked like a sledge-driver's:

"Here he is, here he is! Very glad to see you, Mr. House-painter! Masha has told me all about it; she has been singing your praises. I quite understand and approve," he went on, taking my arm. "To be a good workman is ever so much more honest and more sensible than wasting government paper and wearing a cockade on your head. I myself worked in Belgium with these very hands and then spent two years as a mechanic. . . ."

He was wearing a short reefer jacket and indoor slippers; he walked like a man with the gout, rolling slightly from side to side and rubbing his hands. Humming something he softly purred and hugged himself with satisfaction at being at home again at last, and able to have his beloved shower bath.

"There is no disputing," he said to me at supper, "there is no disputing; you are all nice and charming people, but for some reason, as soon as you take to manual labour, or go in for saving the peasants, in the long run it all comes to no more than being a dissenter. Aren't you a dissenter? Here you don't take vodka. What's the meaning of that if it is not being a dissenter?"

To satisfy him I drank some vodka and I drank some wine, too. We tasted the cheese, the sausage, the pâtés, the pickles, and the savouries of all sorts that the engineer had brought with him, and the wine that had come in his absence from abroad. The wine was first-rate. For some reason the engineer got wine and cigars from abroad without paying duty; the caviare and the dried sturgeon someone sent him for nothing; he did not pay rent for his flat as the owner of the house provided the kerosene for the line; and altogether he and his daughter produced on me the impression that all the best in the world was at their service, and provided for them for nothing.

I went on going to see them, but not with the same eagerness. The engineer made me feel constrained, and in his presence I did not feel free. I could not face his clear, guileless eyes, his reflections wearied and sickened me; I was sickened, too, by the memory that so lately I had been in the employment of this red-faced, well-fed man, and that he had been brutally rude to me. It is true that he put his arm round my waist, slapped me on the shoulder in a friendly way, approved my manner of life, but I felt that, as before, he despised my insignificance, and only put up with me to please his daughter, and I couldn't now laugh and talk as I liked, and I behaved unsociably and kept expecting that in another minute he would address me as Panteley as he did his footman Pavel. How my pride as a provincial and a working man was revolted. I, a proletarian, a house painter, went every day to rich people who were alien to me, and whom the whole town regarded as though they were foreigners, and every day I drank costly wines with them and ate unusual dainties - my conscience refused to be reconciled to it! On my way to the house I sullenly avoided meeting people, and looked at them from under my brows as though I really were a dissenter, and when I was going home from the engineer's I was ashamed of my well-fed condition.

Above all I was afraid of being carried away. Whether I was walking along the street, or working, or talking to the other fellows, I was all the time thinking of one thing only, of going in the evening to see Mariya Viktorovna and was picturing her voice, her laugh, her movements. When I was getting ready to go to her I always spent a long time before my nurse's warped looking-glass, as I fastened my tie; my serge trousers were detestable in my eyes, and I suffered torments, and at the same time despised myself for being so trivial. When she called to me out of the other room that she was not dressed and asked me to wait, I listened to her dressing; it agitated me, I felt as though the ground were giving way under my feet. And when I saw a woman's figure in the street, even at a distance, I invariably compared it. It seemed to me that all our girls and women were vulgar, that they were absurdly dressed, and did not know how to hold themselves; and these comparisons aroused a feeling of pride in me: Mariya Viktorovna was the best of them all! And I dreamed of her and myself at night.

One evening at supper with the engineer we ate a whole lobster As I was going home afterwards I remembered that the engineer twice called me "My dear fellow" at supper, and I reflected that they treated me very kindly in that house, as they might an unfortunate big dog who had been kicked out by its owners, that they were amusing themselves with me, and that when they were tired of me they would turn me out like a dog. I felt ashamed and wounded, wounded to the point of tears as though I had been insulted, and looking up at the sky I took a vow to put an end to all this.

The next day I did not go to the Dolzhikov's. Late in the evening, when it was quite dark and raining, I walked along Great Dvoryansky Street, looking up at the windows. Everyone was asleep at the Azhogins', and the only light was in one of the furthest windows. It was Madame Azhogin in her own room, sewing by the light of three candles, imagining that she was combating superstition. Our house was in darkness, but at the Dolzhikovs', on the contrary, the windows were lighted up, but one could distinguish nothing through the flowers and the curtains. I kept walking up and down the street; the cold March rain drenched me through. I heard my father come home from the club; he stood knocking at the gate. A minute later a light appeared at the window, and I saw my sister, who was hastening down with a lamp, while with the other hand she was twisting her thick hair together as she went. Then my father walked about the drawing-room, talking and rubbing his hands, while my sister sat in a low chair, thinking and not listening to what he said.

But then they went away; the light went out. . . . I glanced round at the engineer's, and there, too, all was darkness now. In the dark and the rain I felt hopelessly alone, abandoned to the whims of destiny; I felt that all my doings, my desires, and everything I had thought and said till then were trivial in comparison with my loneliness, in comparison with my present suffering, and the suffering that lay before me in the future. Alas, the thoughts and doings of living creatures are not nearly so significant as their sufferings! And without clearly realizing what I was doing, I pulled at the bell of the Dolzhikovs' gate, broke it, and ran along the street like some naughty boy, with a feeling of terror in my heart, expecting every moment that they would come out and recognize me. When I stopped at the end of the street to take breath I could hear nothing but the sound of the rain, and somewhere in the distance a watchman striking on a sheet of iron.

For a whole week I did not go to the Dolzhikovs'. My serge trousers were sold. There was nothing doing in the painting trade. I knew the pangs of hunger again, and earned from twopence to fourpence a day, where I could, by heavy and unpleasant work. Struggling up to my knees in the cold mud, straining my chest, I tried to stifle my memories, and, as it were, to punish myself for the cheeses and preserves with which I had been regaled at the engineer's. But all the same, as soon as I lay in bed, wet and hungry, my sinful imagination immediately began to paint exquisite, seductive pictures, and with amazement I acknowledged to myself that I was in love, passionately in love, and I fell into a sound, heavy sleep, feeling that hard labour only made my body stronger and younger.

One evening snow began falling most inappropriately, and the wind blew from the north as though winter had come back again. When I returned from work that evening I found Mariya Viktorovna in my room. She was sitting in her fur coat, and had both hands in her muff.

"Why don't you come to see me?" she asked, raising her clear, clever eyes, and I was utterly confused with delight and stood stiffly upright before her, as I used to stand facing my father when he was going to beat me; she looked into my face and I could see from her eyes that she understood why I was confused.

"Why don't you come to see me?" she repeated. "If you don't want to come, you see, I have come to you."

She got up and came close to me.

"Don't desert me," she said, and her eyes filled with tears. "I am alone, utterly alone."

She began crying; and, hiding her face in her muff, articulated:

"Alone! My life is hard, very hard, and in all the world I have no one but you. Don't desert me!"

Looking for a handkerchief to wipe her tears she smiled; we were silent for some time, then I put my arms round her and kissed her, scratching my cheek till it bled with her hatpin as I did it.

And we began talking to each other as though we had been on the closest terms for ages and ages.

X

Two days later she sent me to Dubetchnya and I was unutterably delighted to go. As I walked towards the station and afterwards, as I was sitting in the train, I kept laughing from no apparent cause, and people looked at me as though I were drunk. Snow was falling, and there were still frosts in the mornings, but the roads were already dark-coloured and rooks hovered over them, cawing.

At first I had intended to fit up an abode for us two, Masha and me, in the lodge at the side opposite Madame Tcheprakov's lodge, but it appeared that the doves and the ducks had been living there for a long time, and it was impossible to clean it without destroying a great number of nests. There was nothing for it but to live in the comfortless rooms of the big house with the sunblinds. The peasants called the house the palace; there were more than twenty rooms in it, and the only furniture was a piano and a child's arm-chair lying in the attic. And if Masha had brought all her furniture from the town we should even then have been unable to get rid of the impression of immense emptiness and cold. I picked out three small rooms with windows looking into the garden, and worked from early morning till night, setting them to rights, putting in new panes, papering the walls, filling up the holes and chinks in the floors. It was easy, pleasant work. I was continually running to the river to see whether the ice were not going; I kept fancying that starlings were flying. And at night, thinking of Masha, I listened with an unutterably sweet feeling, with clutching delight to the noise of the rats and the wind droning and knocking above the ceiling. It seemed as though some old house spirit were coughing in the attic.

The snow was deep; a great deal had fallen even at the end of March, but it melted quickly, as though by magic, and the spring floods passed in a tumultuous rush, so that by the beginning of April the starlings were already noisy, and yellow butterflies were flying in the garden. It was exquisite weather. Every day, towards evening, I used to walk to the town to meet Masha, and what a delight it was to walk with bare feet along the gradually drying, still soft road. Half-way I used to sit down and look towards the town, not venturing to go near it. The sight of it troubled me. I kept wondering how the people I knew would behave to me when they heard of my love. What would my father say? What troubled me particularly was the thought that my life was more complicated, and that I had completely lost all power to set it right, and that, like a balloon, it was bearing me away, God knows whither. I no longer considered the problem how to earn my daily bread, how to live, but thought about - I really don't know what.

Masha used to come in a carriage; I used to get in with her, and we drove to Dubetchnya, feeling light-hearted and free. Or, after waiting till the sun had set, I would go back dissatisfied and dreary, wondering why Masha had not come; at the gate or in the garden I would be met by a sweet, unexpected apparition - it was she! It would turn out that she had come by rail, and had walked from the station. What a festival it was! In a simple woollen dress with a kerchief on her head, with a modest sunshade, but laced in, slender, in expensive foreign boots - it was a talented actress playing the part of a little workgirl. We looked round our domain and decided which should be her room, and which mine, where we would have our avenue, our kitchen garden, our beehives.

We already had hens, ducks, and geese, which we loved because they were ours. We had, all ready for sowing, oats, clover, timothy grass, buckwheat, and vegetable seeds, and we always looked at all these stores and discussed at length the crop we might get; and everything Masha said to me seemed extraordinarily clever, and fine. This was the happiest time of my life.

Soon after St. Thomas's week we were married at our parish church in the village of Kurilovka, two miles from Dubetchnya. Masha wanted everything to be done quietly; at her wish our "best men" were peasant lads, the sacristan sang alone, and we came back from the church in a small, jolting chaise which she drove herself. Our only guest from the town was my sister Kleopatra, to whom Masha sent a note three days before the wedding. My sister came in a white dress and wore gloves. During the wedding she cried quietly from joy and tenderness. Her expression was motherly and infinitely kind. She was intoxicated with our happiness, and smiled as though she were absorbing a sweet delirium, and looking at her during our wedding, I realized that for her there was nothing in the world higher than love, earthly love, and that she was dreaming of it secretly, timidly, but continually and passionately. She embraced and kissed Masha, and, not knowing how to express her rapture, said to her of me: "He is good! He is very good!"

Before she went away she changed into her ordinary dress, and drew me into the garden to talk to me alone.

"Father is very much hurt," she said, "that you have written nothing to him. You ought to have asked for his blessing. But in reality he is very much pleased. He says that this marriage will raise you in the eyes of all society, and that under the influence of Mariya Viktorovna you will begin to take a more serious view of life. We talk of nothing but you in the evenings now, and yesterday he actually used the expression: 'Our Misail.' That pleased me. It seems as though he had some plan in his mind, and I fancy he wants to set you an example of magnanimity and be the first to speak of reconciliation. It is very possible he may come here to see you in a day or two."

She hurriedly made the sign of the cross over me several times and said:

"Well, God be with you. Be happy. Anyuta Blagovo is a very clever girl; she says about your marriage that God is sending you a fresh ordeal. To be sure - married life does not bring only joy but suffering too. That's bound to be so."

Masha and I walked a couple of miles to see her on her way; we walked back slowly and in silence, as though we were resting. Masha held my hand, my heart felt light, and I had no inclination to talk about love; we had become closer and more akin now that we were married, and we felt that nothing now could separate us.

"Your sister is a nice creature," said Masha, "but it seems as though she had been tormented for years. Your father must be a terrible man."

I began telling her how my sister and I had been brought up, and what a senseless torture our childhood had really been. When she heard how my father had so lately beaten me, she shuddered and drew closer to me.

"Don't tell me any more," she said. "It's horrible!"

Now she never left me. We lived together in the three rooms in the big house, and in the evenings we bolted the door which led to the empty part of the house, as though someone were living there whom we did not know, and were afraid of. I got up early, at dawn, and immediately set to work of some sort. I mended the carts, made paths in the garden, dug the flower beds, painted the roof of the house. When the time came to sow the oats I tried to plough the ground over again, to harrow and to sow, and I did it all conscientiously, keeping up with our labourer; I was worn out, the rain and the cold wind made my face and feet burn for hours afterwards. I dreamed of ploughed land at night. But field labour did not attract me. I did not understand farming, and I did not care for it; it was perhaps because my forefathers had not been tillers of the soil, and the very blood that flowed in my veins was purely of the city. I loved nature tenderly; I loved the fields and meadows and kitchen gardens, but the peasant who turned up the soil with his plough and urged on his pitiful horse, wet and tattered, with his craning neck, was to me the expression of coarse, savage, ugly force, and every time I looked at his uncouth movements I involuntarily began thinking of the legendary life of the remote past, before men knew the use of fire. The fierce bull that ran with the peasants' herd, and the horses, when they dashed about the village, stamping their hoofs, moved me to fear, and everything rather big, strong, and angry, whether it was the ram with its horns, the gander, or the yard-dog, seemed to me the expression of the same coarse, savage force. This mood was particularly strong in me in bad weather, when heavy clouds were hanging over the black ploughed land. Above all, when I was ploughing or sowing, and two or three people stood looking how I was doing it, I had not the feeling that this work was inevitable and obligatory, and it seemed to me that I was amusing myself. I preferred doing something in the yard, and there was nothing I liked so much as painting the roof.

I used to walk through the garden and the meadow to our mill. It was let to a peasant of Kurilovka called Stepan, a handsome, dark fellow with a thick black beard, who looked very strong. He did not like the miller's work, and looked upon it as dreary and unprofitable, and only lived at the mill in order not to live at home. He was a leather-worker, and was always surrounded by a pleasant smell of tar and leather. He was not fond of talking, he was listless and sluggish, and was always sitting in the doorway or on the river bank, humming "oo-loo-loo." His wife and mother-in-law, both white-faced, languid, and meek, used sometimes to come from Kurilovka to see him; they made low bows to him and addressed him formally, "Stepan Petrovitch," while he went on sitting on the river bank, softly humming "oo-loo-loo," without responding by word or movement to their bows. One hour and then a second would pass in silence. His mother-in-law and wife, after whispering together, would get up and gaze at him for some time, expecting him to look round; then they would make a low bow, and in sugary, chanting voices, say:

"Good-bye, Stepan Petrovitch!"

And they would go away. After that Stepan, picking up the parcel they had left, containing cracknels or a shirt, would heave a sigh and say, winking in their direction:

"The female sex!"

The mill with two sets of millstones worked day and night. I used to help Stepan; I liked the work, and when he went off I was glad to stay and take his place.

XI

After bright warm weather came a spell of wet; all May it rained and was cold. The sound of the millwheels and of the rain disposed one to indolence and slumber. The floor trembled, there was a smell of flour, and that, too, induced drowsiness. My wife in a short fur-lined jacket, and in men s high golosh boots, would make her appearance twice a day, and she always said the same thing:

"And this is called summer! Worse than it was in October!"

We used to have tea and make the porridge together, or we would sit for hours at a stretch without speaking, waiting for the rain to stop. Once, when Stepan had gone off to the fair, Masha stayed all night at the mill. When we got up we could not tell what time it was, as the rainclouds covered the whole sky; but sleepy cocks were crowing at Dubetchnya, and landrails were calling in the meadows; it was still very, very early. . . . My wife and I went down to the millpond and drew out the net which Stepan had thrown in overnight in our presence. A big pike was struggling in it, and a cray-fish was twisting about, clawing upwards with its pincers.

"Let them go," said Masha. "Let them be happy too."

Because we got up so early and afterwards did nothing, that day seemed very long, the longest day in my life. Towards evening Stepan came back and I went home.

"Your father came to-day," said Masha.

"Where is he?" I asked.

"He has gone away. I would not see him."

Seeing that I remained standing and silent, that I was sorry for my father, she said:

"One must be consistent. I would not see him, and sent word to him not to trouble to come and see us again."

A minute later I was out at the gate and walking to the town to explain things to my father. It was muddy, slippery, cold. For the first time since my marriage I felt suddenly sad, and in my brain exhausted by that long, grey day, there was stirring the thought that perhaps I was not living as I ought. I was worn out; little by little I was overcome by despondency and indolence, I did not want to move or think, and after going on a little I gave it up with a wave of my hand and turned back.

The engineer in a leather overcoat with a hood was standing in the middle of the yard.

"Where's the furniture? There used to be lovely furniture in the Empire style: there used to be pictures, there used to be vases, while now you could play ball in it! I bought the place with the furniture. The devil take her!"

Moisey, a thin pock-marked fellow of twenty-five, with insolent little eyes, who was in the service of the general's widow, stood near him crumpling up his cap in his hands; one of his cheeks was bigger than the other, as though he had lain too long on it.

"Your honour was graciously pleased to buy the place without the furniture," he brought out irresolutely; "I remember."

"Hold your tongue!" shouted the engineer; he turned crimson and shook with anger . . . and the echo in the garden loudly repeated his shout.

XII

When I was doing anything in the garden or the yard, Moisey would stand beside me, and folding his arms behind his back he would stand lazily and impudently staring at me with his little eyes. And this irritated me to such a degree that I threw up my work and went away.

From Stepan we heard that Moisey was Madame Tcheprakov's lover. I noticed that when people came to her to borrow money they addressed themselves first to Moisey, and once I saw a peasant, black from head to foot - he must have been a coalheaver - bow down at Moisey's feet. Sometimes, after a little whispering, he gave out money himself, without consulting his mistress, from which I concluded that he did a little business on his own account.

He used to shoot in our garden under our windows, carried off victuals from our cellar, borrowed our horses without asking permission, and we were indignant and began to feel as though Dubetchnya were not ours, and Masha would say, turning pale:

"Can we really have to go on living with these reptiles another eighteen months?

Madame Tcheprakov's son, Ivan, was serving as a guard on our railway-line. He had grown much thinner and feebler during the winter, so that a single glass was enough to make him drunk, and he shivered out of the sunshine. He wore the guard's uniform with aversion and was ashamed of it, but considered his post a good one, as he could steal the candles and sell them. My new position excited in him a mixed feeling of wonder, envy, and a vague hope that something of the same sort might happen to him. He used to watch Masha with ecstatic eyes, ask me what I had for dinner now, and his lean and ugly face wore a sad and sweetish expression, and he moved his fingers as though he were feeling my happiness with them.

"Listen, Better-than-nothing," he said fussily, relighting his cigarette at every instant; there was always a litter where he stood, for he wasted dozens of matches, lighting one cigarette. "Listen, my life now is the nastiest possible. The worst of it is any subaltern can shout: 'Hi, there, guard!' I have overheard all sorts of things in the train, my boy, and do you know, I have learned that life's a beastly thing! My mother has been the ruin of me! A doctor in the train told me that if parents are immoral, their children are drunkards or criminals. Think of that!"

Once he came into the yard, staggering; his eyes gazed about blankly, his breathing was laboured; he laughed and cried and babbled as though in a high fever, and the only words I could catch in his muddled talk were, "My mother! Where's my mother?" which he uttered with a wail like a child who has lost his mother in a crowd. I led him into our garden and laid him down under a tree, and Masha and I took turns to sit by him all that day and all night. He was very sick, and Masha looked with aversion at his pale, wet face, and said:

"Is it possible these reptiles will go on living another year and a half in our yard? It's awful! it's awful!"

And how many mortifications the peasants caused us! How many bitter disappointments in those early days in the spring months, when we so longed to be happy. My wife built a school. I drew a plan of a school for sixty boys, and the Zemstvo Board approved of it, but advised us to build the school at Kurilovka the big village which was only two miles from us. Moreover, the school at Kurilovka in which children - from four villages, our Dubetchnya being one of the number - were taught, was old and too small, and the floor was scarcely safe to walk upon. At the end of March at Masha's wish, she was appointed guardian of the Kurilovka school, and at the beginning of April we three times summoned the village assembly, and tried to persuade the peasants that their school was old and overcrowded, and that it was essential to build a new one. A member of the Zemstvo Board and the Inspector of Peasant Schools came, and they, too, tried to persuade them. After each meeting the peasants surrounded us, begging for a bucket of vodka; we were hot in the crowd; we were soon exhausted, and returned home dissatisfied and a little ill at ease. In the end the peasants set apart a plot of ground for the school, and were obliged to bring all the building material from the town with their own horses. And the very first Sunday after the spring corn was sown carts set off from Kurilovka and Dubetchnya to fetch bricks for the foundations.

They set off as soon as it was light, and came back late in the evening; the peasants were drunk, and said they were worn out.

As ill-luck would have it, the rain and the cold persisted all through May. The road was in an awful state: it was deep in mud. The carts usually drove into our yard when they came back from the town - and what a horrible ordeal it was. A potbellied horse would appear at the gate, setting its front legs wide apart; it would stumble forward before coming into the yard; a beam, nine yards long, wet and slimy-looking, crept in on a waggon. Beside it, muffled up against the rain, strode a peasant with the skirts of his coat tucked up in his belt, not looking where he was going, but stepping through the puddles. Another cart would appear with boards, then a third with a beam, a fourth . and the space before our house was gradually crowded up with horses, beams, and planks. Men and women, with their heads muffled and their skirts tucked up, would stare angrily at our windows, make an uproar, and clamour for the mistress to come out to them; coarse oaths were audible. Meanwhile Moisey stood at one side, and we fancied he was enjoying our discomfiture.

"We are not going to cart anymore," the peasants would shout. "We are worn out! Let her go and get the stuff herself."

Masha, pale and flustered, expecting every minute that they would break into the house, would send them out a half-pail of vodka; after that the noise would subside and the long beams, one after another, would crawl slowly out of the yard.

When I was setting off to see the building my wife was worried and said:

"The peasants are spiteful; I only hope they won't do you a mischief. Wait a minute, I'll come with you."

We drove to Kurilovka together, and there the carpenters asked us for a drink. The framework of the house was ready. It was time to lay the foundation, but the masons had not come; this caused delay, and the carpenters complained. And when at last the masons did come, it appeared that there was no sand; it had been somehow overlooked that it would be needed. Taking advantage of our helpless position, the peasants demanded thirty kopecks for each cartload, though the distance from the building to the river where they got the sand was less than a quarter of a mile, and more than five hundred cartloads were found to be necessary. There was no end to the misunderstandings, swearing, and importunity; my wife was indignant, and the foreman of the masons, Tit Petrov, an old man of seventy, took her by the arm, and said:

"You look here! You look here! You only bring me the sand; I set ten men on at once, and in two days it will be done! You look here!"

But they brought the sand and two days passed, and four, and a week, and instead of the promised foundations there was still a yawning hole.

"It's enough to drive one out of one's senses, said my wife, in distress. "What people! What people!"

In the midst of these disorderly doings the engineer arrived; he brought with him parcels of wine and savouries, and after a prolonged meal lay down for a nap in the verandah and snored so loudly that the labourers shook their heads and said: "Well!"

Masha was not pleased at his coming, she did not trust him, though at the same time she asked his advice. When, after sleeping too long after dinner, he got up in a bad humour and said unpleasant things about our management of the place, or expressed regret that he had bought Dubetchnya, which had already been a loss to him, poor Masha's face wore an expression of misery. She would complain to him, and he would yawn and say that the peasants ought to be flogged.

He called our marriage and our life a farce, and said it was a caprice, a whim.

"She has done something of the sort before," he said about Masha. "She once fancied herself a great opera singer and left me; I was looking for her for two months, and, my dear soul, I spent a thousand roubles on telegrams alone."

He no longer called me a dissenter or Mr. Painter, and did not as in the past express approval of my living like a workman, but said:

"You are a strange person! You are not a normal person! I won't venture to prophesy, but you will come to a bad end!"

And Masha slept badly at night, and was always sitting at our bedroom window thinking. There was no laughter at supper now, no charming grimaces. I was wretched, and when it rained, every drop that fell seemed to pierce my heart, like small shot, and I felt ready to fall on my knees before Masha and apologize for the weather. When the peasants made a noise in the yard I felt guilty also. For hours at a time I sat still in one place, thinking of nothing but what a splendid person Masha was, what a wonderful person. I loved her passionately, and I was fascinated by everything she did, everything she said. She had a bent for quiet, studious pursuits; she was fond of reading for hours together, of studying. Although her knowledge of farming was only from books she surprised us all by what she knew; and every piece of advice she gave was of value; not one was ever thrown away; and, with all that, what nobility, what taste, what graciousness, that graciousness which is only found in well-educated people.

To this woman, with her sound, practical intelligence, the disorderly surroundings with petty cares and sordid anxieties in which we were living now were an agony: I saw that and could not sleep at night; my brain worked feverishly and I had a lump in my throat. I rushed about not knowing what to do.

I galloped to the town and brought Masha books, newspapers, sweets, flowers; with Stepan I caught fish, wading for hours up to my neck in the cold water in the rain to catch eel-pout to vary our fare; I demeaned myself to beg the peasants not to make a noise; I plied them with vodka, bought them off, made all sorts of promises. And how many other foolish things I did!

At last the rain ceased, the earth dried. One would get up at four o'clock in the morning; one would go out into the garden - where there was dew sparkling on the flowers, the twitter of birds, the hum of insects, not one cloud in the sky; and the garden, the meadows, and the river were so lovely, yet there were memories of the peasants, of their carts, of the engineer. Masha and I drove out together in the racing droshky to the fields to look at the oats. She used to drive, I sat behind; her shoulders were raised and the wind played with her hair.

"Keep to the right!" she shouted to those she met.

"You are like a sledge-driver," I said to her one day.

"Maybe! Why, my grandfather, the engineer's father, was a sledge-driver. Didn't you know that?" she asked, turning to me, and at once she mimicked the way sledge-drivers shout and sing.

"And thank God for that," I thought as I listened to her. "Thank God."

And again memories of the peasants, of the carts, of the engineer. . . .

XIII

Dr. Blagovo arrived on his bicycle. My sister began coming often. Again there were conversations about manual labour, about progress, about a mysterious millennium awaiting mankind in the remote future. The doctor did not like our farmwork, because it interfered with arguments, and said that ploughing, reaping, grazing calves were unworthy of a free man, and all these coarse forms of the struggle for existence men would in time relegate to animals and machines, while they would devote themselves exclusively to scientific investigation. My sister kept begging them to let her go home earlier, and if she stayed on till late in the evening, or spent the night with us, there would be no end to the agitation.

"Good Heavens, what a baby you are still!" said Masha reproachfully. "It is positively absurd."

"Yes, it is absurd," my sister agreed, "I know it's absurd; but what is to be done if I haven't the strength to get over it? I keep feeling as though I were doing wrong."

At haymaking I ached all over from the unaccustomed labour; in the evening, sitting on the verandah and talking with the others, I suddenly dropped asleep, and they laughed aloud at me. They waked me up and made me sit down to supper; I was overpowered with drowsiness and I saw the lights, the faces, and the plates as it were in a dream, heard the voices, but did not understand them. And getting up early in the morning, I took up the scythe at once, or went to the building and worked hard all day.

When I remained at home on holidays I noticed that my sister and Masha were concealing something from me, and even seemed to be avoiding me. My wife was tender to me as before, but she had thoughts of her own apart, which she did not share with me. There was no doubt that her exasperation with the peasants was growing, the life was becoming more and more distasteful to her, and yet she did not complain to me. She talked to the doctor now more readily than she did to me, and I did not understand why it was so.

It was the custom in our province at haymaking and harvest time for the labourers to come to the manor house in the evening and be regaled with vodka; even young girls drank a glass. We did not keep up this practice; the mowers and the peasant women stood about in our yard till late in the evening expecting vodka, and then departed abusing us. And all the time Masha frowned grimly and said nothing, or murmured to the doctor with exasperation: "Savages! Petchenyegs!"

In the country newcomers are met ungraciously, almost with hostility, as they are at school. And we were received in this way. At first we were looked upon as stupid, silly people, who had bought an estate simply because we did not know what to do with our money. We were laughed at. The peasants grazed their cattle in our wood and even in our garden; they drove away our cows and horses to the village, and then demanded money for the damage done by them. They came in whole companies into our yard, and loudly clamoured that at the mowing we had cut some piece of land that did not belong to us; and as we did not yet know the boundaries of our estate very accurately, we took their word for it and paid damages. Afterwards it turned out that there had been no mistake at the mowing. They barked the lime-trees in our wood. One of the Dubetchnya peasants, a regular shark, who did a trade in vodka without a licence, bribed our labourers, and in collaboration with them cheated us in a most treacherous way. They took the new wheels off our carts and replaced them with old ones, stole our ploughing harness and actually sold them to us, and so on. But what was most mortifying of all was what happened at the building; the peasant women stole by night boards, bricks, tiles, pieces of iron. The village elder with witnesses made a search in their huts; the village meeting fined them two roubles each, and afterwards this money was spent on drink by the whole commune.

When Masha heard about this, she would say to the doctor or my sister indignantly:

"What beasts! It's awful! awful!"

And I heard her more than once express regret that she had ever taken it into her head to build the school.

"You must understand," the doctor tried to persuade her, "that if you build this school and do good in general, it's not for the sake of the peasants, but in the name of culture, in the name of the future; and the worse the peasants are the more reason for building the school. Understand that!"

But there was a lack of conviction in his voice, and it seemed to me that both he and Masha hated the peasants.

Masha often went to the mill, taking my sister with her, and they both said, laughing, that they went to have a look at Stepan, he was so handsome. Stepan, it appeared, was torpid and taciturn only with men; in feminine society his manners were free and easy, and he talked incessantly. One day, going down to the river to bathe, I accidentally overheard a conversation. Masha and Kleopatra, both in white dresses, were sitting on the bank in the spreading shade of a willow, and Stepan was standing by them with his hands behind his back, and was saying:

"Are peasants men? They are not men, but, asking your pardon, wild beasts, impostors. What life has a peasant? Nothing but eating and drinking; all he cares for is victuals to be cheaper and swilling liquor at the tavern like a fool; and there's no conversation, no manners, no formality, nothing but ignorance! He lives in filth, his wife lives in filth, and his children live in filth. What he stands up in, he lies down to sleep in; he picks the potatoes out of the soup with his fingers; he drinks kvass with a cockroach in it, and doesn't bother to blow it away!"

"It's their poverty, of course," my sister put in.

"Poverty? There is want to be sure, there's different sorts of want, Madam. If a man is in prison, or let us say blind or crippled, that really is trouble I wouldn't wish anyone, but if a man's free and has all his senses, if he has his eyes and his hands and his strength and God, what more does he want? It's cockering themselves, and it's ignorance, Madam, it's not poverty. If you, let us suppose, good gentlefolk, by your education, wish out of kindness to help him he will drink away your money in his low way; or, what's worse, he will open a drink-shop, and with your money start robbing the people. You say poverty, but does the rich peasant live better? He, too, asking your pardon, lives like a swine: coarse, loud-mouthed, cudgel-headed, broader than he is long, fat, red-faced mug, I'd like to swing my fist and send him flying, the scoundrel. There's Larion, another rich one at Dubetchnya, and I bet he strips the bark off your trees as much as any poor one; and he is a foul-mouthed fellow; his children are the same, and when he has had a drop too much he'll topple with his nose in a puddle and sleep there. They are all a worthless lot, Madam. If you live in a village with them it is like hell. It has stuck in my teeth, that village has, and thank the Lord, the King of Heaven, I've plenty to eat and clothes to wear, I served out my time in the dragoons, I was village elder for three years, and now I am a free Cossack, I live where I like. I don't want to live in the village, and no one has the right to force me. They say - my wife. They say you are bound to live in your cottage with your wife. But why so? I am not her hired man."

"Tell me, Stepan, did you marry for love?" asked Masha.

"Love among us in the village!" answered Stepan, and he gave a laugh. "Properly speaking, Madam, if you care to know, this is my second marriage. I am not a Kurilovka man, I am from Zalegoshtcho, but afterwards I was taken into Kurilovka when I married. You see my father did not want to divide the land among us. There were five of us brothers. I took my leave and went to another village to live with my wife's family, but my first wife died when she was young."

"What did she die of?"

"Of foolishness. She used to cry and cry and cry for no reason, and so she pined away. She was always drinking some sort of herbs to make her better looking, and I suppose she damaged her inside. And my second wife is a Kurilovka woman too, there is nothing in her. She's a village woman, a peasant woman, and nothing more. I was taken in when they plighted me to her. I thought she was young and fair-skinned, and that they lived in a clean way. Her mother was just like a Flagellant and she drank coffee, and the chief thing, to be sure, they were clean in their ways. So I married her, and next day we sat down to dinner; I bade my mother-in-law give me a spoon, and she gives me a spoon, and I see her wipe it out with her finger. So much for you, thought I; nice sort of cleanliness yours is. I lived a year with them and then I went away. I might have married a girl from the town," he went on after a pause. "They say a wife is a helpmate to her husband. What do I want with a helpmate? I help myself; I'd rather she talked to me, and not clack, clack, clack, but circumstantially, feelingly. What is life without good conversation?"

Stepan suddenly paused, and at once there was the sound of his dreary, monotonous "Oo-loo-loo-loo." This meant that he had seen me.

Masha used often to go to the mill, and evidently found pleasure in her conversations with Stepan. Stepan abused the peasants with such sincerity and conviction, and she was attracted to him. Every time she came back from the mill the feeble-minded peasant, who looked after the garden, shouted at her:

"Wench Palashka! Hulla, wench Palashka!" and he would bark like a dog: "Ga! Ga!"

And she would stop and look at him attentively, as though in that idiot's barking she found an answer to her thoughts, and probably he attracted her in the same way as Stepan's abuse. At home some piece of news would await her, such, for instance, as that the geese from the village had ruined our cabbage in the garden, or that Larion had stolen the reins; and shrugging her shoulders, she would say with a laugh:

"What do you expect of these people?"

She was indignant, and there was rancour in her heart, and meanwhile I was growing used to the peasants, and I felt more and more drawn to them. For the most part they were nervous, irritable, downtrodden people; they were people whose imagination had been stifled, ignorant, with a poor, dingy outlook on life, whose thoughts were ever the same - of the grey earth, of grey days, of black bread, people who cheated, but like birds hiding nothing but their head behind the tree - people who could not count. They would not come to mow for us for twenty roubles, but they came for half a pail of vodka, though for twenty roubles they could have bought four pails. There really was filth and drunkenness and foolishness and deceit, but with all that one yet felt that the life of the peasants rested on a firm, sound foundation. However uncouth a wild animal the peasant following the plough seemed, and however he might stupefy himself with vodka, still, looking at him more closely, one felt that there was in him what was needed, something very important, which was lacking in Masha and in the doctor, for instance, and that was that he believed the chief thing on earth was truth and justice, and that his salvation, and that of the whole people, was only to be found in truth and justice, and so more than anything in the world he loved just dealing. I told my wife she saw the spots on the glass, but not the glass itself; she said nothing in reply, or hummed like Stepan "oo-loo-loo-loo." When this good-hearted and clever woman turned pale with indignation, and with a quiver in her voice spoke to the doctor of the drunkenness and dishonesty, it perplexed me, and I was struck by the shortness of her memory. How could she forget that her father the engineer drank too, and drank heavily, and that the money with which Dubetchnya had been bought had been acquired by a whole series of shameless, impudent dishonesties? How could she forget it?

XIV

My sister, too, was leading a life of her own which she carefully hid from me. She was often whispering with Masha. When I went up to her she seemed to shrink into herself, and there was a guilty, imploring look in her eyes; evidently there was something going on in her heart of which she was afraid or ashamed. So as to avoid meeting me in the garden, or being left alone with me, she always kept close to Masha, and I rarely had an opportunity of talking to her except at dinner.

One evening I was walking quietly through the garden on my way back from the building. It was beginning to get dark. Without noticing me, or hearing my step, my sister was walking near a spreading old apple-tree, absolutely noiselessly as though she were a phantom. She was dressed in black, and was walking rapidly backwards and forwards on the same track, looking at the ground. An apple fell from the tree; she started at the sound, stood still and pressed her hands to her temples. At that moment I went up to her.

In a rush of tender affection which suddenly flooded my heart, with tears in my eyes, suddenly remembering my mother and our childhood, I put my arm round her shoulders and kissed her.

"What is the matter?" I asked her. "You are unhappy; I have seen it for a long time. Tell me what's wrong?"

"I am frightened," she said, trembling.

"What is it?" I insisted. "For God's sake, be open!"

"I will, I will be open; I will tell you the whole truth. To hide it from you is so hard, so agonizing. Misail, I love . . ." she went on in a whisper, "I love him . . . I love him. . . . I am happy, but why am I so frightened?"

There was the sound of footsteps; between the trees appeared Dr. Blagovo in his silk shirt with his high top boots. Evidently they had arranged to meet near the apple-tree. Seeing him, she rushed impulsively towards him with a cry of pain as though he were being taken from her.

"Vladimir! Vladimir!"

She clung to him and looked greedily into his face, and only then I noticed how pale and thin she had become of late. It was particularly noticeable from her lace collar which I had known for so long, and which now hung more loosely than ever before about her thin, long neck. The doctor was disconcerted, but at once recovered himself, and, stroking her hair, said:

"There, there. . . . Why so nervous? You see, I'm here."

We were silent, looking with embarrassment at each other, then we walked on, the three of us together, and I heard the doctor say to me:

"Civilized life has not yet begun among us. Old men console themselves by making out that if there is nothing now, there was something in the forties or the sixties; that's the old: you and I are young; our brains have not yet been touched by *marasmus senilis;* we cannot comfort ourselves with such illusions. The beginning of Russia was in 862, but the beginning of civilized Russia has not come yet."

But I did not grasp the meaning of these reflections. It was somehow strange, I could not believe it, that my sister was in love, that she was walking and holding the arm of a stranger and looking tenderly at him. My sister, this nervous, frightened, crushed, fettered creature, loved a man who was married and had children! I felt sorry for something, but what exactly I don't know; the presence of the doctor was for some reason distasteful to me now, and I could not imagine what would come of this love of theirs.

XV

Masha and I drove to Kurilovka to the dedication of the school.

"Autumn, autumn, autumn, . . ." said Masha softly, looking away. "Summer is over. There are no birds and nothing is green but the willows."

Yes, summer was over. There were fine, warm days, but it was fresh in the morning, and the shepherds went out in their sheepskins already; and in our garden the dew did not dry off the asters all day long. There were plaintive sounds all the time, and one could not make out whether they came from the shutters creaking on their rusty hinges, or from the flying cranes - and one's heart felt light, and one was eager for life.

"The summer is over," said Masha. "Now you and I can balance our accounts. We have done a lot of work, a lot of thinking; we are the better for it - all honour and glory to us - we have succeeded in self-improvement; but have our successes had any perceptible influence on the life around us, have they brought any benefit to anyone whatever? No. Ignorance, physical uncleanliness, drunkenness, an appallingly high infant mortality, everything remains as it was, and no one is the better for your having ploughed and sown, and my having wasted money and read books. Obviously we have been working only for ourselves and have had advanced ideas only for ourselves." Such reasonings perplexed me, and I did not know what to think.

"We have been sincere from beginning to end," said I, "and if anyone is sincere he is right."

"Who disputes it? We were right, but we haven't succeeded in properly accomplishing what we were right in. To begin with, our external methods themselves - aren't they mistaken? You want to be of use to men, but by the very fact of your buying an estate, from the very start you cut yourself off from any possibility of doing anything useful for them. Then if you work, dress, eat like a peasant you sanctify, as it were, by your authority, their heavy, clumsy dress, their horrible huts, their stupid beards. . . . On the other hand, if we suppose that you work for long, long years, your whole life, that in the end some practical results are obtained, yet what are they, your results, what can they do against such elemental forces as wholesale ignorance, hunger, cold, degeneration? A drop in the ocean! Other methods of struggle are needed, strong, bold, rapid! If one really wants to be of use one must get out of the narrow circle of ordinary social work, and try to act direct upon the mass! What is wanted, first of all, is a loud, energetic propaganda. Why is it that art - music, for instance - is so living, so popular, and in reality so powerful? Because the musician or the singer affects thousands at once. Precious, precious art!" she went on, looking dreamily at the sky. "Art gives us wings and carries us far, far away! Anyone who is sick of filth, of petty, mercenary interests, anyone who is revolted, wounded, and indignant, can find peace and satisfaction only in the beautiful."

When we drove into Kurilovka the weather was bright and joyous. Somewhere they were threshing; there was a smell of rye straw. A mountain ash was bright red behind the hurdle fences, and all the trees wherever one looked were ruddy or golden. They were ringing the bells, they were carrying the ikons to the school, and we could hear them sing: "Holy Mother, our Defender," and how limpid the air was, and how high the doves were flying.

The service was being held in the classroom. Then the peasants of Kurilovka brought Masha the ikon, and the peasants of Dubetchnya offered her abig loaf and a gilt salt cellar. And Masha broke into sobs.

"If anything has been said that shouldn't have been or anything done not to your liking, forgive us," said an old man, and he bowed down to her and to me.

As we drove home Masha kept looking round at the school; the green roof, which I had painted, and which was glistening in the sun, remained in sight for a long while. And I felt that the look Masha turned upon it now was one of farewell.

XVI

In the evening she got ready to go to the town. Of late she had taken to going often to the town and staying the night there. In her absence I could not work, my hands felt weak and limp; our huge courtyard seemed a dreary, repulsive, empty hole. The garden was full of angry noises, and without her the house, the trees, the horses were no longer "ours."

I did not go out of the house, but went on sitting at her table beside her bookshelf with the books on land work, those old favourites no longer wanted and looking at me now so shamefacedly. For whole hours together, while it struck seven, eight, nine, while the autumn night, black as soot, came on outside, I kept examining her old glove, or the pen with which she always wrote, or her little scissors. I did nothing, and realized clearly that all I had done before, ploughing, mowing, chopping, had only been because she wished it. And if she had sent me to clean a deep well, where I had to stand up to my waist in deep water, I should have crawled into the well without considering whether it was necessary or not. And now when she was not near, Dubetchnya, with its ruins, its untidiness, its banging shutters, with its thieves by day and by night, seemed to me a chaos in which any work would be useless. Besides, what had I to work for here, why anxiety and thought about the future, if I felt that the earth was giving way under my feet, that I had played my part in Dubetchnya, and that the fate of the books on farming was awaiting me too? Oh, what misery it was at night, in hours of solitude, when I was listening every minute in alarm, as though I were expecting someone to shout that it was time for me to go away! I did not grieve for Dubetchnya. I grieved for my love which, too, was threatened with its autumn. What an immense happiness it is to love and be loved, and how awful to feel that one is slipping down from that high pinnacle!

Masha returned from the town towards the evening of the next day. She was displeased with something, but she concealed it, and only said, why was it all the window frames had been put in for the winter it was enough to suffocate one. I took out two frames. We were not hungry, but we sat down to supper.

"Go and wash your hands," said my wife; "you smell of putty."

She had brought some new illustrated papers from the town, and we looked at them together after supper. There were supplements with fashion plates and patterns. Masha looked through them casually, and was putting them aside to examine them properly later on; but one dress, with a flat skirt as full as a bell and large sleeves, interested her, and she looked at it for a minute gravely and attentively.

"That's not bad," she said.

"Yes, that dress would suit you beautifully," I said, "beautifully."

And looking with emotion at the dress, admiring that patch of grey simply because she liked it, I went on tenderly:

"A charming, exquisite dress! Splendid, glorious, Masha! My precious Masha!"

And tears dropped on the fashion plate.

"Splendid Masha . . ." I muttered; "sweet, precious Masha. . . ."

She went to bed, while I sat another hour looking at the illustrations.

"It's a pity you took out the window frames," she said from the bedroom, "I am afraid it may be cold. Oh, dear, what a draught there is!"

I read something out of the column of odds and ends, a receipt for making cheap ink, and an account of the biggest diamond in the world. I came again upon the fashion plate of the dress she liked, and I imagined her at a ball, with a fan, bare shoulders, brilliant, splendid, with a full understanding of painting, music, literature, and how small and how brief my part seemed!

Our meeting, our marriage, had been only one of the episodes of which there would be many more in the life of this vital, richly gifted woman. All the best in the world, as I have said already, was at her service, and she received it absolutely for nothing, and even ideas and the intellectual movement in vogue served simply for her recreation, giving variety to her life, and I was only the sledge-driver who drove her from one entertainment to another. Now she did not need me. She would take flight, and I should be alone.

And as though in response to my thought, there came a despairing scream from the garden.

"He-e-elp!"

It was a shrill, womanish voice, and as though to mimic it the wind whistled in the chimney on the same shrill note. Half a minute passed, and again through the noise of the wind, but coming, it seemed, from the other end of the yard:

"He-e-elp!"

"Misail, do you hear?" my wife asked me softly. "Do you hear?"

She came out from the bedroom in her nightgown, with her hair down, and listened, looking at the dark window.

"Someone is being murdered," she said. "That is the last straw."

I took my gun and went out. It was very dark outside, the wind was high, and it was difficult to stand. I went to the gate and listened, the trees roared, the wind whistled and, probably at the feeble-minded peasant's, a dog howled lazily. Outside the gates the darkness was absolute, not a light on the railway-line. And near the lodge, which a year before had been the office, suddenly sounded a smothered scream:

"He-e-elp!"

"Who's there?" I called.

There were two people struggling. One was thrusting the other out, while the other was resisting, and both were breathing heavily.

"Leave go," said one, and I recognized Ivan Tcheprakov; it was he who was shrieking in a shrill, womanish voice: "Let go, you damned brute, or I'll bite your hand off."

The other I recognized as Moisey. I separated them, and as I did so I could not resist hitting Moisey two blows in the face. He fell down, then got up again, and I hit him once more.

"He tried to kill me," he muttered. "He was trying to get at his mamma's chest. . . . I want to lock him up in the lodge for security."

Tchepraköv was drunk and did not recognize me; he kept drawing deep breaths, as though he were just going to shout "help" again.

I left them and went back to the house; my wife was lying on her bed; she had dressed. I told her what had happened in the yard, and did not conceal the fact that I had hit Moisey.

"It's terrible to live in the country," she said.

"And what a long night it is. Oh dear, if only it were over!"

"He-e-elp!" we heard again, a little later.

"I'll go and stop them," I said.

"No, let them bite each other's throats," she said with an expression of disgust.

She was looking up at the ceiling, listening, while I sat beside her, not daring to speak to her, feeling as though I were to blame for their shouting "help" in the yard and for the night's seeming so long.

We were silent, and I waited impatiently for a gleam of light at the window, and Masha looked all the time as though she had awakened from a trance and now was marvelling how she, so clever, and well-educated, so elegant, had come into this pitiful, provincial, empty hole among a crew of petty, insignificant people, and how she could have so far forgotten herself as ever to be attracted by one of these people, and for more than six months to have been his wife. It seemed to me that at that moment it did not matter to her whether it was I, or Moisey, or Tchepraköv; everything for her was merged in that savage drunken "help" - I and our marriage, and our work together, and the mud and slush of autumn, and when she sighed or moved into a more comfortable position I read in her face: "Oh, that morning would come quickly!"

In the morning she went away. I spent another three days at Dubetchnya expecting her, then I packed all our things in one room, locked it, and walked to the town. It was already evening when I rang at the engineer's, and the street lamps were burning in Great Dvoryansky Street. Pavel told me there was no one at home; Viktor Ivanitch had gone to Petersburg, and Mariya Viktorovna was probably at the rehearsal at the Azhogins'. I remember with what emotion I went on to the Azhogins', how my heart throbbed and fluttered as I mounted the stairs, and stood waiting a long while on the landing at the top, not daring to enter that temple of the muses! In the big room there were lighted candles everywhere, on a little table, on the piano, and on the stage, everywhere in threes; and the first performance was fixed for the thirteenth, and now the first rehearsal was on a Monday, an unlucky day. All part of the war against superstition! All the devotees of the scenic art were gathered together; the eldest, the middle, and the youngest sisters were walking about the stage, reading their parts in exercise books. Apart from all the rest stood Radish, motionless, with the side of his head pressed to the wall as he gazed with adoration at the stage, waiting for the rehearsal to begin. Everything as it used to be.

I was making my way to my hostess; I had to pay my respects to her, but suddenly everyone said "Hush!" and waved me to step quietly. There was a silence. The lid of the piano was raised; a lady sat down at it screwing up her short-sighted eyes at the music, and my Masha walked up to the piano, in a low-necked dress, looking beautiful, but with a special, new sort of beauty not in the least like the Masha who used to come and meet me in the spring at the mill. She sang: "Why do I love the radiant night?"

It was the first time during our whole acquaintance that I had heard her sing. She had a fine, mellow, powerful voice, and while she sang I felt as though I were eating a ripe, sweet, fragrant melon. She ended, the audience applauded, and she smiled, very much pleased, making play with her eyes, turning over the music, smoothing her skirts, like a bird that has at last broken out of its cage and preens its wings in freedom. Her hair was arranged over her ears, and she had an unpleasant, defiant expression in her face, as though she wanted to throw down a challenge to us all, or to shout to us as she did to her horses: "Hey, there, my beauties!"

And she must at that moment have been very much like her grandfather the sledge-driver.

"You here too?" she said, giving me her hand. "Did you hear me sing? Well, what did you think of it?" and without waiting for my answer she went on: "It's a very good thing you are here. I am going to-night to Petersburg for a short time. You'll let me go, won't you?"

At midnight I went with her to the station. She embraced me affectionately, probably feeling grateful to me for not asking unnecessary questions, and she promised to write to me, and I held her hands a long time, and kissed them, hardly able to restrain my tears and not uttering a word.

And when she had gone I stood watching the retreating lights, caressing her in imagination and softly murmuring:

"My darling Masha, glorious Masha. . . ."

I spent the night at Karpovna's, and next morning I was at work with Radish, re-covering the furniture of a rich merchant who was marrying his daughter to a doctor.

XVII

My sister came after dinner on Sunday and had tea with me.

"I read a great deal now," she said, showing me the books which she had fetched from the public library on her way to me. "Thanks to your wife and to Vladimir, they have awakened me to self-realization. They have been my salvation; they have made me feel myself a human being. In old days I used to lie awake at night with worries of all sorts, thinking what a lot of Êsugar we had used in the week, or hoping the cucumbers would not be too salt. And now, too, I lie awake at night, but I have different thoughts. I am distressed that half my life has been passed in such a foolish, cowardly way. I despise my past; I am ashamed of it. And I look upon our father now as my enemy. Oh, how grateful I am to your wife! And Vladimir! He is such a wonderful person! They have opened my eyes!"

"That's bad that you don't sleep at night," I said.

"Do you think I am ill? Not at all. Vladimir sounded me, and said I was perfectly well. But health is not what matters, it is not so important. Tell me: am I right?"

She needed moral support - that was obvious. Masha had gone away. Dr. Blagovo was in Petersburg, and there was no one left in the town but me, to tell her she was right. She looked intently into my face, trying to read my secret thoughts, and if I were absorbed or silent in her presence she thought this was on her account, and was grieved. I always had to be on my guard, and when she asked me whether she was right I hastened to assure her that she was right, and that I had a deep respect for her.

"Do you know they have given me a part at the Azhogins'?" she went on. "I want to act on the stage, I want to live - in fact, I mean to drain the full cup. I have no talent, none, and the part is only ten lines, but still this is immeasurably finer and loftier than pouring out tea five times a day, and looking to see if the cook has eaten too much. Above all, let my father see I am capable of protest."

After tea she lay down on my bed, and lay for a little while with her eyes closed, looking very pale.

"What weakness," she said, getting up. "Vladimir says all city-bred women and girls are anæmic from doing nothing. What a clever man Vladimir is! He is right, absolutely right. We must work!"

Two days later she came to the Azhogins' with her manuscript for the rehearsal. She was wearing a black dress with a string of coral round her neck, and a brooch that in the distance was like a pastry puff, and in her ears earrings sparkling with brilliants. When I looked at her I felt uncomfortable. I was struck by her lack of taste. That she had very inappropriately put on earrings and brilliants, and that she was strangely dressed, was remarked by other people too; I saw smiles on people's faces, and heard someone say with a laugh: "Kleopatra of Egypt."

She was trying to assume society manners, to be unconstrained and at her ease, and so seemed artificial and strange. She had lost simplicity and sweetness.

"I told father just now that I was going to the rehearsal," she began, coming up to me, "and he shouted that he would not give me his blessing, and actually almost struck me. Only fancy, I don't know my part," she said, looking at her manuscript. "I am sure to make a mess of it. So be it, the die is cast," she went on in intense excitement. "The die is cast. . . ."

It seemed to her that everyone was looking at her, and that all were amazed at the momentous step she had taken, that everyone was expecting something special of her, and it would have been impossible to convince her that no one was paying attention to people so petty and insignificant as she and I were.

She had nothing to do till the third act, and her part, that of a visitor, a provincial crony, consisted only in standing at the door as though listening, and then delivering a brief monologue. In the interval before her appearance, an hour and a half at least, while they were moving about on the stage reading their parts, drinking tea and arguing, she did not leave my side, and was all the time muttering her part and nervously crumpling up the manuscript. And imagining that everyone was looking at her and waiting for her appearance, with a trembling hand she smoothed back her hair and said to me:

"I shall certainly make a mess of it. . . . What a load on my heart, if only you knew! I feel frightened, as though I were just going to be led to execution."

At last her turn came.

"Kleopatra Alexyevna, it's your cue!" said the stage manager.

She came forward into the middle of the stage with an expression of horror on her face, looking ugly and angular, and for half a minute stood as though in a trance, perfectly motionless, and only her big earrings shook in her ears.

"The first time you can read it," said someone.

It was clear to me that she was trembling, and trembling so much that she could not speak, and could not unfold her manuscript, and that she was incapable of acting her part; and I was already on the point of going to her and saying something, when she suddenly dropped on her knees in the middle of the stage and broke into loud sobs.

All was commotion and hubbub. I alone stood still, leaning against the side scene, overwhelmed by what had happened, not understanding and not knowing what to do. I saw them lift her up and lead her away. I saw Anyuta Blagovo come up to me; I had not seen her in the room before, and she seemed to have sprung out of the earth. She was wearing her hat and veil, and, as always, had an air of having come only for a moment.

"I told her not to take a part," she said angrily, jerking out each word abruptly and turning crimson. "It's insanity! You ought to have prevented her!"

Madame Azhogin, in a short jacket with short sleeves, with cigarette ash on her breast, looking thin and flat, came rapidly towards me.

"My dear, this is terrible," she brought out, wringing her hands, and, as her habit was, looking intently into my face. "This is terrible! Your sister is in a condition. . . . She is with child. Take her away, I implore you. . . ."

She was breathless with agitation, while on one side stood her three daughters, exactly like her, thin and flat, huddling together in a scared way. They were alarmed, overwhelmed, as though a convict had been caught in their house. What a disgrace, how dreadful! And yet this estimable family had spent its life waging war on superstition; evidently they imagined that all the superstition and error of humanity was limited to the three candles, the thirteenth of the month, and to the unluckiness of Monday!

"I beg you. . . I beg," repeated Madame Azhogin, pursing up her lips in the shape of a heart on the syllable "you." "I beg you to take her home."

XVIII

A little later my sister and I were walking along the street. I covered her with the skirts of my coat; we hastened, choosing back streets where there were no street lamps, avoiding passers-by; it was as though we were running away. She was no longer crying, but looked at me with dry eyes. To Karpovna's, where I took her, it was only twenty minutes' walk, and, strange to say, in that short time we succeeded in thinking of our whole life; we talked over everything, considered our position, reflected. . . .

We decided we could not go on living in this town, and that when I had earned a little money we would move to some other place. In some houses everyone was asleep, in others they were playing cards; we hated these houses; we were afraid of them. We talked of the fanaticism, the coarseness of feeling, the insignificance of these respectable families, these amateurs of dramatic art whom we had so alarmed, and I kept asking in what way these stupid, cruel, lazy, and dishonest people were superior to the drunken and superstitious peasants of Kurilovka, or in what way they were better than animals, who in the same way are thrown into a panic when some incident disturbs the monotony of their life limited by their instincts. What would have happened to my sister now if she had been left to live at home?

What moral agonies would she have experienced, talking with my father, meeting every day with acquaintances? I imagined this to myself, and at once there came into my mind people, all people I knew, who had been slowly done to death by their nearest relations. I remembered the tortured dogs, driven mad, the live sparrows plucked naked by boys and flung into the water, and a long, long series of obscure lingering miseries which I had looked on continually from early childhood in that town; and I could not understand what these sixty thousand people lived for, what they read the gospel for, why they prayed, why they read books and magazines. What good had they gained from all that had been said and written hitherto if they were still possessed by the same spiritual darkness and hatred of liberty, as they were a hundred and three hundred years ago? A master carpenter spends his whole life building houses in the town, and always, to the day of his death, calls a "gallery" a "galdery." So these sixty thousand people have been reading and hearing of truth, of justice, of mercy, of freedom for generations, and yet from morning till night, till the day of their death, they are lying, and tormenting each other, and they fear liberty and hate it as a deadly foe.

"And so my fate is decided," said my sister, as we arrived home. "After what has happened I cannot go back *there*. Heavens, how good that is! My heart feels lighter."

She went to bed at once. Tears were glittering on her eyelashes, but her expression was happy; she fell into a sound sweet sleep, and one could see that her heart was lighter and that she was resting. It was a long, long time since she had slept like that.

And so we began our life together. She was always singing and saying that her life was very happy, and the books I brought her from the public library I took back unread, as now she could not read; she wanted to do nothing but dream and talk of the future, mending my linen, or helping Karpovna near the stove; she was always singing, or talking of her Vladimir, of his cleverness, of his charming manners, of his kindness, of his extraordinary learning, and I assented to all she said, though by now I disliked her doctor. She wanted to work, to lead an independent life on her own account, and she used to say that she would become a school-teacher or a doctor' s assistant as soon as her health would permit her, and would herself do the scrubbing and the washing. Already she was passionately devoted to her child; he was not yet born, but she knew already the colour of his eyes, what his hands would be like, and how he would laugh. She was fond of talking about education, and as her Vladimir was the best man in the world, all her discussion of education could be summed up in the question how to make the boy as fascinating as his father. There was no end to her talk, and everything she said made her intensely joyful. Sometimes I was delighted, too, though I could not have said why.

I suppose her dreaminess infected me. I, too, gave up reading, and did nothing but dream. In the evenings, in spite of my fatigue, I walked up and down the room, with my hands in my pockets, talking of Masha.

"What do you think?" I would ask of my sister. "When will she come back? I think she'll come back at Christmas, not later; what has she to do there?"

"As she doesn't write to you, it's evident she will come back very soon.

"That's true," I assented, though I knew perfectly well that Masha would not return to our town.

I missed her fearfully, and could no longer deceive myself, and tried to get other people to deceive me. My sister was expecting her doctor, and I - Masha; and both of us talked incessantly, laughed, and did not notice that we were preventing Karpovna from sleeping. She lay on the stove and kept muttering:

"The samovar hummed this morning, it did hum! Oh, it bodes no good, my dears, it bodes no good!"

No one ever came to see us but the postman, who brought my sister letters from the doctor, and Prokofy, who sometimes came in to see us in the evening, and after looking at my sister without speaking went away, and when he was in the kitchen said:

"Every class ought to remember its rules, and anyone, who is so proud that he won't understand that, will find it a vale of tears."

He was very fond of the phrase "a vale of tears." One day - it was in Christmas week, when I was walking by the bazaar - he called me into the butcher's shop, and not shaking hands with me, announced that he had to speak to me about something very important. His face was red from the frost and vodka; near him, behind the counter, stood Nikolka, with the expression of a brigand, holding a bloodstained knife in his hand.

"I desire to express my word to you," Prokofy began. "This incident cannot continue, because, as you understand yourself that for such a vale, people will say nothing good of you or of us. Mamma, through pity, cannot say something unpleasant to you, that your sister should move into another lodging on account of her condition, but I won't have it any more, because I can't approve of her behaviour."

I understood him, and I went out of the shop. The same day my sister and I moved to Radish's. We had no money for a cab, and we walked on foot; I carried a parcel of our belongings on my back; my sister had nothing in her hands, but she gasped for breath and coughed, and kept asking whether we should get there soon.

XIX

At last a letter came from Masha.

"Dear, good M. A." (she wrote), "our kind, gentle 'angel' as the old painter calls you, farewell; I am going with my father to America for the exhibition. In a few days I shall see the ocean - so far from Dubetchnya, it's dreadful to think! It's far and unfathomable as the sky, and I long to be there in freedom. I am triumphant, I am mad, and you see how incoherent my letter is. Dear, good one, give me my freedom, make haste to break the thread, which still holds, binding you and me together. My meeting and knowing you was a ray from heaven that lighted up my existence; but my becoming your wife was a mistake, you understand that, and I am oppressed now by the consciousness of the mistake, and I beseech you, on my knees, my generous friend, quickly, quickly, before I start for the ocean, telegraph that you consent to correct our common mistake, to remove the solitary stone from my wings, and my father, who will undertake all the arrangements, promised me not to burden you too much with formalities. And so I am free to fly whither I will? Yes?

"Be happy, and God bless you; forgive me, a sinner.

"I am well, I am wasting money, doing all sorts of silly things, and I thank God every minute that such a bad woman as I has no children. I sing and have success, but it's not an infatuation; no, it's my haven, my cell to which I go for peace. King David had a ring with an inscription on it: 'All things pass.' When one is sad those words make one cheerful, and when one is cheerful it makes one sad. I have got myself a ring like that with Hebrew letters on it, and this talisman keeps me from infatuations. All things pass, life will pass, one wants nothing. Or at least one wants nothing but the sense of freedom, for when anyone is free, he wants nothing, nothing, nothing. Break the thread. A warm hug to you and your sister. Forgive and forget your M."

My sister used to lie down in one room, and Radish, who had been ill again and was now better, in another. Just at the moment when I received this letter my sister went softly into the painter's room, sat down beside him and began reading aloud. She read to him every day, Ostrovsky or Gogol, and he listened, staring at one point, not laughing, but shaking his head and muttering to himself from time to time:

"Anything may happen! Anything may happen!"

If anything ugly or unseemly were depicted in the play he would say as though vindictively, thrusting his finger into the book:

"There it is, lying! That's what it does, lying does."

The plays fascinated him, both from their subjects and their moral, and from their skilful, complex construction, and he marvelled at "him," never calling the author by his name. How neatly *he* has put it all together.

This time my sister read softly only one page, and could read no more: her voice would not last out. Radish took her hand and, moving his parched lips, said, hardly audibly, in a husky voice:

"The soul of a righteous man is white and smooth as chalk, but the soul of a sinful man is like pumice stone. The soul of a righteous man is like clear oil, but the soul of a sinful man is gas tar. We must labour, we must sorrow, we must suffer sickness," he went on, "and he who does not labour and sorrow will not gain the Kingdom of Heaven. Woe, woe to them that are well fed, woe to the mighty, woe to the rich, woe to the moneylenders! Not for them is the Kingdom of Heaven. Lice eat grass, rust eats iron. . ."

"And lying the soul," my sister added laughing. I read the letter through once more. At that moment there walked into the kitchen a soldier who had been bringing us twice a week parcels of tea, French bread and game, which smelt of scent, from some unknown giver. I had no work. I had had to sit at home idle for whole days together, and probably whoever sent us the French bread knew that we were in want.

I heard my sister talking to the soldier and laughing gaily. Then, lying down, she ate some French bread and said to me:

"When you wouldn't go into the service, but became a house painter, Anyuta Blagovo and I knew from the beginning that you were right, but we were frightened to say so aloud. Tell me what force is it that hinders us from saying what one thinks? Take Anyuta Blagovo now, for instance. She loves you, she adores you, she knows you are right, she loves me too, like a sister, and knows that I am right, and I daresay in her soul envies me, but some force prevents her from coming to see us, she shuns us, she is afraid."

My sister crossed her arms over her breast, and said passionately:

"How she loves you, if only you knew! She has confessed her love to no one but me, and then very secretly in the dark. She led me into a dark avenue in the garden, and began whispering how precious you were to her. You will see, she'll never marry, because she loves you. Are you sorry for her?"

"Yes."

"It's she who has sent the bread. She is absurd really, what is the use of being so secret? I used to be absurd and foolish, but now I have got away from that and am afraid of nobody. I think and say aloud what I like, and am happy. When I lived at home I hadn't a conception of happiness, and now I wouldn't change with a queen."

Dr. Blagovo arrived. He had taken his doctor's degree, and was now staying in our town with his father; he was taking a rest, and said that he would soon go back to Petersburg again. He wanted to study anti-toxins against typhus, and, I believe, cholera; he wanted to go abroad to perfect his training, and then to be appointed a professor. He had already left the army service, and wore a roomy serge reefer jacket, very full trousers, and magnificent neckties. My sister was in ecstasies over his scarfpin, his studs, and the red silk handkerchief which he wore, I suppose from foppishness, sticking out of the breast pocket of his jacket. One day, having nothing to do, she and I counted up all the suits we remembered him wearing, and came to the conclusion that he had at least ten. It was clear that he still loved my sister as before, but he never once even in jest spoke of taking her with him to Petersburg or abroad, and I could not picture to myself clearly what would become of her if she remained alive and what would become of her child. She did nothing but dream endlessly, and never thought seriously of the future; she said he might go where he liked, and might abandon her even, so long as he was happy himself; that what had been was enough for her.

As a rule he used to sound her very carefully on his arrival, and used to insist on her taking milk and drops in his presence. It was the same on this occasion. He sounded her and made her drink a glass of milk, and there was a smell of creosote in our room afterwards.

"That's a good girl," he said, taking the glass from her. "You mustn't talk too much now; you've taken to chattering like a magpie of late. Please hold your tongue."

She laughed. Then he came into Radish's room where I was sitting and affectionately slapped me on the shoulder.

"Well, how goes it, old man?" he said, bending down to the invalid.

"Your honour," said Radish, moving his lips slowly, "your honour, I venture to submit. . . . We all walk in the fear of God, we all have to die. . . . Permit me to tell you the truth. . . . Your honour, the Kingdom of Heaven will not be for you!"

"There's no help for it," the doctor said jestingly; "there must be somebody in hell, you know."

And all at once something happened with my consciousness; as though I were in a dream, as though I were standing on a winter night in the slaughterhouse yard, and Prokofy beside me, smelling of pepper cordial; I made an effort to control myself, and rubbed my eyes, and at once it seemed to me that I was going along the road to the interview with the Governor. Nothing of the sort had happened to me before, or has happened to me since, and these strange memories that were like dreams, I ascribed to overexhaustion of my nerves. I lived through the scene at the slaughterhouse, and the interview with the Governor, and at the same time was dimly aware that it was not real.

When I came to myself I saw that I was no longer in the house, but in the street, and was standing with the doctor near a lamp-post.

"It's sad, it's sad," he was saying, and tears were trickling down his cheeks. "She is in good spirits, she's always laughing and hopeful, but her position's hopeless, dear boy. Your Radish hates me, and is always trying to make me feel that I have treated her badly. He is right from his standpoint, but I have my point of view too; and I shall never regret all that has happened. One must love; we ought all to love - oughtn't we? There would be no life without love; anyone who fears and avoids love is not free."

Little by little he passed to other subjects, began talking of science, of his dissertation which had been liked in Petersburg. He was carried away by his subject, and no longer thought of my sister, nor of his grief, nor of me. Life was of absorbing interest to him. She has America and her ring with the inscription on it, I thought, while this fellow has his doctor's degree and a professor's chair to look forward to, and only my sister and I are left with the old things.

When I said good-bye to him, I went up to the lamp-post and read the letter once more. And I remembered, I remembered vividly how that spring morning she had come to me at the mill, lain down and covered herself with her jacket - she wanted to be like a simple peasant woman. And how, another time - it was in the morning also - we drew the net out of the water, and heavy drops of rain fell upon us from the riverside willows, and we laughed.

It was dark in our house in Great Dvoryansky Street. I got over the fence and, as I used to do in the old days, went by the back way to the kitchen to borrow a lantern. There was no one in the kitchen. The samovar hissed near the stove, waiting for my father. "Who pours out my father's tea now?" I thought. Taking the lantern I went out to the shed, built myself up a bed of old newspapers and lay down. The hooks on the walls looked forbidding, as they used to of old, and their shadows flickered. It was cold. I felt that my sister would come in in a minute, and bring me supper, but at once I remembered that she was ill and was lying at Radish's, and it seemed to me strange that I should have climbed over the fence and be lying here in this unheated shed. My mind was in a maze, and I saw all sorts of absurd things.

There was a ring. A ring familiar from childhood: first the wire rustled against the wall, then a short plaintive ring in the kitchen. It was my father come back from the club. I got up and went into the kitchen. Axinya the cook clasped her hands on seeing me, and for some reason burst into tears.

"My own!" she said softly. "My precious! O Lord!"

And she began crumpling up her apron in her agitation. In the window there were standing jars of berries in vodka. I poured myself out a teacupful and greedily drank it off, for I was intensely thirsty. Axinya had quite recently scrubbed the table and benches, and there was that smell in the kitchen which is found in bright, snug kitchens kept by tidy cooks. And that smell and the chirp of the cricket used to lure us as children into the kitchen, and put us in the mood for hearing fairy tales and playing at "Kings" . . .

"Where's Kleopatra?" Axinya asked softly, in a fluster, holding her breath; "and where is your cap, my dear? Your wife, you say, has gone to Petersburg?"

She had been our servant in our mother's time, and used once to give Kleopatra and me our baths, and to her we were still children who had to be talked to for their good. For a quarter of an hour or so she laid before me all the reflections which she had with the sagacity of an old servant been accumulating in the stillness of that kitchen, all the time since we had seen each other. She said that the doctor could be forced to marry Kleopatra; he only needed to be thoroughly frightened; and that if an appeal were promptly written the bishop would annul the first marriage; that it would be a good thing for me to sell Dubetchnya without my wife's knowledge, and put the money in the bank in my own name; that if my sister and I were to bow down at my father's feet and ask him properly, he might perhaps forgive us; that we ought to have a service sung to the Queen of Heaven. . . .

"Come, go along, my dear, and speak to him," she said, when she heard my father's cough. "Go along, speak to him; bow down, your head won't drop off."

I went in. My father was sitting at the table sketching a plan of a summer villa, with Gothic windows, and with a fat turret like a fireman's watch tower - something peculiarly stiff and tasteless. Going into the study I stood still where I could see this drawing. I did not know why I had gone in to my father, but I remember that when I saw his lean face, his red neck, and his shadow on the wall, I wanted to throw myself on his neck, and as Axinya had told me, bow down at his feet; but the sight of the summer villa with the Gothic windows, and the fat turret, restrained me.

"Good evening," I said.

He glanced at me, and at once dropped his eyes on his drawing.

"What do you want?" he asked, after waiting a little.

"I have come to tell you my sister's very ill. She can't live very long," I added in a hollow voice.

"Well," sighed my father, taking off his spectacles, and laying them on the table. "What thou sowest that shalt thou reap. What thou sowest," he repeated, getting up from the table. "that shalt thou reap. I ask you to remember how you came to me two years ago, and on this very spot I begged you, I besought you to give up your errors; I reminded you of your duty, of your honour, of what you owed to your forefathers whose traditions we ought to preserve as sacred. Did you obey me? You scorned my counsels, and obstinately persisted in clinging to your false ideals; worse still you drew your sister into the path of error with you, and led her to lose her moral principles and sense of shame. Now you are both in a bad way. Well, as thou sowest, so shalt thou reap!"

As he said this he walked up and down the room. He probably imagined that I had come to him to confess my wrong doings, and he probably expected that I should begin begging him to forgive my sister and me. I was cold, I was shivering as though I were in a fever, and spoke with difficulty in a husky voice.

"And I beg you, too, to remember," I said, "on this very spot I besought you to understand me, to reflect, to decide with me how and for what we should live, and in answer you began talking about our forefathers, about my grandfather who wrote poems. One tells you now that your only daughter is hopelessly ill, and you go on again about your forefathers, your traditions. . . . And such frivolity in your old age, when death is close at hand, and you haven't more than five or ten years left!"

"What have you come here for?" my father asked sternly, evidently offended at my reproaching him for his frivolity.

"I don't know. I love you, I am unutterably sorry that we are so far apart - so you see I have come. I love you still, but my sister has broken with you completely. She does not forgive you, and will never forgive you now. Your very name arouses her aversion for the past, for life."

"And who is to blame for it?" cried my father. "It's your fault, you scoundrel!

"Well, suppose it is my fault?" I said. "I admit I have been to blame in many things, but why is it that this life of yours, which you think binding upon us, too - why is it so dreary, so barren? How is it that in not one of these houses you have been building for the last thirty years has there been anyone from whom I might have learnt how to live, so as not to be to blame? There is not one honest man in the whole town! These houses of yours are nests of damnation, where mothers and daughters are made away with, where children are tortured. . . . My poor mother!" I went on in despair. "My poor sister! One has to stupefy oneself with vodka, with cards, with scandal; one must become a scoundrel, a hypocrite, or go on drawing plans for years and years, so as not to notice all the horrors that lie hidden in these houses. Our town has existed for hundreds of years, and all that time it has not produced one man of service to our country - not one. You have stifled in the germ everything in the least living and bright. It's a town of shopkeepers, publicans, counting-house clerks, canting hypocrites; it's a useless, unnecessary town, which not one soul would regret if it suddenly sank through the earth."

"I don't want to listen to you, you scoundrel!" said my father, and he took up his ruler from the table. "You are drunk. Don't dare come and see your father in such a state! I tell you for the last time, and you can repeat it to your depraved sister, that you'll get nothing from me, either of you. I have torn my disobedient children out of my heart, and if they suffer for their disobedience and obstinacy I do not pity them. You can go whence you came. It has pleased God to chastise me with you, but I will bear the trial with resignation, and, like Job, I will find consolation in my sufferings and in unremitting labour. You must not cross my threshold till you have mended your ways. I am a just man, all I tell you is for your benefit, and if you desire your own good you ought to remember all your life what I say and have said to you. . . ."

I waved my hand in despair and went away. I don't remember what happened afterwards, that night and next day.

I am told that I walked about the streets bareheaded, staggering, and singing aloud, while a crowd of boys ran after me, shouting:

"Better-than-nothing!"

XX

If I wanted to order a ring for myself, the inscription I should choose would be: "Nothing passes away." I believe that nothing passes away without leaving a trace, and that every step we take, however small, has significance for our present and our future existence.

What I have been through has not been for nothing. My great troubles, my patience, have touched people's hearts, and now they don't call me "Better-than-nothing," they don't laugh at me, and when I walk by the shops they don't throw water over me. They have grown used to my being a workman, and see nothing strange in my carrying a pail of paint and putting in windows, though I am of noble rank; on the contrary, people are glad to give me orders, and I am now considered a first-rate workman, and the best foreman after Radish, who, though he has regained his health, and though, as before, he paints the cupola on the belfry without scaffolding, has no longer the force to control the workmen; instead of him I now run about the town looking for work, I engage the workmen and pay them, borrow money at a high rate of interest, and now that I myself am a contractor, I understand how it is that one may have to waste three days racing about the town in search of tilers on account of some twopenny-halfpenny job. People are civil to me, they address me politely, and in the houses where I work, they offer me tea, and send to enquire whether I wouldn't like dinner. Children and young girls often come and look at me with curiosity and compassion.

One day I was working in the Governor's garden, painting an arbour there to look like marble. The Governor, walking in the garden, came up to the arbour and, having nothing to do, entered into conversation with me, and I reminded him how he had once summoned me to an interview with him. He looked into my face intently for a minute, then made his mouth like a round "O," flung up his hands, and said: "I don't remember!"

I have grown older, have become silent, stern, and austere, I rarely laugh, and I am told that I have grown like Radish, and that like him I bore the workmen by my useless exhortations.

Mariya Viktorovna, my former wife, is living now abroad, while her father is constructing a railway somewhere in the eastern provinces, and is buying estates there. Dr. Blagovo is also abroad. Dubetchnya has passed again into the possession of Madame Tcheprakov, who has bought it after forcing the engineer to knock the price down twenty per cent. Moisey goes about now in a bowler hat; he often drives into the town in a racing droshky on business of some sort, and stops near the bank. They say he has already bought up a mortgaged estate, and is constantly making enquiries at the bank about Dubetchnya, which he means to buy too. Poor Ivan Tcheprakov was for a long while out of work, staggering about the town and drinking. I tried to get him into our work, and for a time he painted roofs and put in window-panes in our company, and even got to like it, and stole oil, asked for tips, and drank like a regular painter. But he soon got sick of the work, and went back to Dubetchnya, and afterwards the workmen confessed to me that he had tried to persuade them to join him one night and murder Moisey and rob Madame Tcheprakov.

My father has greatly aged; he is very bent, and in the evenings walks up and down near his house. I never go to see him.

During an epidemic of cholera Prokofy doctored some of the shopkeepers with pepper cordial and pitch, and took money for doing so, and, as I learned from the newspapers, was flogged for abusing the doctors as he sat in his shop. His shop boy Nikolka died of cholera. Karpovna is still alive and, as always, she loves and fears her Prokofy. When she sees me, she always shakes her head mournfully, and says with a sigh: "Your life is ruined."

On working days I am busy from morning till night. On holidays, in fine weather, I take my tiny niece (my sister reckoned on a boy, but the child is a girl) and walk in a leisurely way to the cemetery. There I stand or sit down, and stay a long time gazing at the grave that is so dear to me, and tell the child that her mother lies here.

Sometimes, by the graveside, I find Anyuta Blagovo. We greet each other and stand in silence, or talk of Kleopatra, of her child, of how sad life is in this world; then, going out of the cemetery we walk along in silence and she slackens her pace on purpose to walk beside me a little longer. The little girl, joyous and happy, pulls at her hand, laughing and screwing up her eyes in the bright sunlight, and we stand still and join in caressing the dear child.

When we reach the town Anyuta Blagovo, agitated and flushing crimson, says good-bye to me and walks on alone, austere and respectable. . . . And no one who met her could, looking at her, imagine that she had just been walking beside me and even caressing the child.

PEASANTS

I

Nikolay Tchikildyeev, a waiter in the Moscow hotel, Slavyansky Bazaar, was taken ill. His legs went numb and his gait was affected, so that on one occasion, as he was going along the corridor, he tumbled and fell down with a tray full of ham and peas. He had to leave his job. All his own savings and his wife's were spent on doctors and medicines; they had nothing left to live upon. He felt dull with no work to do, and he made up his mind he must go home to the village. It is better to be ill at home, and living there is cheaper; and it is a true saying that the walls of home are a help.

He reached Zhukovo towards evening. In his memories of childhood he had pictured his home as bright, snug, comfortable. Now, going into the hut, he was positively frightened; it was so dark, so crowded, so unclean. His wife Olga and his daughter Sasha, who had come with him, kept looking in bewilderment at the big untidy stove, which filled up almost half the hut and was black with soot and flies. What lots of flies! The stove was on one side, the beams lay slanting on the walls, and it looked as though the hut were just going to fall to pieces. In the corner, facing the door, under the holy images, bottle labels and newspaper cuttings were stuck on the walls instead of pictures. The poverty, the poverty! Of the grown-up people there were none at home; all were at work at the harvest. On the stove was sitting a white-headed girl of eight, unwashed and apathetic; she did not even glance at them as they came in. On the floor a white cat was rubbing itself against the oven fork.

"Puss, puss!" Sasha called to her. "Puss!"

"She can't hear," said the little girl; "she has gone deaf."

"How is that?"

"Oh, she was beaten."

Nikolay and Olga realized from the first glance what life was like here, but said nothing to one another; in silence they put down their bundles, and went out into the village street. Their hut was the third from the end, and seemed the very poorest and oldest-looking; the second was not much better; but the last one had an iron roof, and curtains in the windows. That hut stood apart, not enclosed; it was a tavern. The huts were in a single row, and the whole of the little village - quiet and dreamy, with willows, elders, and mountain-ash trees peeping out from the yards - had an attractive look.

Beyond the peasants homesteads there was a slope down to the river, so steep and precipitous that huge stones jutted out bare here and there through the clay. Down the slope, among the stones and holes dug by the potters, ran winding paths; bits of broken pottery, some brown, some red, lay piled up in heaps, and below there stretched a broad, level, bright green meadow, from which the hay had been already carried, and in which the peasants' cattle were wandering. The river, three-quarters of a mile from the village, ran twisting and turning, with beautiful leafy banks; beyond it was again a broad meadow, a herd of cattle, long strings of white geese; then, just as on the near side, a steep ascent uphill, and on the top of the hill a hamlet, and a church with five domes, and at a little distance the manor-house.

"It's lovely here in your parts!" said Olga, crossing herself at the sight of the church. "What space, oh Lord!"

Just at that moment the bell began ringing for service (it was Saturday evening). Two little girls, down below, who were dragging up a pail of water, looked round at the church to listen to the bell.

"At this time they are serving the dinners at the Slavyansky Bazaar," said Nikolay dreamily.

Sitting on the edge of the slope, Nikolay and Olga watched the sun setting, watched the gold and crimson sky reflected in the river, in the church windows, and in the whole air - which was soft and still and unutterably pure as it never was in Moscow. And when the sun had set the flocks and herds passed, bleating and lowing; geese flew across from the further side of the river, and all sank into silence; the soft light died away in the air, and the dusk of evening began quickly moving down upon them.

Meanwhile Nikolay's father and mother, two gaunt, bent, toothless old people, just of the same height, came back. The women - the sisters-in-law Marya and Fyokla - who had been working on the landowner's estate beyond the river, arrived home, too. Marya, the wife of Nikolay's brother Kiryak, had six children, and Fyokla, the wife of Nikolay's brother Denis - who had gone for a soldier - had two; and when Nikolay, going into the hut, saw all the family, all those bodies big and little moving about on the lockers, in the hanging cradles and in all the corners, and when he saw the greed with which the old father and the women ate the black bread, dipping it in water, he realized he had made a mistake in coming here, sick, penniless, and with a family, too - a great mistake!

"And where is Kiryak?" he asked after they had exchanged greetings.

"He is in service at the merchant's," answered his father; "a keeper in the woods. He is not a bad peasant, but too fond of his glass."

"He is no great help!" said the old woman tearfully. "Our men are a grievous lot; they bring nothing into the house, but take plenty out. Kiryak drinks, and so does the old man; it is no use hiding a sin; he knows his way to the tavern. The Heavenly Mother is wroth."

In honour of the visitors they brought out the samovar. The tea smelt of fish; the sugar was grey and looked as though it had been nibbled; cockroaches ran to and fro over the bread and among the crockery. It was disgusting to drink, and the conversation was disgusting, too - about nothing but poverty and illnesses. But before they had time to empty their first cups there came a loud, prolonged, drunken shout from the yard:

"Ma-arya!"

"It looks as though Kiryak were coming," said the old man. "Speak of the devil."

All were hushed. And again, soon afterwards, the same shout, coarse and drawn-out as though it came out of the earth:

"Ma-arya!"

Marya, the elder sister-in-law, turned pale and huddled against the stove, and it was strange to see the look of terror on the face of the strong, broad-shouldered, ugly woman. Her daughter, the child who had been sitting on the stove and looked so apathetic, suddenly broke into loud weeping.

"What are you howling for, you plague?" Fyokla, a handsome woman, also strong and broad-shouldered, shouted to her. "He won't kill you, no fear!"

From his old father Nikolay learned that Marya was afraid to live in the forest with Kiryak, and that when he was drunk he always came for her, made a row, and beat her mercilessly.

"Ma-arya!" the shout sounded close to the door.

"Protect me, for Christ's sake, good people!" faltered Marya, breathing as though she had been plunged into very cold water. "Protect me, kind people. . . ."

All the children in the hut began crying, and looking at them, Sasha, too, began to cry. They heard a drunken cough, and a tall, black-bearded peasant wearing a winter cap came into the hut, and was the more terrible because his face could not be seen in the dim light of the little lamp. It was Kiryak. Going up to his wife, he swung his arm and punched her in the face with his fist. Stunned by the blow, she did not utter a sound, but sat down, and her nose instantly began bleeding.

"What a disgrace! What a disgrace!" muttered the old man, clambering up on to the stove. "Before visitors, too! It's a sin!"

The old mother sat silent, bowed, lost in thought; Fyokla rocked the cradle.

Evidently conscious of inspiring fear, and pleased at doing so, Kiryak seized Marya by the arm, dragged her towards the door, and bellowed like an animal in order to seem still more terrible; but at that moment he suddenly caught sight of the visitors and stopped.

"Oh, they have come, . . ." he said, letting his wife go; "my own brother and his family. . . ."

Staggering and opening wide his red, drunken eyes, he said his prayer before the image and went on:

"My brother and his family have come to the parental home . . . from Moscow, I suppose. The great capital Moscow, to be sure, the mother of cities. . . . Excuse me."

He sank down on the bench near the samovar and began drinking tea, sipping it loudly from the saucer in the midst of general silence. . . . He drank off a dozen cups, then reclined on the bench and began snoring.

They began going to bed. Nikolay, as an invalid, was put on the stove with his old father; Sasha lay down on the floor, while Olga went with the other women into the barn.

"Aye, aye, dearie," she said, lying down on the hay beside Marya; "you won't mend your trouble with tears. Bear it in patience, that is all. It is written in the Scriptures: 'If anyone smite thee on the right cheek, offer him the left one also.' . . . Aye, aye, dearie."

Then in a low singsong murmur she told them about Moscow, about her own life, how she had been a servant in furnished lodgings.

"And in Moscow the houses are big, built of brick," she said; "and there are ever so many churches, forty times forty, dearie; and they are all gentry in the houses, so handsome and so proper!"

Marya told her that she had not only never been in Moscow, but had not even been in their own district town; she could not read or write, and knew no prayers, not even "Our Father." Both she and Fyokla, the other sister-in-law, who was sitting a little way off listening, were extremely ignorant and could understand nothing. They both disliked their husbands; Marya was afraid of Kiryak, and whenever he stayed with her she was shaking with fear, and always got a headache from the fumes of vodka and tobacco with which he reeked. And in answer to the question whether she did not miss her husband, Fyokla answered with vexation:

"Miss him!"

They talked a little and sank into silence.

It was cool, and a cock crowed at the top of his voice near the barn, preventing them from sleeping. When the bluish morning light was already peeping through all the crevices, Fyokla got up stealthily and went out, and then they heard the sound of her bare feet running off somewhere.

II

Olga went to church, and took Marya with her. As they went down the path towards the meadow both were in good spirits. Olga liked the wide view, and Marya felt that in her sister-in-law she had someone near and akin to her. The sun was rising. Low down over the meadow floated a drowsy hawk. The river looked gloomy; there was a haze hovering over it here and there, but on the further bank a streak of light already stretched across the hill. The church was gleaming, and in the manor garden the rooks were cawing furiously.

"The old man is all right," Marya told her, "but Granny is strict; she is continually nagging. Our own grain lasted till Carnival. We buy flour now at the tavern. She is angry about it; she says we eat too much."

"Aye, aye, dearie! Bear it in patience, that is all. It is written: 'Come unto Me, all ye that labour and are heavy laden.' "

Olga spoke sedately, rhythmically, and she walked like a pilgrim woman, with a rapid, anxious step. Every day she read the gospel, read it aloud like a deacon; a great deal of it she did not understand, but the words of the gospel moved her to tears, and words like "forasmuch as" and "verily" she pronounced with a sweet flutter at her heart. She believed in God, in the Holy Mother, in the Saints; she believed one must not offend anyone in the world - not simple folks, nor Germans, nor gypsies, nor Jews - and woe even to those who have no compassion on the beasts. She believed this was written in the Holy Scriptures; and so, when she pronounced phrases from Holy Writ, even though she did not understand them, her face grew softened, compassionate, and radiant.

"What part do you come from?" Marya asked her.

"I am from Vladimir. Only I was taken to Moscow long ago, when I was eight years old."

They reached the river. On the further side a woman was standing at the water's edge, undressing.

"It's our Fyokla," said Marya, recognizing her. "She has been over the river to the manor yard. To the stewards. She is a shameless hussy and foul-mouthed - fearfully!"

Fyokla, young and vigorous as a girl, with her black eyebrows and her loose hair, jumped off the bank and began splashing the water with her feet, and waves ran in all directions from her.

"Shameless - dreadfully!" repeated Marya.

The river was crossed by a rickety little bridge of logs, and exactly below it in the clear, limpid water was a shoal of broad-headed mullets. The dew was glistening on the green bushes that looked into the water. There was a feeling of warmth; it was comforting! What a lovely morning! And how lovely life would have been in this world, in all likelihood, if it were not for poverty, horrible, hopeless poverty, from which one can find no refuge! One had only to look round at the village to remember vividly all that had happened the day before, and the illusion of happiness which seemed to surround them vanished instantly.

They reached the church. Marya stood at the entrance, and did not dare to go farther. She did not dare to sit down either. Though they only began ringing for mass between eight and nine, she remained standing the whole time.

While the gospel was being read the crowd suddenly parted to make way for the family from the great house. Two young girls in white frocks and wide-brimmed hats walked in; with them a chubby, rosy boy in a sailor suit. Their appearance touched Olga; she made up her mind from the first glance that they were refined, well-educated, handsome people. Marya looked at them from under her brows, sullenly, dejectedly, as though they were not human beings coming in, but monsters who might crush her if she did not make way for them.

And every time the deacon boomed out something in his bass voice she fancied she heard "Ma-arya!" and she shuddered.

III

The arrival of the visitors was already known in the village, and directly after mass a number of people gathered together in the hut. The Leonytchevs and Matvyeitchevs and the Ilyitchovs came to inquire about their relations who were in service in Moscow. All the lads of Zhukovo who could read and write were packed off to Moscow and hired out as butlers or waiters (while from the village on the other side of the river the boys all became bakers), and that had been the custom from the days of serfdom long ago when a certain Luka Ivanitch, a peasant from Zhukovo, now a legendary figure, who had been a waiter in one of the Moscow clubs, would take none but his fellow-villagers into his service, and found jobs for them in taverns and restaurants; and from that time the village of Zhukovo was always called among the inhabitants of the surrounding districts Slaveytown. Nikolay had been taken to Moscow when he was eleven, and Ivan Makaritch, one of the Matvyeitchevs, at that time a headwaiter in the "Hermitage" garden, had put him into a situation. And now, addressing the Matvyeitchevs, Nikolay said emphatically:

"Ivan Makaritch was my benefactor, and I am bound to pray for him day and night, as it is owing to him I have become a good man."

"My good soul!" a tall old woman, the sister of Ivan Makaritch, said tearfully, "and not a word have we heard about him, poor dear."

"In the winter he was in service at Omon's, and this season there was a rumour he was somewhere out of town, in gardens. . . . He has aged! In old days he would bring home as much as ten roubles a day in the summer-time, but now things are very quiet everywhere. The old man frets."

The women looked at Nikolay's feet, shod in felt boots, and at his pale face, and said mournfully:

"You are not one to get on, Nikolay Osipitch; you are not one to get on! No, indeed!"

And they all made much of Sasha. She was ten years old, but she was little and very thin, and might have been taken for no more than seven. Among the other little girls, with their sunburnt faces and roughly cropped hair, dressed in long faded smocks, she with her white little face, with her big dark eyes, with a red ribbon in her hair, looked funny, as though she were some little wild creature that had been caught and brought into the hut.

"She can read, too," Olga said in her praise, looking tenderly at her daughter. "Read a little, child!" she said, taking the gospel from the corner. "You read, and the good Christian people will listen."

The testament was an old and heavy one in leather binding, with dog's-eared edges, and it exhaled a smell as though monks had come into the hut. Sasha raised her eyebrows and began in a loud rhythmic chant:

" 'And the angel of the Lord . . . appeared unto Joseph, saying unto him: Rise up, and take the Babe and His mother.' "

"The Babe and His mother," Olga repeated, and flushed all over with emotion.

" 'And flee into Egypt, . . . and tarry there until such time as . . .' "

At the word "tarry" Olga could not refrain from tears. Looking at her, Marya began to whimper, and after her Ivan Makaritch's sister. The old father cleared his throat, and bustled about to find something to give his grand-daughter, but, finding nothing, gave it up with a wave of his hand. And when the reading was over the neighbours dispersed to their homes, feeling touched and very much pleased with Olga and Sasha.

As it was a holiday, the family spent the whole day at home. The old woman, whom her husband, her daughters-in-law, her grandchildren all alike called Granny, tried to do everything herself; she heated the stove and set the samovar with her own hands, even waited at the midday meal, and then complained that she was worn out with work. And all the time she was uneasy for fear someone should eat a piece too much, or that her husband and daughters-in-law would sit idle. At one time she would hear the tavern-keeper's geese going at the back of the huts to her kitchen-garden, and she would run out of the hut with a long stick and spend half an hour screaming shrilly by her cabbages, which were as gaunt and scraggy as herself; at another time she fancied that a crow had designs on her chickens, and she rushed to attack it with loud words of abuse. She was cross and grumbling from morning till night.

And often she raised such an outcry that passers-by stopped in the street.

She was not affectionate towards the old man, reviling him as a lazy-bones and a plague. He was not a responsible, reliable peasant, and perhaps if she had not been continually nagging at him he would not have worked at all, but would have simply sat on the stove and talked. He talked to his son at great length about certain enemies of his, complained of the insults he said he had to put up with every day from the neighbours, and it was tedious to listen to him.

"Yes," he would say, standing with his arms akimbo, "yes. . . . A week after the Exaltation of the Cross I sold my hay willingly at thirty kopecks a pound. . . . Well and good. . . . So you see I was taking the hay in the morning with a good will; I was interfering with no one. In an unlucky hour I see the village elder, Antip Syedelnikov, coming out of the tavern. 'Where are you taking it, you ruffian?' says he, and takes me by the ear."

Kiryak had a fearful headache after his drinking bout, and was ashamed to face his brother.

"What vodka does! Ah, my God!" he muttered, shaking his aching head. "For Christ's sake, forgive me, brother and sister; I'm not happy myself."

As it was a holiday, they bought a herring at the tavern and made a soup of the herring's head. At midday they all sat down to drink tea, and went on drinking it for a long time, till they were all perspiring; they looked positively swollen from the tea-drinking, and after it began sipping the broth from the herring's head, all helping themselves out of one bowl. But the herring itself Granny had hidden.

In the evening a potter began firing pots on the ravine. In the meadow below the girls got up a choral dance and sang songs. They played the concertina. And on the other side of the river a kiln for baking pots was lighted, too, and the girls sang songs, and in the distance the singing sounded soft and musical. The peasants were noisy in and about the tavern. They were singing with drunken voices, each on his own account, and swearing at one another, so that Olga could only shudder and say:

"Oh, holy Saints!"

She was amazed that the abuse was incessant, and those who were loudest and most persistent in this foul language were the old men who were so near their end. And the girls and children heard the swearing, and were not in the least disturbed by it, and it was evident that they were used to it from their cradles.

It was past midnight, the kilns on both sides of the river were put out, but in the meadow below and in the tavern the merrymaking still went on. The old father and Kiryak, both drunk, walking arm-in-arm and jostling against each other's shoulders, went to the barn where Olga and Marya were lying.

"Let her alone," the old man persuaded him; "let her alone. . . . She is a harmless woman. . . . It's a sin. . . ."

"Ma-arya! " shouted Kiryak.

"Let her be. . . . It's a sin. . . . She is not a bad woman."

Both stopped by the barn and went on.

"I lo-ove the flowers of the fi-ield," the old man began singing suddenly in a high, piercing tenor. "I lo-ove to gather them in the meadows!"

Then he spat, and with a filthy oath went into the hut.

IV

Granny put Sasha by her kitchen-garden and told her to keep watch that the geese did not go in. It was a hot August day. The tavernkeeper's geese could make their way into the kitchen-garden by the backs of the huts, but now they were busily engaged picking up oats by the tavern, peacefully conversing together, and only the gander craned his head high as though trying to see whether the old woman were coming with her stick. The other geese might come up from below, but they were now grazing far away the other side of the river, stretched out in a long white garland about the meadow. Sasha stood about a little, grew weary, and, seeing that the geese were not coming, went away to the ravine.

There she saw Marya's eldest daughter Motka, who was standing motionless on a big stone, staring at the church. Marya had given birth to thirteen children, but she only had six living, all girls, not one boy, and the eldest was eight. Motka in a long smock was standing barefooted in the full sunshine; the sun was blazing down right on her head, but she did not notice that, and seemed as though turned to stone. Sasha stood beside her and said, looking at the church:

"God lives in the church. Men have lamps and candles, but God has little green and red and blue lamps like little eyes. At night God walks about the church, and with Him the Holy Mother of God and Saint Nikolay, thud, thud, thud! . . . And the watchman is terrified, terrified! Aye, aye, dearie," she added, imitating her mother. "And when the end of the world comes all the churches will be carried up to heaven."

"With the-ir be-ells?" Motka asked in her deep voice, drawling every syllable.

"With their bells. And when the end of the world comes the good will go to Paradise, but the angry will burn in fire eternal and unquenchable, dearie. To my mother as well as to Marya God will say: 'You never offended anyone, and for that go to the right to Paradise'; but to Kiryak and Granny He will say: 'You go to the left into the fire.' And anyone who has eaten meat in Lent will go into the fire, too."

She looked upwards at the sky, opening wide her eyes, and said:

"Look at the sky without winking, you will see angels."

Motka began looking at the sky, too, and a minute passed in silence.

"Do you see them?" asked Sasha.

"I don't," said Motka in her deep voice.

"But I do. Little angels are flying about the sky and flap, flap with their little wings as though they were gnats."

Motka thought for a little, with her eyes on the ground, and asked:

"Will Granny burn?"

"She will, dearie."

From the stone an even gentle slope ran down to the bottom, covered with soft green grass, which one longed to lie down on or to touch with one's hands. . . Sasha lay down and rolled to the bottom. Motka with a grave, severe face, taking a deep breath, lay down, too, and rolled to the bottom, and in doing so tore her smock from the hem to the shoulder.

"What fun it is!" said Sasha, delighted.

They walked up to the top to roll down again, but at that moment they heard a shrill, familiar voice. Oh, how awful it was! Granny, a toothless, bony, hunchbacked figure, with short grey hair which was fluttering in the wind, was driving the geese out of the kitchen-garden with a long stick, shouting.

"They have trampled all the cabbages, the damned brutes! I'd cut your throats, thrice accursed plagues! Bad luck to you!"

She saw the little girls, flung down the stick and picked up a switch, and, seizing Sasha by the neck with her fingers, thin and hard as the gnarled branches of a tree, began whipping her. Sasha cried with pain and terror, while the gander, waddling and stretching his neck, went up to the old woman and hissed at her, and when he went back to his flock all the geese greeted him approvingly with "Ga-ga-ga!" Then Granny proceeded to whip Motka, and in this Motka's smock was torn again. Feeling in despair, and crying loudly, Sasha went to the hut to complain. Motka followed her; she, too, was crying on a deeper note, without wiping her tears, and her face was as wet as though it had been dipped in water.

"Holy Saints!" cried Olga, aghast, as the two came into the hut. "Queen of Heaven!"

Sasha began telling her story, while at the same time Granny walked in with a storm of shrill cries and abuse; then Fyokla flew into a rage, and there was an uproar in the hut.

"Never mind, never mind!" Olga, pale and upset, tried to comfort them, stroking Sasha's head. "She is your grandmother; it's a sin to be angry with her. Never mind, my child."

Nikolay, who was worn out already by the everlasting hubbub, hunger, stifling fumes, filth, who hated and despised the poverty, who was ashamed for his wife and daughter to see his father and mother, swung his legs off the stove and said in an irritable, tearful voice, addressing his mother:

"You must not beat her! You have no right to beat her!"

"You lie rotting on the stove, you wretched creature!" Fyokla shouted at him spitefully. "The devil brought you all on us, eating us out of house and home."

Sasha and Motka and all the little girls in the hut huddled on the stove in the corner behind Nikolay's back, and from that refuge listened in silent terror, and the beating of their little hearts could be distinctly heard. Whenever there is someone in a family who has long been ill, and hopelessly ill, there come painful moments when all timidly, secretly, at the bottom of their hearts long for his death; and only the children fear the death of someone near them, and always feel horrified at the thought of it. And now the children, with bated breath, with a mournful look on their faces, gazed at Nikolay and thought that he was soon to die; and they wanted to cry and to say something friendly and compassionate to him.

He pressed close to Olga, as though seeking protection, and said to her softly in a quavering voice:

"Olya darling, I can't stay here longer. It's more than I can bear. For God's sake, for Christ's sake, write to your sister Klavdia Abramovna. Let her sell and pawn everything she has; let her send us the money. We will go away from here. Oh, Lord," he went on miserably, "to have one peep at Moscow! If I could see it in my dreams, the dear place!

And when the evening came on, and it was dark in the hut, it was so dismal that it was hard to utter a word. Granny, very ill-tempered, soaked some crusts of rye bread in a cup, and was a long time, a whole hour, sucking at them. Marya, after milking the cow, brought in a pail of milk and set it on a bench; then Granny poured it from the pail into a jug just as slowly and deliberately, evidently pleased that it was now the Fast of the Assumption, so that no one would drink milk and it would be left untouched. And she only poured out a very little in a saucer for Fyokla's baby. When Marya and she carried the jug down to the cellar Motka suddenly stirred, clambered down from the stove, and going to the bench where stood the wooden cup full of crusts, sprinkled into it some milk from the saucer.

Granny, coming back into the hut, sat down to her soaked crusts again, while Sasha and Motka, sitting on the stove, gazed at her, and they were glad that she had broken her fast and now would go to hell. They were comforted and lay down to sleep, and Sasha as she dozed off to sleep imagined the Day of Judgment: a huge fire was burning, somewhat like a potter's kiln, and the Evil One, with horns like a cow's, and black all over, was driving Granny into the fire with a long stick, just as Granny herself had been driving the geese.

V

On the day of the Feast of the Assumption, between ten and eleven in the evening, the girls and lads who were merrymaking in the meadow suddenly raised a clamour and outcry, and ran in the direction of the village; and those who were above on the edge of the ravine could not for the first moment make out what was the matter.

"Fire! Fire!" they heard desperate shouts from below. "The village is on fire!"

Those who were sitting above looked round, and a terrible and extraordinary spectacle met their eyes. On the thatched roof of one of the end cottages stood a column of flame, seven feet high, which curled round and scattered sparks in all directions as though it were a fountain. And all at once the whole roof burst into bright flame, and the crackling of the fire was audible.

The light of the moon was dimmed, and the whole village was by now bathed in a red quivering glow: black shadows moved over the ground, there was a smell of burning, and those who ran up from below were all gasping and could not speak for trembling; they jostled against each other, fell down, and they could hardly see in the unaccustomed light, and did not recognize each other. It was terrible. What seemed particularly dreadful was that doves were flying over the fire in the smoke; and in the tavern, where they did not yet know of the fire, they were still singing and playing the concertina as though there were nothing the matter.

"Uncle Semyon's on fire," shouted a loud, coarse voice.

Marya was fussing about round her hut, weeping and wringing her hands, while her teeth chattered, though the fire was a long way off at the other end of the village. Nikolay came out in high felt boots, the children ran out in their little smocks. Near the village constable's hut an iron sheet was struck. Boom, boom, boom! . . . floated through the air, and this repeated, persistent sound sent a pang to the heart and turned one cold. The old women stood with the holy ikons. Sheep, calves, cows were driven out of the back-yards into the street; boxes, sheepskins, tubs were carried out. A black stallion, who was kept apart from the drove of horses because he kicked and injured them, on being set free ran once or twice up and down the village, neighing and pawing the ground; then suddenly stopped short near a cart and began kicking it with his hind-legs.

They began ringing the bells in the church on the other side of the river.

Near the burning hut it was hot and so light that one could distinctly see every blade of grass. Semyon, a red-haired peasant with a long nose, wearing a reefer-jacket and a cap pulled down right over his ears, sat on one of the boxes which they had succeeded in bringing out: his wife was lying on her face, moaning and unconscious. A little old man of eighty, with a big beard, who looked like a gnome - not one of the villagers, though obviously connected in some way with the fire - walked about bareheaded, with a white bundle in his arms. The glare was reflected on his bald head. The village elder, Antip Syedelnikov, as swarthy and black-haired as a gypsy, went up to the hut with an axe, and hacked out the windows one after another - no one knew why - then began chopping up the roof.

"Women, water!" he shouted. "Bring the engine! Look sharp!"

The peasants, who had been drinking in the tavern just before, dragged the engine up. They were all drunk; they kept stumbling and falling down, and all had a helpless expression and tears in their eyes.

"Wenches, water! " shouted the elder, who was drunk, too. "Look sharp, wenches!"

The women and the girls ran downhill to where there was a spring, and kept hauling pails and buckets of water up the hill, and, pouring it into the engine, ran down again. Olga and Marya and Sasha and Motka all brought water. The women and the boys pumped the water; the pipe hissed, and the elder, directing it now at the door, now at the windows, held back the stream with his finger, which made it hiss more sharply still.

"Bravo, Antip!" voices shouted approvingly. "Do your best."

Antip went inside the hut into the fire and shouted from within.

"Pump! Bestir yourselves, good Christian folk, in such a terrible mischance!"

The peasants stood round in a crowd, doing nothing but staring at the fire. No one knew what to do, no one had the sense to do anything, though there were stacks of wheat, hay, barns, and piles of faggots standing all round. Kiryak and old Osip, his father, both tipsy, were standing there, too. And as though to justify his doing nothing, old Osip said, addressing the woman who lay on the ground:

"What is there to trouble about, old girl! The hut is insured - why are you taking on?"

Semyon, addressing himself first to one person and then to another, kept describing how the fire had started.

"That old man, the one with the bundle, a house-serf of General Zhukov's. . . . He was cook at our general's, God rest his soul! He came over this evening: 'Let me stay the night,' says he. . . . Well, we had a glass, to be sure. . . . The wife got the samovar - she was going to give the old fellow a cup of tea, and in an unlucky hour she set the samovar in the entrance. The sparks from the chimney must have blown straight up to the thatch; that's how it was. We were almost burnt ourselves. And the old fellow's cap has been burnt; what a shame!"

And the sheet of iron was struck indefatigably, and the bells kept ringing in the church the other side of the river. In the glow of the fire Olga, breathless, looking with horror at the red sheep and the pink doves flying in the smoke, kept running down the hill and up again. It seemed to her that the ringing went to her heart with a sharp stab, that the fire would never be over, that Sasha was lost. . . . And when the ceiling of the hut fell in with a crash, the thought that now the whole village would be burnt made her weak and faint, and she could not go on fetching water, but sat down on the ravine, setting the pail down near her; beside her and below her, the peasant women sat wailing as though at a funeral.

Then the stewards and watchmen from the estate the other side of the river arrived in two carts, bringing with them a fire-engine. A very young student in an unbuttoned white tunic rode up on horseback. There was the thud of axes. They put a ladder to the burning framework of the house, and five men ran up it at once. Foremost of them all was the student, who was red in the face and shouting in a harsh hoarse voice, and in a tone as though putting out fires was a thing he was used to. They pulled the house to pieces, a beam at a time; they dragged away the corn, the hurdles, and the stacks that were near.

"Don't let them break it up! " cried stern voices in the crowd. "Don't let them."

Kiryak made his way up to the hut with a resolute air, as though he meant to prevent the newcomers from breaking up the hut, but one of the workmen turned him back with a blow in his neck. There was the sound of laughter, the workman dealt him another blow, Kiryak fell down, and crawled back into the crowd on his hands and knees.

Two handsome girls in hats, probably the student's sisters, came from the other side of the river. They stood a little way off, looking at the fire. The beams that had been dragged apart were no longer burning, but were smoking vigorously; the student, who was working the hose, turned the water, first on the beams, then on the peasants, then on the women who were bringing the water.

"George!" the girls called to him reproachfully in anxiety, "George!"

The fire was over. And only when they began to disperse they noticed that the day was breaking, that everyone was pale and rather dark in the face, as it always seems in the early morning when the last stars are going out. As they separated, the peasants laughed and made jokes about General Zhukov's cook and his cap which had been burnt; they already wanted to turn the fire into a joke, and even seemed sorry that it had so soon been put out.

"How well you extinguished the fire, sir!" said Olga to the student. "You ought to come to us in Moscow: there we have a fire every day."

"Why, do you come from Moscow?" asked one of the young ladies.

"Yes, miss. My husband was a waiter at the Slavyansky Bazaar. And this is my daughter," she said, indicating Sasha, who was cold and huddling up to her. "She is a Moscow girl, too."

The two young ladies said something in French to the student, and he gave Sasha a twenty-kopeck piece.

Old Father Osip saw this, and there was a gleam of hope in his face.

"We must thank God, your honour, there was no wind," he said, addressing the student, "or else we should have been all burnt up together. Your honour, kind gentlefolks," he added in embarrassment in a lower tone, "the morning's chilly . . . something to warm one . . . half a bottle to your honour's health."

Nothing was given him, and clearing his throat he slouched home. Olga stood afterwards at the end of the street and watched the two carts crossing the river by the ford and the gentlefolks walking across the meadow; a carriage was waiting for them the other side of the river. Going into the hut, she described to her husband with enthusiasm:

"Such good people! And so beautiful! The young ladies were like cherubim."

"Plague take them!" Fyokla, sleepy, said spitefully.

VI

Marya thought herself unhappy, and said that she would be very glad to die; Fyokla, on the other hand, found all this life to her taste: the poverty, the uncleanliness, and the incessant quarrelling. She ate what was given her without discrimination; slept anywhere, on whatever came to hand. She would empty the slops just at the porch, would splash them out from the doorway, and then walk barefoot through the puddle. And from the very first day she took a dislike to Olga and Nikolay just because they did not like this life.

"We shall see what you'll find to eat here, you Moscow gentry!" she said malignantly. "We shall see!"

One morning, it was at the beginning of September, Fyokla, vigorous, good-looking, and rosy from the cold, brought up two pails of water; Marya and Olga were sitting meanwhile at the table drinking tea.

"Tea and sugar," said Fyokla sarcastically. "The fine ladies!" she added, setting down the pails. "You have taken to the fashion of tea every day. You better look out that you don't burst with your tea-drinking," she went on, looking with hatred at Olga. "That's how you have come by your fat mug, having a good time in Moscow, you lump of flesh!" She swung the yoke and hit Olga such a blow on the shoulder that the two sisters-in-law could only clasp their hands and say:

"Oh, holy Saints!"

Then Fyokla went down to the river to wash the clothes, swearing all the time so loudly that she could be heard in the hut.

The day passed and was followed by the long autumn evening. They wound silk in the hut; everyone did it except Fyokla; she had gone over the river. They got the silk from a factory close by, and the whole family working together earned next to nothing, twenty kopecks a week.

"Things were better in the old days under the gentry," said the old father as he wound silk. "You worked and ate and slept, everything in its turn. At dinner you had cabbage-soup and boiled grain, and at supper the same again. Cucumbers and cabbage in plenty: you could eat to your heart's content, as much as you wanted. And there was more strictness. Everyone minded what he was about."

The hut was lighted by a single little lamp, which burned dimly and smoked. When someone screened the lamp and a big shadow fell across the window, the bright moonlight could be seen. Old Osip, speaking slowly, told them how they used to live before the emancipation; how in those very parts, where life was now so poor and so dreary, they used to hunt with harriers, greyhounds,. retrievers, and when they went out as beaters the peasants were given vodka; how whole waggonloads of game used to be sent to Moscow for the young masters; how the bad were beaten with rods or sent away to the Tver estate, while the good were rewarded. And Granny told them something, too. She remembered everything, positively everything. She described her mistress, a kind, God-fearing woman, whose husband was a profligate and a rake, and all of whose daughters made unlucky marriages: one married a drunkard, another married a workman, the other eloped secretly (Granny herself, at that time a young girl, helped in the elopement), and they had all three as well as their mother died early from grief. And remembering all this, Granny positively began to shed tears.

All at once someone knocked at the door, and they all started.

"Uncle Osip, give me a night's lodging."

The little bald old man, General Zhukov's cook, the one whose cap had been burnt, walked in. He sat down and listened, then he, too, began telling stories of all sorts. Nikolay, sitting on the stove with his legs hanging down, listened and asked questions about the dishes that were prepared in the old days for the gentry. They talked of rissoles, cutlets, various soups and sauces, and the cook, who remembered everything very well, mentioned dishes that are no longer served. There was one, for instance - a dish made of bulls' eyes, which was called "waking up in the morning."

"And used you to do cutlets à la maréchal?" asked Nikolay.

"No."

Nikolay shook his head reproachfully and said:

"Tut, tut! You were not much of a cook!"

The little girls sitting and lying on the stove stared down without blinking; it seemed as though there were a great many of them, like cherubim in the clouds. They liked the stories: they were breathless; they shuddered and turned pale with alternate rapture and terror, and they listened breathlessly, afraid to stir, to Granny, whose stories were the most interesting of all.

They lay down to sleep in silence; and the old people, troubled and excited by their reminiscences, thought how precious was youth, of which, whatever it might have been like, nothing was left in the memory but what was living, joyful, touching, and how terribly cold was death, which was not far off, better not think of it! The lamp died down. And the dusk, and the two little windows sharply defined by the moonlight, and the stillness and the creak of the cradle, reminded them for some reason that life was over, that nothing one could do would bring it back. . . . You doze off, you forget yourself, and suddenly someone touches your shoulder or breathes on your cheek - and sleep is gone; your body feels cramped, and thoughts of death keep creeping into your mind. You turn on the other side: death is forgotten, but old dreary, sickening thoughts of poverty, of food, of how dear flour is getting, stray through the mind, and a little later again you remember that life is over and you cannot bring it back. . . .

"Oh, Lord!" sighed the cook.

Someone gave a soft, soft tap at the window. It must be Fyokla come back. Olga got up, and yawning and whispering a prayer, opened the door, then drew the bolt in the outer room, but no one came in; only from the street came a cold draught and a sudden brightness from the moonlight. The street, still and deserted, and the moon itself floating across the sky, could be seen at the open door.

"Who is there?" called Olga.

"I," she heard the answer - "it is I."

Near the door, crouching against the wall, stood Fyokla, absolutely naked. She was shivering with cold, her teeth were chattering, and in the bright moonlight she looked very pale, strange, and beautiful. The shadows on her, and the bright moonlight on her skin, stood out vividly, and her dark eyebrows and firm, youthful bosom were defined with peculiar distinctness.

"The ruffians over there undressed me and turned me out like this," she said. "I've come home without my clothes . . . naked as my mother bore me. Bring me something to put on."

"But go inside!" Olga said softly, beginning to shiver, too.

"I don't want the old folks to see." Granny was, in fact, already stirring and muttering, and the old father asked: "Who is there?" Olga brought her own smock and skirt, dressed Fyokla, and then both went softly into the inner room, trying not to make a noise with the door.

"Is that you, you sleek one?" Granny grumbled angrily, guessing who it was. "Fie upon you, nightwalker! . . . Bad luck to you!"

"It's all right, it's all right," whispered Olga, wrapping Fyokla up; "it's all right, dearie."

All was stillness again. They always slept badly; everyone was kept awake by something worrying and persistent: the old man by the pain in his back, Granny by anxiety and anger, Marya by terror, the children by itch and hunger. Now, too, their sleep was troubled; they kept turning over from one side to the other, talking in their sleep, getting up for a drink.

Fyokla suddenly broke into a loud, coarse howl, but immediately checked herself, and only uttered sobs from time to time, growing softer and on a lower note, until she relapsed into silence. From time to time from the other side of the river there floated the sound of the beating of the hours; but the time seemed somehow strange - five was struck and then three.

"Oh Lord!" sighed the cook.

Looking at the windows, it was difficult to tell whether it was still moonlight or whether the dawn had begun. Marya got up and went out, and she could be heard milking the cows and saying, "Stea-dy!"

Granny went out, too. It was still dark in the hut, but all the objects in it could be discerned.

Nikolay, who had not slept all night, got down from the stove. He took his dress-coat out of a green box, put it on, and going to the window, stroked the sleeves and took hold of the coat-tails - and smiled. Then he carefully took off the coat, put it away in his box, and lay down again.

Marya came in again and began lighting the stove. She was evidently hardly awake, and seemed dropping asleep as she walked. Probably she had had some dream, or the stories of the night before came into her mind as, stretching luxuriously before the stove, she said:

"No, freedom is better."

VII

The master arrived - that was what they called the police inspector. When he would come and what he was coming for had been known for the last week. There were only forty households in Zhukovo, but more than two thousand roubles of arrears of rates and taxes had accumulated.

The police inspector stopped at the tavern. He drank there two glasses of tea, and then went on foot to the village elder's hut, near which a crowd of those who were in debt stood waiting. The elder, Antip Syedelnikov, was, in spite of his youth - he was only a little over thirty - strict and always on the side of the authorities, though he himself was poor and did not pay his taxes regularly. Evidently he enjoyed being elder, and liked the sense of authority, which he could only display by strictness. In the village council the peasants were afraid of him and obeyed him. It would sometimes happen that he would pounce on a drunken man in the street or near the tavern, tie his hands behind him, and put him in the lock-up. On one occasion he even put Granny in the lock-up because she went to the village council instead of Osip, and began swearing, and he kept her there for a whole day and night. He had never lived in a town or read a book, but somewhere or other had picked up various learned expressions, and loved to make use of them in conversation, and he was respected for this though he was not always understood.

When Osip came into the village elder's hut with his tax book, the police inspector, a lean old man with a long grey beard, in a grey tunic, was sitting at a table in the passage, writing something. It was clean in the hut; all the walls were dotted with pictures cut out of the illustrated papers, and in the most conspicuous place near the ikon there was a portrait of the Battenburg who was the Prince of Bulgaria. By the table stood Antip Syedelnikov with his arms folded.

"There is one hundred and nineteen roubles standing against him," he said when it came to Osip's turn. "Before Easter he paid a rouble, and he has not paid a kopeck since."

The police inspector raised his eyes to Osip and asked:

"Why is this, brother?"

"Show Divine mercy, your honour," Osip began, growing agitated. "Allow me to say last year the gentleman at Lutorydsky said to me, 'Osip,' he said, 'sell your hay . . . you sell it,' he said. Well, I had a hundred poods for sale; the women mowed it on the water-meadow. Well, we struck a bargain all right, willingly. . . ."

He complained of the elder, and kept turning round to the peasants as though inviting them to bear witness; his face flushed red and perspired, and his eyes grew sharp and angry.

"I don't know why you are saying all this," said the police inspector. "I am asking you . . . I am asking you why you don't pay your arrears. You don't pay, any of you, and am I to be responsible for you?"

"I can't do it."

"His words have no sequel, your honour," said the elder. "The Tchikildyeevs certainly are of a defective class, but if you will just ask the others, the root of it all is vodka, and they are a very bad lot. With no sort of understanding."

The police inspector wrote something down, and said to Osip quietly, in an even tone, as though he were asking him for water:

"Be off."

Soon he went away; and when he got into his cheap chaise and cleared his throat, it could be seen from the very expression of his long thin back that he was no longer thinking of Osip or of the village elder, nor of the Zhukovo arrears, but was thinking of his own affairs. Before he had gone three-quarters of a mile Antip was already carrying off the samovar from the Tchikildyeevs' cottage, followed by Granny, screaming shrilly and straining her throat:

"I won't let you have it. I won't let you have it, damn you!"

He walked rapidly with long steps, and she pursued him panting, almost falling over, a bent, ferocious figure; her kerchief slipped on to her shoulders, her grey hair with greenish lights on it was blown about in the wind. She suddenly stopped short, and like a genuine rebel, fell to beating her breast with her fists and shouting louder than ever in a sing-song voice, as though she were sobbing:

"Good Christians and believers in God! Neighbours, they have ill-treated me! Kind friends, they have oppressed me! Oh, oh! dear people, take my part."

"Granny, Granny!" said the village elder sternly, "have some sense in your head!"

It was hopelessly dreary in the Tchikildyeevs' hut without the samovar; there was something humiliating in this loss, insulting, as though the honour of the hut had been outraged. Better if the elder had carried off the table, all the benches, all the pots - it would not have seemed so empty. Granny screamed, Marya cried, and the little girls, looking at her, cried, too. The old father, feeling guilty, sat in the corner with bowed head and said nothing. And Nikolay, too, was silent. Granny loved him and was sorry for him, but now, forgetting her pity, she fell upon him with abuse, with reproaches, shaking her fist right in his face. She shouted that it was all his fault; why had he sent them so little when he boasted in his letters that he was getting fifty roubles a month at the Slavyansky Bazaar? Why had he come, and with his family, too? If he died, where was the money to come from for his funeral . . . ? And it was pitiful to look at Nikolay, Olga, and Sasha.

The old father cleared his throat, took his cap, and went off to the village elder. Antip was soldering something by the stove, puffing out his cheeks; there was a smell of burning. His children, emaciated and unwashed, no better than the Tchikildyeevs, were scrambling about the floor; his wife, an ugly, freckled woman with a prominent stomach, was winding silk. They were a poor, unlucky family, and Antip was the only one who looked vigorous and handsome. On a bench there were five samovars standing in a row. The old man said his prayer to Battenburg and said:

"Antip, show the Divine mercy. Give me back the samovar, for Christ's sake!"

"Bring three roubles, then you shall have it.

"I can't do it!"

Antip puffed out his cheeks, the fire roared and hissed, and the glow was reflected in the samovar. The old man crumpled up his cap and said after a moment's thought:

"You give it me back."

The swarthy elder looked quite black, and was like a magician; he turned round to Osip and said sternly and rapidly:

"It all depends on the rural captain. On the twenty-sixth instant you can state the grounds for your dissatisfaction before the administrative session, verbally or in writing."

Osip did not understand a word, but he was satisfied with that and went home.

Ten days later the police inspector came again, stayed an hour and went away. During those days the weather had changed to cold and windy; the river had been frozen for some time past, but still there was no snow, and people found it difficult to get about. On the eve of a holiday some of the neighbours came in to Osip's to sit and have a talk. They did not light the lamp, as it would have been a sin to work, but talked in the darkness. There were some items of news, all rather unpleasant. In two or three households hens had been taken for the arrears, and had been sent to the district police station, and there they had died because no one had fed them; they had taken sheep, and while they were being driven away tied to one another, shifted into another cart at each village, one of them had died. And now they were discussing the question, who was to blame?

"The Zemstvo," said Osip. "Who else?"

"Of course it is the Zemstvo."

The Zemstvo was blamed for everything - for the arrears, and for the oppressions, and for the failure of the crops, though no one of them knew what was meant by the Zemstvo. And this dated from the time when well-to-do peasants who had factories, shops, and inns of their own were members of the Zemstvos, were dissatisfied with them, and took to swearing at the Zemstvos in their factories and inns.

They talked of God's not sending the snow; they had to bring in wood for fuel, and there was no driving nor walking in the frozen ruts. In old days fifteen to twenty years ago conversation was much more interesting in Zhukovo. In those days every old man looked as though he were treasuring some secret; as though he knew something and was expecting something. They used to talk about an edict in golden letters, about the division of lands, about new land, about treasures; they hinted at something. Now the people of Zhukovo had no mystery at all; their whole life was bare and open in the sight of all, and they could talk of nothing but poverty, food, there being no snow yet. . . .

There was a pause. Then they thought again of the hens, of the sheep, and began discussing whose fault it was.

"The Zemstvo," said Osip wearily. "Who else?"

VIII

The parish church was nearly five miles away at Kosogorovo, and the peasants only attended it when they had to do so for baptisms, weddings, or funerals; they went to the services at the church across the river. On holidays in fine weather the girls dressed up in their best and went in a crowd together to church, and it was a cheering sight to see them in their red, yellow, and green dresses cross the meadow; in bad weather they all stayed at home. They went for the sacrament to the parish church. From each of those who did not manage in Lent to go to confession in readiness for the sacrament the parish priest, going the round of the huts with the cross at Easter, took fifteen kopecks.

The old father did not believe in God, for he hardly ever thought about Him; he recognized the supernatural, but considered it was entirely the women's concern, and when religion or miracles were discussed before him, or a question were put to him, he would say reluctantly, scratching himself:

"Who can tell!"

Granny believed, but her faith was somewhat hazy; everything was mixed up in her memory, and she could scarcely begin to think of sins, of death, of the salvation of the soul, before poverty and her daily cares took possession of her mind, and she instantly forgot what she was thinking about. She did not remember the prayers, and usually in the evenings, before lying down to sleep, she would stand before the ikons and whisper:

"Holy Mother of Kazan, Holy Mother of Smolensk, Holy Mother of Troerutchitsy. . ."

Marya and Fyokla crossed themselves, fasted, and took the sacrament every year, but understood nothing. The children were not taught their prayers, nothing was told them about God, and no moral principles were instilled into them; they were only forbidden to eat meat or milk in Lent. In the other families it was much the same: there were few who believed, few who understood. At the same time everyone loved the Holy Scripture, loved it with a tender, reverent love; but they had no Bible, there was no one to read it and explain it, and because Olga sometimes read them the gospel, they respected her, and they all addressed her and Sasha as though they were superior to themselves.

For church holidays and services Olga often went to neighbouring villages, and to the district town, in which there were two monasteries and twenty-seven churches. She was dreamy, and when she was on these pilgrimages she quite forgot her family, and only when she got home again suddenly made the joyful discovery that she had a husband and daughter, and then would say, smiling and radiant:

"God has sent me blessings!"

What went on in the village worried her and seemed to her revolting. On Elijah's Day they drank, at the Assumption they drank, at the Ascension they drank. The Feast of the Intercession was the parish holiday for Zhukovo, and the peasants used to drink then for three days; they squandered on drink fifty roubles of money belonging to the Mir, and then collected more for vodka from all the households. On the first day of the feast the Tchikildyeevs killed a sheep and ate of it in the morning, at dinner-time, and in the evening; they ate it ravenously, and the children got up at night to eat more. Kiryak was fearfully drunk for three whole days; he drank up everything, even his boots and cap, and beat Marya so terribly that they had to pour water over her. And then they were all ashamed and sick.

However, even in Zhukovo, in this "Slaveytown," there was once an outburst of genuine religious enthusiasm. It was in August, when throughout the district they carried from village to village the Holy Mother, the giver of life. It was still and overcast on the day when they expected *Her* at Zhukovo. The girls set off in the morning to meet the ikon, in their bright holiday dresses, and brought Her towards the evening, in procession with the cross and with singing, while the bells pealed in the church across the river. An immense crowd of villagers and strangers flooded the street; there was noise, dust, a great crush. . . . And the old father and Granny and Kiryak - all stretched out their hands to the ikon, looked eagerly at it and said, weeping:

"Defender! Mother! Defender!"

All seemed suddenly to realize that there was not an empty void between earth and heaven, that the rich and the powerful had not taken possession of everything, that there was still a refuge from injury, from slavish bondage, from crushing, unendurable poverty, from the terrible vodka.

"Defender! Mother!" sobbed Marya. "Mother!"

But the thanksgiving service ended and the ikon was carried away, and everything went on as before; and again there was a sound of coarse drunken oaths from the tavern.

Only the well-to-do peasants were afraid of death; the richer they were the less they believed in God, and in the salvation of souls, and only through fear of the end of the world put up candles and had services said for them, to be on the safe side. The peasants who were rather poorer were not afraid of death. The old father and Granny were told to their faces that they had lived too long, that it was time they were dead, and they did not mind. They did not hinder Fyokla from saying in Nikolay's presence that when Nikolay died her husband Denis would get exemption - to return home from the army. And Marya, far from fearing death, regretted that it was so slow in coming, and was glad when her children died.

Death they did not fear, but of every disease they had an exaggerated terror. The merest trifle was enough - a stomach upset, a slight chill, and Granny would be wrapped up on the stove, and would begin moaning loudly and incessantly:

"I am dy-ing!"

The old father hurried off for the priest, and Granny received the sacrament and extreme unction. They often talked of colds, of worms, of tumours which move in the stomach and coil round to the heart. Above all, they were afraid of catching cold, and so put on thick clothes even in the summer and warmed themselves at the stove. Granny was fond of being doctored, and often went to the hospital, where she used to say she was not seventy, but fifty-eight; she supposed that if the doctor knew her real age he would not treat her, but would say it was time she died instead of taking medicine. She usually went to the hospital early in the morning, taking with her two or three of the little girls, and came back in the evening, hungry and ill-tempered - with drops for herself and ointments for the little girls. Once she took Nikolay, who swallowed drops for a fortnight afterwards, and said he felt better.

Granny knew all the doctors and their assistants and the wise men for twenty miles round, and not one of them she liked. At the Intercession, when the priest made the round of the huts with the cross, the deacon told her that in the town near the prison lived an old man who had been a medical orderly in the army, and who made wonderful cures, and advised her to try him. Granny took his advice. When the first snow fell she drove to the town and fetched an old man with a big beard, a converted Jew, in a long gown, whose face was covered with blue veins. There were outsiders at work in the hut at the time: an old tailor, in terrible spectacles, was cutting a waistcoat out of some rags, and two young men were making felt boots out of wool; Kiryak, who had been dismissed from his place for drunkenness, and now lived at home, was sitting beside the tailor mending a bridle. And it was crowded, stifling, and noisome in the hut. The converted Jew examined Nikolay and said that it was necessary to try cupping.

He put on the cups, and the old tailor, Kiryak, and the little girls stood round and looked on, and it seemed to them that they saw the disease being drawn out of Nikolay; and Nikolay, too, watched how the cups suckling at his breast gradually filled with dark blood, and felt as though there really were something coming out of him, and smiled with pleasure.

"It's a good thing," said the tailor. "Please God, it will do you good."

The Jew put on twelve cups and then another twelve, drank some tea, and went away. Nikolay began shivering; his face looked drawn, and, as the women expressed it, shrank up like a fist; his fingers turned blue. He wrapped himself up in a quilt and in a sheepskin, but got colder and colder. Towards the evening he began to be in great distress; asked to be laid on the ground, asked the tailor not to smoke; then he subsided under the sheepskin and towards morning he died.

IX

Oh, what a grim, what a long winter!

Their own grain did not last beyond Christmas, and they had to buy flour. Kiryak, who lived at home now, was noisy in the evenings, inspiring terror in everyone, and in the mornings he suffered from headache and was ashamed; and he was a pitiful sight. In the stall the starved cows bellowed day and night - a heart-rending sound to Granny and Marya. And as ill-luck would have it, there was a sharp frost all the winter, the snow drifted in high heaps, and the winter dragged on. At Annunciation there was a regular blizzard, and there was a fall of snow at Easter.

But in spite of it all the winter did end. At the beginning of April there came warm days and frosty nights. Winter would not give way, but one warm day overpowered it at last, and the streams began to flow and the birds began to sing. The whole meadow and the bushes near the river were drowned in the spring floods, and all the space between Zhukovo and the further side was filled up with a vast sheet of water, from which wild ducks rose up in flocks here and there. The spring sunset, flaming among gorgeous clouds, gave every evening something new, extraordinary, incredible - just what one does not believe in afterwards, when one sees those very colours and those very clouds in a picture.

The cranes flew swiftly, swiftly, with mournful cries, as though they were calling themselves. Standing on the edge of the ravine, Olga looked a long time at the flooded meadow, at the sunshine, at the bright church, that looked as though it had grown younger; and her tears flowed and her breath came in gasps from her passionate longing to go away, to go far away to the end of the world. It was already settled that she should go back to Moscow to be a servant, and that Kiryak should set off with her to get a job as a porter or something. Oh, to get away quickly!

As soon as it dried up and grew warm they got ready to set off. Olga and Sasha, with wallets on their backs and shoes of plaited bark on their feet, came out before daybreak: Marya came out, too, to see them on their way. Kiryak was not well, and was kept at home for another week. For the last time Olga prayed at the church and thought of her husband, and though she did not shed tears, her face puckered up and looked ugly like an old woman's. During the winter she had grown thinner and plainer, and her hair had gone a little grey, and instead of the old look of sweetness and the pleasant smile on her face, she had the resigned, mournful expression left by the sorrows she had been through, and there was something blank and irresponsive in her eyes, as though she did not hear what was said. She was sorry to part from the village and the peasants. She remembered how they had carried out Nikolay, and how a requiem had been ordered for him at almost every hut, and all had shed tears in sympathy with her grief. In the course of the summer and the winter there had been hours and days when it seemed as though these people lived worse than the beasts, and to live with them was terrible; they were coarse, dishonest, filthy, and drunken; they did not live in harmony, but quarrelled continually, because they distrusted and feared and did not respect one another. Who keeps the tavern and makes the people drunken? A peasant. Who wastes and spends on drink the funds of the commune, of the schools, of the church? A peasant. Who stole from his neighbours, set fire to their property, gave false witness at the court for a bottle of vodka? At the meetings of the Zemstvo and other local bodies, who was the first to fall foul of the peasants? A peasant. Yes, to live with them was terrible; but yet, they were human beings, they suffered and wept like human beings, and there was nothing in their lives for which one could not find excuse. Hard labour that made the whole body ache at night, the cruel winters, the scanty harvests, the overcrowding; and they had no help and none to whom they could look for help. Those of them who were a little stronger and better off could be no help, as they were themselves coarse, dishonest, drunken, and abused one another just as revoltingly; the paltriest little clerk or official treated the peasants as though they were tramps, and addressed even the village elders and church wardens as inferiors, and considered they had a right to do so. And, indeed, can any sort of help or good example be given by mercenary, greedy, depraved, and idle persons who only visit the village in order to insult, to despoil, and to terrorize? Olga remembered the pitiful, humiliated look of the old people when in the winter Kiryak had been taken to be flogged. . . . And now she felt sorry for all these people, painfully so, and as she walked on she kept looking back at the huts.

After walking two miles with them Marya said good-bye, then kneeling, and falling forward with her face on the earth, she began wailing:

"Again I am left alone. Alas, for poor me! poor, unhappy! . . ."

And she wailed like this for a long time, and for a long way Olga and Sasha could still see her on her knees, bowing down to someone at the side and clutching her head in her hands, while the rooks flew over her head.

The sun rose high; it began to get hot. Zhukovo was left far behind. Walking was pleasant. Olga and Sasha soon forgot both the village and Marya; they were gay and everything entertained them. Now they came upon an ancient barrow, now upon a row of telegraph posts running one after another into the distance and disappearing into the horizon, and the wires hummed mysteriously. Then they saw a homestead, all wreathed in green foliage; there came a scent from it of dampness, of hemp, and it seemed for some reason that happy people lived there. Then they came upon a horse's skeleton whitening in solitude in the open fields. And the larks trilled unceasingly, the corncrakes called to one another, and the landrail cried as though someone were really scraping at an old iron rail.

At midday Olga and Sasha reached a big village. There in the broad street they met the little old man who was General Zhukov's cook. He was hot, and his red, perspiring bald head shone in the sunshine. Olga and he did not recognize each other, then looked round at the same moment, recognized each other, and went their separate ways without saying a word. Stopping near the hut which looked newest and most prosperous, Olga bowed down before the open windows, and said in a loud, thin, chanting voice:

"Good Christian folk, give alms, for Christ's sake, that God's blessing may be upon you, and that your parents may be in the Kingdom of Heaven in peace eternal."

"Good Christian folk," Sasha began chanting, "give, for Christ's sake, that God's blessing, the Heavenly Kingdom . . ."

THE PETCHENYEG

Ivan Abramitch Zhmuhin, a retired Cossack officer, who had once served in the Caucasus, but now lived on his own farm, and who had once been young, strong, and vigorous, but now was old, dried up, and bent, with shaggy eyebrows and a greenish-grey moustache, was returning from the town to his farm one hot summer's day. In the town he had confessed and received absolution, and had made his will at the notary's (a fortnight before he had had a slight stroke), and now all the while he was in the railway carriage he was haunted by melancholy, serious thoughts of approaching death, of the vanity of vanities, of the transitoriness of all things earthly. At the station of Provalye - there is such a one on the Donetz line - a fair-haired, plump, middle-aged gentleman with a shabby portfolio stepped into the carriage and sat down opposite. They got into conversation.

"Yes," said Ivan Abramitch, looking pensively out of window, "it is never too late to marry. I myself married when I was forty-eight; I was told it was late, but it has turned out that it was not late or early, but simply that it would have been better not to marry at all. Everyone is soon tired of his wife, but not everyone tells the truth, because, you know, people are ashamed of an unhappy home life and conceal it. It's 'Manya this' and 'Manya that' with many a man by his wife's side, but if he had his way he'd put that Manya in a sack and drop her in the water. It's dull with one's wife, it's mere foolishness. And it's no better with one's children, I make bold to assure you. I have two of them, the rascals. There's nowhere for them to be taught out here in the steppe; I haven't the money to send them to school in Novo Tcherkask, and they live here like young wolves. Next thing they will be murdering someone on the highroad."

The fair-haired gentleman listened attentively, answered questions briefly in a low voice, and was apparently a gentleman of gentle and modest disposition. He mentioned that he was a lawyer, and that he was going to the village Dyuevka on business.

"Why, merciful heavens, that is six miles from me!" said Zhmuhin in a tone of voice as though someone were disputing with him. "But excuse me, you won't find horses at the station now. To my mind, the very best thing you can do, you know, is to come straight to me, stay the night, you know, and in the morning drive over with my horses."

The lawyer thought a moment and accepted the invitation.

When they reached the station the sun was already low over the steppe. They said nothing all the way from the station to the farm: the jolting prevented conversation. The trap bounded up and down, squeaked, and seemed to be sobbing, and the lawyer, who was sitting very uncomfortably, stared before him, miserably hoping to see the farm. After they had driven five or six miles there came into view in the distance a low-pitched house and a yard enclosed by a fence made of dark, flat stones standing on end; the roof was green, the stucco was peeling off, and the windows were little narrow slits like screwed-up eyes. The farm stood in the full sunshine, and there was no sign either of water or trees anywhere round. Among the neighbouring landowners and the peasants it was known as the Petchenyegs' farm. Many years before, a land surveyor, who was passing through the neighbourhood and put up at the farm, spent the whole night talking to Ivan Abramitch, was not favourably impressed, and as he was driving away in the morning said to him grimly:

"You are a Petchenyeg, my good sir!"

From this came the nickname, the Petchenyegs' farm, which stuck to the place even more when Zhmuhin's boys grew up and began to make raids on the orchards and kitchen-gardens. Ivan Abramitch was called "You Know," as he usually talked a very great deal and frequently made use of that expression.

In the yard near a barn Zhmuhin's sons were standing, one a young man of nineteen, the other a younger lad, both barefoot and bareheaded. Just at the moment when the trap drove into the yard the younger one flung high up a hen which, cackling, described an arc in the air; the elder shot at it with a gun and the hen fell dead on the earth.

"Those are my boys learning to shoot birds flying," said Zhmuhin.

In the entry the travellers were met by a little thin woman with a pale face, still young and beautiful; from her dress she might have been taken for a servant.

"And this, allow me to introduce her," said Zhmuhin, "is the mother of my young cubs. Come, Lyubov Osipovna," he said, addressing her, "you must be spry, mother, and get something for our guest. Let us have supper. Look sharp!"

The house consisted of two parts: in one was the parlour and beside it old Zhmuhin's bedroom, both stuffy rooms with low ceilings and multitudes of flies and wasps, and in the other was the kitchen in which the cooking and washing was done and the labourers had their meals; here geese and turkey-hens were sitting on their eggs under the benches, and here were the beds of Lyubov Osipovna and her two sons. The furniture in the parlour was unpainted and evidently roughly made by a carpenter; guns, game-bags, and whips were hanging on the walls, and all this old rubbish was covered with the rust of years and looked grey with dust. There was not one picture; in the corner was a dingy board which had at one time been an ikon.

A young Little Russian woman laid the table and handed ham, then beetroot soup. The visitor refused vodka and ate only bread and cucumbers.

"How about ham?" asked Zhmuhin.

"Thank you, I don't eat it," answered the visitor, "I don't eat meat at all."

"Why is that?"

"I am a vegetarian. Killing animals is against my principles."

Zhmuhin thought a minute and then said slowly with a sigh:

"Yes . . . to be sure. . . . I saw a man who did not eat meat in town, too. It's a new religion they've got now. Well, it's good. We can't go on always shooting and slaughtering, you know; we must give it up some day and leave even the beasts in peace. It's a sin to kill, it's a sin, there is no denying it. Sometimes one kills a hare and wounds him in the leg, and he cries like a child. . . . So it must hurt him!"

"Of course it hurts him; animals suffer just like human beings."

"That's true," Zhmuhin assented. "I understand that very well," he went on, musing, "only there is this one thing I don't understand: suppose, you know, everyone gave up eating meat, what would become of the domestic animals - fowls and geese, for instance?"

"Fowls and geese would live in freedom like wild birds."

"Now I understand. To be sure, crows and jackdaws get on all right without us. Yes. . . . Fowls and geese and hares and sheep, all will live in freedom, rejoicing, you know, and praising God; and they will not fear us, peace and concord will come. Only there is one thing, you know, I can't understand," Zhmuhin went on, glancing at the ham. "How will it be with the pigs? What is to be done with them?"

"They will be like all the rest - that is, they will live in freedom."

"Ah! Yes. But allow me to say, if they were not slaughtered they would multiply, you know, and then good-bye to the kitchen-gardens and the meadows. Why, a pig, if you let it free and don't look after it, will ruin everything in a day. A pig is a pig, and it is not for nothing it is called a pig. . . ."

They finished supper. Zhmuhin got up from the table and for a long while walked up and down the room, talking and talking. . . . He was fond of talking of something important or serious and was fond of meditating, and in his old age he had a longing to reach some haven, to be reassured, that he might not be so frightened of dying. He had a longing for meekness, spiritual calm, and confidence in himself, such as this guest of theirs had, who had satisfied his hunger on cucumbers and bread, and believed that doing so made him more perfect; he was sitting on a chest, plump and healthy, keeping silent and patiently enduring his boredom, and in the dusk when one glanced at him from the entry he looked like a big round stone which one could not move from its place. If a man has something to lay hold of in life he is all right.

Zhmuhin went through the entry to the porch, and then he could be heard sighing and saying reflectively to himself: "Yes. . . . To be sure. . . . By now it was dark, and here and there stars could be seen in the sky. They had not yet lighted up indoors. Someone came into the parlour as noiselessly as a shadow and stood still near the door. It was Lyubov Osipovna, Zhmuhin's wife.

"Are you from the town?" she asked timidly, not looking at her visitor.

"Yes, I live in the town."

"Perhaps you are something in the learned way, sir; be so kind as to advise us. We ought to send in a petition."

"To whom?" asked the visitor.

"We have two sons, kind gentleman, and they ought to have been sent to school long ago, but we never see anyone and have no one to advise us. And I know nothing. For if they are not taught they will have to serve in the army as common Cossacks. It's not right, sir! They can't read and write, they are worse than peasants, and Ivan Abramitch himself can't stand them and won't let them indoors. But they are not to blame. The younger one, at any rate, ought to be sent to school, it is such a pity!" she said slowly, and there was a quiver in her voice; and it seemed incredible that a woman so small and so youthful could have grown-up children. "Oh, it's such a pity!"

"You don't know anything about it, mother, and it is not your affair," said Zhmuhin, appearing in the doorway. "Don't pester our guest with your wild talk. Go away, mother!"

Lyubov Osipovna went out, and in the entry repeated once more in a thin little voice: "Oh, it's such a pity!"

A bed was made up for the visitor on the sofa in the parlour, and that it might not be dark for him they lighted the lamp before the ikon. Zhmuhin went to bed in his own room. And as he lay there he thought of his soul, of his age, of his recent stroke which had so frightened him and made him think of death. He was fond of philosophizing when he was in quietness by himself, and then he fancied that he was a very earnest, deep thinker, and that nothing in this world interested him but serious questions. And now he kept thinking and he longed to pitch upon some one significant thought unlike others, which would be a guide to him in life, and he wanted to think out principles of some sort for himself so as to make his life as deep and earnest as he imagined that he felt himself to be. It would be a good thing for an old man like him to abstain altogether from meat, from superfluities of all sorts. The time when men give up killing each other and animals would come sooner or later, it could not but be so, and he imagined that time to himself and clearly pictured himself living in peace with all the animals, and suddenly he thought again of the pigs, and everything was in a tangle in his brain.

"It's a queer business, Lord have mercy upon us," he muttered, sighing heavily. "Are you asleep?" he asked.

"No."

Zhmuhin got out of bed and stopped in the doorway with nothing but his shirt on, displaying to his guest his sinewy legs, that looked as dry as sticks.

"Nowadays, you know," he began, "all sorts of telegraphs, telephones, and marvels of all kinds, in fact, have come in, but people are no better than they were. They say that in our day, thirty or forty years ago, men were coarse and cruel; but isn't it just the same now? We certainly did not stand on ceremony in our day. I remember in the Caucasus when we were stationed by a little river with nothing to do for four whole months - I was an under-officer at that time - something queer happened, quite in the style of a novel. Just on the banks of that river, you know, where our division was encamped, a wretched prince whom we had killed not long before was buried. And at night, you know, the princess used to come to his grave and weep. She would wail and wail, and moan and moan, and make us so depressed we couldn't sleep, and that's the fact. We couldn't sleep one night, we couldn't sleep a second; well, we got sick of it. And from a common-sense point of view you really can't go without your sleep for the devil knows what (excuse the expression). We took that princess and gave her a good thrashing, and she gave up coming. There's an instance for you. Nowadays, of course, there is not the same class of people, and they are not given to thrashing and they live in cleaner style, and there is more learning, but, you know, the soul is just the same: there is no change. Now, look here, there's a landowner living here among us; he has mines, you know; all sorts of tramps without passports who don't know where to go work for him. On Saturdays he has to settle up with the workmen, but he doesn't care to pay them, you know, he grudges the money. So he's got hold of a foreman who is a tramp too, though he does wear a hat. 'Don't you pay them anything,' he says, 'not a kopeck; they'll beat you, and let them beat you,' says he, 'but you put up with it, and I'll pay you ten roubles every Saturday for it.' So on the Saturday evening the workmen come to settle up in the usual way; the foreman says to them: 'Nothing!' Well, word for word, as the master said, they begin swearing and using their fists. . . . They beat him and they kick him . . . you know, they are a set of men brutalized by hunger - they beat him till he is senseless, and then they go each on his way. The master gives orders for cold water to be poured on the foreman, then flings ten roubles in his face. And he takes it and is pleased too, for indeed he'd be ready to be hanged for three roubles, let alone ten. Yes . . . and on Monday a new gang of workmen arrive; they work, for they have nowhere to go. . . . On Saturday it is the same story over again."

The visitor turned over on the other side with his face to the back of the sofa and muttered something.

"And here's another instance," Zhmuhin went on. "We had the Siberian plague here, you know - the cattle die off like flies, I can tell you - and the veterinary surgeons came here, and strict orders were given that the dead cattle were to be buried at a distance deep in the earth, that lime was to be thrown over them, and so on, you know, on scientific principles. My horse died too. I buried it with every precaution, and threw over three hundredweight of lime over it. And what do you think? My fine fellows - my precious sons, I mean - dug it up, skinned it, and sold the hide for three roubles; there's an instance for you. So people have grown no better, and however you feed a wolf he will always look towards the forest; there it is. It gives one something to think about, eh? How do you look at it?"

On one side a flash of lightning gleamed through a chink in the window-blinds. There was the stifling feeling of a storm coming, the gnats were biting, and Zhmuhin, as he lay in his bedroom meditating, sighed and groaned and said to himself: "Yes, to be sure --" and there was no possibility of getting to sleep. Somewhere far, far away there was a growl of thunder.

"Are you asleep?"

"No," answered the visitor.

Zhmuhin got up, and thudding with his heels walked through the parlour and the entry to the kitchen to get a drink of water.

"The worst thing in the world, you know, is stupidity," he said a little later, coming back with a dipper. "My Lyubov Osipovna is on her knees saying her prayers. She prays every night, you know, and bows down to the ground, first that her children may be sent to school; she is afraid her boys will go into the army as simple Cossacks, and that they will be whacked across their backs with sabres. But for teaching one must have money, and where is one to get it? You may break the floor beating your head against it, but if you haven't got it you haven't. And the other reason she prays is because, you know, every woman imagines there is no one in the world as unhappy as she is. I am a plain-spoken man, and I don't want to conceal anything from you. She comes of a poor family, a village priest's daughter. I married her when she was seventeen, and they accepted my offer chiefly because they hadn't enough to eat; it was nothing but poverty and misery, while I have anyway land, you see - a farm - and after all I am an officer; it was a step up for her to marry me, you know. On the very first day when she was married she cried, and she has been crying ever since, all these twenty years; she has got a watery eye. And she's always sitting and thinking, and what do you suppose she is thinking about? What can a woman think about? Why, nothing. I must own I don't consider a woman a human being."

The visitor got up abruptly and sat on the bed.

"Excuse me, I feel stifled," he said; "I will go outside."

Zhmuhin, still talking about women, drew the bolt in the entry and they both went out. A full moon was floating in the sky just over the yard, and in the moonlight the house and barn looked whiter than by day; and on the grass brilliant streaks of moonlight, white too, stretched between the black shadows. Far away on the right could be seen the steppe, above it the stars were softly glowing - and it was all mysterious, infinitely far away, as though one were gazing into a deep abyss; while on the left heavy storm-clouds, black as soot, were piling up one upon another above the steppe; their edges were lighted up by the moon, and it looked as though there were mountains there with white snow on their peaks, dark forests, the sea. There was a flash of lightning, a faint rumble of thunder, and it seemed as though a battle were being fought in the mountains.

Quite close to the house a little night-owl screeched monotonously:

"Asleep! asleep!"

"What time is it now?" asked the visitor.

"Just after one."

"How long it is still to dawn!"

They went back to the house and lay down again. It was time to sleep, and one can usually sleep so splendidly before rain; but the old man had a hankering after serious, weighty thoughts; he wanted not simply to think but to meditate, and he meditated how good it would be, as death was near at hand, for the sake of his soul to give up the idleness which so imperceptibly swallowed up day after day, year after year, leaving no trace; to think out for himself some great exploit - for instance, to walk on foot far, far away, or to give up meat like this young man. And again he pictured to himself the time when animals would not be killed, pictured it clearly and distinctly as though he were living through that time himself; but suddenly it was all in a tangle again in his head and all was muddled.

The thunderstorm had passed over, but from the edges of the storm-clouds came rain softly pattering on the roof. Zhmuhin got up, stretching and groaning with old age, and looked into the parlour. Noticing that his visitor was not asleep, he said:

"When we were in the Caucasus, you know, there was a colonel there who was a vegetarian, too; he didn't eat meat, never went shooting, and would not let his servants catch fish. Of course, I understand that every animal ought to live in freedom and enjoy its life; only I don't understand how a pig can go about where it likes without being looked after. . . ."

The visitor got up and sat down. His pale, haggard face expressed weariness and vexation; it was evident that he was exhausted, and only his gentleness and the delicacy of his soul prevented him from expressing his vexation in words.

"It's getting light," he said mildly. "Please have the horse brought round for me."

"Why so? Wait a little and the rain will be over."

"No, I entreat you," said the visitor in horror, with a supplicating voice; "it is essential for me to go at once."

And he began hurriedly dressing.

By the time the horse was harnessed the sun was rising. It had just left off raining, the clouds were racing swiftly by, and the patches of blue were growing bigger and bigger in the sky. The first rays of the sun were timidly reflected below in the big puddles. The visitor walked through the entry with his portfolio to get into the trap, and at that moment Zhmuhin's wife, pale, and it seemed paler than the day before, with tear-stained eyes, looked at him intently without blinking, with the naïve expression of a little girl, and it was evident from her dejected face that she was envying him his freedom - oh, with what joy she would have gone away from there! - and she wanted to say something to him, most likely to ask advice about her children. And what a pitiable figure she was! This was not a wife, not the head of a house, not even a servant, but more like a dependent, a poor relation not wanted by anyone, a nonentity. . . . Her husband, fussing about, talking unceasingly, was seeing his visitor off, continually running in front of him, while she huddled up to the wall with a timid, guilty air, waiting for a convenient minute to speak.

"Please come again another time," the old man kept repeating incessantly; "what we have we are glad to offer, you know."

The visitor hurriedly got into the trap, evidently with relief, as though he were afraid every minute that they would detain him. The trap lurched about as it had the day before, squeaked, and furiously rattled the pail that was tied on at the back. He glanced round at Zhmuhin with a peculiar expression; it looked as though he wanted to call him a Petchenyeg, as the surveyor had once done, or some such name, but his gentleness got the upper hand. He controlled himself and said nothing. But in the gateway he suddenly could not restrain himself; he got up and shouted loudly and angrily:

"You have bored me to death."

And he disappeared through the gate.

Near the barn Zhmuhin's sons were standing; the elder held a gun, while the younger had in his hands a grey cockerel with a bright red comb. The younger flung up the cockerel with all his might; the bird flew upwards higher than the house and turned over in the air like a pigeon. The elder boy fired and the cockerel fell like a stone.

The old man, overcome with confusion, not knowing how to explain the visitor's strange, unexpected shout, went slowly back into the house. And sitting down at the table he spent a long while meditating on the intellectual tendencies of the day, on the universal immorality, on the telegraph, on the telephone, on velocipedes, on how unnecessary it all was; little by little he regained his composure, then slowly had a meal, drank five glasses of tea, and lay down for a nap.

AT HOME

I

The Don railway. A quiet, cheerless station, white and solitary in the steppe, with its walls baking in the sun, without a speck of shade, and, it seems, without a human being. The train goes on after leaving one here; the sound of it is scarcely audible and dies away at last. Outside the station it is a desert, and there are no horses but one's own. One gets into the carriage - which is so pleasant after the train - and is borne along the road through the steppe, and by degrees there are unfolded before one views such as one does not see near Moscow - immense, endless, fascinating in their monotony. The steppe, the steppe, and nothing more; in the distance an ancient barrow or a windmill; ox-waggons laden with coal trail by. . . . Solitary birds fly low over the plain, and a drowsy feeling comes with the monotonous beat of their wings. It is hot. Another hour or so passes, and still the steppe, the steppe, and still in the distance the barrow. The driver tells you something, some long unnecessary tale, pointing into the distance with his whip. And tranquillity takes possession of the soul; one is loth to think of the past. . . .

A carriage with three horses had been sent to fetch Vera Ivanovna Kardin. The driver put in her luggage and set the harness to rights.

"Everything just as it always has been," said Vera, looking about her. "I was a little girl when I was here last, ten years ago. I remember old Boris came to fetch me then. Is he still living, I wonder?"

The driver made no reply, but, like a Little Russian, looked at her angrily and clambered on to the box.

It was a twenty-mile drive from the station, and Vera, too, abandoned herself to the charm of the steppe, forgot the past, and thought only of the wide expanse, of the freedom. Healthy, clever, beautiful, and young - she was only three-and-twenty - she had hitherto lacked nothing in her life but just this space and freedom.

The steppe, the steppe. . . . The horses trotted, the sun rose higher and higher; and it seemed to Vera that never in her childhood had the steppe been so rich, so luxuriant in June; the wild flowers were green, yellow, lilac, white, and a fragrance rose from them and from the warmed earth; and there were strange blue birds along the roadside. . . . Vera had long got out of the habit of praying, but now, struggling with drowsiness, she murmured:

"Lord, grant that I may be happy here."

And there was peace and sweetness in her soul, and she felt as though she would have been glad to drive like that all her life, looking at the steppe.

Suddenly there was a deep ravine overgrown with oak saplings and alder-trees; there was a moist feeling in the air - there must have been a spring at the bottom. On the near side, on the very edge of the ravine, a covey of partridges rose noisily. Vera remembered that in old days they used to go for evening walks to this ravine; so it must be near home! And now she could actually see the poplars, the barn, black smoke rising on one side - they were burning old straw. And there was Auntie Dasha coming to meet her and waving her handkerchief; grandfather was on the terrace. Oh dear, how happy she was!

"My darling, my darling!" cried her aunt, shrieking as though she were in hysterics. "Our real mistress has come! You must understand you are our mistress, you are our queen! Here everything is yours! My darling, my beauty, I am not your aunt, but your willing slave!"

Vera had no relations but her aunt and her grandfather; her mother had long been dead; her father, an engineer, had died three months before at Kazan, on his way from Siberia. Her grandfather had a big grey beard. He was stout, red-faced, and asthmatic, and walked leaning on a cane and sticking his stomach out. Her aunt, a lady of forty-two, drawn in tightly at the waist and fashionably dressed with sleeves high on the shoulder, evidently tried to look young and was still anxious to be charming; she walked with tiny steps with a wriggle of her spine.

"Will you love us?" she said, embracing Vera, "You are not proud?"

At her grandfather's wish there was a thanksgiving service, then they spent a long while over dinner - and Vera's new life began. She was given the best room. All the rugs in the house had been put in it, and a great many flowers; and when at night she lay down in her snug, wide, very soft bed and covered herself with a silk quilt that smelt of old clothes long stored away, she laughed with pleasure. Auntie Dasha came in for a minute to wish her good-night.

"Here you are home again, thank God," she said, sitting down on the bed. "As you see, we get along very well and have everything we want. There's only one thing: your grandfather is in a poor way! A terribly poor way! He is short of breath and he has begun to lose his memory. And you remember how strong, how vigorous, he used to be! There was no doing anything with him. . . . In old days, if the servants didn't please him or anything else went wrong, he would jump up at once and shout: 'Twenty-five strokes! The birch!' But now he has grown milder and you never hear him. And besides, times are changed, my precious; one mayn't beat them nowadays. Of course, they oughtn't to be beaten, but they need looking after."

"And are they beaten now, auntie?" asked Vera.

"The steward beats them sometimes, but I never do, bless their hearts! And your grandfather sometimes lifts his stick from old habit, but he never beats them."

Auntie Dasha yawned and crossed herself over her mouth and her right ear.

"It's not dull here?" Vera inquired.

"What shall I say? There are no landowners living here now, but there have been works built near, darling, and there are lots of engineers, doctors, and mine managers. Of course, we have theatricals and concerts, but we play cards more than anything. They come to us, too. Dr. Neshtchapov from the works comes to see us - such a handsome, interesting man! He fell in love with your photograph. I made up my mind: he is Verotchka's destiny, I thought. He's young, handsome, he has means - a good match, in fact. And of course you're a match for any one. You're of good family. The place is mortgaged, it's true, but it's in good order and not neglected; there is my share in it, but it will all come to you; I am your willing slave. And my brother, your father, left you fifteen thousand roubles. . . . But I see you can't keep your eyes open. Sleep, my child."

Next day Vera spent a long time walking round the house. The garden, which was old and unattractive, lying inconveniently upon the slope, had no paths, and was utterly neglected; probably the care of it was regarded as an unnecessary item in the management. There were numbers of grass-snakes. Hoopoes flew about under the trees calling "Oo-too-toot!" as though they were trying to remind her of something. At the bottom of the hill there was a river overgrown with tall reeds, and half a mile beyond the river was the village. From the garden Vera went out into the fields; looking into the distance, thinking of her new life in her own home, she kept trying to grasp what was in store for her. The space, the lovely peace of the steppe, told her that happiness was near at hand, and perhaps was here already; thousands of people, in fact, would have said: "What happiness to be young, healthy, well-educated, to be living on one's own estate!" And at the same time the endless plain, all alike, without one living soul, frightened her, and at moments it was clear to her that its peaceful green vastness would swallow up her life and reduce it to nothingness. She was very young, elegant, fond of life; she had finished her studies at an aristocratic boarding-school, had learnt three languages, had read a great deal, had travelled with her father - and could all this have been meant to lead to nothing but settling down in a remote country-house in the steppe, and wandering day after day from the garden into the fields and from the fields into the garden to while away the time, and then sitting at home listening to her grandfather's breathing? But what could she do? Where could she go? She could find no answer, and as she was returning home she doubted whether she would be happy here, and thought that driving from the station was far more interesting than living here.

Dr. Neshtchapov drove over from the works. He was a doctor, but three years previously he had taken a share in the works, and had become one of the partners; and now he no longer looked upon medicine as his chief vocation, though he still practised. In appearance he was a pale, dark man in a white waistcoat, with a good figure; but to guess what there was in his heart and his brain was difficult. He kissed Auntie Dasha's hand on greeting her, and was continually leaping up to set a chair or give his seat to some one. He was very silent and grave all the while, and, when he did speak, it was for some reason impossible to hear and understand his first sentence, though he spoke correctly and not in a low voice.

"You play the piano?" he asked Vera, and immediately leapt up, as she had dropped her handkerchief.

He stayed from midday to midnight without speaking, and Vera found him very unattractive. She thought that a white waistcoat in the country was bad form, and his elaborate politeness, his manners, and his pale, serious face with dark eyebrows, were mawkish; and it seemed to her that he was perpetually silent, probably because he was stupid. When he had gone her aunt said enthusiastically:

"Well? Isn't he charming?"

II

Auntie Dasha looked after the estate. Tightly laced, with jingling bracelets on her wrists, she went into the kitchen, the granary, the cattle-yard, tripping along with tiny steps, wriggling her spine; and whenever she talked to the steward or to the peasants, she used, for some reason, to put on a pince-nez. Vera's grandfather always sat in the same place, playing patience or dozing. He ate a very great deal at dinner and supper; they gave him the dinner cooked to-day and what was left from yesterday, and cold pie left from Sunday, and salt meat from the servants' dinner, and he ate it all greedily. And every dinner left on Vera such an impression, that when she saw afterwards a flock of sheep driven by, or flour being brought from the mill, she thought, "Grandfather will eat that." For the most part he was silent, absorbed in eating or in patience; but it sometimes happened at dinner that at the sight of Vera he would be touched and say tenderly:

"My only grandchild! Verotchka!"

And tears would glisten in his eyes. Or his face would turn suddenly crimson, his neck would swell, he would look with fury at the servants, and ask, tapping with his stick:

"Why haven't you brought the horse-radish?"

In winter he led a perfectly inactive existence; in summer he sometimes drove out into the fields to look at the oats and the hay; and when he came back he would flourish his stick and declare that everything was neglected now that he was not there to look after it.

"Your grandfather is out of humour," Auntie Dasha would whisper. "But it's nothing now to what it used to be in the old days: 'Twenty-five strokes! The birch!' "

Her aunt complained that everyone had grown lazy, that no one did anything, and that the estate yielded no profit. Indeed, there was no systematic farming; they ploughed and sowed a little simply from habit, and in reality did nothing and lived in idleness. Meanwhile there was a running to and fro, reckoning and worrying all day long; the bustle in the house began at five o'clock in the morning; there were continual sounds of "Bring it," "Fetch it," "Make haste," and by the evening the servants were utterly exhausted. Auntie Dasha changed her cooks and her housemaids every week; sometimes she discharged them for immorality; sometimes they went of their own accord, complaining that they were worked to death. None of the village people would come to the house as servants; Auntie Dasha had to hire them from a distance. There was only one girl from the village living in the house, Alyona, and she stayed because her whole family - old people and children - were living upon her wages. This Alyona, a pale, rather stupid little thing, spent the whole day turning out the rooms, waiting at table, heating the stoves, sewing, washing; but it always seemed as though she were only pottering about, treading heavily with her boots, and were nothing but a hindrance in the house. In her terror that she might be dismissed and sent home, she often dropped and broke the crockery, and they stopped the value of it out of her wages, and then her mother and grandmother would come and bow down at Auntie Dasha's feet.

Once a week or sometimes oftener visitors would arrive. Her aunt would come to Vera and say:

"You should sit a little with the visitors, or else they'll think that you are stuck up."

Vera would go in to the visitors and play *vint* with them for hours together, or play the piano for the visitors to dance; her aunt, in high spirits and breathless from dancing, would come up and whisper to her:

"Be nice to Marya Nikiforovna."

On the sixth of December, St. Nikolay's Day, a large party of about thirty arrived all at once; they played *vint* until late at night, and many of them stayed the night. In the morning they sat down to cards again, then they had dinner, and when Vera went to her room after dinner to rest from conversation and tobacco smoke, there were visitors there too, and she almost wept in despair. And when they began to get ready to go in the evening, she was so pleased they were going at last, that she said:

"Do stay a little longer."

She felt exhausted by the visitors and constrained by their presence; yet every day, as soon as it began to grow dark, something drew her out of the house, and she went out to pay visits either at the works or at some neighbours', and then there were cards, dancing, forfeits, suppers. . . .The young people in the works or in the mines sometimes sang Little Russian songs, and sang them very well. It made one sad to hear them sing. Or they all gathered together in one room and talked in the dusk of the mines, of the treasures that had once been buried in the steppes, of Saur's Grave. . . . Later on, as they talked, a shout of "Help!" sometimes reached them. It was a drunken man going home, or some one was being robbed by the pit near by. Or the wind howled in the chimneys, the shutters banged; then, soon afterwards, they would hear the uneasy church bell, as the snow-storm began.

At all the evening parties, picnics, and dinners, Auntie Dasha was invariably the most interesting woman and the doctor the most interesting man. There was very little reading either at the works or at the country-houses; they played only marches and polkas; and the young people always argued hotly about things they did not understand, and the effect was crude. The discussions were loud and heated, but, strange to say, Vera had nowhere else met people so indifferent and careless as these. They seemed to have no fatherland, no religion, no public interests. When they talked of literature or debated some abstract question, it could be seen from Dr. Neshtchapov's face that the question had no interest for him whatever, and that for long, long years he had read nothing and cared to read nothing. Serious and expressionless, like a badly painted portrait, for ever in his white waistcoat, he was silent and incomprehensible as before; but the ladies, young and old, thought him interesting and were enthusiastic over his manners. They envied Vera, who appeared to attract him very much. And Vera always came away from the visits with a feeling of vexation, vowing inwardly to remain at home; but the day passed, the evening came, and she hurried off to the works again, and it was like that almost all the winter.

She ordered books and magazines, and used to read them in her room. And she read at night, lying in bed. When the clock in the corridor struck two or three, and her temples were beginning to ache from reading, she sat up in bed and thought, "What am I to do? Where am I to go?" Accursed, importunate question, to which there were a number of ready-made answers, and in reality no answer at all.

Oh, how noble, how holy, how picturesque it must be to serve the people, to alleviate their sufferings, to enlighten them! But she, Vera, did not know the people. And how could she go to them? They were strange and uninteresting to her; she could not endure the stuffy smell of the huts, the pot-house oaths, the unwashed children, the women's talk of illnesses. To walk over the snow-drifts, to feel cold, then to sit in a stifling hut, to teach children she disliked - no, she would rather die! And to teach the peasants' children while Auntie Dasha made money out of the pot-houses and fined the peasants - it was too great a farce! What a lot of talk there was of schools, of village libraries, of universal education; but if all these engineers, these mine-owners and ladies of her acquaintance, had not been hypocrites, and really had believed that enlightenment was necessary, they would not have paid the schoolmasters fifteen roubles a month as they did now, and would not have let them go hungry. And the schools and the talk about ignorance - it was all only to stifle the voice of conscience because they were ashamed to own fifteen or thirty thousand acres and to be indifferent to the peasants' lot. Here the ladies said about Dr. Neshtchapov that he was a kind man and had built a school at the works. Yes, he had built a school out of the old bricks at the works for some eight hundred roubles, and they sang the prayer for "long life" to him when the building was opened, but there was no chance of his giving up his shares, and it certainly never entered his head that the peasants were human beings like himself, and that they, too, needed university teaching, and not merely lessons in these wretched schools.

And Vera felt full of anger against herself and everyone else. She took up a book again and tried to read it, but soon afterwards sat down and thought again. To become a doctor? But to do that one must pass an examination in Latin; besides, she had an invincible repugnance to corpses and disease. It would be nice to become a mechanic, a judge, a commander of a steamer, a scientist; to do something into which she could put all her powers, physical and spiritual, and to be tired out and sleep soundly at night; to give up her life to something that would make her an interesting person, able to attract interesting people, to love, to have a real family of her own. . . . But what was she to do? How was she to begin?

One Sunday in Lent her aunt came into her room early in the morning to fetch her umbrella. Vera was sitting up in bed clasping her head in her hands, thinking.

"You ought to go to church, darling," said her aunt, "or people will think you are not a believer."

Vera made no answer.

"I see you are dull, poor child," said Auntie Dasha, sinking on her knees by the bedside; she adored Vera. "Tell me the truth, are you bored?"

"Dreadfully."

"My beauty, my queen, I am your willing slave, I wish you nothing but good and happiness. . . . Tell me, why don't you want to marry Nestchapov? What more do you want, my child? You must forgive me, darling; you can't pick and choose like this, we are not princes. . . . Time is passing, you are not seventeen. . . . And I don't understand it! He loves you, idolises you!"

"Oh, mercy!" said Vera with vexation. "How can I tell? He sits dumb and never says a word."

"He's shy, darling. . . . He's afraid you'll refuse him!"

And when her aunt had gone away, Vera remained standing in the middle of her room uncertain whether to dress or to go back to bed.

The bed was hateful; if one looked out of the window there were the bare trees, the grey snow, the hateful jackdaws, the pigs that her grandfather would eat. . . .

"Yes, after all, perhaps I'd better get married!" she thought.

III

For two days Auntie Dasha went about with a tear-stained and heavily powdered face, and at dinner she kept sighing and looking towards the ikon. And it was impossible to make out what was the matter with her. But at last she made up her mind, went in to Vera, and said in a casual way:

"The fact is, child, we have to pay interest on the bank loan, and the tenant hasn't paid his rent. Will you let me pay it out of the fifteen thousand your papa left you?"

All day afterwards Auntie Dasha spent in making cherry jam in the garden. Alyona, with her cheeks flushed with the heat, ran to and from the garden to the house and back again to the cellar.

When Auntie Dasha was making jam with a very serious face as though she were performing a religious rite, and her short sleeves displayed her strong, little, despotic hands and arms, and when the servants ran about incessantly, bustling about the jam which they would never taste, there was always a feeling of martyrdom in the air. . . .

The garden smelt of hot cherries. The sun had set, the charcoal stove had been carried away, but the pleasant, sweetish smell still lingered in the air. Vera sat on a bench in the garden and watched a new labourer, a young soldier, not of the neighbourhood, who was, by her express orders, making new paths. He was cutting the turf with a spade and heaping it up on a barrow.

"Where were you serving?" Vera asked him.

"At Berdyansk."

"And where are you going now? Home?"

"No," answered the labourer. "I have no home."

"But where were you born and brought up?"

"In the province of Oryol. Till I went into the army I lived with my mother, in my step-father's house; my mother was the head of the house, and people looked up to her, and while she lived I was cared for. But while I was in the army I got a letter telling me my mother was dead. . . . And now I don't seem to care to go home. It's not my own father, so it's not like my own home."

"Then your father is dead?"

"I don't know. I am illegitimate."

At that moment Auntie Dasha appeared at the window and said:

"*Il ne faut pas parler aux gens.* . . . Go into the kitchen, my good man. You can tell your story there," she said to the soldier.

And then came as yesterday and every day supper, reading, a sleepless night, and endless thinking about the same thing. At three o'clock the sun rose; Alyona was already busy in the corridor, and Vera was not asleep yet and was trying to read. She heard the creak of the barrow: it was the new labourer at work in the garden. . . . Vera sat at the open window with a book, dozed, and watched the soldier making the paths for her, and that interested her. The paths were as even and level as a leather strap, and it was pleasant to imagine what they would be like when they were strewn with yellow sand.

She could see her aunt come out of the house soon after five o'clock, in a pink wrapper and curl-papers. She stood on the steps for three minutes without speaking, and then said to the soldier:

"Take your passport and go in peace. I can't have any one illegitimate in my house."

An oppressive, angry feeling sank like a stone on Vera's heart. She was indignant with her aunt, she hated her; she was so sick of her aunt that her heart was full of misery and loathing. But what was she to do? To stop her mouth? To be rude to her? But what would be the use? Suppose she struggled with her, got rid of her, made her harmless, prevented her grandfather from flourishing his stick - what would be the use of it? It would be like killing one mouse or one snake in the boundless steppe. The vast expanse, the long winters, the monotony and dreariness of life, instil a sense of helplessness; the position seems hopeless, and one wants to do nothing - everything is useless.

Alyona came in, and bowing low to Vera, began carrying out the arm-chairs to beat the dust out of them.

"You have chosen a time to clean up," said Vera with annoyance. "Go away."

Alyona was overwhelmed, and in her terror could not understand what was wanted of her. She began hurriedly tidying up the dressing-table.

"Go out of the room, I tell you," Vera shouted, turning cold; she had never had such an oppressive feeling before. "Go away!"

Alyona uttered a sort of moan, like a bird, and dropped Vera's gold watch on the carpet.

"Go away!" Vera shrieked in a voice not her own, leaping up and trembling all over. "Send her away; she worries me to death!" she went on, walking rapidly after Alyona down the passage, stamping her feet. "Go away! Birch her! Beat her!" Then suddenly she came to herself, and just as she was, unwashed, uncombed, in her dressing-gown and slippers, she rushed out of the house. She ran to the familiar ravine and hid herself there among the sloe-trees, so that she might see no one and be seen by no one. Lying there motionless on the grass, she did not weep, she was not horror-stricken, but gazing at the sky open-eyed, she reflected coldly and clearly that something had happened which she could never forget and for which she could never forgive herself all her life.

"No, I can't go on like this," she thought. "It's time to take myself in hand, or there'll be no end to it. . . . I can't go on like this. . . ."

At midday Dr. Neshtchapov drove by the ravine on his way to the house. She saw him and made up her mind that she would begin a new life, and that she would make herself begin it, and this decision calmed her. And following with her eyes the doctor's well-built figure, she said, as though trying to soften the crudity of her decision:

"He's a nice man. . . . We shall get through life somehow."

She returned home. While she was dressing, Auntie Dasha came into the room, and said:

"Alyona upset you, darling; I've sent her home to the village. Her mother's given her a good beating and has come here, crying."

"Auntie," said Vera quickly, "I'm going to marry Dr. Neshtchapov. Only talk to him yourself . . . I can't."

And again she went out into the fields. And wandering aimlessly about, she made up her mind that when she was married she would look after the house, doctor the peasants, teach in the school, that she would do all the things that other women of her circle did. And this perpetual dissatisfaction with herself and everyone else, this series of crude mistakes which stand up like a mountain before one whenever one looks back upon one's past, she would accept as her real life to which she was fated, and she would expect nothing better. . . . Of course there was nothing better! Beautiful nature, dreams, music, told one story, but reality another. Evidently truth and happiness existed somewhere outside real life. . . . One must give up one's own life and merge oneself into this luxuriant steppe, boundless and indifferent as eternity, with its flowers, its ancient barrows, and its distant horizon, and then it would be well with one. . . .

A month later Vera was living at the works.

THE SCHOOLMISTRESS

At half-past eight they drove out of the town.

The highroad was dry, a lovely April sun was shining warmly, but the snow was still lying in the ditches and in the woods. Winter, dark, long, and spiteful, was hardly over; spring had come all of a sudden. But neither the warmth nor the languid transparent woods, warmed by the breath of spring, nor the black flocks of birds flying over the huge puddles that were like lakes, nor the marvelous fathomless sky, into which it seemed one would have gone away so joyfully, presented anything new or interesting to Marya Vassilyevna who was sitting in the cart. For thirteen years she had been schoolmistress, and there was no reckoning how many times during all those years she had been to the town for her salary; and whether it were spring as now, or a rainy autumn evening, or winter, it was all the same to her, and she always - invariably - longed for one thing only, to get to the end of her journey as quickly as could be.

She felt as though she had been living in that part of the country for ages and ages, for a hundred years, and it seemed to her that she knew every stone, every tree on the road from the town to her school. Her past was here, her present was here, and she could imagine no other future than the school, the road to the town and back again, and again the school and again the road. . . .

She had got out of the habit of thinking of her past before she became a schoolmistress, and had almost forgotten it. She had once had a father and mother; they had lived in Moscow in a big flat near the Red Gate, but of all that life there was left in her memory only something vague and fluid like a dream. Her father had died when she was ten years old, and her mother had died soon after. . . . She had a brother, an officer; at first they used to write to each other, then her brother had given up answering her letters, he had got out of the way of writing. Of her old belongings, all that was left was a photograph of her mother, but it had grown dim from the dampness of the school, and now nothing could be seen but the hair and the eyebrows.

When they had driven a couple of miles, old Semyon, who was driving, turned round and said:

"They have caught a government clerk in the town. They have taken him away. The story is that with some Germans he killed Alexeyev, the Mayor, in Moscow."

"Who told you that?"

"They were reading it in the paper, in Ivan Ionov's tavern."

And again they were silent for a long time. Marya Vassilyevna thought of her school, of the examination that was coming soon, and of the girl and four boys she was sending up for it. And just as she was thinking about the examination, she was overtaken by a neighboring landowner called Hanov in a carriage with four horses, the very man who had been examiner in her school the year before. When he came up to her he recognized her and bowed.

"Good-morning," he said to her. "You are driving home, I suppose."

This Hanov, a man of forty with a listless expression and a face that showed signs of wear, was beginning to look old, but was still handsome and admired by women. He lived in his big homestead alone, and was not in the service; and people used to say of him that he did nothing at home but walk up and down the room whistling, or play chess with his old footman. People said, too, that he drank heavily. And indeed at the examination the year before the very papers he brought with him smelt of wine and scent. He had been dressed all in new clothes on that occasion, and Marya Vassilyevna thought him very attractive, and all the while she sat beside him she had felt embarrassed. She was accustomed to see frigid and sensible examiners at the school, while this one did not remember a single prayer, or know what to ask questions about, and was exceedingly courteous and delicate, giving nothing but the highest marks.

"I am going to visit Bakvist," he went on, addressing Marya Vassilyevna, "but I am told he is not at home."

They turned off the highroad into a by-road to the village, Hanov leading the way and Semyon following. The four horses moved at a walking pace, with effort dragging the heavy carriage through the mud. Semyon tacked from side to side, keeping to the edge of the road, at one time through a snowdrift, at another through a pool, often jumping out of the cart and helping the horse. Marya Vassilyevna was still thinking about the school, wondering whether the arithmetic questions at the examination would be difficult or easy. And she felt annoyed with the Zemstvo board at which she had found no one the day before. How unbusiness-like! Here she had been asking them for the last two years to dismiss the watchman, who did nothing, was rude to her, and hit the schoolboys; but no one paid any attention. It was hard to find the president at the office, and when one did find him he would say with tears in his eyes that he hadn't a moment to spare; the inspector visited the school at most once in three years, and knew nothing whatever about his work, as he had been in the Excise Duties Department, and had received the post of school inspector through influence. The School Council met very rarely, and there was no knowing where it met; the school guardian was an almost illiterate peasant, the head of a tanning business, unintelligent, rude, and a great friend of the watchman's - and goodness knows to whom she could appeal with complaints or inquiries . . . .

"He really is handsome," she thought, glancing at Hanov.

The road grew worse and worse. . . . They drove into the wood. Here there was no room to turn round, the wheels sank deeply in, water splashed and gurgled through them, and sharp twigs struck them in the face.

"What a road!" said Hanov, and he laughed.

The schoolmistress looked at him and could not understand why this queer man lived here. What could his money, his interesting appearance, his refined bearing do for him here, in this mud, in this God-forsaken, dreary place? He got no special advantages out of life, and here, like Semyon, was driving at a jog-trot on an appalling road and enduring the same discomforts. Why live here if one could live in Petersburg or abroad? And one would have thought it would be nothing for a rich man like him to make a good road instead of this bad one, to avoid enduring this misery and seeing the despair on the faces of his coachman and Semyon; but he only laughed, and apparently did not mind, and wanted no better life. He was kind, soft, naïve, and he did not understand this coarse life, just as at the examination he did not know the prayers. He subscribed nothing to the schools but globes, and genuinely regarded himself as a useful person and a prominent worker in the cause of popular education. And what use were his globes here?

"Hold on, Vassilyevna!" said Semyon.

The cart lurched violently and was on the point of upsetting; something heavy rolled on to Marya Vassilyevna's feet - it was her parcel of purchases. There was a steep ascent uphill through the clay; here in the winding ditches rivulets were gurgling. The water seemed to have gnawed away the road; and how could one get along here! The horses breathed hard. Hanov got out of his carriage and walked at the side of the road in his long overcoat. He was hot.

"What a road!" he said, and laughed again. "It would soon smash up one's carriage."

"Nobody obliges you to drive about in such weather," said Semyon surlily. "You should stay at home."

"I am dull at home, grandfather. I don't like staying at home."

Beside old Semyon he looked graceful and vigorous, but yet in his walk there was something just perceptible which betrayed in him a being already touched by decay, weak, and on the road to ruin. And all at once there was a whiff of spirits in the wood. Marya Vassilyevna was filled with dread and pity for this man going to his ruin for no visible cause or reason, and it came into her mind that if she had been his wife or sister she would have devoted her whole life to saving him from ruin. His wife! Life was so ordered that here he was living in his great house alone, and she was living in a God-forsaken village alone, and yet for some reason the mere thought that he and she might be close to one another and equals seemed impossible and absurd. In reality, life was arranged and human relations were complicated so utterly beyond all understanding that when one thought about it one felt uncanny and one's heart sank.

"And it is beyond all understanding," she thought, "why God gives beauty, this graciousness, and sad, sweet eyes to weak, unlucky, useless people - why they are so charming."

"Here we must turn off to the right," said Hanov, getting into his carriage. "Good-by! I wish you all things good!"

And again she thought of her pupils, of the examination, of the watchman, of the School Council; and when the wind brought the sound of the retreating carriage these thoughts were mingled with others. She longed to think of beautiful eyes, of love, of the happiness which would never be. . . .

His wife? It was cold in the morning, there was no one to heat the stove, the watchman disappeared; the children came in as soon as it was light, bringing in snow and mud and making a noise: it was all so inconvenient, so comfortless. Her abode consisted of one little room and the kitchen close by. Her head ached every day after her work, and after dinner she had heart-burn. She had to collect money from the school-children for wood and for the watchman, and to give it to the school guardian, and then to entreat him - that overfed, insolent peasant - for God's sake to send her wood. And at night she dreamed of examinations, peasants, snowdrifts. And this life was making her grow old and coarse, making her ugly, angular, and awkward, as though she were made of lead. She was always afraid, and she would get up from her seat and not venture to sit down in the presence of a member of the Zemstvo or the school guardian. And she used formal, deferential expressions when she spoke of any one of them. And no one thought her attractive, and life was passing drearily, without affection, without friendly sympathy, without interesting acquaintances. How awful it would have been in her position if she had fallen in love!

"Hold on, Vassilyevna!"

Again a sharp ascent uphill. . . .

She had become a schoolmistress from necessity, without feeling any vocation for it; and she had never thought of a vocation, of serving the cause of enlightenment; and it always seemed to her that what was most important in her work was not the children, nor enlightenment, but the examinations. And what time had she for thinking of vocation, of serving the cause of enlightenment? Teachers, badly paid doctors, and their assistants, with their terribly hard work, have not even the comfort of thinking that they are serving an idea or the people, as their heads are always stuffed with thoughts of their daily bread, of wood for the fire, of bad roads, of illnesses. It is a hard-working, an uninteresting life, and only silent, patient cart-horses like Mary Vassilyevna could put up with it for long; the lively, nervous, impressionable people who talked about vocation and serving the idea were soon weary of it and gave up the work.

Semyon kept picking out the driest and shortest way, first by a meadow, then by the backs of the village huts; but in one place the peasants would not let them pass, in another it was the priest's land and they could not cross it, in another Ivan Ionov had bought a plot from the landowner and had dug a ditch round it. They kept having to turn back.

They reached Nizhneye Gorodistche. Near the tavern on the dung-strewn earth, where the snow was still lying, there stood wagons that had brought great bottles of crude sulphuric acid. There were a great many people in the tavern, all drivers, and there was a smell of vodka, tobacco, and sheepskins. There was a loud noise of conversation and the banging of the swing-door. Through the wall, without ceasing for a moment, came the sound of a concertina being played in the shop. Marya Vassilyevna sat down and drank some tea, while at the next table peasants were drinking vodka and beer, perspiring from the tea they had just swallowed and the stifling fumes of the tavern.

"I say, Kuzma!" voices kept shouting in confusion. "What there!" "The Lord bless us!" "Ivan Dementyitch, I can tell you that!" "Look out, old man!"

A little pock-marked man with a black beard, who was quite drunk, was suddenly surprised by something and began using bad language.

"What are you swearing at, you there?" Semyon, who was sitting some way off, responded angrily. "Don't you see the young lady?"

"The young lady!" someone mimicked in another corner.

"Swinish crow!"

"We meant nothing . . ." said the little man in confusion. "I beg your pardon. We pay with our money and the young lady with hers. Good-morning!"

"Good-morning," answered the schoolmistress.

"And we thank you most feelingly."

Marya Vassilyevna drank her tea with satisfaction, and she, too, began turning red like the peasants, and fell to thinking again about firewood, about the watchman. . . .

"Stay, old man," she heard from the next table, "it's the schoolmistress from Vyazovye. . . . We know her; she's a good young lady."

"She's all right!"

The swing-door was continually banging, some coming in, others going out. Marya Vassilyevna sat on, thinking all the time of the same things, while the concertina went on playing and playing. The patches of sunshine had been on the floor, then they passed to the counter, to the wall, and disappeared altogether; so by the sun it was past midday. The peasants at the next table were getting ready to go. The little man, somewhat unsteadily, went up to Marya Vassilyevna and held out his hand to her; following his example, the others shook hands, too, at parting, and went out one after another, and the swing-door squeaked and slammed nine times.

"Vassilyevna, get ready," Semyon called to her.

They set off. And again they went at a walking pace.

"A little while back they were building a school here in their Nizhneye Gorodistche," said Semyon, turning round. "It was a wicked thing that was done!"

"Why, what?"

"They say the president put a thousand in his pocket, and the school guardian another thousand in his, and the teacher five hundred."

"The whole school only cost a thousand. It's wrong to slander people, grandfather. That's all nonsense."

"I don't know, . . . I only tell you what folks say."

But it was clear that Semyon did not believe the schoolmistress. The peasants did not believe her. They always thought she received too large a salary, twenty-one roubles a month (five would have been enough), and that of the money that she collected from the children for the firewood and the watchman the greater part she kept for herself. The guardian thought the same as the peasants, and he himself made a profit off the firewood and received payments from the peasants for being a guardian - without the knowledge of the authorities.

The forest, thank God! was behind them, and now it would be flat, open ground all the way to Vyazovye, and there was not far to go now. They had to cross the river and then the railway line, and then Vyazovye was in sight.

"Where are you driving?" Marya Vassilyevna asked Semyon. "Take the road to the right to the bridge."

"Why, we can go this way as well. It's not deep enough to matter."

"Mind you don't drown the horse."

"What?"

"Look, Hanov is driving to the bridge," said Marya Vassilyevna, seeing the four horses far away to the right. "It is he, I think."

"It is. So he didn't find Bakvist at home. What a pig-headed fellow he is. Lord have mercy upon us! He's driven over there, and what for? It's fully two miles nearer this way."

They reached the river. In the summer it was a little stream easily crossed by wading. It usually dried up in August, but now, after the spring floods, it was a river forty feet in breadth, rapid, muddy, and cold; on the bank and right up to the water there were fresh tracks of wheels, so it had been crossed here.

"Go on!" shouted Semyon angrily and anxiously, tugging violently at the reins and jerking his elbows as a bird does its wings. "Go on!"

The horse went on into the water up to his belly and stopped, but at once went on again with an effort, and Marya Vassilyevna was aware of a keen chilliness in her feet.

"Go on!" she, too, shouted, getting up. "Go on!"

They got out on the bank.

"Nice mess it is, Lord have mercy upon us!" muttered Semyon, setting straight the harness. "It's a perfect plague with this Zemstvo. . . ."

Her shoes and goloshes were full of water, the lower part of her dress and of her coat and one sleeve were wet and dripping: the sugar and flour had got wet, and that was worst of all, and Marya Vassilyevna could only clasp her hands In despair and say:

Oh, Semyon, Semyon! How tiresome you are really! . . ."

The barrier was down at the railway crossing. A train was coming out of the station. Marya Vassilyevna stood at the crossing waiting till it should pass, and shivering all over with cold. Vyazovye was in sight now, and the school with the green roof, and the church with its crosses flashing in the evening sun: and the station windows flashed too, and a pink smoke rose from the engine . . . and it seemed to her that everything was trembling with cold.

Here was the train; the windows reflected the gleaming light like the crosses on the church: it made her eyes ache to look at them. On the little platform between two first-class carriages a lady was standing, and Marya Vassilyevna glanced at her as she passed. Her mother! What a resemblance! Her mother had had just such luxuriant hair, just such a brow and bend of the head. And with amazing distinctness, for the first time in those thirteen years, there rose before her mind a vivid picture of her mother, her father, her brother, their flat in Moscow, the aquarium with little fish, everything to the tiniest detail; she heard the sound of the piano, her father's voice; she felt as she had been then, young, good-looking, well-dressed, in a bright warm room among her own people. A feeling of joy and happiness suddenly came over her, she pressed her hands to her temples in an ecstacy, and called softly, beseechingly:

"Mother!"

And she began crying, she did not know why. Just at that instant Hanov drove up with his team of four horses, and seeing him she imagined happiness such as she had never had, and smiled and nodded to him as an equal and a friend, and it seemed to her that her happiness, her triumph, was glowing in the sky and on all sides, in the windows and on the trees. Her father and mother had never died, she had never been a schoolmistress, it was a long, tedious, strange dream, and now she had awakened. . . .

"Vassilyevna, get in!"

And at once it all vanished. The barrier was slowly raised. Marya Vassilyevna, shivering and numb with cold, got into the cart. The carriage with the four horses crossed the railway line; Semyon followed it. The signalman took off his cap.

"And here is Vyazovye. Here we are."

THE MAN IN A CASE

At the furthest end of the village of Mironositskoe some belated sportsmen lodged for the night in the elder Prokofy's barn. There were two of them, the veterinary surgeon Ivan Ivanovitch and the schoolmaster Burkin. Ivan Ivanovitch had a rather strange double-barrelled surname - Tchimsha-Himalaisky - which did not suit him at all, and he was called simply Ivan Ivanovitch all over the province. He lived at a stud-farm near the town, and had come out shooting now to get a breath of fresh air. Burkin, the high-school teacher, stayed every summer at Count P---'s, and had been thoroughly at home in this district for years.

They did not sleep. Ivan Ivanovitch, a tall, lean old fellow with long moustaches, was sitting outside the door, smoking a pipe in the moonlight. Burkin was lying within on the hay, and could not be seen in the darkness.

They were telling each other all sorts of stories. Among other things, they spoke of the fact that the elder's wife, Mavra, a healthy and by no means stupid woman, had never been beyond her native village, had never seen a town nor a railway in her life, and had spent the last ten years sitting behind the stove, and only at night going out into the street.

"What is there wonderful in that!" said Burkin. "There are plenty of people in the world, solitary by temperament, who try to retreat into their shell like a hermit crab or a snail. Perhaps it is an instance of atavism, a return to the period when the ancestor of man was not yet a social animal and lived alone in his den, or perhaps it is only one of the diversities of human character - who knows? I am not a natural science man, and it is not my business to settle such questions; I only mean to say that people like Mavra are not uncommon. There is no need to look far; two months ago a man called Byelikov, a colleague of mine, the Greek master, died in our town. You have heard of him, no doubt. He was remarkable for always wearing goloshes and a warm wadded coat, and carrying an umbrella even in the very finest weather. And his umbrella was in a case, and his watch was in a case made of grey chamois leather, and when he took out his penknife to sharpen his pencil, his penknife, too, was in a little case; and his face seemed to be in a case too, because he always hid it in his turned-up collar. He wore dark spectacles and flannel vests, stuffed up his ears with cotton-wool, and when he got into a cab always told the driver to put up the hood. In short, the man displayed a constant and insurmountable impulse to wrap himself in a covering, to make himself, so to speak, a case which would isolate him and protect him from external influences. Reality irritated him, frightened him, kept him in continual agitation, and, perhaps to justify his timidity, his aversion for the actual, he always praised the past and what had never existed; and even the classical languages which he taught were in reality for him goloshes and umbrellas in which he sheltered himself from real life.

" 'Oh, how sonorous, how beautiful is the Greek language!' he would say, with a sugary expression; and as though to prove his words he would screw up his eyes and, raising his finger, would pronounce 'Anthropos!'

"And Byelikov tried to hide his thoughts also in a case. The only things that were clear to his mind were government circulars and newspaper articles in which something was forbidden. When some proclamation prohibited the boys from going out in the streets after nine o'clock in the evening, or some article declared carnal love unlawful, it was to his mind clear and definite; it was forbidden, and that was enough. For him there was always a doubtful element, something vague and not fully expressed, in any sanction or permission. When a dramatic club or a reading-room or a tea-shop was licensed in the town, he would shake his head and say softly:

"It is all right, of course; it is all very nice, but I hope it won't lead to anything!"

"Every sort of breach of order, deviation or departure from rule, depressed him, though one would have thought it was no business of his. If one of his colleagues was late for church or if rumours reached him of some prank of the high-school boys, or one of the mistresses was seen late in the evening in the company of an officer, he was much disturbed, and said he hoped that nothing would come of it. At the teachers' meetings he simply oppressed us with his caution, his circumspection, and his characteristic reflection on the ill-behaviour of the young people in both male and female high-schools, the uproar in the classes.

"Oh, he hoped it would not reach the ears of the authorities; oh, he hoped nothing would come of it; and he thought it would be a very good thing if Petrov were expelled from the second class and Yegorov from the fourth. And, do you know, by his sighs, his despondency, his black spectacles on his pale little face, a little face like a pole-cat's, you know, he crushed us all, and we gave way, reduced Petrov's and Yegorov's marks for conduct, kept them in, and in the end expelled them both. He had a strange habit of visiting our lodgings. He would come to a teacher's, would sit down, and remain silent, as though he were carefully inspecting something. He would sit like this in silence for an hour or two and then go away. This he called 'maintaining good relations with his colleagues'; and it was obvious that coming to see us and sitting there was tiresome to him, and that he came to see us simply because he considered it his duty as our colleague. We teachers were afraid of him. And even the headmaster was afraid of him. Would you believe it, our teachers were all intellectual, right-minded people, brought up on Turgenev and Shtchedrin, yet this little chap, who always went about with goloshes and an umbrella, had the whole high-school under his thumb for fifteen long years! High-school, indeed - he had the whole town under his thumb! Our ladies did not get up private theatricals on Saturdays for fear he should hear of it, and the clergy dared not eat meat or play cards in his presence. Under the influence of people like Byelikov we have got into the way of being afraid of everything in our town for the last ten or fifteen years. They are afraid to speak aloud, afraid to send letters, afraid to make acquaintances, afraid to read books, afraid to help the poor, to teach people to read and write. . . ."

Ivan Ivanovitch cleared his throat, meaning to say something, but first lighted his pipe, gazed at the moon, and then said, with pauses:

"Yes, intellectual, right minded people read Shtchedrin and Turgenev, Buckle, and all the rest of them, yet they knocked under and put up with it. . . that's just how it is."

"Byelikov lived in the same house as I did," Burkin went on, "on the same storey, his door facing mine; we often saw each other, and I knew how he lived when he was at home. And at home it was the same story: dressing-gown, nightcap, blinds, bolts, a perfect succession of prohibitions and restrictions of all sorts, and -'Oh, I hope nothing will come of it!' Lenten fare was bad for him, yet he could not eat meat, as people might perhaps say Byelikov did not keep the fasts, and he ate freshwater fish with butter - not a Lenten dish, yet one could not say that it was meat. He did not keep a female servant for fear people might think evil of him, but had as cook an old man of sixty, called Afanasy, half-witted and given to tippling, who had once been an officer's servant and could cook after a fashion. This Afanasy was usually standing at the door with his arms folded; with a deep sigh, he would mutter always the same thing:

" 'There are plenty of *them* about nowadays!'

"Byelikov had a little bedroom like a box; his bed had curtains. When he went to bed he covered his head over; it was hot and stuffy; the wind battered on the closed doors; there was a droning noise in the stove and a sound of sighs from the kitchen - ominous sighs. . . . And he felt frightened under the bed-clothes. He was afraid that something might happen, that Afanasy might murder him, that thieves might break in, and so he had troubled dreams all night, and in the morning, when we went together to the high-school, he was depressed and pale, and it was evident that the high-school full of people excited dread and aversion in his whole being, and that to walk beside me was irksome to a man of his solitary temperament.

" 'They make a great noise in our classes,' he used to say, as though trying to find an explanation for his depression. 'It's beyond anything.'

"And the Greek master, this man in a case - would you believe it? - almost got married."

Ivan Ivanovitch glanced quickly into the barn, and said:

"You are joking!"

"Yes, strange as it seems, he almost got married. A new teacher of history and geography, Milhail Savvitch Kovalenko, a Little Russian, was appointed. He came, not alone, but with his sister Varinka. He was a tall, dark young man with huge hands, and one could see from his face that he had a bass voice, and, in fact, he had a voice that seemed to come out of a barrel - 'boom, boom, boom!' And she was not so young, about thirty, but she, too, was tall, well-made, with black eyebrows and red cheeks - in fact, she was a regular sugar-plum, and so sprightly, so noisy; she was always singing Little Russian songs and laughing. For the least thing she would go off into a ringing laugh - 'Ha-ha-ha!' We made our first thorough acquaintance with the Kovalenkos at the headmaster's name-day party. Among the glum and intensely bored teachers who came even to the name-day party as a duty we suddenly saw a new Aphrodite risen from the waves; she walked with her arms akimbo, laughed, sang, danced. . . . She sang with feeling 'The Winds do Blow,' then another song, and another, and she fascinated us all - all, even Byelikov. He sat down by her and said with a honeyed smile:

" 'The Little Russian reminds one of the ancient Greek in its softness and agreeable resonance.'

"That flattered her, and she began telling him with feeling and earnestness that they had a farm in the Gadyatchsky district, and that her mamma lived at the farm, and that they had such pears, such melons, such *kabaks!* The Little Russians call pumpkins *kabaks* (i.e., pothouses), while their pothouses they call *shinki,* and they make a beetroot soup with tomatoes and aubergines in it, 'which was so nice - awfully nice!'

"We listened and listened, and suddenly the same idea dawned upon us all:

" 'It would be a good thing to make a match of it,' the headmaster's wife said to me softly.

"We all for some reason recalled the fact that our friend Byelikov was not married, and it now seemed to us strange that we had hitherto failed to observe, and had in fact completely lost sight of, a detail so important in his life. What was his attitude to woman? How had he settled this vital question for himself? This had not interested us in the least till then; perhaps we had not even admitted the idea that a man who went out in all weathers in goloshes and slept under curtains could be in love.

" 'He is a good deal over forty and she is thirty,' the headmaster's wife went on, developing her idea. 'I believe she would marry him.'

"All sorts of things are done in the provinces through boredom, all sorts of unnecessary and nonsensical things! And that is because what is necessary is not done at all. What need was there for instance, for us to make a match for this Byelikov, whom one could not even imagine married? The headmaster's wife, the inspector's wife, and all our high-school ladies, grew livelier and even better-looking, as though they had suddenly found a new object in life. The headmaster's wife would take a box at the theatre, and we beheld sitting in her box Varinka, with such a fan, beaming and happy, and beside her Byelikov, a little bent figure, looking as though he had been extracted from his house by pincers. I would give an evening party, and the ladies would insist on my inviting Byelikov and Varinka. In short, the machine was set in motion. It appeared that Varinka was not averse to matrimony. She had not a very cheerful life with her brother; they could do nothing but quarrel and scold one another from morning till night. Here is a scene, for instance. Kovalenko would be coming along the street, a tall, sturdy young ruffian, in an embroidered shirt, his love-locks falling on his forehead under his cap, in one hand a bundle of books, in the other a thick knotted stick, followed by his sister, also with books in her hand.

" 'But you haven't read it, Mihalik!' she would be arguing loudly. 'I tell you, I swear you have not read it at all!'

" 'And I tell you I have read it,' cries Kovalenko, thumping his stick on the pavement.

" 'Oh, my goodness, Mihalik! why are you so cross? We are arguing about principles.'

" 'I tell you that I have read it!' Kovalenko would shout, more loudly than ever.

"And at home, if there was an outsider present, there was sure to be a skirmish. Such a life must have been wearisome, and of course she must have longed for a home of her own. Besides, there was her age to be considered; there was no time left to pick and choose; it was a case of marrying anybody, even a Greek master. And, indeed, most of our young ladies don't mind whom they marry so long as they do get married. However that may be, Varinka began to show an unmistakable partiality for Byelikov.

"And Byelikov? He used to visit Kovalenko just as he did us. He would arrive, sit down, and remain silent. He would sit quiet, and Varinka would sing to him 'The Winds do Blow,' or would look pensively at him with her dark eyes, or would suddenly go off into a peal - 'Ha-ha-ha!'

"Suggestion plays a great part in love affairs, and still more in getting married. Everybody - both his colleagues and the ladies - began assuring Byelikov that he ought to get married, that there was nothing left for him in life but to get married; we all congratulated him, with solemn countenances delivered ourselves of various platitudes, such as 'Marriage is a serious step.' Besides, Varinka was good-looking and interesting; she was the daughter of a civil councillor, and had a farm; and what was more, she was the first woman who had been warm and friendly in her manner to him. His head was turned, and he decided that he really ought to get married."

"Well, at that point you ought to have taken away his goloshes and umbrella," said Ivan Ivanovitch.

"Only fancy! that turned out to be impossible. He put Varinka's portrait on his table, kept coming to see me and talking about Varinka, and home life, saying marriage was a serious step. He was frequently at Kovalenko's, but he did not alter his manner of life in the least; on the contrary, indeed, his determination to get married seemed to have a depressing effect on him. He grew thinner and paler, and seemed to retreat further and further into his case.

" 'I like Varvara Savvishna,' he used to say to me, with a faint and wry smile, 'and I know that everyone ought to get married, but . . . you know all this has happened so suddenly. . . . One must think a little.'

" 'What is there to think over?' I used to say to him. 'Get married - that is all.'

" 'No; marriage is a serious step. One must first weigh the duties before one, the responsibilities . . . that nothing may go wrong afterwards. It worries me so much that I don't sleep at night. And I must confess I am afraid: her brother and she have a strange way of thinking; they look at things strangely, you know, and her disposition is very impetuous. One may get married, and then, there is no knowing, one may find oneself in an unpleasant position.'

"And he did not make an offer; he kept putting it off, to the great vexation of the headmaster's wife and all our ladies; he went on weighing his future duties and responsibilities, and meanwhile he went for a walk with Varinka almost every day - possibly he thought that this was necessary in his position - and came to see me to talk about family life. And in all probability in the end he would have proposed to her, and would have made one of those unnecessary, stupid marriages such as are made by thousands among us from being bored and having nothing to do, if it had not been for a *kolossalische scandal.* I must mention that Varinka's brother, Kovalenko, detested Byelikov from the first day of their acquaintance, and could not endure him.

" 'I don't understand,' he used to say to us, shrugging his shoulders -'I don't understand how you can put up with that sneak, that nasty phiz. Ugh! how can you live here! The atmosphere is stifling and unclean! Do you call yourselves schoolmasters, teachers? You are paltry government clerks. You keep, not a temple of science, but a department for red tape and loyal behaviour, and it smells as sour as a police-station. No, my friends; I will stay with you for a while, and then I will go to my farm and there catch crabs and teach the Little Russians. I shall go, and you can stay here with your Judas - damn his soul!'

"Or he would laugh till he cried, first in a loud bass, then in a shrill, thin laugh, and ask me, waving his hands:

" 'What does he sit here for? What does he want? He sits and stares.'

"He even gave Byelikov a nickname, 'The Spider.' And it will readily be understood that we avoided talking to him of his sister's being about to marry 'The Spider.'

"And on one occasion, when the headmaster's wife hinted to him what a good thing it would be to secure his sister's future with such a reliable, universally respected man as Byelikov, he frowned and muttered:

" 'It's not my business; let her marry a reptile if she likes. I don't like meddling in other people's affairs.'

"Now hear what happened next. Some mischievous person drew a caricature of Byelikov walking along in his goloshes with his trousers tucked up, under his umbrella, with Varinka on his arm; below, the inscription 'Anthropos in love.' The expression was caught to a marvel, you know. The artist must have worked for more than one night, for the teachers of both the boys' and girls' high-schools, the teachers of the seminary, the government officials, all received a copy. Byelikov received one, too. The caricature made a very painful impression on him.

"We went out together; it was the first of May, a Sunday, and all of us, the boys and the teachers, had agreed to meet at the high-school and then to go for a walk together to a wood beyond the town. We set off, and he was green in the face and gloomier than a storm-cloud.

'What wicked, ill-natured people there are!' he said, and his lips quivered.

"I felt really sorry for him. We were walking along, and all of a sudden - would you believe it? - Kovalenko came bowling along on a bicycle, and after him, also on a bicycle, Varinka, flushed and exhausted, but good-humoured and gay.

" 'We are going on ahead,' she called. 'What lovely weather! Awfully lovely!'

"And they both disappeared from our sight. Byelikov turned white instead of green, and seemed petrified. He stopped short and stared at me. . . .

" 'What is the meaning of it? Tell me, please!' he asked. 'Can my eyes have deceived me? Is it the proper thing for high-school masters and ladies to ride bicycles?'

" 'What is there improper about it?' I said. 'Let them ride and enjoy themselves.'

" 'But how can that be?' he cried, amazed at my calm. 'What are you saying?'

"And he was so shocked that he was unwilling to go on, and returned home.

"Next day he was continually twitching and nervously rubbing his hands, and it was evident from his face that he was unwell. And he left before his work was over, for the first time in his life. And he ate no dinner. Towards evening he wrapped himself up warmly, though it was quite warm weather, and sallied out to the Kovalenkos'. Varinka was out; he found her brother, however.

" 'Pray sit down,' Kovalenko said coldly, with a frown. His face looked sleepy; he had just had a nap after dinner, and was in a very bad humour.

"Byelikov sat in silence for ten minutes, and then began:

" 'I have come to see you to relieve my mind. I am very, very much troubled. Some scurrilous fellow has drawn an absurd caricature of me and another person, in whom we are both deeply interested. I regard it as a duty to assure you that I have had no hand in it. . . . I have given no sort of ground for such ridicule - on the contrary, I have always behaved in every way like a gentleman.'

"Kovalenko sat sulky and silent. Byelikov waited a little, and went on slowly in a mournful voice:

" 'And I have something else to say to you. I have been in the service for years, while you have only lately entered it, and I consider it my duty as an older colleague to give you a warning. You ride on a bicycle, and that pastime is utterly unsuitable for an educator of youth.'

" 'Why so?' asked Kovalenko in his bass.

" 'Surely that needs no explanation, Mihail Savvitch - surely you can understand that? If the teacher rides a bicycle, what can you expect the pupils to do? You will have them walking on their heads next! And so long as there is no formal permission to do so, it is out of the question.

I was horrified yesterday! When I saw your sister everything seemed dancing before my eyes. A lady or a young girl on a bicycle - it's awful!'

" 'What is it you want exactly?'

" 'All I want is to warn you, Mihail Savvitch. You are a young man, you have a future before you, you must be very, very careful in your behaviour, and you are so careless - oh, so careless! You go about in an embroidered shirt, are constantly seen in the street carrying books, and now the bicycle, too. The headmaster will learn that you and your sister ride the bicycle, and then it will reach the higher authorities. . . . Will that be a good thing?'

" 'It's no business of anybody else if my sister and I do bicycle!' said Kovalenko, and he turned crimson. 'And damnation take any one who meddles in my private affairs!'

"Byelikov turned pale and got up.

" 'If you speak to me in that tone I cannot continue,' he said. 'And I beg you never to express yourself like that about our superiors in my presence; you ought to be respectful to the authorities.'

" 'Why, have I said any harm of the authorities?' asked Kovalenko, looking at him wrathfully. 'Please leave me alone. I am an honest man, and do not care to talk to a gentleman like you. I don't like sneaks!'

"Byelikov flew into a nervous flutter, and began hurriedly putting on his coat, with an expression of horror on his face. It was the first time in his life he had been spoken to so rudely.

" 'You can say what you please,' he said, as he went out from the entry to the landing on the staircase. 'I ought only to warn you: possibly some one may have overheard us, and that our conversation may not be misunderstood and harm come of it, I shall be compelled to inform our headmaster of our conversation . . . in its main features. I am bound to do so.'

" 'Inform him? You can go and make your report!'

"Kovalenko seized him from behind by the collar and gave him a push, and Byelikov rolled downstairs, thudding with his goloshes. The staircase was high and steep, but he rolled to the bottom unhurt, got up, and touched his nose to see whether his spectacles were all right. But just as he was falling down the stairs Varinka came in, and with her two ladies; they stood below staring, and to Byelikov this was more terrible than anything. I believe he would rather have broken his neck or both legs than have been an object of ridicule. 'Why, now the whole town would hear of it; it would come to the headmaster's ears, would reach the higher authorities - oh, it might lead to something! There would be another caricature, and it would all end in his being asked to resign his post. . . .

"When he got up, Varinka recognized him, and, looking at his ridiculous face, his crumpled overcoat, and his goloshes, not understanding what had happened and supposing that he had slipped down by accident, could not restrain herself, and laughed loud enough to be heard by all the flats:

" 'Ha-ha-ha!'

"And this pealing, ringing 'Ha-ha-ha!' was the last straw that put an end to everything: to the proposed match and to Byelikov's earthly existence. He did not hear what Varinka said to him; he saw nothing. On reaching home, the first thing he did was to remove her portrait from the table; then he went to bed, and he never got up again.

"Three days later Afanasy came to me and asked whether we should not send for the doctor, as there was something wrong with his master. I went in to Byelikov. He lay silent behind the curtain, covered with a quilt; if one asked him a question, he said 'Yes' or 'No' and not another sound. He lay there while Afanasy, gloomy and scowling, hovered about him, sighing heavily, and smelling like a pothouse.

"A month later Byelikov died. We all went to his funeral - that is, both the high-schools and the seminary. Now when he was lying in his coffin his expression was mild, agreeable, even cheerful, as though he were glad that he had at last been put into a case which he would never leave again. Yes, he had attained his ideal! And, as though in his honour, it was dull, rainy weather on the day of his funeral, and we all wore goloshes and took our umbrellas. Varinka, too, was at the funeral, and when the coffin was lowered into the grave she burst into tears. I have noticed that Little Russian women are always laughing or crying - no intermediate mood.

"One must confess that to bury people like Byelikov is a great pleasure. As we were returning from the cemetery we wore discreet Lenten faces; no one wanted to display this feeling of pleasure - a feeling like that we had experienced long, long ago as children when our elders had gone out and we ran about the garden for an hour or two, enjoying complete freedom. Ah, freedom, freedom! The merest hint, the faintest hope of its possibility gives wings to the soul, does it not?

"We returned from the cemetery in a good humour. But not more than a week had passed before life went on as in the past, as gloomy, oppressive, and senseless - a life not forbidden by government prohibition, but not fully permitted, either: it was no better. And, indeed, though we had buried Byelikov, how many such men in cases were left, how many more of them there will be!"

"That's just how it is," said Ivan Ivanovitch and he lighted his pipe.

"How many more of them there will be!" repeated Burkin.

The schoolmaster came out of the barn. He was a short, stout man, completely bald, with a black beard down to his waist. The two dogs came out with him.

"What a moon!" he said, looking upwards.

It was midnight. On the right could be seen the whole village, a long street stretching far away for four miles. All was buried in deep silent slumber; not a movement, not a sound; one could hardly believe that nature could be so still. When on a moonlight night you see a broad village street, with its cottages, haystacks, and slumbering willows, a feeling of calm comes over the soul; in this peace, wrapped away from care, toil, and sorrow in the darkness of night, it is mild, melancholy, beautiful, and it seems as though the stars look down upon it kindly and with tenderness, and as though there were no evil on earth and all were well. On the left the open country began from the end of the village; it could be seen stretching far away to the horizon, and there was no movement, no sound in that whole expanse bathed in moonlight.

"Yes, that is just how it is," repeated Ivan Ivanovitch; "and isn't our living in town, airless and crowded, our writing useless papers, our playing *vint* - isn't that all a sort of case for us? And our spending our whole lives among trivial, fussy men and silly, idle women, our talking and our listening to all sorts of nonsense - isn't that a case for us, too? If you like, I will tell you a very edifying story."

"No; it's time we were asleep," said Burkin. "Tell it tomorrow."

They went into the barn and lay down on the hay. And they were both covered up and beginning to doze when they suddenly heard light footsteps - patter, patter. . . . Some one was walking not far from the barn, walking a little and stopping, and a minute later, patter, patter again. . . . The dogs began growling.

"That's Mavra," said Burkin.

The footsteps died away.

"You see and hear that they lie," said Ivan Ivanovitch, turning over on the other side, "and they call you a fool for putting up with their lying. You endure insult and humiliation, and dare not openly say that you are on the side of the honest and the free, and you lie and smile yourself; and all that for the sake of a crust of bread, for the sake of a warm corner, for the sake of a wretched little worthless rank in the service. No, one can't go on living like this."

"Well, you are off on another tack now, Ivan Ivanovitch," said the schoolmaster. "Let us go to sleep!

And ten minutes later Burkin was asleep. But Ivan Ivanovitch kept sighing and turning over from side to side; then he got up, went outside again, and, sitting in the doorway, lighted his pipe.

GOOSEBERRIES

The whole sky had been overcast with rain-clouds from early morning; it was a still day, not hot, but heavy, as it is in grey dull weather when the clouds have been hanging over the country for a long while, when one expects rain and it does not come. Ivan Ivanovitch, the veterinary surgeon, and Burkin, the high-school teacher, were already tired from walking, and the fields seemed to them endless. Far ahead of them they could just see the windmills of the village of Mironositskoe; on the right stretched a row of hillocks which disappeared in the distance behind the village, and they both knew that this was the bank of the river, that there were meadows, green willows, homesteads there, and that if one stood on one of the hillocks one could see from it the same vast plain, telegraph-wires, and a train which in the distance looked like a crawling caterpillar, and that in clear weather one could even see the town. Now, in still weather, when all nature seemed mild and dreamy, Ivan Ivanovitch and Burkin were filled with love of that countryside, and both thought how great, how beautiful a land it was.

"Last time we were in Prokofy's barn," said Burkin, "you were about to tell me a story."

"Yes; I meant to tell you about my brother."

Ivan Ivanovitch heaved a deep sigh and lighted a pipe to begin to tell his story, but just at that moment the rain began. And five minutes later heavy rain came down, covering the sky, and it was hard to tell when it would be over. Ivan Ivanovitch and Burkin stopped in hesitation; the dogs, already drenched, stood with their tails between their legs gazing at them feelingly.

"We must take shelter somewhere," said Burkin. "Let us go to Alehin's; it's close by."

"Come along."

They turned aside and walked through mown fields, sometimes going straight forward, sometimes turning to the right, till they came out on the road. Soon they saw poplars, a garden, then the red roofs of barns; there was a gleam of the river, and the view opened on to a broad expanse of water with a windmill and a white bath-house: this was Sofino, where Alehin lived.

The watermill was at work, drowning the sound of the rain; the dam was shaking. Here wet horses with drooping heads were standing near their carts, and men were walking about covered with sacks. It was damp, muddy, and desolate; the water looked cold and malignant. Ivan Ivanovitch and Burkin were already conscious of a feeling of wetness, messiness, and discomfort all over; their feet were heavy with mud, and when, crossing the dam, they went up to the barns, they were silent, as though they were angry with one another.

In one of the barns there was the sound of a winnowing machine, the door was open, and clouds of dust were coming from it. In the doorway was standing Alehin himself, a man of forty, tall and stout, with long hair, more like a professor or an artist than a landowner. He had on a white shirt that badly needed washing, a rope for a belt, drawers instead of trousers, and his boots, too, were plastered up with mud and straw. His eyes and nose were black with dust. He recognized Ivan Ivanovitch and Burkin, and was apparently much delighted to see them.

"Go into the house, gentlemen," he said, smiling; "I'll come directly, this minute."

It was a big two-storeyed house. Alehin lived in the lower storey, with arched ceilings and little windows, where the bailiffs had once lived; here everything was plain, and there was a smell of rye bread, cheap vodka, and harness. He went upstairs into the best rooms only on rare occasions, when visitors came. Ivan Ivanovitch and Burkin were met in the house by a maid-servant, a young woman so beautiful that they both stood still and looked at one another.

"You can't imagine how delighted I am to see you, my friends," said Alehin, going into the hall with them. "It is a surprise! Pelagea," he said, addressing the girl, "give our visitors something to change into. And, by the way, I will change too. Only I must first go and wash, for I almost think I have not washed since spring. Wouldn't you like to come into the bath-house? and meanwhile they will get things ready here."

Beautiful Pelagea, looking so refined and soft, brought them towels and soap, and Alehin went to the bath-house with his guests.

"It's a long time since I had a wash," he said, undressing. "I have got a nice bath-house, as you see - my father built it - but I somehow never have time to wash."

He sat down on the steps and soaped his long hair and his neck, and the water round him turned brown.

"Yes, I must say," said Ivan Ivanovitch meaningly, looking at his head.

"It's a long time since I washed . . ." said Alehin with embarrassment, giving himself a second soaping, and the water near him turned dark blue, like ink.

Ivan Ivanovitch went outside, plunged into the water with a loud splash, and swam in the rain, flinging his arms out wide. He stirred the water into waves which set the white lilies bobbing up and down; he swam to the very middle of the millpond and dived, and came up a minute later in another place, and swam on, and kept on diving, trying to touch the bottom.

"Oh, my goodness!" he repeated continually, enjoying himself thoroughly. "Oh, my goodness!" He swam to the mill, talked to the peasants there, then returned and lay on his back in the middle of the pond, turning his face to the rain. Burkin and Alehin were dressed and ready to go, but he still went on swimming and diving. "Oh, my goodness! . . ." he said. "Oh, Lord, have mercy on me! . . ."

"That's enough!" Burkin shouted to him.

They went back to the house. And only when the lamp was lighted in the big drawing-room upstairs, and Burkin and Ivan Ivanovitch, attired in silk dressing-gowns and warm slippers, were sitting in arm-chairs; and Alehin, washed and combed, in a new coat, was walking about the drawing-room, evidently enjoying the feeling of warmth, cleanliness, dry clothes, and light shoes; and when lovely Pelagea, stepping noiselessly on the carpet and smiling softly, handed tea and jam on a tray - only then Ivan Ivanovitch began on his story, and it seemed as though not only Burkin and Alehin were listening, but also the ladies, young and old, and the officers who looked down upon them sternly and calmly from their gold frames.

"There are two of us brothers," he began -"I, Ivan Ivanovitch, and my brother, Nikolay Ivanovitch, two years younger. I went in for a learned profession and became a veterinary surgeon, while Nikolay sat in a government office from the time he was nineteen. Our father, Tchimsha-Himalaisky, was a kantonist, but he rose to be an officer and left us a little estate and the rank of nobility. After his death the little estate went in debts and legal expenses; but, anyway, we had spent our childhood running wild in the country. Like peasant children, we passed our days and nights in the fields and the woods, looked after horses, stripped the bark off the trees, fished, and so on. . . . And, you know, whoever has once in his life caught perch or has seen the migrating of the thrushes in autumn, watched how they float in flocks over the village on bright, cool days, he will never be a real townsman, and will have a yearning for freedom to the day of his death. My brother was miserable in the government office. Years passed by, and he went on sitting in the same place, went on writing the same papers and thinking of one and the same thing - how to get into the country. And this yearning by degrees passed into a definite desire, into a dream of buying himself a little farm somewhere on the banks of a river or a lake.

"He was a gentle, good-natured fellow, and I was fond of him, but I never sympathized with this desire to shut himself up for the rest of his life in a little farm of his own. It's the correct thing to say that a man needs no more than six feet of earth. But six feet is what a corpse needs, not a man. And they say, too, now, that if our intellectual classes are attracted to the land and yearn for a farm, it's a good thing. But these farms are just the same as six feet of earth. To retreat from town, from the struggle, from the bustle of life, to retreat and bury oneself in one's farm - it's not life, it's egoism, laziness, it's monasticism of a sort, but monasticism without good works. A man does not need six feet of earth or a farm, but the whole globe, all nature, where he can have room to display all the qualities and peculiarities of his free spirit.

"My brother Nikolay, sitting in his government office, dreamed of how he would eat his own cabbages, which would fill the whole yard with such a savoury smell, take his meals on the green grass, sleep in the sun, sit for whole hours on the seat by the gate gazing at the fields and the forest. Gardening books and the agricultural hints in calendars were his delight, his favourite spiritual sustenance; he enjoyed reading newspapers, too, but the only things he read in them were the advertisements of so many acres of arable land and a grass meadow with farm-houses and buildings, a river, a garden, a mill and millponds, for sale. And his imagination pictured the garden-paths, flowers and fruit, starling cotes, the carp in the pond, and all that sort of thing, you know. These imaginary pictures were of different kinds according to the advertisements which he came across, but for some reason in everyone of them he had always to have gooseberries. He could not imagine a homestead, he could not picture an idyllic nook, without gooseberries.

" 'Country life has its conveniences,' he would sometimes say. 'You sit on the verandah and you drink tea, while your ducks swim on the pond, there is a delicious smell everywhere, and . . . and the gooseberries are growing.'

"He used to draw a map of his property, and in every map there were the same things - (a) house for the family, (b) servants' quarters, (c) kitchen-garden, (d) gooseberry-bushes. He lived parsimoniously, was frugal in food and drink, his clothes were beyond description; he looked like a beggar, but kept on saving and putting money in the bank. He grew fearfully avaricious. I did not like to look at him, and I used to give him something and send him presents for Christmas and Easter, but he used to save that too. Once a man is absorbed by an idea there is no doing anything with him.

"Years passed: he was transferred to another province. He was over forty, and he was still reading the advertisements in the papers and saving up. Then I heard he was married. Still with the same object of buying a farm and having gooseberries, he married an elderly and ugly widow without a trace of feeling for her, simply because she had filthy lucre. He went on living frugally after marrying her, and kept her short of food, while he put her money in the bank in his name.

"Her first husband had been a postmaster, and with him she was accustomed to pies and home-made wines, while with her second husband she did not get enough black bread; she began to pine away with this sort of life, and three years later she gave up her soul to God. And I need hardly say that my brother never for one moment imagined that he was responsible for her death. Money, like vodka, makes a man queer. In our town there was a merchant who, before he died, ordered a plateful of honey and ate up all his money and lottery tickets with the honey, so that no one might get the benefit of it. While I was inspecting cattle at a railway-station, a cattle-dealer fell under an engine and had his leg cut off. We carried him into the waiting-room, the blood was flowing - it was a horrible thing - and he kept asking them to look for his leg and was very much worried about it; there were twenty roubles in the boot on the leg that had been cut off, and he was afraid they would be lost."

"That's a story from a different opera," said Burkin.

"After his wife's death," Ivan Ivanovitch went on, after thinking for half a minute, "my brother began looking out for an estate for himself. Of course, you may look about for five years and yet end by making a mistake, and buying something quite different from what you have dreamed of. My brother Nikolay bought through an agent a mortgaged estate of three hundred and thirty acres, with a house for the family, with servants' quarters, with a park, but with no orchard, no gooseberry-bushes, and no duck-pond; there was a river, but the water in it was the colour of coffee, because on one side of the estate there was a brickyard and on the other a factory for burning bones. But Nikolay Ivanovitch did not grieve much; he ordered twenty gooseberry-bushes, planted them, and began living as a country gentleman.

"Last year I went to pay him a visit. I thought I would go and see what it was like. In his letters my brother called his estate 'Tchumbaroklov Waste, alias Himalaiskoe.' I reached 'alias Himalaiskoe' in the afternoon. It was hot. Everywhere there were ditches, fences, hedges, fir-trees planted in rows, and there was no knowing how to get to the yard, where to put one's horse. I went up to the house, and was met by a fat red dog that looked like a pig. It wanted to bark, but it was too lazy. The cook, a fat, barefooted woman, came out of the kitchen, and she, too, looked like a pig, and said that her master was resting after dinner. I went in to see my brother. He was sitting up in bed with a quilt over his legs; he had grown older, fatter, wrinkled; his cheeks, his nose, and his mouth all stuck out - he looked as though he might begin grunting into the quilt at any moment.

"We embraced each other, and shed tears of joy and of sadness at the thought that we had once been young and now were both grey-headed and near the grave. He dressed, and led me out to show me the estate.

" 'Well, how are you getting on here?' I asked.

" 'Oh, all right, thank God; I am getting on very well.'

"He was no more a poor timid clerk, but a real landowner, a gentleman. He was already accustomed to it, had grown used to it, and liked it. He ate a great deal, went to the bath-house, was growing stout, was already at law with the village commune and both factories, and was very much offended when the peasants did not call him 'Your Honour.' And he concerned himself with the salvation of his soul in a substantial, gentlemanly manner, and performed deeds of charity, not simply, but with an air of consequence. And what deeds of charity! He treated the peasants for every sort of disease with soda and castor oil, and on his name-day had a thanksgiving service in the middle of the village, and then treated the peasants to a gallon of vodka - he thought that was the thing to do. Oh, those horrible gallons of vodka! One day the fat landowner hauls the peasants up before the district captain for trespass, and next day, in honour of a holiday, treats them to a gallon of vodka, and they drink and shout 'Hurrah!' and when they are drunk bow down to his feet. A change of life for the better, and being well-fed and idle develop in a Russian the most insolent self-conceit. Nikolay Ivanovitch, who at one time in the government office was afraid to have any views of his own, now could say nothing that was not gospel truth, and uttered such truths in the tone of a prime minister. 'Education is essential, but for the peasants it is premature.' 'Corporal punishment is harmful as a rule, but in some cases it is necessary and there is nothing to take its place.'

" 'I know the peasants and understand how to treat them,' he would say. 'The peasants like me. I need only to hold up my little finger and the peasants will do anything I like.'

"And all this, observe, was uttered with a wise, benevolent smile. He repeated twenty times over 'We noblemen,' 'I as a noble'; obviously he did not remember that our grandfather was a peasant, and our father a soldier. Even our surname Tchimsha-Himalaisky, in reality so incongruous, seemed to him now melodious, distinguished, and very agreeable.

"But the point just now is not he, but myself. I want to tell you about the change that took place in me during the brief hours I spent at his country place. In the evening, when we were drinking tea, the cook put on the table a plateful of gooseberries. They were not bought, but his own gooseberries, gathered for the first time since the bushes were planted. Nikolay Ivanovitch laughed and looked for a minute in silence at the gooseberries, with tears in his eyes; he could not speak for excitement. Then he put one gooseberry in his mouth, looked at me with the triumph of a child who has at last received his favourite toy, and said:

" 'How delicious!'

"And he ate them greedily, continually repeating, 'Ah, how delicious! Do taste them!'

"They were sour and unripe, but, as Pushkin says:

" 'Dearer to us the falsehood that exalts

Than hosts of baser truths.'

"I saw a happy man whose cherished dream was so obviously fulfilled, who had attained his object in life, who had gained what he wanted, who was satisfied with his fate and himself. There is always, for some reason, an element of sadness mingled with my thoughts of human happiness, and, on this occasion, at the sight of a happy man I was overcome by an oppressive feeling that was close upon despair. It was particularly oppressive at night. A bed was made up for me in the room next to my brother's bedroom, and I could hear that he was awake, and that he kept getting up and going to the plate of gooseberries and taking one. I reflected how many satisfied, happy people there really are! 'What a suffocating force it is! You look at life: the insolence and idleness of the strong, the ignorance and brutishness of the weak, incredible poverty all about us, overcrowding, degeneration, drunkenness, hypocrisy, lying. . . . Yet all is calm and stillness in the houses and in the streets; of the fifty thousand living in a town, there is not one who would cry out, who would give vent to his indignation aloud. We see the people going to market for provisions, eating by day, sleeping by night, talking their silly nonsense, getting married, growing old, serenely escorting their dead to the cemetery; but we do not see and we do not hear those who suffer, and what is terrible in life goes on somewhere behind the scenes. . . . Everything is quiet and peaceful, and nothing protests but mute statistics: so many people gone out of their minds, so many gallons of vodka drunk, so many children dead from malnutrition. . . . And this order of things is evidently necessary; evidently the happy man only feels at ease because the unhappy bear their burdens in silence, and without that silence happiness would be impossible. It's a case of general hypnotism. There ought to be behind the door of every happy, contented man some one standing with a hammer continually reminding him with a tap that there are unhappy people; that however happy he may be, life will show him her laws sooner or later, trouble will come for him - disease, poverty, losses, and no one will see or hear, just as now he neither sees nor hears others. But there is no man with a hammer; the happy man lives at his ease, and trivial daily cares faintly agitate him like the wind in the aspen-tree - and all goes well.

"That night I realized that I, too, was happy and contented," Ivan Ivanovitch went on, getting up. "I, too, at dinner and at the hunt liked to lay down the law on life and religion, and the way to manage the peasantry. I, too, used to say that science was light, that culture was essential, but for the simple people reading and writing was enough for the time. Freedom is a blessing, I used to say; we can no more do without it than without air, but we must wait a little. Yes, I used to talk like that, and now I ask, 'For what reason are we to wait?' " asked Ivan Ivanovitch, looking angrily at Burkin. "Why wait, I ask you? What grounds have we for waiting? I shall be told, it can't be done all at once; every idea takes shape in life gradually, in its due time. But who is it says that? Where is the proof that it's right? You will fall back upon the natural order of things, the uniformity of phenomena; but is there order and uniformity in the fact that I, a living, thinking man, stand over a chasm and wait for it to close of itself, or to fill up with mud at the very time when perhaps I might leap over it or build a bridge across it? And again, wait for the sake of what? Wait till there's no strength to live? And meanwhile one must live, and one wants to live!

"I went away from my brother's early in the morning, and ever since then it has been unbearable for me to be in town. I am oppressed by its peace and quiet; I am afraid to look at the windows, for there is no spectacle more painful to me now than the sight of a happy family sitting round the table drinking tea. I am old and am not fit for the struggle; I am not even capable of hatred; I can only grieve inwardly, feel irritated and vexed; but at night my head is hot from the rush of ideas, and I cannot sleep. . . . Ah, if I were young!"

Ivan Ivanovitch walked backwards and forwards in excitement, and repeated: "If I were young!"

He suddenly went up to Alehin and began pressing first one of his hands and then the other.

"Pavel Konstantinovitch," he said in an imploring voice, "don't be calm and contented, don't let yourself be put to sleep! While you are young, strong, confident, be not weary in well-doing! There is no happiness, and there ought not to be; but if there is a meaning and an object in life, that meaning and object is not our happiness, but something greater and more rational. Do good!"

And all this Ivan Ivanovitch said with a pitiful, imploring smile, as though he were asking him a personal favour.

Then all three sat in arm-chairs at different ends of the drawing-room and were silent. Ivan Ivanovitch's story had not satisfied either Burkin or Alehin. When the generals and ladies gazed down from their gilt frames, looking in the dusk as though they were alive, it was dreary to listen to the story of the poor clerk who ate gooseberries. They felt inclined, for some reason, to talk about elegant people, about women. And their sitting in the drawing-room where everything - the chandeliers in their covers, the arm-chairs, and the carpet under their feet - reminded them that those very people who were now looking down from their frames had once moved about, sat, drunk tea in this room, and the fact that lovely Pelagea was moving noiselessly about was better than any story.

Alehin was fearfully sleepy; he had got up early, before three o'clock in the morning, to look after his work, and now his eyes were closing; but he was afraid his visitors might tell some interesting story after he had gone, and he lingered on. He did not go into the question whether what Ivan Ivanovitch had just said was right and true. His visitors did not talk of groats, nor of hay, nor of tar, but of something that had no direct bearing on his life, and he was glad and wanted them to go on.

"It's bed-time, though," said Burkin, getting up. "Allow me to wish you good-night."

Alehin said good-night and went downstairs to his own domain, while the visitors remained upstairs. They were both taken for the night to a big room where there stood two old wooden beds decorated with carvings, and in the corner was an ivory crucifix. The big cool beds, which had been made by the lovely Pelagea, smelt agreeably of clean linen.

Ivan Ivanovitch undressed in silence and got into bed.

"Lord forgive us sinners!" he said, and put his head under the quilt.

His pipe lying on the table smelt strongly of stale tobacco, and Burkin could not sleep for a long while, and kept wondering where the oppressive smell came from.

The rain was pattering on the window-panes all night.

ABOUT LOVE

At lunch next day there were very nice pies, crayfish, and mutton cutlets; and while we were eating, Nikanor, the cook, came up to ask what the visitors would like for dinner. He was a man of medium height, with a puffy face and little eyes; he was close-shaven, and it looked as though his moustaches had not been shaved, but had been pulled out by the roots. Alehin told us that the beautiful Pelagea was in love with this cook. As he drank and was of a violent character, she did not want to marry him, but was willing to live with him without. He was very devout, and his religious convictions would not allow him to "live in sin"; he insisted on her marrying him, and would consent to nothing else, and when he was drunk he used to abuse her and even beat her. Whenever he got drunk she used to hide upstairs and sob, and on such occasions Alehin and the servants stayed in the house to be ready to defend her in case of necessity.

We began talking about love.

"How love is born," said Alehin, "why Pelagea does not love somebody more like herself in her spiritual and external qualities, and why she fell in love with Nikanor, that ugly snout - we all call him 'The Snout' - how far questions of personal happiness are of consequence in love - all that is known; one can take what view one likes of it. So far only one incontestable truth has been uttered about love: 'This is a great mystery.' Everything else that has been written or said about love is not a conclusion, but only a statement of questions which have remained unanswered. The explanation which would seem to fit one case does not apply in a dozen others, and the very best thing, to my mind, would be to explain every case individually without attempting to generalize. We ought, as the doctors say, to individualize each case."

"Perfectly true," Burkin assented.

"We Russians of the educated class have a partiality for these questions that remain unanswered. Love is usually poeticized, decorated with roses, nightingales; we Russians decorate our loves with these momentous questions, and select the most uninteresting of them, too. In Moscow, when I was a student, I had a friend who shared my life, a charming lady, and every time I took her in my arms she was thinking what I would allow her a month for housekeeping and what was the price of beef a pound. In the same way, when we are in love we are never tired of asking ourselves questions: whether it is honourable or dishonourable, sensible or stupid, what this love is leading up to, and so on. Whether it is a good thing or not I don't know, but that it is in the way, unsatisfactory, and irritating, I do know."

It looked as though he wanted to tell some story. People who lead a solitary existence always have something in their hearts which they are eager to talk about. In town bachelors visit the baths and the restaurants on purpose to talk, and sometimes tell the most interesting things to bath attendants and waiters; in the country, as a rule, they unbosom themselves to their guests. Now from the window we could see a grey sky, trees drenched in the rain; in such weather we could go nowhere, and there was nothing for us to do but to tell stories and to listen.

"I have lived at Sofino and been farming for a long time," Alehin began, "ever since I left the University. I am an idle gentleman by education, a studious person by disposition; but there was a big debt owing on the estate when I came here, and as my father was in debt partly because he had spent so much on my education, I resolved not to go away, but to work till I paid off the debt. I made up my mind to this and set to work, not, I must confess, without some repugnance. The land here does not yield much, and if one is not to farm at a loss one must employ serf labour or hired labourers, which is almost the same thing, or put it on a peasant footing - that is, work the fields oneself and with one's family. There is no middle path. But in those days I did not go into such subtleties. I did not leave a clod of earth unturned; I gathered together all the peasants, men and women, from the neighbouring villages; the work went on at a tremendous pace. I myself ploughed and sowed and reaped, and was bored doing it, and frowned with disgust, like a village cat driven by hunger to eat cucumbers in the kitchen-garden. My body ached, and I slept as I walked. At first it seemed to me that I could easily reconcile this life of toil with my cultured habits; to do so, I thought, all that is necessary is to maintain a certain external order in life. I established myself upstairs here in the best rooms, and ordered them to bring me there coffee and liquor after lunch and dinner, and when I went to bed I read every night the *Yyesnik Evropi.* But one day our priest, Father Ivan, came and drank up all my liquor at one sitting; and the *Yyesnik Evropi* went to the priest's daughters; as in the summer, especially at the haymaking, I did not succeed in getting to my bed at all, and slept in the sledge in the barn, or somewhere in the forester's lodge, what chance was there of reading? Little by little I moved downstairs, began dining in the servants' kitchen, and of my former luxury nothing is left but the servants who were in my father's service, and whom it would be painful to turn away.

"In the first years I was elected here an honorary justice of the peace. I used to have to go to the town and take part in the sessions of the congress and of the circuit court, and this was a pleasant change for me. When you live here for two or three months without a break, especially in the winter, you begin at last to pine for a black coat. And in the circuit court there were frock-coats, and uniforms, and dress-coats, too, all lawyers, men who have received a general education; I had some one to talk to. After sleeping in the sledge and dining in the kitchen, to sit in an arm-chair in clean linen, in thin boots, with a chain on one's waistcoat, is such luxury!

"I received a warm welcome in the town. I made friends eagerly. And of all my acquaintanceships the most intimate and, to tell the truth, the most agreeable to me was my acquaintance with Luganovitch, the vice-president of the circuit court. You both know him: a most charming personality. It all happened just after a celebrated case of incendiarism; the preliminary investigation lasted two days; we were exhausted. Luganovitch looked at me and said:

" 'Look here, come round to dinner with me.'

"This was unexpected, as I knew Luganovitch very little, only officially, and I had never been to his house. I only just went to my hotel room to change and went off to dinner. And here it was my lot to meet Anna Alexyevna, Luganovitch's wife. At that time she was still very young, not more than twenty-two, and her first baby had been born just six months before. It is all a thing of the past; and now I should find it difficult to define what there was so exceptional in her, what it was in her attracted me so much; at the time, at dinner, it was all perfectly clear to me. I saw a lovely young, good, intelligent, fascinating woman, such as I had never met before; and I felt her at once some one close and already familiar, as though that face, those cordial, intelligent eyes, I had seen somewhere in my childhood, in the album which lay on my mother's chest of drawers.

"Four Jews were charged with being incendiaries, were regarded as a gang of robbers, and, to my mind, quite groundlessly. At dinner I was very much excited, I was uncomfortable, and I don't know what I said, but Anna Alexyevna kept shaking her head and saying to her husband:

" 'Dmitry, how is this?'

"Luganovitch is a good-natured man, one of those simple-hearted people who firmly maintain the opinion that once a man is charged before a court he is guilty, and to express doubt of the correctness of a sentence cannot be done except in legal form on paper, and not at dinner and in private conversation.

" 'You and I did not set fire to the place,' he said softly, 'and you see we are not condemned, and not in prison.'

"And both husband and wife tried to make me eat and drink as much as possible. From some trifling details, from the way they made the coffee together, for instance, and from the way they understood each other at half a word, I could gather that they lived in harmony and comfort, and that they were glad of a visitor. After dinner they played a duet on the piano; then it got dark, and I went home. That was at the beginning of spring.

"After that I spent the whole summer at Sofino without a break, and I had no time to think of the town, either, but the memory of the graceful fair-haired woman remained in my mind all those days; I did not think of her, but it was as though her light shadow were lying on my heart.

"In the late autumn there was a theatrical performance for some charitable object in the town. I went into the governor's box (I was invited to go there in the interval); I looked, and there was Anna Alexyevna sitting beside the governor's wife; and again the same irresistible, thrilling impression of beauty and sweet, caressing eyes, and again the same feeling of nearness. We sat side by side, then went to the foyer.

" 'You've grown thinner,' she said; 'have you been ill?'

" 'Yes, I've had rheumatism in my shoulder, and in rainy weather I can't sleep.'

" 'You look dispirited. In the spring, when you came to dinner, you were younger, more confident. You were full of eagerness, and talked a great deal then; you were very interesting, and I really must confess I was a little carried away by you. For some reason you often came back to my memory during the summer, and when I was getting ready for the theatre today I thought I should see you.'

"And she laughed.

" 'But you look dispirited today,' she repeated; 'it makes you seem older.'

"The next day I lunched at the Luganovitchs'. After lunch they drove out to their summer villa, in order to make arrangements there for the winter, and I went with them. I returned with them to the town, and at midnight drank tea with them in quiet domestic surroundings, while the fire glowed, and the young mother kept going to see if her baby girl was asleep. And after that, every time I went to town I never failed to visit the Luganovitchs. They grew used to me, and I grew used to them. As a rule I went in unannounced, as though I were one of the family.

" 'Who is there?' I would hear from a faraway room, in the drawling voice that seemed to me so lovely.

" 'It is Pavel Konstantinovitch,' answered the maid or the nurse.

"Anna Alexyevna would come out to me with an anxious face, and would ask every time:

" 'Why is it so long since you have been? Has anything happened?'

"Her eyes, the elegant refined hand she gave me, her indoor dress, the way she did her hair, her voice, her step, always produced the same impression on me of something new and extraordinary in my life, and very important. We talked together for hours, were silent, thinking each our own thoughts, or she played for hours to me on the piano. If there were no one at home I stayed and waited, talked to the nurse, played with the child, or lay on the sofa in the study and read; and when Anna Alexyevna came back I met her in the hall, took all her parcels from her, and for some reason I carried those parcels every time with as much love, with as much solemnity, as a boy.

"There is a proverb that if a peasant woman has no troubles she will buy a pig. The Luganovitchs had no troubles, so they made friends with me. If I did not come to the town I must be ill or something must have happened to me, and both of them were extremely anxious. They were worried that I, an educated man with a knowledge of languages, should, instead of devoting myself to science or literary work, live in the country, rush round like a squirrel in a rage, work hard with never a penny to show for it. They fancied that I was unhappy, and that I only talked, laughed, and ate to conceal my sufferings, and even at cheerful moments when I felt happy I was aware of their searching eyes fixed upon me. They were particularly touching when I really was depressed, when I was being worried by some creditor or had not money enough to pay interest on the proper day. The two of them, husband and wife, would whisper together at the window; then he would come to me and say with a grave face:

" 'If you really are in need of money at the moment, Pavel Konstantinovitch, my wife and I beg you not to hesitate to borrow from us.'

"And he would blush to his ears with emotion. And it would happen that, after whispering in the same way at the window, he would come up to me, with red ears, and say:

" 'My wife and I earnestly beg you to accept this present.'

"And he would give me studs, a cigar-case, or a lamp, and I would send them game, butter, and flowers from the country. They both, by the way, had considerable means of their own. In early days I often borrowed money, and was not very particular about it - borrowed wherever I could - but nothing in the world would have induced me to borrow from the Luganovitchs. But why talk of it?

"I was unhappy. At home, in the fields, in the barn, I thought of her; I tried to understand the mystery of a beautiful, intelligent young woman's marrying some one so uninteresting, almost an old man (her husband was over forty), and having children by him; to understand the mystery of this uninteresting, good, simple-hearted man, who argued with such wearisome good sense, at balls and evening parties kept near the more solid people, looking listless and superfluous, with a submissive, uninterested expression, as though he had been brought there for sale, who yet believed in his right to be happy, to have children by her; and I kept trying to understand why she had met him first and not me, and why such a terrible mistake in our lives need have happened.

"And when I went to the town I saw every time from her eyes that she was expecting me, and she would confess to me herself that she had had a peculiar feeling all that day and had guessed that I should come. We talked a long time, and were silent, yet we did not confess our love to each other, but timidly and jealously concealed it. We were afraid of everything that might reveal our secret to ourselves. I loved her tenderly, deeply, but I reflected and kept asking myself what our love could lead to if we had not the strength to fight against it. It seemed to be incredible that my gentle, sad love could all at once coarsely break up the even tenor of the life of her husband, her children, and all the household in which I was so loved and trusted. Would it be honourable? She would go away with me, but where? Where could I take her? It would have been a different matter if I had had a beautiful, interesting life - if, for instance, I had been struggling for the emancipation of my country, or had been a celebrated man of science, an artist or a painter; but as it was it would mean taking her from one everyday humdrum life to another as humdrum or perhaps more so. And how long would our happiness last? What would happen to her in case I was ill, in case I died, or if we simply grew cold to one another?

"And she apparently reasoned in the same way. She thought of her husband, her children, and of her mother, who loved the husband like a son. If she abandoned herself to her feelings she would have to lie, or else to tell the truth, and in her position either would have been equally terrible and inconvenient. And she was tormented by the question whether her love would bring me happiness - would she not complicate my life, which, as it was, was hard enough and full of all sorts of trouble? She fancied she was not young enough for me, that she was not industrious nor energetic enough to begin a new life, and she often talked to her husband of the importance of my marrying a girl of intelligence and merit who would be a capable housewife and a help to me - and she would immediately add that it would be difficult to find such a girl in the whole town.

"Meanwhile the years were passing. Anna Alexyevna already had two children. When I arrived at the Luganovitchs' the servants smiled cordially, the children shouted that Uncle Pavel Konstantinovitch had come, and hung on my neck; everyone was overjoyed. They did not understand what was passing in my soul, and thought that I, too, was happy. Everyone looked on me as a noble being. And grown-ups and children alike felt that a noble being was walking about their rooms, and that gave a peculiar charm to their manner towards me, as though in my presence their life, too, was purer and more beautiful. Anna Alexyevna and I used to go to the theatre together, always walking there; we used to sit side by side in the stalls, our shoulders touching. I would take the opera-glass from her hands without a word, and feel at that minute that she was near me, that she was mine, that we could not live without each other; but by some strange misunderstanding, when we came out of the theatre we always said good-bye and parted as though we were strangers. Goodness knows what people were saying about us in the town already, but there was not a word of truth in it all!

"In the latter years Anna Alexyevna took to going away for frequent visits to her mother or to her sister; she began to suffer from low spirits, she began to recognize that her life was spoilt and unsatisfied, and at times she did not care to see her husband nor her children. She was already being treated for neurasthenia.

"We were silent and still silent, and in the presence of outsiders she displayed a strange irritation in regard to me; whatever I talked about, she disagreed with me, and if I had an argument she sided with my opponent. If I dropped anything, she would say coldly:

" 'I congratulate you.'

"If I forgot to take the opera-glass when we were going to the theatre, she would say afterwards:

" 'I knew you would forget it.'

"Luckily or unluckily, there is nothing in our lives that does not end sooner or later. The time of parting came, as Luganovitch was appointed president in one of the western provinces. They had to sell their furniture, their horses, their summer villa. When they drove out to the villa, and afterwards looked back as they were going away, to look for the last time at the garden, at the green roof, everyone was sad, and I realized that I had to say goodbye not only to the villa. It was arranged that at the end of August we should see Anna Alexyevna off to the Crimea, where the doctors were sending her, and that a little later Luganovitch and the children would set off for the western province.

"We were a great crowd to see Anna Alexyevna off. When she had said good-bye to her husband and her children and there was only a minute left before the third bell, I ran into her compartment to put a basket, which she had almost forgotten, on the rack, and I had to say good-bye. When our eyes met in the compartment our spiritual fortitude deserted us both; I took her in my arms, she pressed her face to my breast, and tears flowed from her eyes. Kissing her face, her shoulders, her hands wet with tears - oh, how unhappy we were! - I confessed my love for her, and with a burning pain in my heart I realized how unnecessary, how petty, and how deceptive all that had hindered us from loving was. I understood that when you love you must either, in your reasonings about that love, start from what is highest, from what is more important than happiness or unhappiness, sin or virtue in their accepted meaning, or you must not reason at all.

"I kissed her for the last time, pressed her hand, and parted for ever. The train had already started. I went into the next compartment - it was empty - and until I reached the next station I sat there crying. Then I walked home to Sofino. . . ."

While Alehin was telling his story, the rain left off and the sun came out. Burkin and Ivan Ivanovitch went out on the balcony, from which there was a beautiful view over the garden and the mill-pond, which was shining now in the sunshine like a mirror. They admired it, and at the same time they were sorry that this man with the kind, clever eyes, who had told them this story with such genuine feeling, should be rushing round and round this huge estate like a squirrel on a wheel instead of devoting himself to science or something else which would have made his life more pleasant; and they thought what a sorrowful face Anna Alexyevna must have had when he said good-bye to her in the railway-carriage and kissed her face and shoulders. Both of them had met her in the town, and Burkin knew her and thought her beautiful.

IONITCH

I

When visitors to the provincial town S-- complained of the dreariness and monotony of life, the inhabitants of the town, as though defending themselves, declared that it was very nice in S--, that there was a library, a theatre, a club; that they had balls; and, finally, that there were clever, agreeable, and interesting families with whom one could make acquaintance. And they used to point to the family of the Turkins as the most highly cultivated and talented.

This family lived in their own house in the principal street, near the Governor's. Ivan Petrovitch Turkin himself - a stout, handsome, dark man with whiskers - used to get up amateur performances for benevolent objects, and used to take the part of an elderly general and cough very amusingly. He knew a number of anecdotes, charades, proverbs, and was fond of being humorous and witty, and he always wore an expression from which it was impossible to tell whether he were joking or in earnest. His wife, Vera Iosifovna - a thin, nice-looking lady who wore a pince-nez - used to write novels and stories, and was very fond of reading them aloud to her visitors. The daughter, Ekaterina Ivanovna, a young girl, used to play on the piano. In short, every member of the family had a special talent. The Turkins welcomed visitors, and good-humouredly displayed their talents with genuine simplicity. Their stone house was roomy and cool in summer; half of the windows looked into a shady old garden, where nightingales used to sing in the spring. When there were visitors in the house, there was a clatter of knives in the kitchen and a smell of fried onions in the yard - and that was always a sure sign of a plentiful and savoury supper to follow.

And as soon as Dmitri Ionitch Startsev was appointed the district doctor, and took up his abode at Dyalizh, six miles from S--, he, too, was told that as a cultivated man it was essential for him to make the acquaintance of the Turkins. In the winter he was introduced to Ivan Petrovitch in the street; they talked about the weather, about the theatre, about the cholera; an invitation followed. On a holiday in the spring - it was Ascension Day - after seeing his patients, Startsev set off for town in search of a little recreation and to make some purchases.

He walked in a leisurely way (he had not yet set up his carriage), humming all the time:

" 'Before I'd drunk the tears from life's goblet. . . .' "

In town he dined, went for a walk in the gardens, then Ivan Petrovitch's invitation came into his mind, as it were of itself, and he decided to call on the Turkins and see what sort of people they were.

"How do you do, if you please?" said Ivan Petrovitch, meeting him on the steps. "Delighted, delighted to see such an agreeable visitor. Come along; I will introduce you to my better half. I tell him, Verotchka," he went on, as he presented the doctor to his wife -"I tell him that he has no human right to sit at home in a hospital; he ought to devote his leisure to society. Oughtn't he, darling?"

"Sit here," said Vera Iosifovna, making her visitor sit down beside her. "You can dance attendance on me. My husband is jealous - he is an Othello; but we will try and behave so well that he will notice nothing."

"Ah, you spoilt chicken!" Ivan Petrovitch muttered tenderly, and he kissed her on the forehead. "You have come just in the nick of time," he said, addressing the doctor again. "My better half has written a 'hugeous' novel, and she is going to read it aloud to-day."

"Petit Jean," said Vera Iosifovna to her husband, "dites que l'on nous donne du thé."

Startsev was introduced to Ekaterina Ivanovna, a girl of eighteen, very much like her mother, thin and pretty. Her expression was still childish and her figure was soft and slim; and her developed girlish bosom, healthy and beautiful, was suggestive of spring, real spring.

Then they drank tea with jam, honey, and sweetmeats, and with very nice cakes, which melted in the mouth. As the evening came on, other visitors gradually arrived, and Ivan Petrovitch fixed his laughing eyes on each of them and said:

"How do you do, if you please?"

Then they all sat down in the drawing-room with very serious faces, and Vera Iosifovna read her novel. It began like this: "The frost was intense. . . ." The windows were wide open; from the kitchen came the clatter of knives and the smell of fried onions. . . . It was comfortable in the soft deep arm-chair; the lights had such a friendly twinkle in the twilight of the drawing-room, and at the moment on a summer evening when sounds of voices and laughter floated in from the street and whiffs of lilac from the yard, it was difficult to grasp that the frost was intense, and that the setting sun was lighting with its chilly rays a solitary wayfarer on the snowy plain. Vera Iosifovna read how a beautiful young countess founded a school, a hospital, a library, in her village, and fell in love with a wandering artist; she read of what never happens in real life, and yet it was pleasant to listen - it was comfortable, and such agreeable, serene thoughts kept coming into the mind, one had no desire to get up.

"Not badsome . . ." Ivan Petrovitch said softly.

And one of the visitors hearing, with his thoughts far away, said hardly audibly:

"Yes . . . truly. . . ."

One hour passed, another. In the town gardens close by a band was playing and a chorus was singing. When Vera Iosifovna shut her manuscript book, the company was silent for five minutes, listening to "Lutchina" being sung by the chorus, and the song gave what was not in the novel and is in real life.

"Do you publish your stories in magazines?" Startsev asked Vera Iosifovna.

"No," she answered. "I never publish. I write it and put it away in my cupboard. Why publish?" she explained. "We have enough to live on."

And for some reason everyone sighed.

"And now, Kitten, you play something," Ivan Petrovitch said to his daughter.

The lid of the piano was raised and the music lying ready was opened. Ekaterina Ivanovna sat down and banged on the piano with both hands, and then banged again with all her might, and then again and again; her shoulders and bosom shook. She obstinately banged on the same notes, and it sounded as if she would not leave off until she had hammered the keys into the piano. The drawing-room was filled with the din; everything was resounding; the floor, the ceiling, the furniture. . . . Ekaterina Ivanovna was playing a difficult passage, interesting simply on account of its difficulty, long and monotonous, and Startsev, listening, pictured stones dropping down a steep hill and going on dropping, and he wished they would leave off dropping; and at the same time Ekaterina Ivanovna, rosy from the violent exercise, strong and vigorous, with a lock of hair falling over her forehead, attracted him very much. After the winter spent at Dyalizh among patients and peasants, to sit in a drawing-room, to watch this young, elegant, and, in all probability, pure creature, and to listen to these noisy, tedious but still cultured sounds, was so pleasant, so novel. . . .

"Well, Kitten, you have played as never before," said Ivan Petrovitch, with tears in his eyes, when his daughter had finished and stood up. "Die, Denis; you won't write anything better."

All flocked round her, congratulated her, expressed astonishment, declared that it was long since they had heard such music, and she listened in silence with a faint smile, and her whole figure was expressive of triumph.

"Splendid, superb!"

"Splendid," said Startsev, too, carried away by the general enthusiasm. "Where have you studied?" he asked Ekaterina Ivanovna. "At the Conservatoire?"

"No, I am only preparing for the Conservatoire, and till now have been working with Madame Zavlovsky."

"Have you finished at the high school here?"

"Oh, no," Vera Iosifovna answered for her, "We have teachers for her at home; there might be bad influences at the high school or a boarding school, you know. While a young girl is growing up, she ought to be under no influence but her mother's."

"All the same, I'm going to the Conservatoire," said Ekaterina Ivanovna.

"No. Kitten loves her mamma. Kitten won't grieve papa and mamma."

"No, I'm going, I'm going," said Ekaterina Ivanovna, with playful caprice and stamping her foot.

And at supper it was Ivan Petrovitch who displayed his talents. Laughing only with his eyes, he told anecdotes, made epigrams, asked ridiculous riddles and answered them himself, talking the whole time in his extraordinary language, evolved in the course of prolonged practice in witticism and evidently now become a habit: "Badsome," "Hugeous," "Thank you most dumbly," and so on.

But that was not all. When the guests, replete and satisfied, trooped into the hall, looking for their coats and sticks, there bustled about them the footman Pavlusha, or, as he was called in the family, Pava - a lad of fourteen with shaven head and chubby cheeks.

Come, Pava, perform!" Ivan Petrovitch said to him.

Pava struck an attitude, flung up his arm, and said in a tragic tone: "Unhappy woman, die!"

And everyone roared with laughter.

"It's entertaining," thought Startsev, as he went out into the street.

He went to a restaurant and drank some beer, then set off to walk home to Dyalizh; he walked all the way singing:

" 'Thy voice to me so languid and caressing. . . .' "

On going to bed, he felt not the slightest fatigue after the six miles' walk. On the contrary, he felt as though he could with pleasure have walked another twenty.

"Not badsome," he thought, and laughed as he fell asleep.

II

Startsev kept meaning to go to the Turkins' again, but there was a great deal of work in the hospital, and he was unable to find free time. In this way more than a year passed in work and solitude. But one day a letter in a light blue envelope was brought him from the town.

Vera Iosifovna had been suffering for some time from migraine, but now since Kitten frightened her every day by saying that she was going away to the Conservatoire, the attacks began to be more frequent. All the doctors of the town had been at the Turkins'; at last it was the district doctor's turn. Vera Iosifovna wrote him a touching letter in which she begged him to come and relieve her sufferings. Startsev went, and after that he began to be often, very often at the Turkins'. . . . He really did something for Vera Iosifovna, and she was already telling all her visitors that he was a wonderful and exceptional doctor. But it was not for the sake of her migraine that he visited the Turkins' now. . . .

It was a holiday. Ekaterina Ivanovna finished her long, wearisome exercises on the piano. Then they sat a long time in the dining-room, drinking tea, and Ivan Petrovitch told some amusing story. Then there was a ring and he had to go into the hall to welcome a guest; Startsev took advantage of the momentary commotion, and whispered to Ekaterina Ivanovna in great agitation:

"For God's sake, I entreat you, don't torment me; let us go into the garden!"

She shrugged her shoulders, as though perplexed and not knowing what he wanted of her, but she got up and went.

"You play the piano for three or four hours," he said, following her; "then you sit with your mother, and there is no possibility of speaking to you. Give me a quarter of an hour at least, I beseech you."

Autumn was approaching, and it was quiet and melancholy in the old garden; the dark leaves lay thick in the walks. It was already beginning to get dark early.

"I haven't seen you for a whole week," Startsev went on, "and if you only knew what suffering it is! Let us sit down. Listen to me."

They had a favourite place in the garden; a seat under an old spreading maple. And now they sat down on this seat.

"What do you want?" said Ekaterina Ivanovna drily, in a matter-of-fact tone.

"I have not seen you for a whole week; I have not heard you for so long. I long passionately, I thirst for your voice. Speak."

She fascinated him by her freshness, the naïve expression of her eyes and cheeks. Even in the way her dress hung on her, he saw something extraordinarily charming, touching in its simplicity and naïve grace; and at the same time, in spite of this naïveté, she seemed to him intelligent and developed beyond her years. He could talk with her about literature, about art, about anything he liked; could complain to her of life, of people, though it sometimes happened in the middle of serious conversation she would laugh inappropriately or run away into the house. Like almost all girls of her neighbourhood, she had read a great deal (as a rule, people read very little in S--, and at the lending library they said if it were not for the girls and the young Jews, they might as well shut up the library). This afforded Startsev infinite delight; he used to ask her eagerly every time what she had been reading the last few days, and listened enthralled while she told him.

"What have you been reading this week since I saw you last?" he asked now. "Do please tell me."

"I have been reading Pisemsky."

"What exactly?"

" 'A Thousand Souls,' "answered Kitten. "And what a funny name Pisemsky had - Alexey Feofilaktitch!

"Where are you going?" cried Startsev in horror, as she suddenly got up and walked towards the house. "I must talk to you; I want to explain myself. . . . Stay with me just five minutes, I supplicate you!"

She stopped as though she wanted to say something, then awkwardly thrust a note into his hand, ran home and sat down to the piano again.

"Be in the cemetery," Startsev read, "at eleven o'clock to-night, near the tomb of Demetti."

"Well, that's not at all clever," he thought, coming to himself. "Why the cemetery? What for?"

It was clear: Kitten was playing a prank. Who would seriously dream of making an appointment at night in the cemetery far out of the town, when it might have been arranged in the street or in the town gardens? And was it in keeping with him - a district doctor, an intelligent, staid man - to be sighing, receiving notes, to hang about cemeteries, to do silly things that even schoolboys think ridiculous nowadays? What would this romance lead to? What would his colleagues say when they heard of it? Such were Startsev's reflections as he wandered round the tables at the club, and at half-past ten he suddenly set off for the cemetery.

By now he had his own pair of horses, and a coachman called Panteleimon, in a velvet waistcoat. The moon was shining. It was still warm, warm as it is in autumn. Dogs were howling in the suburb near the slaughter-house. Startsev left his horses in one of the side-streets at the end of the town, and walked on foot to the cemetery.

"We all have our oddities," he thought. "Kitten is odd, too; and - who knows? - perhaps she is not joking, perhaps she will come"; and he abandoned himself to this faint, vain hope, and it intoxicated him.

He walked for half a mile through the fields; the cemetery showed as a dark streak in the distance, like a forest or a big garden. The wall of white stone came into sight, the gate. . . . In the moonlight he could read on the gate: "The hour cometh." Startsev went in at the little gate, and before anything else he saw the white crosses and monuments on both sides of the broad avenue, and the black shadows of them and the poplars; and for a long way round it was all white and black, and the slumbering trees bowed their branches over the white stones. It seemed as though it were lighter here than in the fields; the maple-leaves stood out sharply like paws on the yellow sand of the avenue and on the stones, and the inscriptions on the tombs could be clearly read. For the first moments Startsev was struck now by what he saw for the first time in his life, and what he would probably never see again; a world not like anything else, a world in which the moonlight was as soft and beautiful, as though slumbering here in its cradle, where there was no life, none whatever; but in every dark poplar, in every tomb, there was felt the presence of a mystery that promised a life peaceful, beautiful, eternal. The stones and faded flowers, together with the autumn scent of the leaves, all told of forgiveness, melancholy, and peace.

All was silence around; the stars looked down from the sky in the profound stillness, and Startsev's footsteps sounded loud and out of place, and only when the church clock began striking and he imagined himself dead, buried there for ever, he felt as though some one were looking at him, and for a moment he thought that it was not peace and tranquillity, but stifled despair, the dumb dreariness of non-existence. . . .

Demetti's tomb was in the form of a shrine with an angel at the top. The Italian opera had once visited S-- and one of the singers had died; she had been buried here, and this monument put up to her. No one in the town remembered her, but the lamp at the entrance reflected the moonlight, and looked as though it were burning.

There was no one, and, indeed, who would come here at midnight? But Startsev waited, and as though the moonlight warmed his passion, he waited passionately, and, in imagination, pictured kisses and embraces. He sat near the monument for half an hour, then paced up and down the side avenues, with his hat in his hand, waiting and thinking of the many women and girls buried in these tombs who had been beautiful and fascinating, who had loved, at night burned with passion, yielding themselves to caresses. How wickedly Mother Nature jested at man's expense, after all! How humiliating it was to recognise it!

Startsev thought this, and at the same time he wanted to cry out that he wanted love, that he was eager for it at all costs. To his eyes they were not slabs of marble, but fair white bodies in the moonlight; he saw shapes hiding bashfully in the shadows of the trees, felt their warmth, and the languor was oppressive. . . .

And as though a curtain were lowered, the moon went behind a cloud, and suddenly all was darkness. Startsev could scarcely find the gate - by now it was as dark as it is on an autumn night. Then he wandered about for an hour and a half, looking for the side-street in which he had left his horses.

"I am tired; I can scarcely stand on my legs," he said to Panteleimon.

And settling himself with relief in his carriage, he thought: "Och! I ought not to get fat!"

III

The following evening he went to the Turkins' to make an offer. But it turned out to be an inconvenient moment, as Ekaterina Ivanovna was in her own room having her hair done by a hair-dresser. She was getting ready to go to a dance at the club.

He had to sit a long time again in the dining-room drinking tea. Ivan Petrovitch, seeing that his visitor was bored and preoccupied, drew some notes out of his waistcoat pocket, read a funny letter from a German steward, saying that all the ironmongery was ruined and the plasticity was peeling off the walls.

"I expect they will give a decent dowry," thought Startsev, listening absent-mindedly.

After a sleepless night, he found himself in a state of stupefaction, as though he had been given something sweet and soporific to drink; there was fog in his soul, but joy and warmth, and at the same time a sort of cold, heavy fragment of his brain was reflecting:

"Stop before it is too late! Is she the match for you? She is spoilt, whimsical, sleeps till two o'clock in the afternoon, while you are a deacon's son, a district doctor. . . ."

"What of it?" he thought. "I don't care."

"Besides, if you marry her," the fragment went on, "then her relations will make you give up the district work and live in the town."

"After all," he thought, "if it must be the town, the town it must be. They will give a dowry; we can establish ourselves suitably."

At last Ekaterina Ivanovna came in, dressed for the ball, with a low neck, looking fresh and pretty; and Startsev admired her so much, and went into such ecstasies, that he could say nothing, but simply stared at her and laughed.

She began saying good-bye, and he - he had no reason for staying now - got up, saying that it was time for him to go home; his patients were waiting for him.

"Well, there's no help for that," said Ivan Petrovitch. "Go, and you might take Kitten to the club on the way."

It was spotting with rain; it was very dark, and they could only tell where the horses were by Panteleimon's husky cough. The hood of the carriage was put up.

"I stand upright; you lie down right; he lies all right," said Ivan Petrovitch as he put his daughter into the carriage.

They drove off.

"I was at the cemetery yesterday," Startsev began. "How ungenerous and merciless it was on your part! . . ."

"You went to the cemetery?"

"Yes, I went there and waited almost till two o'clock. I suffered . . ."

"Well, suffer, if you cannot understand a joke."

Ekaterina Ivanovna, pleased at having so cleverly taken in a man who was in love with her, and at being the object of such intense love, burst out laughing and suddenly uttered a shriek of terror, for, at that very minute, the horses turned sharply in at the gate of the club, and the carriage almost tilted over. Startsev put his arm round Ekaterina Ivanovna's waist; in her fright she nestled up to him, and he could not restrain himself, and passionately kissed her on the lips and on the chin, and hugged her more tightly.

"That's enough," she said drily.

And a minute later she was not in the carriage, and a policeman near the lighted entrance of the club shouted in a detestable voice to Panteleimon:

"What are you stopping for, you crow? Drive on."

Startsev drove home, but soon afterwards returned. Attired in another man's dress suit and a stiff white tie which kept sawing at his neck and trying to slip away from the collar, he was sitting at midnight in the club drawing-room, and was saying with enthusiasm to Ekaterina Ivanovna.

"Ah, how little people know who have never loved! It seems to me that no one has ever yet written of love truly, and I doubt whether this tender, joyful, agonising feeling can be described, and any one who has once experienced it would not attempt to put it into words. What is the use of preliminaries and introductions? What is the use of unnecessary fine words? My love is immeasurable. I beg, I beseech you," Startsev brought out at last, "be my wife!"

"Dmitri Ionitch," said Ekaterina Ivanovna, with a very grave face, after a moment's thought - "Dmitri Ionitch, I am very grateful to you for the honour. I respect you, but . . ." she got up and continued standing, "but, forgive me, I cannot be your wife. Let us talk seriously. Dmitri Ionitch, you know I love art beyond everything in life. I adore music; I love it frantically; I have dedicated my whole life to it. I want to be an artist; I want fame, success, freedom, and you want me to go on living in this town, to go on living this empty, useless life, which has become insufferable to me. To become a wife - oh, no, forgive me! One must strive towards a lofty, glorious goal, and married life would put me in bondage for ever. Dmitri Ionitch" (she faintly smiled as she pronounced his name; she thought of "Alexey Feofilaktitch") - "Dmitri Ionitch, you are a good, clever, honourable man; you are better than any one. . . ." Tears came into her eyes. "I feel for you with my whole heart, but . . . but you will understand. . . ."

And she turned away and went out of the drawing-room to prevent herself from crying.

Startsev's heart left off throbbing uneasily. Going out of the club into the street, he first of all tore off the stiff tie and drew a deep breath. He was a little ashamed and his vanity was wounded - he had not expected a refusal - and could not believe that all his dreams, his hopes and yearnings, had led him up to such a stupid end, just as in some little play at an amateur performance, and he was sorry for his feeling, for that love of his, so sorry that he felt as though he could have burst into sobs or have violently belaboured Panteleimon's broad back with his umbrella.

For three days he could not get on with anything, he could not eat nor sleep; but when the news reached him that Ekaterina Ivanovna had gone away to Moscow to enter the Conservatoire, he grew calmer and lived as before.

Afterwards, remembering sometimes how he had wandered about the cemetery or how he had driven all over the town to get a dress suit, he stretched lazily and said:

"What a lot of trouble, though!"

IV

Four years had passed. Startsev already had a large practice in the town. Every morning he hurriedly saw his patients at Dyalizh, then he drove in to see his town patients. By now he drove, not with a pair, but with a team of three with bells on them, and he returned home late at night. He had grown broader and stouter, and was not very fond of walking, as he was somewhat asthmatic. And Panteleimon had grown stout, too, and the broader he grew, the more mournfully he sighed and complained of his hard luck: he was sick of driving! Startsev used to visit various households and met many people, but did not become intimate with any one. The inhabitants irritated him by their conversation, their views of life, and even their appearance. Experience taught him by degrees that while he played cards or lunched with one of these people, the man was a peaceable, friendly, and even intelligent human being; that as soon as one talked of anything not eatable, for instance, of politics or science, he would be completely at a loss, or would expound a philosophy so stupid and ill-natured that there was nothing else to do but wave one's hand in despair and go away. Even when Startsev tried to talk to liberal citizens, saying, for instance, that humanity, thank God, was progressing, and that one day it would be possible to dispense with passports and capital punishment, the liberal citizen would look at him askance and ask him mistrustfully: "Then any one could murder any one he chose in the open street?" And when, at tea or supper, Startsev observed in company that one should work, and that one ought not to live without working, everyone took this as a reproach, and began to get angry and argue aggressively. With all that, the inhabitants did nothing, absolutely nothing, and took no interest in anything, and it was quite impossible to think of anything to say. And Startsev avoided conversation, and confined himself to eating and playing *vint;* and when there was a family festivity in some household and he was invited to a meal, then he sat and ate in silence, looking at his plate.

And everything that was said at the time was uninteresting, unjust, and stupid; he felt irritated and disturbed, but held his tongue, and, because he sat glumly silent and looked at his plate, he was nicknamed in the town "the haughty Pole," though he never had been a Pole.

All such entertainments as theatres and concerts he declined, but he played *vint* every evening for three hours with enjoyment. He had another diversion to which he took imperceptibly, little by little: in the evening he would take out of his pockets the notes he had gained by his practice, and sometimes there were stuffed in his pockets notes - yellow and green, and smelling of scent and vinegar and incense and fish oil - up to the value of seventy roubles; and when they amounted to some hundreds he took them to the Mutual Credit Bank and deposited the money there to his account.

He was only twice at the Turkins' in the course of the four years after Ekaterina Ivanovna had gone away, on each occasion at the invitation of Vera Iosifovna, who was still undergoing treatment for migraine. Every summer Ekaterina Ivanovna came to stay with her parents, but he did not once see her; it somehow never happened.

But now four years had passed. One still, warm morning a letter was brought to the hospital. Vera Iosifovna wrote to Dmitri Ionitch that she was missing him very much, and begged him to come and see them, and to relieve her sufferings; and, by the way, it was her birthday. Below was a postscript: "I join in mother's request.- K."

Startsev considered, and in the evening he went to the Turkins'.

"How do you do, if you please?" Ivan Petrovitch met him, smiling with his eyes only. "Bongjour."

Vera Iosifovna, white-haired and looking much older, shook Startsev's hand, sighed affectedly, and said:

"You don't care to pay attentions to me, doctor. You never come and see us; I am too old for you. But now some one young has come; perhaps she will be more fortunate."

And Kitten? She had grown thinner, paler, had grown handsomer and more graceful; but now she was Ekaterina Ivanovna, not Kitten; she had lost the freshness and look of childish naïveté. And in her expression and manners there was something new - guilty and diffident, as though she did not feel herself at home here in the Turkins' house.

"How many summers, how many winters!" she said, giving Startsev her hand, and he could see that her heart was beating with excitement; and looking at him intently and curiously, she went on: "How much stouter you are! You look sunburnt and more manly, but on the whole you have changed very little."

Now, too, he thought her attractive, very attractive, but there was something lacking in her, or else something superfluous - he could not himself have said exactly what it was, but something prevented him from feeling as before. He did not like her pallor, her new expression, her faint smile, her voice, and soon afterwards he disliked her clothes, too, the low chair in which she was sitting; he disliked something in the past when he had almost married her. He thought of his love, of the dreams and the hopes which had troubled him four years before - and he felt awkward.

They had tea with cakes. Then Vera Iosifovna read aloud a novel; she read of things that never happen in real life, and Startsev listened, looked at her handsome grey head, and waited for her to finish.

People are not stupid because they can't write novels, but because they can't conceal it when they do," he thought.

"Not badsome," said Ivan Petrovitch.

Then Ekaterina Ivanovna played long and noisily on the piano, and when she finished she was profusely thanked and warmly praised.

"It's a good thing I did not marry her," thought Startsev.

She looked at him, and evidently expected him to ask her to go into the garden, but he remained silent.

"Let us have a talk," she said, going up to him. "How are you getting on? What are you doing? How are things? I have been thinking about you all these days," she went on nervously. "I wanted to write to you, wanted to come myself to see you at Dyalizh. I quite made up my mind to go, but afterwards I thought better of it. God knows what your attitude is towards me now; I have been looking forward to seeing you to-day with such emotion. For goodness' sake let us go into the garden."

They went into the garden and sat down on the seat under the old maple, just as they had done four years before. It was dark.

"How are you getting on?" asked Ekaterina Ivanovna.

"Oh, all right; I am jogging along," answered Startsev.

And he could think of nothing more. They were silent.

"I feel so excited!" said Ekaterina Ivanovna, and she hid her face in her hands. "But don't pay attention to it. I am so happy to be at home; I am so glad to see everyone. I can't get used to it. So many memories! I thought we should talk without stopping till morning."

Now he saw her face near, her shining eyes, and in the darkness she looked younger than in the room, and even her old childish expression seemed to have come back to her. And indeed she was looking at him with naïve curiosity, as though she wanted to get a closer view and understanding of the man who had loved her so ardently, with such tenderness, and so unsuccessfully; her eyes thanked him for that love.

And he remembered all that had been, every minute detail; how he had wandered about the cemetery, how he had returned home in the morning exhausted, and he suddenly felt sad and regretted the past. A warmth began glowing in his heart.

"Do you remember how I took you to the dance at the club?" he asked. "It was dark and rainy then. . ."

The warmth was glowing now in his heart, and he longed to talk, to rail at life. . . .

"Ech!" he said with a sigh. "You ask how I am living. How do we live here? Why, not at all. We grow old, we grow stout, we grow slack. Day after day passes; life slips by without colour, without expressions, without thoughts. . . . In the daytime working for gain, and in the evening the club, the company of card-players, alcoholic, raucous-voiced gentlemen whom I can't endure. What is there nice in it?"

"Well, you have work - a noble object in life. You used to be so fond of talking of your hospital. I was such a queer girl then; I imagined myself such a great pianist. Nowadays all young ladies play the piano, and I played, too, like everybody else, and there was nothing special about me. I am just such a pianist as my mother is an authoress. And of course I didn't understand you then, but afterwards in Moscow I often thought of you. I thought of no one but you. What happiness to be a district doctor; to help the suffering; to be serving the people! What happiness!" Ekaterina Ivanovna repeated with enthusiasm. "When I thought of you in Moscow, you seemed to me so ideal, so lofty. . . ."

Startsev thought of the notes he used to take out of his pockets in the evening with such pleasure, and the glow in his heart was quenched.

He got up to go into the house. She took his arm.

"You are the best man I've known in my life," she went on. "We will see each other and talk, won't we? Promise me. I am not a pianist; I am not in error about myself now, and I will not play before you or talk of music."

When they had gone into the house, and when Startsev saw in the lamplight her face, and her sad, grateful, searching eyes fixed upon him, he felt uneasy and thought again:

"It's a good thing I did not marry her then."

He began taking leave.

"You have no human right to go before supper," said Ivan Petrovitch as he saw him off. "It's extremely perpendicular on your part. Well, now, perform!" he added, addressing Pava in the hall.

Pava, no longer a boy, but a young man with moustaches, threw himself into an attitude, flung up his arm, and said in a tragic voice:

"Unhappy woman, die!"

All this irritated Startsev. Getting into his carriage, and looking at the dark house and garden which had once been so precious and so dear, he thought of everything at once - Vera Iosifovna's novels and Kitten's noisy playing, and Ivan Petrovitch's jokes and Pava's tragic posturing, and thought if the most talented people in the town were so futile, what must the town be?

Three days later Pava brought a letter from Ekaterina Ivanovna.

"You don't come and see us - why?" she wrote to him. "I am afraid that you have changed towards us. I am afraid, and I am terrified at the very thought of it. Reassure me; come and tell me that everything is well.

"I must talk to you.- Your E. I."

--

He read this letter, thought a moment, and said to Pava:

"Tell them, my good fellow, that I can't come to-day; I am very busy. Say I will come in three days or so."

But three days passed, a week passed; he still did not go. Happening once to drive past the Turkins' house, he thought he must go in, if only for a moment, but on second thoughts . . . did not go in.

And he never went to the Turkins' again.

V

Several more years have passed. Startsev has grown stouter still, has grown corpulent, breathes heavily, and already walks with his head thrown back. When stout and red in the face, he drives with his bells and his team of three horses, and Panteleimon, also stout and red in the face with his thick beefy neck, sits on the box, holding his arms stiffly out before him as though they were made of wood, and shouts to those he meets: "Keep to the ri-i-ight!" it is an impressive picture; one might think it was not a mortal, but some heathen deity in his chariot. He has an immense practice in the town, no time to breathe, and already has an estate and two houses in the town, and he is looking out for a third more profitable; and when at the Mutual Credit Bank he is told of a house that is for sale, he goes to the house without ceremony, and, marching through all the rooms, regardless of half-dressed women and children who gaze at him in amazement and alarm, he prods at the doors with his stick, and says:

"Is that the study? Is that a bedroom? And what's here?"

And as he does so he breathes heavily and wipes the sweat from his brow.

He has a great deal to do, but still he does not give up his work as district doctor; he is greedy for gain, and he tries to be in all places at once. At Dyalizh and in the town he is called simply "Ionitch": "Where is Ionitch off to?" or "Should not we call in Ionitch to a consultation?"

Probably because his throat is covered with rolls of fat, his voice has changed; it has become thin and sharp. His temper has changed, too: he has grown ill-humoured and irritable. When he sees his patients he is usually out of temper; he impatiently taps the floor with his stick, and shouts in his disagreeable voice:

"Be so good as to confine yourself to answering my questions! Don't talk so much!"

He is solitary. He leads a dreary life; nothing interests him.

During all the years he had lived at Dyalizh his love for Kitten had been his one joy, and probably his last. In the evenings he plays *vint* at the club, and then sits alone at a big table and has supper. Ivan, the oldest and most respectable of the waiters, serves him, hands him Lafitte No. 17, and everyone at the club - the members of the committee, the cook and waiters - know what he likes and what he doesn't like and do their very utmost to satisfy him, or else he is sure to fly into a rage and bang on the floor with his stick.

As he eats his supper, he turns round from time to time and puts in his spoke in some conversation:

"What are you talking about? Eh? Whom?"

And when at a neighbouring table there is talk of the Turkins, he asks:

"What Turkins are you speaking of? Do you mean the people whose daughter plays on the piano?"

That is all that can be said about him.

And the Turkins? Ivan Petrovitch has grown no older; he is not changed in the least, and still makes jokes and tells anecdotes as of old. Vera Iosifovna still reads her novels aloud to her visitors with eagerness and touching simplicity. And Kitten plays the piano for four hours every day. She has grown visibly older, is constantly ailing, and every autumn goes to the Crimea with her mother. When Ivan Petrovitch sees them off at the station, he wipes his tears as the train starts, and shouts:

"Good-bye, if you please."

And he waves his handkerchief.

A DOCTOR'S VISIT

The Professor received a telegram from the Lyalikovs' factory; he was asked to come as quickly as possible. The daughter of some Madame Lyalikov, apparently the owner of the factory, was ill, and that was all that one could make out of the long, incoherent telegram. And the Professor did not go himself, but sent instead his assistant, Korolyov.

It was two stations from Moscow, and there was a drive of three miles from the station. A carriage with three horses had been sent to the station to meet Korolyov; the coachman wore a hat with a peacock's feather on it, and answered every question in a loud voice like a soldier: "No, sir!" "Certainly, sir!"

It was Saturday evening; the sun was setting, the workpeople were coming in crowds from the factory to the station, and they bowed to the carriage in which Korolyov was driving. And he was charmed with the evening, the farmhouses and villas on the road, and the birch-trees, and the quiet atmosphere all around, when the fields and woods and the sun seemed preparing, like the workpeople now on the eve of the holiday, to rest, and perhaps to pray. . . .

He was born and had grown up in Moscow; he did not know the country, and he had never taken any interest in factories, or been inside one, but he had happened to read about factories, and had been in the houses of manufacturers and had talked to them; and whenever he saw a factory far or near, he always thought how quiet and peaceable it was outside, but within there was always sure to be impenetrable ignorance and dull egoism on the side of the owners, wearisome, unhealthy toil on the side of the workpeople, squabbling, vermin, vodka. And now when the workpeople timidly and respectfully made way for the carriage, in their faces, their caps, their walk, he read physical impurity, drunkenness, nervous exhaustion, bewilderment.

They drove in at the factory gates. On each side he caught glimpses of the little houses of workpeople, of the faces of women, of quilts and linen on the railings. "Look out!" shouted the coachman, not pulling up the horses. It was a wide courtyard without grass, with five immense blocks of buildings with tall chimneys a little distance one from another, warehouses and barracks, and over everything a sort of grey powder as though from dust. Here and there, like oases in the desert, there were pitiful gardens, and the green and red roofs of the houses in which the managers and clerks lived. The coachman suddenly pulled up the horses, and the carriage stopped at the house, which had been newly painted grey; here was a flower garden, with a lilac bush covered with dust, and on the yellow steps at the front door there was a strong smell of paint.

"Please come in, doctor," said women's voices in the passage and the entry, and at the same time he heard sighs and whisperings. "Pray walk in. . . . We've been expecting you so long. . . we're in real trouble. Here, this way."

Madame Lyalikov - a stout elderly lady wearing a black silk dress with fashionable sleeves, but, judging from her face, a simple uneducated woman - looked at the doctor in a flutter, and could not bring herself to hold out her hand to him; she did not dare. Beside her stood a personage with short hair and a pince-nez; she was wearing a blouse of many colours, and was very thin and no longer young. The servants called her Christina Dmitryevna, and Korolyov guessed that this was the governess. Probably, as the person of most education in the house, she had been charged to meet and receive the doctor, for she began immediately, in great haste, stating the causes of the illness, giving trivial and tiresome details, but without saying who was ill or what was the matter.

The doctor and the governess were sitting talking while the lady of the house stood motionless at the door, waiting. From the conversation Korolyov learned that the patient was Madame Lyalikov's only daughter and heiress, a girl of twenty, called Liza; she had been ill for a long time, and had consulted various doctors, and the previous night she had suffered till morning from such violent palpitations of the heart, that no one in the house had slept, and they had been afraid she might die.

"She has been, one may say, ailing from a child," said Christina Dmitryevna in a sing-song voice, continually wiping her lips with her hand. "The doctors say it is nerves; when she was a little girl she was scrofulous, and the doctors drove it inwards, so I think it may be due to that."

They went to see the invalid. Fully grown up, big and tall, but ugly like her mother, with the same little eyes and disproportionate breadth of the lower part of the face, lying with her hair in disorder, muffled up to the chin, she made upon Korolyov at the first minute the impression of a poor, destitute creature, sheltered and cared for here out of charity, and he could hardly believe that this was the heiress of the five huge buildings.

"I am the doctor come to see you," said Korolyov. "Good evening."

He mentioned his name and pressed her hand, a large, cold, ugly hand; she sat up, and, evidently accustomed to doctors, let herself be sounded, without showing the least concern that her shoulders and chest were uncovered.

"I have palpitations of the heart," she said, "It was so awful all night. . . . I almost died of fright! Do give me something."

"I will, I will; don't worry yourself."

Korolyov examined her and shrugged his shoulders.

"The heart is all right," he said; "it's all going on satisfactorily; everything is in good order. Your nerves must have been playing pranks a little, but that's so common. The attack is over by now, one must suppose; lie down and go to sleep."

At that moment a lamp was brought into the bed-room. The patient screwed up her eyes at the light, then suddenly put her hands to her head and broke into sobs. And the impression of a destitute, ugly creature vanished, and Korolyov no longer noticed the little eyes or the heavy development of the lower part of the face. He saw a soft, suffering expression which was intelligent and touching: she seemed to him altogether graceful, feminine, and simple; and he longed to soothe her, not with drugs, not with advice, but with simple, kindly words. Her mother put her arms round her head and hugged her. What despair, what grief was in the old woman's face! She, her mother, had reared her and brought her up, spared nothing, and devoted her whole life to having her daughter taught French, dancing, music: had engaged a dozen teachers for her; had consulted the best doctors, kept a governess. And now she could not make out the reason of these tears, why there was all this misery, she could not understand, and was bewildered; and she had a guilty, agitated, despairing expression, as though she had omitted something very important, had left something undone, had neglected to call in somebody - and whom, she did not know.

"Lizanka, you are crying again . . . again," she said, hugging her daughter to her. "My own, my darling, my child, tell me what it is! Have pity on me! Tell me."

Both wept bitterly. Korolyov sat down on the side of the bed and took Liza's hand.

"Come, give over; it's no use crying," he said kindly. "Why, there is nothing in the world that is worth those tears. Come, we won't cry; that's no good. . . ."

And inwardly he thought:

"It's high time she was married. . . ."

"Our doctor at the factory gave her kalibromati," said the governess, "but I notice it only makes her worse. I should have thought that if she is given anything for the heart it ought to be drops. . . . I forget the name. . . . Convallaria, isn't it?"

And there followed all sorts of details. She interrupted the doctor, preventing his speaking, and there was a look of effort on her face, as though she supposed that, as the woman of most education in the house, she was duty bound to keep up a conversation with the doctor, and on no other subject but medicine.

Korolyov felt bored.

"I find nothing special the matter," he said, addressing the mother as he went out of the bedroom. "If your daughter is being attended by the factory doctor, let him go on attending her. The treatment so far has been perfectly correct, and I see no reason for changing your doctor. Why change? It's such an ordinary trouble; there's nothing seriously wrong."

He spoke deliberately as he put on his gloves, while Madame Lyalikov stood without moving, and looked at him with her tearful eyes.

"I have half an hour to catch the ten o'clock train," he said. "I hope I am not too late."

"And can't you stay?" she asked, and tears trickled down her cheeks again. "I am ashamed to trouble you, but if you would be so good. . . . For God's sake," she went on in an undertone, glancing towards the door, "do stay to-night with us! She is all I have . . . my only daughter. . . . She frightened me last night; I can't get over it. . . . Don't go away, for goodness' sake! . . ."

He wanted to tell her that he had a great deal of work in Moscow, that his family were expecting him home; it was disagreeable to him to spend the evening and the whole night in a strange house quite needlessly; but he looked at her face, heaved a sigh, and began taking off his gloves without a word.

All the lamps and candles were lighted in his honour in the drawing-room and the dining-room. He sat down at the piano and began turning over the music. Then he looked at the pictures on the walls, at the portraits. The pictures, oil-paintings in gold frames, were views of the Crimea - a stormy sea with a ship, a Catholic monk with a wineglass; they were all dull, smooth daubs, with no trace of talent in them. There was not a single good-looking face among the portraits, nothing but broad cheekbones and astonished-looking eyes. Lyalikov, Liza's father, had a low forehead and a self-satisfied expression; his uniform sat like a sack on his bulky plebeian figure; on his breast was a medal and a Red Cross Badge. There was little sign of culture, and the luxury was senseless and haphazard, and was as ill fitting as that uniform. The floors irritated him with their brilliant polish, the lustres on the chandelier irritated him, and he was reminded for some reason of the story of the merchant who used to go to the baths with a medal on his neck. . . .

He heard a whispering in the entry; some one was softly snoring. And suddenly from outside came harsh, abrupt, metallic sounds, such as Korolyov had never heard before, and which he did not understand now; they roused strange, unpleasant echoes in his soul.

"I believe nothing would induce me to remain here to live . . ." he thought, and went back to the music-books again.

"Doctor, please come to supper!" the governess called him in a low voice.

He went into supper. The table was large and laid with a vast number of dishes and wines, but there were only two to supper: himself and Christina Dmitryevna. She drank Madeira, ate rapidly, and talked, looking at him through her pince-nez:

"Our workpeople are very contented. We have performances at the factory every winter; the workpeople act themselves. They have lectures with a magic lantern, a splendid tea-room, and everything they want. They are very much attached to us, and when they heard that Lizanka was worse they had a service sung for her. Though they have no education, they have their feelings, too."

"It looks as though you have no man in the house at all," said Korolyov.

"Not one. Pyotr Nikanoritch died a year and a half ago, and left us alone. And so there are the three of us. In the summer we live here, and in winter we live in Moscow, in Polianka. I have been living with them for eleven years - as one of the family."

At supper they served sterlet, chicken rissoles, and stewed fruit; the wines were expensive French wines.

"Please don't stand on ceremony, doctor," said Christina Dmitryevna, eating and wiping her mouth with her fist, and it was evident she found her life here exceedingly pleasant. "Please have some more."

After supper the doctor was shown to his room, where a bed had been made up for him, but he did not feel sleepy. The room was stuffy and it smelt of paint; he put on his coat and went out.

It was cool in the open air; there was already a glimmer of dawn, and all the five blocks of buildings, with their tall chimneys, barracks, and warehouses, were distinctly outlined against the damp air. As it was a holiday, they were not working, and the windows were dark, and in only one of the buildings was there a furnace burning; two windows were crimson, and fire mixed with smoke came from time to time from the chimney. Far away beyond the yard the frogs were croaking and the nightingales singing.

Looking at the factory buildings and the barracks, where the workpeople were asleep, he thought again what he always thought when he saw a factory. They may have performances for the workpeople, magic lanterns, factory doctors, and improvements of all sorts, but, all the same, the workpeople he had met that day on his way from the station did not look in any way different from those he had known long ago in his childhood, before there were factory performances and improvements. As a doctor accustomed to judging correctly of chronic complaints, the radical cause of which was incomprehensible and incurable, he looked upon factories as something baffling, the cause of which also was obscure and not removable, and all the improvements in the life of the factory hands he looked upon not as superfluous, but as comparable with the treatment of incurable illnesses.

"There is something baffling in it, of course . . ." he thought, looking at the crimson windows. "Fifteen hundred or two thousand workpeople are working without rest in unhealthy surroundings, making bad cotton goods, living on the verge of starvation, and only waking from this nightmare at rare intervals in the tavern; a hundred people act as overseers, and the whole life of that hundred is spent in imposing fines, in abuse, in injustice, and only two or three so-called owners enjoy the profits, though they don't work at all, and despise the wretched cotton. But what are the profits, and how do they enjoy them? Madame Lyalikov and her daughter are unhappy - it makes one wretched to look at them; the only one who enjoys her life is Christina Dmitryevna, a stupid, middle-aged maiden lady in pince-nez. And so it appears that all these five blocks of buildings are at work, and inferior cotton is sold in the Eastern markets, simply that Christina Dmitryevna may eat sterlet and drink Madeira."

Suddenly there came a strange noise, the same sound Korolyov had heard before supper. Some one was striking on a sheet of metal near one of the buildings; he struck a note, and then at once checked the vibrations, so that short, abrupt, discordant sounds were produced, rather like "Dair . . . dair . . . dair. . . ." Then there was half a minute of stillness, and from another building there came sounds equally abrupt and unpleasant, lower bass notes: "Drin . . . drin . . . drin. . ." Eleven times. Evidently it was the watchman striking the hour. Near the third building he heard: "Zhuk . . . zhuk . . . zhuk. . . ." And so near all the buildings, and then behind the barracks and beyond the gates. And in the stillness of the night it seemed as though these sounds were uttered by a monster with crimson eyes - the devil himself, who controlled the owners and the work-people alike, and was deceiving both.

Korolyov went out of the yard into the open country.

"Who goes there?" some one called to him at the gates in an abrupt voice.

"It's just like being in prison," he thought, and made no answer.

Here the nightingales and the frogs could be heard more distinctly, and one could feel it was a night in May. From the station came the noise of a train; somewhere in the distance drowsy cocks were crowing; but, all the same, the night was still, the world was sleeping tranquilly. In a field not far from the factory there could be seen the framework of a house and heaps of building material:

Korolyov sat down on the planks and went on thinking.

"The only person who feels happy here is the governess, and the factory hands are working for her gratification. But that's only apparent: she is only the figurehead. The real person, for whom everything is being done, is the devil."

And he thought about the devil, in whom he did not believe, and he looked round at the two windows where the fires were gleaming. It seemed to him that out of those crimson eyes the devil himself was looking at him - that unknown force that had created the mutual relation of the strong and the weak, that coarse blunder which one could never correct. The strong must hinder the weak from living - such was the law of Nature; but only in a newspaper article or in a school book was that intelligible and easily accepted. In the hotchpotch which was everyday life, in the tangle of trivialities out of which human relations were woven, it was no longer a law, but a logical absurdity, when the strong and the weak were both equally victims of their mutual relations, unwillingly submitting to some directing force, unknown, standing outside life, apart from man.

So thought Korolyov, sitting on the planks, and little by little he was possessed by a feeling that this unknown and mysterious force was really close by and looking at him. Meanwhile the east was growing paler, time passed rapidly; when there was not a soul anywhere near, as though everything were dead, the five buildings and their chimneys against the grey background of the dawn had a peculiar look - not the same as by day; one forgot altogether that inside there were steam motors, electricity, telephones, and kept thinking of lake-dwellings, of the Stone Age, feeling the presence of a crude, unconscious force. . . .

And again there came the sound: "Dair . . . dair . . . dair . . . dair . . ." twelve times. Then there was stillness, stillness for half a minute, and at the other end of the yard there rang out.

"Drin . . . drin . . . drin. . . ."

"Horribly disagreeable," thought Korolyov.

"Zhuk . . . zhuk . . ." there resounded from a third place, abruptly, sharply, as though with annoyance - "Zhuk . . . zhuk. . . ."

And it took four minutes to strike twelve. Then there was a hush; and again it seemed as though everything were dead.

Korolyov sat a little longer, then went to the house, but sat up for a good while longer. In the adjoining rooms there was whispering, there was a sound of shuffling slippers and bare feet.

"Is she having another attack?" thought Korolyov.

He went out to have a look at the patient. By now it was quite light in the rooms, and a faint glimmer of sunlight, piercing through the morning mist, quivered on the floor and on the wall of the drawing-room. The door of Liza's room was open, and she was sitting in a low chair beside her bed, with her hair down, wearing a dressing-gown and wrapped in a shawl. The blinds were down on the windows.

"How do you feel?" asked Korolyov.

"Well, thank you."

He touched her pulse, then straightened her hair, that had fallen over her forehead.

"You are not asleep," he said. "It's beautiful weather outside. It's spring. The nightingales are singing, and you sit in the dark and think of something."

She listened and looked into his face; her eyes were sorrowful and intelligent, and it was evident she wanted to say something to him.

"Does this happen to you often?" he said.

She moved her lips, and answered:

"Often, I feel wretched almost every night."

At that moment the watchman in the yard began striking two o'clock. They heard: "Dair . . . dair . . ." and she shuddered.

"Do those knockings worry you?" he asked.

"I don't know. Everything here worries me," she answered, and pondered. "Everything worries me. I hear sympathy in your voice; it seemed to me as soon as I saw you that I could tell you all about it."

"Tell me, I beg you."

"I want to tell you of my opinion. It seems to me that I have no illness, but that I am weary and frightened, because it is bound to be so and cannot be otherwise. Even the healthiest person can't help being uneasy if, for instance, a robber is moving about under his window. I am constantly being doctored," she went on, looking at her knees, and she gave a shy smile. "I am very grateful, of course, and I do not deny that the treatment is a benefit; but I should like to talk, not with a doctor, but with some intimate friend who would understand me and would convince me that I was right or wrong."

"Have you no friends?" asked Korolyov.

"I am lonely. I have a mother; I love her, but, all the same, I am lonely. That's how it happens to be. . . . Lonely people read a great deal, but say little and hear little. Life for them is mysterious; they are mystics and often see the devil where he is not. Lermontov's Tamara was lonely and she saw the devil."

"Do you read a great deal?"

"Yes. You see, my whole time is free from morning till night. I read by day, and by night my head is empty; instead of thoughts there are shadows in it."

"Do you see anything at night?" asked Korolyov.

"No, but I feel. . . ."

She smiled again, raised her eyes to the doctor, and looked at him so sorrowfully, so intelligently; and it seemed to him that she trusted him, and that she wanted to speak frankly to him, and that she thought the same as he did. But she was silent, perhaps waiting for him to speak.

And he knew what to say to her. It was clear to him that she needed as quickly as possible to give up the five buildings and the million if she had it - to leave that devil that looked out at night; it was clear to him, too, that she thought so herself, and was only waiting for some one she trusted to confirm her.

But he did not know how to say it. How? One is shy of asking men under sentence what they have been sentenced for; and in the same way it is awkward to ask very rich people what they want so much money for, why they make such a poor use of their wealth, why they don't give it up, even when they see in it their unhappiness; and if they begin a conversation about it themselves, it is usually embarrassing, awkward, and long.

"How is one to say it?" Korolyov wondered. "And is it necessary to speak?"

And he said what he meant in a roundabout way:

"You in the position of a factory owner and a wealthy heiress are dissatisfied; you don't believe in your right to it; and here now you can't sleep. That, of course, is better than if you were satisfied, slept soundly, and thought everything was satisfactory. Your sleeplessness does you credit; in any case, it is a good sign. In reality, such a conversation as this between us now would have been unthinkable for our parents. At night they did not talk, but slept sound; we, our generation, sleep badly, are restless, but talk a great deal, and are always trying to settle whether we are right or not. For our children or grandchildren that question - whether they are right or not - will have been settled. Things will be clearer for them than for us. Life will be good in fifty years' time; it's only a pity we shall not last out till then. It would be interesting to have a peep at it."

"What will our children and grandchildren do?" asked Liza.

"I don't know. . . . I suppose they will throw it all up and go away."

"Go where?"

"Where? . . . Why, where they like," said Korolyov; and he laughed. "There are lots of places a good, intelligent person can go to."

He glanced at his watch.

"The sun has risen, though," he said. "It is time you were asleep. Undress and sleep soundly. Very glad to have made your acquaintance," he went on, pressing her hand. "You are a good, interesting woman. Good-night!"

He went to his room and went to bed.

In the morning when the carriage was brought round they all came out on to the steps to see him off. Liza, pale and exhausted, was in a white dress as though for a holiday, with a flower in her hair; she looked at him, as yesterday, sorrowfully and intelligently, smiled and talked, and all with an expression as though she wanted to tell him something special, important - him alone. They could hear the larks trilling and the church bells pealing. The windows in the factory buildings were sparkling gaily, and, driving across the yard and afterwards along the road to the station, Korolyov thought neither of the workpeople nor of lake dwellings, nor of the devil, but thought of the time, perhaps close at hand, when life would be as bright and joyous as that still Sunday morning; and he thought how pleasant it was on such a morning in the spring to drive with three horses in a good carriage, and to bask in the sunshine.

THE DARLING

Olenka, the daughter of the retired collegiate assessor, Plemyanniakov, was sitting in her back porch, lost in thought. It was hot, the flies were persistent and teasing, and it was pleasant to reflect that it would soon be evening. Dark rainclouds were gathering from the east, and bringing from time to time a breath of moisture in the air.

Kukin, who was the manager of an open-air theatre called the Tivoli, and who lived in the lodge, was standing in the middle of the garden looking at the sky.

"Again!" he observed despairingly. "It's going to rain again! Rain every day, as though to spite me. I might as well hang myself! It's ruin! Fearful losses every day."

He flung up his hands, and went on, addressing Olenka:

"There! that's the life we lead, Olga Semyonovna. It's enough to make one cry. One works and does one's utmost, one wears oneself out, getting no sleep at night, and racks one's brain what to do for the best. And then what happens? To begin with, one's public is ignorant, boorish. I give them the very best operetta, a dainty masque, first rate music-hall artists. But do you suppose that's what they want! They don't understand anything of that sort. They want a clown; what they ask for is vulgarity. And then look at the weather! Almost every evening it rains. It started on the tenth of May, and it's kept it up all May and June. It's simply awful! The public doesn't come, but I've to pay the rent just the same, and pay the artists."

The next evening the clouds would gather again, and Kukin would say with an hysterical laugh:

"Well, rain away, then! Flood the garden, drown me! Damn my luck in this world and the next! Let the artists have me up! Send me to prison! - to Siberia! - the scaffold! Ha, ha, ha!"

And next day the same thing.

Olenka listened to Kukin with silent gravity, and sometimes tears came into her eyes. In the end his misfortunes touched her; she grew to love him. He was a small thin man, with a yellow face, and curls combed forward on his forehead. He spoke in a thin tenor; as he talked his mouth worked on one side, and there was always an expression of despair on his face; yet he aroused a deep and genuine affection in her. She was always fond of some one, and could not exist without loving. In earlier days she had loved her papa, who now sat in a darkened room, breathing with difficulty; she had loved her aunt who used to come every other year from Bryansk; and before that, when she was at school, she had loved her French master. She was a gentle, soft-hearted, compassionate girl, with mild, tender eyes and very good health. At the sight of her full rosy cheeks, her soft white neck with a little dark mole on it, and the kind, naïve smile, which came into her face when she listened to anything pleasant, men thought, "Yes, not half bad," and smiled too, while lady visitors could not refrain from seizing her hand in the middle of a conversation, exclaiming in a gush of delight, "You darling!"

The house in which she had lived from her birth upwards, and which was left her in her father's will, was at the extreme end of the town, not far from the Tivoli. In the evenings and at night she could head the band playing, and the crackling and banging of fireworks, and it seemed to her that it was Kukin struggling with his destiny, storming the entrenchments of his chief foe, the indifferent public; there was a sweet thrill at her heart, she had no desire to sleep, and when he returned home at day-break, she tapped softly at her bedroom window, and showing him only her face and one shoulder through the curtain, she gave him a friendly smile. . . .

He proposed to her, and they were married. And when he had a closer view of her neck and her plump, fine shoulders, he threw up his hands, and said:

"You darling!"

He was happy, but as it rained on the day and night of his wedding, his face still retained an expression of despair.

They got on very well together. She used to sit in his office, to look after things in the Tivoli, to put down the accounts and pay the wages. And her rosy cheeks, her sweet, naïve, radiant smile, were to be seen now at the office window, now in the refreshment bar or behind the scenes of the theatre. And already she used to say to her acquaintances that the theatre was the chief and most important thing in life and that it was only through the drama that one could derive true enjoyment and become cultivated and humane.

"But do you suppose the public understands that?" she used to say. "What they want is a clown. Yesterday we gave 'Faust Inside Out,' and almost all the boxes were empty; but if Vanitchka and I had been producing some vulgar thing, I assure you the theatre would have been packed. Tomorrow Vanitchka and I are doing 'Orpheus in Hell.' Do come."

And what Kukin said about the theatre and the actors she repeated. Like him she despised the public for their ignorance and their indifference to art; she took part in the rehearsals, she corrected the actors, she kept an eye on the behaviour of the musicians, and when there was an unfavourable notice in the local paper, she shed tears, and then went to the editor's office to set things right.

The actors were fond of her and used to call her "Vanitchka and I," and "the darling"; she was sorry for them and used to lend them small sums of money, and if they deceived her, she used to shed a few tears in private, but did not complain to her husband.

They got on well in the winter too. They took the theatre in the town for the whole winter, and let it for short terms to a Little Russian company, or to a conjurer, or to a local dramatic society. Olenka grew stouter, and was always beaming with satisfaction, while Kukin grew thinner and yellower, and continually complained of their terrible losses, although he had not done badly all the winter. He used to cough at night, and she used to give him hot raspberry tea or lime-flower water, to rub him with eau-de-Cologne and to wrap him in her warm shawls.

"You're such a sweet pet!" she used to say with perfect sincerity, stroking his hair. "You're such a pretty dear!"

Towards Lent he went to Moscow to collect a new troupe, and without him she could not sleep, but sat all night at her window, looking at the stars, and she compared herself with the hens, who are awake all night and uneasy when the cock is not in the hen-house. Kukin was detained in Moscow, and wrote that he would be back at Easter, adding some instructions about the Tivoli. But on the Sunday before Easter, late in the evening, came a sudden ominous knock at the gate; some one was hammering on the gate as though on a barrel - boom, boom, boom! The drowsy cook went flopping with her bare feet through the puddles, as she ran to open the gate.

"Please open," said some one outside in a thick bass. "There is a telegram for you."

Olenka had received telegrams from her husband before, but this time for some reason she felt numb with terror. With shaking hands she opened the telegram and read as follows:

"IVAN PETROVITCH DIED SUDDENLY TO-DAY. AWAITING IMMATE INSTRUCTIONS FUFUNERAL TUESDAY."

That was how it was written in the telegram - "fufuneral," and the utterly incomprehensible word "immate." It was signed by the stage manager of the operatic company.

"My darling!" sobbed Olenka. "Vanka, my precious, my darling! Why did I ever meet you! Why did I know you and love you! Your poor heart-broken Olenka is alone without you!"

Kukin's funeral took place on Tuesday in Moscow, Olenka returned home on Wednesday, and as soon as she got indoors, she threw herself on her bed and sobbed so loudly that it could be heard next door, and in the street.

"Poor darling!" the neighbours said, as they crossed themselves. "Olga Semyonovna, poor darling! How she does take on!"

Three months later Olenka was coming home from mass, melancholy and in deep mourning. It happened that one of her neighbours, Vassily Andreitch Pustovalov, returning home from church, walked back beside her. He was the manager at Babakayev's, the timber merchant's. He wore a straw hat, a white waistcoat, and a gold watch-chain, and looked more a country gentleman than a man in trade.

"Everything happens as it is ordained, Olga Semyonovna," he said gravely, with a sympathetic note in his voice; "and if any of our dear ones die, it must be because it is the will of God, so we ought have fortitude and bear it submissively."

After seeing Olenka to her gate, he said good-bye and went on. All day afterwards she heard his sedately dignified voice, and whenever she shut her eyes she saw his dark beard. She liked him very much. And apparently she had made an impression on him too, for not long afterwards an elderly lady, with whom she was only slightly acquainted, came to drink coffee with her, and as soon as she was seated at table began to talk about Pustovalov, saying that he was an excellent man whom one could thoroughly depend upon, and that any girl would be glad to marry him. Three days later Pustovalov came himself. He did not stay long, only about ten minutes, and he did not say much, but when he left, Olenka loved him - loved him so much that she lay awake all night in a perfect fever, and in the morning she sent for the elderly lady. The match was quickly arranged, and then came the wedding.

Pustovalov and Olenka got on very well together when they were married.

Usually he sat in the office till dinner-time, then he went out on business, while Olenka took his place, and sat in the office till evening, making up accounts and booking orders.

"Timber gets dearer every year; the price rises twenty per cent," she would say to her customers and friends. "Only fancy we used to sell local timber, and now Vassitchka always has to go for wood to the Mogilev district. And the freight!" she would add, covering her cheeks with her hands in horror. "The freight!"

It seemed to her that she had been in the timber trade for ages and ages, and that the most important and necessary thing in life was timber; and there was something intimate and touching to her in the very sound of words such as "baulk," "post," "beam," "pole," "scantling," "batten," "lath," "plank," etc.

At night when she was asleep she dreamed of perfect mountains of planks and boards, and long strings of wagons, carting timber somewhere far away. She dreamed that a whole regiment of six-inch beams forty feet high, standing on end, was marching upon the timber-yard; that logs, beams, and boards knocked together with the resounding crash of dry wood, kept falling and getting up again, piling themselves on each other. Olenka cried out in her sleep, and Pustovalov said to her tenderly: "Olenka, what's the matter, darling? Cross yourself!"

Her husband's ideas were hers. If he thought the room was too hot, or that business was slack, she thought the same. Her husband did not care for entertainments, and on holidays he stayed at home. She did likewise.

"You are always at home or in the office," her friends said to her. "You should go to the theatre, darling, or to the circus."

"Vassitchka and I have no time to go to theatres," she would answer sedately. "We have no time for nonsense. What's the use of these theatres?"

On Saturdays Pustovalov and she used to go to the evening service; on holidays to early mass, and they walked side by side with softened faces as they came home from church. There was a pleasant fragrance about them both, and her silk dress rustled agreeably. At home they drank tea, with fancy bread and jams of various kinds, and afterwards they ate pie. Every day at twelve o'clock there was a savoury smell of beet-root soup and of mutton or duck in their yard, and on fast-days of fish, and no one could pass the gate without feeling hungry. In the office the samovar was always boiling, and customers were regaled with tea and cracknels. Once a week the couple went to the baths and returned side by side, both red in the face.

"Yes, we have nothing to complain of, thank God," Olenka used to say to her acquaintances. "I wish everyone were as well off as Vassitchka and I."

When Pustovalov went away to buy wood in the Mogilev district, she missed him dreadfully, lay awake and cried. A young veterinary surgeon in the army, called Smirnin, to whom they had let their lodge, used sometimes to come in in the evening. He used to talk to her and play cards with her, and this entertained her in her husband's absence. She was particularly interested in what he told her of his home life. He was married and had a little boy, but was separated from his wife because she had been unfaithful to him, and now he hated her and used to send her forty roubles a month for the maintenance of their son. And hearing of all this, Olenka sighed and shook her head. She was sorry for him.

"Well, God keep you," she used to say to him at parting, as she lighted him down the stairs with a candle. "Thank you for coming to cheer me up, and may the Mother of God give you health."

And she always expressed herself with the same sedateness and dignity, the same reasonableness, in imitation of her husband. As the veterinary surgeon was disappearing behind the door below, she would say:

"You know, Vladimir Platonitch, you'd better make it up with your wife. You should forgive her for the sake of your son. You may be sure the little fellow understands."

And when Pustovalov came back, she told him in a low voice about the veterinary surgeon and his unhappy home life, and both sighed and shook their heads and talked about the boy, who, no doubt, missed his father, and by some strange connection of ideas, they went up to the holy ikons, bowed to the ground before them and prayed that God would give them children.

And so the Pustovalovs lived for six years quietly and peaceably in love and complete harmony.

But behold! one winter day after drinking hot tea in the office, Vassily Andreitch went out into the yard without his cap on to see about sending off some timber, caught cold and was taken ill. He had the best doctors, but he grew worse and died after four months' illness. And Olenka was a widow once more.

"I've nobody, now you've left me, my darling," she sobbed, after her husband's funeral. "How can I live without you, in wretchedness and misery! Pity me, good people, all alone in the world!"

She went about dressed in black with long "weepers," and gave up wearing hat and gloves for good. She hardly ever went out, except to church, or to her husband's grave, and led the life of a nun. It was not till six months later that she took off the weepers and opened the shutters of the windows. She was sometimes seen in the mornings, going with her cook to market for provisions, but what went on in her house and how she lived now could only be surmised. People guessed, from seeing her drinking tea in her garden with the veterinary surgeon, who read the newspaper aloud to her, and from the fact that, meeting a lady she knew at the post-office, she said to her:

"There is no proper veterinary inspection in our town, and that's the cause of all sorts of epidemics. One is always hearing of people's getting infection from the milk supply, or catching diseases from horses and cows. The health of domestic animals ought to be as well cared for as the health of human beings."

She repeated the veterinary surgeon's words, and was of the same opinion as he about everything. It was evident that she could not live a year without some attachment, and had found new happiness in the lodge. In any one else this would have been censured, but no one could think ill of Olenka; everything she did was so natural. Neither she nor the veterinary surgeon said anything to other people of the change in their relations, and tried, indeed, to conceal it, but without success, for Olenka could not keep a secret. When he had visitors, men serving in his regiment, and she poured out tea or served the supper, she would begin talking of the cattle plague, of the foot and mouth disease, and of the municipal slaughterhouses. He was dreadfully embarrassed, and when the guests had gone, he would seize her by the hand and hiss angrily:

"I've asked you before not to talk about what you don't understand. When we veterinary surgeons are talking among ourselves, please don't put your word in. It's really annoying."

And she would look at him with astonishment and dismay, and ask him in alarm: "But, Voloditchka, what *am* I to talk about?"

And with tears in her eyes she would embrace him, begging him not to be angry, and they were both happy.

But this happiness did not last long. The veterinary surgeon departed, departed for ever with his regiment, when it was transferred to a distant place - to Siberia, it may be. And Olenka was left alone.

Now she was absolutely alone. Her father had long been dead, and his armchair lay in the attic, covered with dust and lame of one leg. She got thinner and plainer, and when people met her in the street they did not look at her as they used to, and did not smile to her; evidently her best years were over and left behind, and now a new sort of life had begun for her, which did not bear thinking about. In the evening Olenka sat in the porch, and heard the band playing and the fireworks popping in the Tivoli, but now the sound stirred no response. She looked into her yard without interest, thought of nothing, wished for nothing, and afterwards, when night came on she went to bed and dreamed of her empty yard. She ate and drank as it were unwillingly.

And what was worst of all, she had no opinions of any sort. She saw the objects about her and understood what she saw, but could not form any opinion about them, and did not know what to talk about. And how awful it is not to have any opinions! One sees a bottle, for instance, or the rain, or a peasant driving in his cart, but what the bottle is for, or the rain, or the peasant, and what is the meaning of it, one can't say, and could not even for a thousand roubles. When she had Kukin, or Pustovalov, or the veterinary surgeon, Olenka could explain everything, and give her opinion about anything you like, but now there was the same emptiness in her brain and in her heart as there was in her yard outside. And it was as harsh and as bitter as wormwood in the mouth.

Little by little the town grew in all directions. The road became a street, and where the Tivoli and the timber-yard had been, there were new turnings and houses. How rapidly time passes! Olenka's house grew dingy, the roof got rusty, the shed sank on one side, and the whole yard was overgrown with docks and stinging-nettles. Olenka herself had grown plain and elderly; in summer she sat in the porch, and her soul, as before, was empty and dreary and full of bitterness. In winter she sat at her window and looked at the snow. When she caught the scent of spring, or heard the chime of the church bells, a sudden rush of memories from the past came over her, there was a tender ache in her heart, and her eyes brimmed over with tears; but this was only for a minute, and then came emptiness again and the sense of the futility of life. The black kitten, Briska, rubbed against her and purred softly, but Olenka was not touched by these feline caresses. That was not what she needed. She wanted a love that would absorb her whole being, her whole soul and reason - that would give her ideas and an object in life, and would warm her old blood. And she would shake the kitten off her skirt and say with vexation:

"Get along; I don't want you!"

And so it was, day after day and year after year, and no joy, and no opinions. Whatever Mavra, the cook, said she accepted.

One hot July day, towards evening, just as the cattle were being driven away, and the whole yard was full of dust, some one suddenly knocked at the gate. Olenka went to open it herself and was dumbfounded when she looked out: she saw Smirnin, the veterinary surgeon, grey-headed, and dressed as a civilian. She suddenly remembered everything. She could not help crying and letting her head fall on his breast without uttering a word, and in the violence of her feeling she did not notice how they both walked into the house and sat down to tea.

"My dear Vladimir Platonitch! What fate has brought you?" she muttered, trembling with joy.

"I want to settle here for good, Olga Semyonovna," he told her. "I have resigned my post, and have come to settle down and try my luck on my own account. Besides, it's time for my boy to go to school. He's a big boy. I am reconciled with my wife, you know."

"Where is she?' asked Olenka.

"She's at the hotel with the boy, and I'm looking for lodgings."

"Good gracious, my dear soul! Lodgings? Why not have my house? Why shouldn't that suit you? Why, my goodness, I wouldn't take any rent!" cried Olenka in a flutter, beginning to cry again. "You live here, and the lodge will do nicely for me. Oh dear! how glad I am!"

Next day the roof was painted and the walls were whitewashed, and Olenka, with her arms akimbo walked about the yard giving directions. Her face was beaming with her old smile, and she was brisk and alert as though she had waked from a long sleep. The veterinary's wife arrived - a thin, plain lady, with short hair and a peevish expression. With her was her little Sasha, a boy of ten, small for his age, blue-eyed, chubby, with dimples in his cheeks. And scarcely had the boy walked into the yard when he ran after the cat, and at once there was the sound of his gay, joyous laugh.

"Is that your puss, auntie?" he asked Olenka. "When she has little ones, do give us a kitten. Mamma is awfully afraid of mice."

Olenka talked to him, and gave him tea. Her heart warmed and there was a sweet ache in her bosom, as though the boy had been her own child. And when he sat at the table in the evening, going over his lessons, she looked at him with deep tenderness and pity as she murmured to herself:

"You pretty pet! . . . my precious! . . . Such a fair little thing, and so clever."

" 'An island is a piece of land which is entirely surrounded by water,' " he read aloud.

"An island is a piece of land," she repeated, and this was the first opinion to which she gave utterance with positive conviction after so many years of silence and dearth of ideas.

Now she had opinions of her own, and at supper she talked to Sasha's parents, saying how difficult the lessons were at the high schools, but that yet the high school was better than a commercial one, since with a high-school education all careers were open to one, such as being a doctor or an engineer.

Sasha began going to the high school. His mother departed to Harkov to her sister's and did not return; his father used to go off every day to inspect cattle, and would often be away from home for three days together, and it seemed to Olenka as though Sasha was entirely abandoned, that he was not wanted at home, that he was being starved, and she carried him off to her lodge and gave him a little room there.

And for six months Sasha had lived in the lodge with her. Every morning Olenka came into his bedroom and found him fast asleep, sleeping noiselessly with his hand under his cheek. She was sorry to wake him.

"Sashenka," she would say mournfully, "get up, darling. It's time for school."

He would get up, dress and say his prayers, and then sit down to breakfast, drink three glasses of tea, and eat two large cracknels and a half a buttered roll. All this time he was hardly awake and a little ill-humoured in consequence.

"You don't quite know your fable, Sashenka," Olenka would say, looking at him as though he were about to set off on a long journey. "What a lot of trouble I have with you! You must work and do your best, darling, and obey your teachers."

"Oh, do leave me alone!" Sasha would say.

Then he would go down the street to school, a little figure, wearing a big cap and carrying a satchel on his shoulder. Olenka would follow him noiselessly.

"Sashenka!" she would call after him, and she would pop into his hand a date or a caramel. When he reached the street where the school was, he would feel ashamed of being followed by a tall, stout woman, he would turn round and say:

"You'd better go home, auntie. I can go the rest of the way alone."

She would stand still and look after him fixedly till he had disappeared at the school-gate.

Ah, how she loved him! Of her former attachments not one had been so deep; never had her soul surrendered to any feeling so spontaneously, so disinterestedly, and so joyously as now that her maternal instincts were aroused. For this little boy with the dimple in his cheek and the big school cap, she would have given her whole life, she would have given it with joy and tears of tenderness. Why? Who can tell why?

When she had seen the last of Sasha, she returned home, contented and serene, brimming over with love; her face, which had grown younger during the last six months, smiled and beamed; people meeting her looked at her with pleasure.

"Good-morning, Olga Semyonovna, darling. How are you, darling?"

"The lessons at the high school are very difficult now," she would relate at the market. "It's too much; in the first class yesterday they gave him a fable to learn by heart, and a Latin translation and a problem. You know it's too much for a little chap."

And she would begin talking about the teachers, the lessons, and the school books, saying just what Sasha said.

At three o'clock they had dinner together: in the evening they learned their lessons together and cried. When she put him to bed, she would stay a long time making the Cross over him and murmuring a prayer; then she would go to bed and dream of that far-away misty future when Sasha would finish his studies and become a doctor or an engineer, would have a big house of his own with horses and a carriage, would get married and have children. . . . She would fall asleep still thinking of the same thing, and tears would run down her cheeks from her closed eyes, while the black cat lay purring beside her: "Mrr, mrr, mrr."

Suddenly there would come a loud knock at the gate.

Olenka would wake up breathless with alarm, her heart throbbing. Half a minute later would come another knock.

"It must be a telegram from Harkov," she would think, beginning to tremble from head to foot. "Sasha's mother is sending for him from Harkov. . . . Oh, mercy on us!"

She was in despair. Her head, her hands, and her feet would turn chill, and she would feel that she was the most unhappy woman in the world. But another minute would pass, voices would be heard: it would turn out to be the veterinary surgeon coming home from the club.

"Well, thank God!" she would think.

And gradually the load in her heart would pass off, and she would feel at ease. She would go back to bed thinking of Sasha, who lay sound asleep in the next room, sometimes crying out in his sleep:

"I'll give it you! Get away! Shut up!"

THE NEW VILLA

I

Two miles from the village of Obrutchanovo a huge bridge was being built. From the village, which stood up high on the steep river-bank, its trellis-like skeleton could be seen, and in foggy weather and on still winter days, when its delicate iron girders and all the scaffolding around was covered with hoar frost, it presented a picturesque and even fantastic spectacle. Kutcherov, the engineer who was building the bridge, a stout, broad-shouldered, bearded man in a soft crumpled cap drove through the village in his racing droshky or his open carriage. Now and then on holidays navvies working on the bridge would come to the village; they begged for alms, laughed at the women, and sometimes carried off something. But that was rare; as a rule the days passed quietly and peacefully as though no bridge-building were going on, and only in the evening, when camp fires gleamed near the bridge, the wind faintly wafted the songs of the navvies. And by day there was sometimes the mournful clang of metal, don-don-don.

It happened that the engineer's wife came to see him. She was pleased with the river-banks and the gorgeous view over the green valley with trees, churches, flocks, and she began begging her husband to buy a small piece of ground and to build them a cottage on it. Her husband agreed. They bought sixty acres of land, and on the high bank in a field, where in earlier days the cows of Obrutchanovo used to wander, they built a pretty house of two storeys with a terrace and a verandah, with a tower and a flagstaff on which a flag fluttered on Sundays - they built it in about three months, and then all the winter they were planting big trees, and when spring came and everything began to be green there were already avenues to the new house, a gardener and two labourers in white aprons were digging near it, there was a little fountain, and a globe of looking-glass flashed so brilliantly that it was painful to look at. The house had already been named the New Villa.

On a bright, warm morning at the end of May two horses were brought to Obrutchanovo to the village blacksmith, Rodion Petrov. They came from the New Villa. The horses were sleek, graceful beasts, as white as snow, and strikingly alike.

"Perfect swans!" said Rodion, gazing at them with reverent admiration.

His wife Stepanida, his children and grandchildren came out into the street to look at them. By degrees a crowd collected. The Lytchkovs, father and son, both men with swollen faces and entirely beardless, came up bareheaded. Kozov, a tall, thin old man with a long, narrow beard, came up leaning on a stick with a crook handle: he kept winking with his crafty eyes and smiling ironically as though he knew something.

"It's only that they are white; what is there in them?" he said. "Put mine on oats, and they will be just as sleek. They ought to be in a plough and with a whip, too. . . ."

The coachman simply looked at him with disdain, but did not utter a word. And afterwards, while they were blowing up the fire at the forge, the coachman talked while he smoked cigarettes. The peasants learned from him various details: his employers were wealthy people; his mistress, Elena Ivanovna, had till her marriage lived in Moscow in a poor way as a governess; she was kind-hearted, compassionate, and fond of helping the poor. On the new estate, he told them, they were not going to plough or to sow, but simply to live for their pleasure, live only to breathe the fresh air. When he had finished and led the horses back a crowd of boys followed him, the dogs barked, and Kozov, looking after him, winked sarcastically.

"Landowners, too-oo!" he said. "They have built a house and set up horses, but I bet they are nobodies - landowners, too-oo."

Kozov for some reason took a dislike from the first to the new house, to the white horses, and to the handsome, well-fed coachman. Kozov was a solitary man, a widower; he had a dreary life (he was prevented from working by a disease which he sometimes called a rupture and sometimes worms) he was maintained by his son, who worked at a confectioner's in Harkov and sent him money; and from early morning till evening he sauntered at leisure about the river or about the village; if he saw, for instance, a peasant carting a log, or fishing, he would say: "That log's dry wood - it is rotten," or, "They won't bite in weather like this." In times of drought he would declare that there would not be a drop of rain till the frost came; and when the rains came he would say that everything would rot in the fields, that everything was ruined. And as he said these things he would wink as though he knew something.

At the New Villa they burned Bengal lights and sent up fireworks in the evenings, and a sailing-boat with red lanterns floated by Obrutchanovo. One morning the engineer's wife, Elena Ivanovna, and her little daughter drove to the village in a carriage with yellow wheels and a pair of dark bay ponies; both mother and daughter were wearing broad-brimmed straw hats, bent down over their ears.

This was exactly at the time when they were carting manure, and the blacksmith Rodion, a tall, gaunt old man, bareheaded and barefooted, was standing near his dirty and repulsive-looking cart and, flustered, looked at the ponies, and it was evident by his face that he had never seen such little horses before.

"The Kutcherov lady has come!" was whispered around. "Look, the Kutcherov lady has come!"

Elena Ivanovna looked at the huts as though she were selecting one, and then stopped at the very poorest, at the windows of which there were so many children's heads - flaxen, red, and dark. Stepanida, Rodion's wife, a stout woman, came running out of the hut; her kerchief slipped off her grey head; she looked at the carriage facing the sun, and her face smiled and wrinkled up as though she were blind.

"This is for your children," said Elena Ivanovna, and she gave her three roubles.

Stepanida suddenly burst into tears and bowed down to the ground. Rodion, too, flopped to the ground, displaying his brownish bald head, and as he did so he almost caught his wife in the ribs with the fork. Elena Ivanovna was overcome with confusion and drove back.

II

The Lytchkovs, father and son, caught in their meadows two cart-horses, a pony, and a broad-faced Aalhaus bull-calf, and with the help of red-headed Volodka, son of the blacksmith Rodion, drove them to the village. They called the village elder, collected witnesses, and went to look at the damage.

"All right, let 'em!" said Kozov, winking, "le-et em! Let them get out of it if they can, the engineers! Do you think there is no such thing as law? All right! Send for the police inspector, draw up a statement! . . ."

"Draw up a statement," repeated Volodka.

"I don't want to let this pass!" shouted the younger Lytchkov. He shouted louder and louder, and his beardless face seemed to be more and more swollen. "They've set up a nice fashion! Leave them free, and they will ruin all the meadows! You've no sort of right to ill-treat people! We are not serfs now!"

"We are not serfs now!" repeated Volodka.

"We got on all right without a bridge," said the elder Lytchkov gloomily; "we did not ask for it. What do we want a bridge for? We don't want it!"

"Brothers, good Christians, we cannot leave it like this!"

"All right, let 'em!" said Kozov, winking. "Let them get out of it if they can! Landowners, indeed!"

They went back to the village, and as they walked the younger Lytchkov beat himself on the breast with his fist and shouted all the way, and Volodka shouted, too, repeating his words. And meanwhile quite a crowd had gathered in the village round the thoroughbred bull-calf and the horses. The bullcalf was embarrassed and looked up from under his brows, but suddenly lowered his muzzle to the ground and took to his heels, kicking up his hind legs; Kozov was frightened and waved his stick at him, and they all burst out laughing. Then they locked up the beasts and waited.

In the evening the engineer sent five roubles for the damage, and the two horses, the pony and the bull-calf, without being fed or given water, returned home, their heads hanging with a guilty air as though they were convicted criminals.

On getting the five roubles the Lytchkovs, father and son, the village elder and Volodka, punted over the river in a boat and went to a hamlet on the other side where there was a tavern, and there had a long carousal. Their singing and the shouting of the younger Lytchkov could be heard from the village. Their women were uneasy and did not sleep all night. Rodion did not sleep either.

"It's a bad business," he said, sighing and turning from side to side. "The gentleman will be angry, and then there will be trouble. . . . They have insulted the gentleman. . . . Oh, they've insulted him. It's a bad business. . ."

It happened that the peasants, Rodion amongst them, went into their forest to divide the clearings for mowing, and as they were returning home they were met by the engineer. He was wearing a red cotton shirt and high boots; a setter dog with its long tongue hanging out, followed behind him.

"Good-day, brothers," he said.

The peasants stopped and took off their hats.

"I have long wanted to have a talk with you, friends," he went on. "This is what it is. Ever since the early spring your cattle have been in my copse and garden every day. Everything is trampled down; the pigs have rooted up the meadow, are ruining everything in the kitchen garden, and all the undergrowth in the copse is destroyed. There is no getting on with your herdsmen; one asks them civilly, and they are rude. Damage is done on my estate every day and I do nothing - I don't fine you or make a complaint; meanwhile you impounded my horses and my bull calf and exacted five roubles. Was that right? Is that neighbourly?" he went on, and his face was so soft and persuasive, and his expression was not forbidding. "Is that the way decent people behave? A week ago one of your people cut down two oak saplings in my copse. You have dug up the road to Eresnevo, and now I have to go two miles round. Why do you injure me at every step? What harm have I done you? For God's sake, tell me! My wife and I do our utmost to live with you in peace and harmony; we help the peasants as we can. My wife is a kind, warm-hearted woman; she never refuses you help. That is her dream - to be of use to you and your children. You reward us with evil for our good. You are unjust, my friends. Think of that. I ask you earnestly to think it over. We treat you humanely; repay us in the same coin."

He turned and went away. The peasants stood a little longer, put on their caps and walked away. Rodion, who always understood everything that was said to him in some peculiar way of his own, heaved a sigh and said:

"We must pay. 'Repay in coin, my friends' . . . he said."

They walked to the village in silence. On reaching home Rodion said his prayer, took off his boots, and sat down on the bench beside his wife. Stepanida and he always sat side by side when they were at home, and always walked side by side in the street; they ate and they drank and they slept always together, and the older they grew the more they loved one another. It was hot and crowded in their hut, and there were children everywhere - on the floors, in the windows, on the stove. . . . In spite of her advanced years Stepanida was still bearing children, and now, looking at the crowd of children, it was hard to distinguish which were Rodion's and which were Volodka's. Volodka's wife, Lukerya, a plain young woman with prominent eyes and a nose like the beak of a bird, was kneading dough in a tub; Volodka was sitting on the stove with his legs hanging.

"On the road near Nikita's buckwheat . . . the engineer with his dog . . ." Rodion began, after a rest, scratching his ribs and his elbow. " 'You must pay,' says he . . . 'coin,' says he. . . . Coin or no coin, we shall have to collect ten kopecks from every hut. We've offended the gentleman very much. I am sorry for him. . . ."

"We've lived without a bridge," said Volodka, not looking at anyone, "and we don't want one."

"What next; the bridge is a government business."

"We don't want it."

"Your opinion is not asked. What is it to you?"

" 'Your opinion is not asked,' " Volodka mimicked him. "We don't want to drive anywhere; what do we want with a bridge? If we have to, we can cross by the boat."

Someone from the yard outside knocked at the window so violently that it seemed to shake the whole hut.

"Is Volodka at home?" he heard the voice of the younger Lytchkov. "Volodka, come out, come along."

Volodka jumped down off the stove and began looking for his cap.

"Don't go, Volodka," said Rodion diffidently. "Don't go with them, son. You are foolish, like a little child; they will teach you no good; don't go!"

"Don't go, son," said Stepanida, and she blinked as though about to shed tears. "I bet they are calling you to the tavern."

" 'To the tavern,' " Volodka mimicked.

"You'll come back drunk again, you currish Herod," said Lukerya, looking at him angrily. "Go along, go along, and may you burn up with vodka, you tailless Satan!"

"You hold your tongue," shouted Volodka.

"They've married me to a fool, they've ruined me, a luckless orphan, you red-headed drunkard . . ." wailed Lukerya, wiping her face with a hand covered with dough. "I wish I had never set eyes on you."

Volodka gave her a blow on the ear and went off.

III

Elena Ivanovna and her little daughter visited the village on foot. They were out for a walk. It was a Sunday, and the peasant women and girls were walking up and down the street in their brightly-coloured dresses. Rodion and Stepanida, sitting side by side at their door, bowed and smiled to Elena Ivanovna and her little daughter as to acquaintances. From the windows more than a dozen children stared at them; their faces expressed amazement and curiosity, and they could be heard whispering:

"The Kutcherov lady has come! The Kutcherov lady!"

"Good-morning," said Elena Ivanovna, and she stopped; she paused, and then asked: "Well, how are you getting on?"

"We get along all right, thank God," answered Rodion, speaking rapidly. "To be sure we get along."

"The life we lead!" smiled Stepanida. "You can see our poverty yourself, dear lady! The family is fourteen souls in all, and only two bread-winners. We are supposed to be blacksmiths, but when they bring us a horse to shoe we have no coal, nothing to buy it with. We are worried to death, lady," she went on, and laughed. "Oh, oh, we are worried to death."

Elena Ivanovna sat down at the entrance and, putting her arm round her little girl, pondered something, and judging from the little girl's expression, melancholy thoughts were straying through her mind, too; as she brooded she played with the sumptuous lace on the parasol she had taken out of her mother's hands.

"Poverty," said Rodion, "a great deal of anxiety - you see no end to it. Here, God sends no rain . . . our life is not easy, there is no denying it."

"You have a hard time in this life," said Elena Ivanovna, "but in the other world you will be happy."

Rodion did not understand her, and simply coughed into his clenched hand by way of reply. Stepanida said:

"Dear lady, the rich men will be all right in the next world, too. The rich put up candles, pay for services; the rich give to beggars, but what can the poor man do? He has no time to make the sign of the cross. He is the beggar of beggars himself; how can he think of his soul? And many sins come from poverty; from trouble we snarl at one another like dogs, we haven't a good word to say to one another, and all sorts of things happen, dear lady - God forbid! It seems we have no luck in this world nor the next. All the luck has fallen to the rich."

She spoke gaily; she was evidently used to talking of her hard life. And Rodion smiled, too; he was pleased that his old woman was so clever, so ready of speech.

"It is only on the surface that the rich seem to be happy," said Elena Ivanovna. "Every man has his sorrow. Here my husband and I do not live poorly, we have means, but are we happy? I am young, but I have had four children; my children are always being ill. I am ill, too, and constantly being doctored."

"And what is your illness?" asked Rodion.

"A woman's complaint. I get no sleep; a continual headache gives me no peace. Here I am sitting and talking, but my head is bad, I am weak all over, and I should prefer the hardest labour to such a condition. My soul, too, is troubled; I am in continual fear for my children, my husband. Every family has its own trouble of some sort; we have ours. I am not of noble birth. My grandfather was a simple peasant, my father was a tradesman in Moscow; he was a plain, uneducated man, too, while my husband's parents were wealthy and distinguished. They did not want him to marry me, but he disobeyed them, quarrelled with them, and they have not forgiven us to this day. That worries my husband; it troubles him and keeps him in constant agitation; he loves his mother, loves her dearly. So I am uneasy, too, my soul is in pain."

Peasants, men and women, were by now standing round Rodion's hut and listening. Kozov came up, too, and stood twitching his long, narrow beard. The Lytchkovs, father and son, drew near.

"And say what you like, one cannot be happy and satisfied if one does not feel in one's proper place." Elena Ivanovna went on. "Each of you has his strip of land, each of you works and knows what he is working for; my husband builds bridges - in short, everyone has his place, while I, I simply walk about. I have not my bit to work. I don't work, and feel as though I were an outsider. I am saying all this that you may not judge from outward appearances; if a man is expensively dressed and has means it does not prove that he is satisfied with his life."

She got up to go away and took her daughter by the hand.

"I like your place here very much," she said, and smiled, and from that faint, diffident smile one could tell how unwell she really was, how young and how pretty; she had a pale, thinnish face with dark eyebrows and fair hair. And the little girl was just such another as her mother: thin, fair, and slender. There was a fragrance of scent about them.

"I like the river and the forest and the village," Elena Ivanovna went on; "I could live here all my life, and I feel as though here I should get strong and find my place. I want to help you - I want to dreadfully - to be of use, to be a real friend to you. I know your need, and what I don't know I feel, my heart guesses. I am sick, feeble, and for me perhaps it is not possible to change my life as I would. But I have children. I will try to bring them up that they may be of use to you, may love you. I shall impress upon them continually that their life does not belong to them, but to you. Only I beg you earnestly, I beseech you, trust us, live in friendship with us. My husband is a kind, good man. Don't worry him, don't irritate him. He is sensitive to every trifle, and yesterday, for instance, your cattle were in our vegetable garden, and one of your people broke down the fence to the bee-hives, and such an attitude to us drives my husband to despair. I beg you," she went on in an imploring voice, and she clasped her hands on her bosom - "I beg you to treat us as good neighbours; let us live in peace! There is a saying, you know, that even a bad peace is better than a good quarrel, and, 'Don't buy property, but buy neighbours.' I repeat my husband is a kind man and good; if all goes well we promise to do everything in our power for you; we will mend the roads, we will build a school for your children. I promise you."

"Of course we thank you humbly, lady," said Lytchkov the father, looking at the ground; "you are educated people; it is for you to know best. Only, you see, Voronov, a rich peasant at Eresnevo, promised to build a school; he, too, said, 'I will do this for you,' 'I will do that for you,' and he only put up the framework and refused to go on. And then they made the peasants put the roof on and finish it; it cost them a thousand roubles. Voronov did not care; he only stroked his beard, but the peasants felt it a bit hard."

"That was a crow, but now there's a rook, too," said Kozov, and he winked.

There was the sound of laughter.

"We don't want a school," said Volodka sullenly. "Our children go to Petrovskoe, and they can go on going there; we don't want it."

Elena Ivanovna seemed suddenly intimidated; her face looked paler and thinner, she shrank into herself as though she had been touched with something coarse, and walked away without uttering another word. And she walked more and more quickly, without looking round.

"Lady," said Rodion, walking after her, "lady, wait a bit; hear what I would say to you."

He followed her without his cap, and spoke softly as though begging.

"Lady, wait and hear what I will say to you."

They had walked out of the village, and Elena Ivanovna stopped beside a cart in the shade of an old mountain ash.

"Don't be offended, lady," said Rodion. "What does it mean? Have patience. Have patience for a couple of years. You will live here, you will have patience, and it will all come round. Our folks are good and peaceable; there's no harm in them; it's God's truth I'm telling you. Don't mind Kozov and the Lytchkovs, and don't mind Volodka. He's a fool; he listens to the first that speaks. The others are quiet folks; they are silent. Some would be glad, you know, to say a word from the heart and to stand up for themselves, but cannot. They have a heart and a conscience, but no tongue. Don't be offended . . . have patience. . . . What does it matter?"

Elena Ivanovna looked at the broad, tranquil river, pondering, and tears flowed down her cheeks. And Rodion was troubled by those tears; he almost cried himself.

"Never mind . . ." he muttered. "Have patience for a couple of years. You can have the school, you can have the roads, only not all at once. If you went, let us say, to sow corn on that mound you would first have to weed it out, to pick out all the stones, and then to plough, and work and work . . . and with the people, you see, it is the same . . . you must work and work until you overcome them."

The crowd had moved away from Rodion's hut, and was coming along the street towards the mountain ash. They began singing songs and playing the concertina, and they kept coming closer and closer. . . .

"Mamma, let us go away from here," said the little girl, huddling up to her mother, pale and shaking all over; "let us go away, mamma!

"Where?"

"To Moscow. . . . Let us go, mamma."

The child began crying.

Rodion was utterly overcome; his face broke into profuse perspiration; he took out of his pocket a little crooked cucumber, like a half-moon, covered with crumbs of rye bread, and began thrusting it into the little girl's hands.

"Come, come," he muttered, scowling severely; "take the little cucumber, eat it up. . . . You mustn't cry. Mamma will whip you. . . . She'll tell your father of you when you get home. Come, come. . . ."

They walked on, and he still followed behind them, wanting to say something friendly and persuasive to them. And seeing that they were both absorbed in their own thoughts and their own griefs, and not noticing him, he stopped and, shading his eyes from the sun, looked after them for a long time till they disappeared into their copse.

IV

The engineer seemed to grow irritable and petty, and in every trivial incident saw an act of robbery or outrage. His gate was kept bolted even by day, and at night two watchmen walked up and down the garden beating a board; and they gave up employing anyone from Obrutchanovo as a labourer. As ill-luck would have it someone (either a peasant or one of the workmen) took the new wheels off the cart and replaced them by old ones, then soon afterwards two bridles and a pair of pincers were carried off, and murmurs arose even in the village. People began to say that a search should be made at the Lytchkovs' and at Volodka's, and then the bridles and the pincers were found under the hedge in the engineer's garden; someone had thrown them down there.

It happened that the peasants were coming in a crowd out of the forest, and again they met the engineer on the road. He stopped, and without wishing them good-day he began, looking angrily first at one, then at another:

"I have begged you not to gather mushrooms in the park and near the yard, but to leave them for my wife and children, but your girls come before daybreak and there is not a mushroom left. . . .Whether one asks you or not it makes no difference. Entreaties, and friendliness, and persuasion I see are all useless."

He fixed his indignant eyes on Rodion and went on:

"My wife and I behaved to you as human beings, as to our equals, and you? But what's the use of talking! It will end by our looking down upon you. There is nothing left!"

And making an effort to restrain his anger, not to say too much, he turned and went on.

On getting home Rodion said his prayer, took off his boots, and sat down beside his wife.

"Yes . . ." he began with a sigh. "We were walking along just now, and Mr. Kutcherov met us. . . . Yes. . . . He saw the girls at daybreak. . . 'Why don't they bring mushrooms,' . . . he said 'to my wife and children?' he said. . . . And then he looked at me and he said: 'I and my wife will look after you,' he said. I wanted to fall down at his feet, but I hadn't the courage. . . . God give him health. . . God bless him! . . ."

Stephania crossed herself and sighed.

"They are kind, simple-hearted people," Rodion went on. " 'We shall look after you.' . . . He promised me that before everyone. In our old age . . . it wouldn't be a bad thing. . . . I should always pray for them. . . . Holy Mother, bless them. . . ."

The Feast of the Exaltation of the Cross, the fourteenth of September, was the festival of the village church. The Lytchkovs, father and son, went across the river early in the morning and returned to dinner drunk; they spent a long time going about the village, alternately singing and swearing; then they had a fight and went to the New Villa to complain. First Lytchkov the father went into the yard with a long ashen stick in his hands. He stopped irresolutely and took off his hat. Just at that moment the engineer and his family were sitting on the verandah, drinking tea.

"What do you want?" shouted the engineer.

"Your honour . . ." Lytchkov began, and burst into tears. "Show the Divine mercy, protect me . . . my son makes my life a misery . . . your honour. . ."

Lytchkov the son walked up, too; he, too, was bareheaded and had a stick in his hand; he stopped and fixed his drunken senseless eyes on the verandah.

"It is not my business to settle your affairs," said the engineer. "Go to the rural captain or the police officer."

"I have been everywhere. . . . I have lodged a petition . . ." said Lytchkov the father, and he sobbed. "Where can I go now? He can kill me now, it seems. He can do anything. Is that the way to treat a father? A father?"

He raised his stick and hit his son on the head; the son raised his stick and struck his father just on his bald patch such a blow that the stick bounced back. The father did not even flinch, but hit his son again and again on the head. And so they stood and kept hitting one another on the head, and it looked not so much like a fight as some sort of a game. And peasants, men and women, stood in a crowd at the gate and looked into the garden, and the faces of all were grave. They were the peasants who had come to greet them for the holiday, but seeing the Lytchkovs, they were ashamed and did not go in.

The next morning Elena Ivanovna went with the children to Moscow. And there was a rumour that the engineer was selling his house. . . .

V

The peasants had long ago grown used to the sight of the bridge, and it was difficult to imagine the river at that place without a bridge. The heap of rubble left from the building of it had long been overgrown with grass, the navvies were forgotten, and instead of the strains of the

"Dubinushka" that they used to sing, the peasants heard almost every hour the sounds of a passing train.

The New Villa has long ago been sold; now it belongs to a government clerk who comes here from the town for the holidays with his family, drinks tea on the terrace, and then goes back to the town again. He wears a cockade on his cap; he talks and clears his throat as though he were a very important official, though he is only of the rank of a collegiate secretary, and when the peasants bow he makes no response.

In Obrutchanovo everyone has grown older; Kozov is dead. In Rodion's hut there are even more children. Volodka has grown a long red beard. They are still as poor as ever.

In the early spring the Obrutchanovo peasants were sawing wood near the station. And after work they were going home; they walked without haste one after the other. Broad saws curved over their shoulders; the sun was reflected in them. The nightingales were singing in the bushes on the bank, larks were trilling in the heavens. It was quiet at the New Villa; there was not a soul there, and only golden pigeons - golden because the sunlight was streaming upon them - were flying over the house. All of them - Rodion, the two Lytchkovs, and Volodka - thought of the white horses, the little ponies, the fireworks, the boat with the lanterns; they remembered how the engineer's wife, so beautiful and so grandly dressed, had come into the village and talked to them in such a friendly way. And it seemed as though all that had never been; it was like a dream or a fairy-tale.

They trudged along, tired out, and mused as they went. . . . In their village, they mused, the people were good, quiet, sensible, fearing God, and Elena Ivanovna, too, was quiet, kind, and gentle; it made one sad to look at her, but why had they not got on together? Why had they parted like enemies? How was it that some mist had shrouded from their eyes what mattered most, and had let them see nothing but damage done by cattle, bridles, pincers, and all those trivial things which now, as they remembered them, seemed so nonsensical? How was it that with the new owner they lived in peace, and yet had been on bad terms with the engineer?

And not knowing what answer to make to these questions they were all silent except Volodka, who muttered something.

"What is it?" Rodion asked.

"We lived without a bridge . . ." said Volodka gloomily. "We lived without a bridge, and did not ask for one . . . and we don't want it. . . ."

No one answered him and they walked on in silence with drooping heads.

ON OFFICIAL DUTY

The deputy examining magistrate and the district doctor were going to an inquest in the village of Syrnya. On the road they were overtaken by a snowstorm; they spent a long time going round and round, and arrived, not at midday, as they had intended, but in the evening when it was dark. They put up for the night at the Zemstvo hut. It so happened that it was in this hut that the dead body was lying - the corpse of the Zemstvo insurance agent, Lesnitsky, who had arrived in Syrnya three days before and, ordering the samovar in the hut, had shot himself, to the great surprise of everyone; and the fact that he had ended his life so strangely, after unpacking his eatables and laying them out on the table, and with the samovar before him, led many people to suspect that it was a case of murder; an inquest was necessary.

In the outer room the doctor and the examining magistrate shook the snow off themselves and knocked it off their boots. And meanwhile the old village constable, Ilya Loshadin, stood by, holding a little tin lamp. There was a strong smell of paraffin.

"Who are you?" asked the doctor.

"Conshtable, . . ." answered the constable.

He used to spell it "conshtable" when he signed the receipts at the post office.

"And where are the witnesses?"

"They must have gone to tea, your honor."

On the right was the parlor, the travelers' or gentry's room; on the left the kitchen, with a big stove and sleeping shelves under the rafters. The doctor and the examining magistrate, followed by the constable, holding the lamp high above his head, went into the parlor. Here a still, long body covered with white linen was lying on the floor close to the table-legs. In the dim light of the lamp they could clearly see, besides the white covering, new rubber goloshes, and everything about it was uncanny and sinister: the dark walls, and the silence, and the goloshes, and the stillness of the dead body. On the table stood a samovar, cold long ago; and round it parcels, probably the eatables.

"To shoot oneself in the Zemstvo hut, how tactless!" said the doctor. "If one does want to put a bullet through one's brains, one ought to do it at home in some outhouse."

He sank on to a bench, just as he was, in his cap, his fur coat, and his felt overboots; his fellow-traveler, the examining magistrate, sat down opposite.

"These hysterical, neurasthenic people are great egoists," the doctor went on hotly. "If a neurasthenic sleeps in the same room with you, he rustles his newspaper; when he dines with you, he gets up a scene with his wife without troubling about your presence; and when he feels inclined to shoot himself, he shoots himself in a village in a Zemstvo hut, so as to give the maximum of trouble to everybody. These gentlemen in every circumstance of life think of no one but themselves! That's why the elderly so dislike our 'nervous age.'"

"The elderly dislike so many things," said the examining magistrate, yawning. "You should point out to the elder generation what the difference is between the suicides of the past and the suicides of to-day. In the old days the so-called gentleman shot himself because he had made away with Government money, but nowadays it is because he is sick of life, depressed. . . . Which is better?"

"Sick of life, depressed; but you must admit that he might have shot himself somewhere else."

"Such trouble!" said the constable, "such trouble! It's a real affliction. The people are very much upset, your honor; they haven't slept these three nights. The children are crying. The cows ought to be milked, but the women won't go to the stall - they are afraid . . . for fear the gentleman should appear to them in the darkness. Of course they are silly women, but some of the men are frightened too. As soon as it is dark they won't go by the hut one by one, but only in a flock together. And the witnesses too. . . ."

Dr. Startchenko, a middle-aged man in spectacles with a dark beard, and the examining magistrate Lyzhin, a fair man, still young, who had only taken his degree two years before and looked more like a student than an official, sat in silence, musing. They were vexed that they were late. Now they had to wait till morning, and to stay here for the night, though it was not yet six o'clock; and they had before them a long evening, a dark night, boredom, uncomfortable beds, beetles, and cold in the morning; and listening to the blizzard that howled in the chimney and in the loft, they both thought how unlike all this was the life which they would have chosen for themselves and of which they had once dreamed, and how far away they both were from their contemporaries, who were at that moment walking about the lighted streets in town without noticing the weather, or were getting ready for the theatre, or sitting in their studies over a book. Oh, how much they would have given now only to stroll along the Nevsky Prospect, or along Petrovka in Moscow, to listen to decent singing, to sit for an hour or so in a restaurant!

"Oo-oo-oo-oo!" sang the storm in the loft, and something outside slammed viciously, probably the signboard on the hut. "Oo-oo-oo-oo!"

"You can do as you please, but I have no desire to stay here," said Startchenko, getting up. "It's not six yet, it's too early to go to bed; I am off. Von Taunitz lives not far from here, only a couple of miles from Syrnya. I shall go to see him and spend the evening there. Constable, run and tell my coachman not to take the horses out. And what are you going to do?" he asked Lyzhin.

"I don't know; I expect I shall go to sleep."

The doctor wrapped himself in his fur coat and went out. Lyzhin could hear him talking to the coachman and the bells beginning to quiver on the frozen horses. He drove off.

"It is not nice for you, sir, to spend the night in here," said the constable; "come into the other room. It's dirty, but for one night it won't matter. I'll get a samovar from a peasant and heat it directly. I'll heap up some hay for you, and then you go to sleep, and God bless you, your honor."

A little later the examining magistrate was sitting in the kitchen drinking tea, while Loshadin, the constable, was standing at the door talking. He was an old man about sixty, short and very thin, bent and white, with a naïve smile on his face and watery eyes, and he kept smacking with his lips as though he were sucking a sweetmeat. He was wearing a short sheepskin coat and high felt boots, and held his stick in his hands all the time. The youth of the examining magistrate aroused his compassion, and that was probably why he addressed him familiarly.

"The elder gave orders that he was to be informed when the police superintendent or the examining magistrate came," he said, "so I suppose I must go now. . . . It's nearly three miles to the *volost*, and the storm, the snowdrifts, are something terrible - maybe one won't get there before midnight. Ough! how the wind roars!"

"I don't need the elder," said Lyzhin. "There is nothing for him to do here."

He looked at the old man with curiosity, and asked:

"Tell me, grandfather, how many years have you been constable? "

"How many? Why, thirty years. Five years after the Freedom I began going as constable, that's how I reckon it. And from that time I have been going every day since. Other people have holidays, but I am always going. When it's Easter and the church bells are ringing and Christ has risen, I still go about with my bag - to the treasury, to the post, to the police superintendent's lodgings, to the rural captain, to the tax inspector, to the municipal office, to the gentry, to the peasants, to all orthodox Christians. I carry parcels, notices, tax papers, letters, forms of different sorts, circulars, and to be sure, kind gentleman, there are all sorts of forms nowadays, so as to note down the numbers - yellow, white, and red - and every gentleman or priest or well-to-do peasant must write down a dozen times in the year how much he has sown and harvested, how many quarters or poods he has of rye, how many of oats, how many of hay, and what the weather's like, you know, and insects, too, of all sorts. To be sure you can write what you like, it's only a regulation, but one must go and give out the notices and then go again and collect them. Here, for instance, there's no need to cut open the gentleman; you know yourself it's a silly thing, it's only dirtying your hands, and here you have been put to trouble, your honor; you have come because it's the regulation; you can't help it. For thirty years I have been going round according to regulation. In the summer it is all right, it is warm and dry; but in winter and autumn it's uncomfortable At times I have been almost drowned and almost frozen; all sorts of things have happened - wicked people set on me in the forest and took away my bag; I have been beaten, and I have been before a court of law."

"What were you accused of?"

"Of fraud."

"How do you mean?"

"Why, you see, Hrisanf Grigoryev, the clerk, sold the contractor some boards belonging to someone else - cheated him, in fact. I was mixed up in it. They sent me to the tavern for vodka; well, the clerk did not share with me - did not even offer me a glass; but as through my poverty I was - in appearance, I mean - not a man to be relied upon, not a man of any worth, we were both brought to trial; he was sent to prison, but, praise God! I was acquitted on all points. They read a notice, you know, in the court. And they were all in uniforms - in the court, I mean. I can tell you, your honor, my duties for anyone not used to them are terrible, absolutely killing; but to me it is nothing. In fact, my feet ache when I am not walking. And at home it is worse for me. At home one has to heat the stove for the clerk in the *volost* office, to fetch water for him, to clean his boots."

"And what wages do you get?" Lyzhin asked.

"Eighty-four roubles a year."

"I'll bet you get other little sums coming in. You do, don't you?"

"Other little sums? No, indeed! Gentlemen nowadays don't often give tips. Gentlemen nowadays are strict, they take offense at anything. If you bring them a notice they are offended, if you take off your cap before them they are offended. 'You have come to the wrong entrance,' they say. 'You are a drunkard,' they say. 'You smell of onion; you are a blockhead; you are the son of a bitch.' There are kind-hearted ones, of course; but what does one get from them? They only laugh and call one all sorts of names. Mr. Altuhin, for instance, he is a good-natured gentleman; and if you look at him he seems sober and in his right mind, but so soon as he sees me he shouts and does not know what he means himself. He gave me such a name 'You,' said he, . . ." The constable uttered some word, but in such a low voice that it was impossible to make out what he said.

"What?" Lyzhin asked. "Say it again."

" 'Administration,' " the constable repeated aloud. "He has been calling me that for a long while, for the last six years. 'Hullo, Administration!' But I don't mind; let him, God bless him! Sometimes a lady will send one a glass of vodka and a bit of pie and one drinks to her health. But peasants give more; peasants are more kind-hearted, they have the fear of God in their hearts: one will give a bit of bread, another a drop of cabbage soup, another will stand one a glass. The village elders treat one to tea in the tavern. Here the witnesses have gone to their tea. 'Loshadin,' they said, 'you stay here and keep watch for us,' and they gave me a kopeck each. You see, they are frightened, not being used to it, and yesterday they gave me fifteen kopecks and offered me a glass."

"And you, aren't you frightened?"

"I am, sir; but of course it is my duty, there is no getting away from it. In the summer I was taking a convict to the town, and he set upon me and gave me such a drubbing! And all around were fields, forest - how could I get away from him? It's just the same here. I remember the gentleman, Mr. Lesnitsky, when he was so high, and I knew his father and mother. I am from the village of Nedoshtchotova, and they, the Lesnitsky family, were not more than three-quarters of a mile from us and less than that, their ground next to ours, and Mr. Lesnitsky had a sister, a God-fearing and tender-hearted lady. Lord keep the soul of Thy servant Yulya, eternal memory to her! She was never married, and when she was dying she divided all her property; she left three hundred acres to the monastery, and six hundred to the commune of peasants of Nedoshtchotova to commemorate her soul; but her brother hid the will, they do say burnt it in the stove, and took all this land for himself. He thought, to be sure, it was for his benefit; but - nay, wait a bit, you won't get on in the world through injustice, brother. The gentleman did not go to confession for twenty years after. He kept away from the church, to be sure, and died impenitent. He burst. He was a very fat man, so he burst lengthways. Then everything was taken from the young master, from Seryozha, to pay the debts - everything there was. Well, he had not gone very far in his studies, he couldn't do anything, and the president of the Rural Board, his uncle - 'I'll take him' - Seryozha, I mean - thinks he, 'for an agent; let him collect the insurance, that's not a difficult job,' and the gentleman was young and proud, he wanted to be living on a bigger scale and in better style and with more freedom. To be sure it was a come-down for him to be jolting about the district in a wretched cart and talking to the peasants; he would walk and keep looking on the ground, looking on the ground and saying nothing; if you called his name right in his ear, 'Sergey Sergeyitch!' he would look round like this, 'Eh?' and look down on the ground again, and now you see he has laid hands on himself. There's no sense in it, your honor, it's not right, and there's no making out what's the meaning of it, merciful Lord! Say your father was rich and you are poor; it is mortifying, there's no doubt about it, but there, you must make up your mind to it. I used to live in good style, too; I had two horses, your honor, three cows, I used to keep twenty head of sheep; but the time has come, and I am left with nothing but a wretched bag, and even that is not mine but Government property. And now in our Nedoshtchotova, if the truth is to be told, my house is the worst of the lot. Makey had four footmen, and now Makey is a footman himself. Petrak had four laborers, and now Petrak is a laborer himself."

"How was it you became poor?" asked the examining magistrate.

"My sons drink terribly. I could not tell you how they drink, you wouldn't believe it."

Lyzhin listened and thought how he, Lyzhin, would go back sooner or later to Moscow, while this old man would stay here for ever, and would always be walking and walking. And how many times in his life he would come across such battered, unkempt old men, not "men of any worth," in whose souls fifteen kopecks, glasses of vodka, and a profound belief that you can't get on in this life by dishonesty, were equally firmly rooted.

Then he grew tired of listening, and told the old man to bring him some hay for his bed, There was an iron bedstead with a pillow and a quilt in the traveler's room, and it could be fetched in; but the dead man had been lying by it for nearly three days (and perhaps sitting on it just before his death), and it would be disagreeable to sleep upon it now. . . .

"It's only half-past seven," thought Lyzhin, glancing at his watch. "How awful it is!"

He was not sleepy, but having nothing to do to pass away the time, he lay down and covered himself with a rug. Loshadin went in and out several times, clearing away the tea-things; smacking his lips and sighing, he kept tramping round the table; at last he took his little lamp and went out, and, looking at his long, gray-headed, bent figure from behind, Lyzhin thought:

"Just like a magician in an opera."

It was dark. The moon must have been behind the clouds, as the windows and the snow on the window-frames could be seen distinctly.

"Oo-oo-oo!" sang the storm, "Oo-oo-oo-oo!"

"Ho-ho-ly sa-aints!" wailed a woman in the loft, or it sounded like it. "Ho-ho-ly sa-aints!"

"B-booh!" something outside banged against the wall. "Trah!"

The examining magistrate listened: there was no woman up there, it was the wind howling. It was rather cold, and he put his fur coat over his rug. As he got warm he thought how remote all this - the storm, and the hut, and the old man, and the dead body lying in the next room - how remote it all was from the life he desired for himself, and how alien it all was to him, how petty, how uninteresting. If this man had killed himself in Moscow or somewhere in the neighborhood, and he had had to hold an inquest on him there, it would have been interesting, important, and perhaps he might even have been afraid to sleep in the next room to the corpse. Here, nearly a thousand miles from Moscow, all this was seen somehow in a different light; it was not life, they were not human beings, but something only existing "according to the regulation," as Loshadin said; it would leave not the faintest trace in the memory, and would be forgotten as soon as he, Lyzhin, drove away from Syrnya. The fatherland, the real Russia, was Moscow, Petersburg; but here he was in the provinces, the colonies.

When one dreamed of playing a leading part, of becoming a popular figure, of being, for instance, examining magistrate in particularly important cases or prosecutor in a circuit court, of being a society lion, one always thought of Moscow. To live, one must be in Moscow; here one cared for nothing, one grew easily resigned to one's insignificant position, and only expected one thing of life - to get away quickly, quickly. And Lyzhin mentally moved about the Moscow streets, went into the familiar houses, met his kindred, his comrades, and there was a sweet pang at his heart at the thought that he was only twenty-six, and that if in five or ten years he could break away from here and get to Moscow, even then it would not be too late and he would still have a whole life before him. And as he sank into unconsciousness, as his thoughts began to be confused, he imagined the long corridor of the court at Moscow, himself delivering a speech, his sisters, the orchestra which for some reason kept droning: "Oo-oo-oo-oo! Oo-oooo-oo!"

"Booh! Trah!" sounded again. "Booh!"

And he suddenly recalled how one day, when he was talking to the bookkeeper in the little office of the Rural Board, a thin, pale gentleman with black hair and dark eyes walked in; he had a disagreeable look in his eyes such as one sees in people who have slept too long after dinner, and it spoilt his delicate, intelligent profile; and the high boots he was wearing did not suit him, but looked clumsy. The bookkeeper had introduced him: "This is our insurance agent."

"So that was Lesnitsky, . . . this same man," Lyzhin reflected now.

He recalled Lesnitsky's soft voice, imagined his gait, and it seemed to him that someone was walking beside him now with a step like Lesnitsky's.

All at once he felt frightened, his head turned cold.

"Who's there?" he asked in alarm.

"The conshtable!"

"What do you want here?"

"I have come to ask, your honor - you said this evening that you did not want the elder, but I am afraid he may be angry. He told me to go to him. Shouldn't I go?"

"That's enough, you bother me," said Lyzhin with vexation, and he covered himself up again.

"He may be angry. . . . I'll go, your honor. I hope you will be comfortable," and Loshadin went out.

In the passage there was coughing and subdued voices. The witnesses must have returned.

"We'll let those poor beggars get away early to-morrow, . . ." thought the examining magistrate; "we'll begin the inquest as soon as it is daylight."

He began sinking into forgetfulness when suddenly there were steps again, not timid this time but rapid and noisy. There was the slam of a door, voices, the scratching of a match. . . .

"Are you asleep? Are you asleep?" Dr. Startchenko was asking him hurriedly and angrily as he struck one match after another; he was covered with snow, and brought a chill air in with him. "Are you asleep? Get up! Let us go to Von Taunitz's. He has sent his own horses for you. Come along. There, at any rate, you will have supper, and sleep like a human being. You see I have come for you myself. The horses are splendid, we shall get there in twenty minutes."

"And what time is it now?"

"A quarter past ten."

Lyzhin, sleepy and discontented, put on his felt overboots, his furlined coat, his cap and hood, and went out with the doctor. There was not a very sharp frost, but a violent and piercing wind was blowing and driving along the street the clouds of snow which seemed to be racing away in terror: high drifts were heaped up already under the fences and at the doorways. The doctor and the examining magistrate got into the sledge, and the white coachman bent over them to button up the cover. They were both hot.

"Ready!"

They drove through the village. "Cutting a feathery furrow," thought the examining magistrate, listlessly watching the action of the trace horse's legs. There were lights in all the huts, as though it were the eve of a great holiday: the peasants had not gone to bed because they were afraid of the dead body. The coachman preserved a sullen silence, probably he had felt dreary while he was waiting by the Zemstvo hut, and now he, too, was thinking of the dead man.

"At the Von Taunitz's," said Startchenko, "they all set upon me when they heard that you were left to spend the night in the hut, and asked me why I did not bring you with me."

As they drove out of the village, at the turning the coachman suddenly shouted at the top of his voice: "Out of the way!"

They caught a glimpse of a man: he was standing up to his knees in the snow, moving off the road and staring at the horses. The examining magistrate saw a stick with a crook, and a beard and a bag, and he fancied that it was Loshadin, and even fancied that he was smiling. He flashed by and disappeared.

The road ran at first along the edge of the forest, then along a broad forest clearing; they caught glimpses of old pines and a young birch copse, and tall, gnarled young oak trees standing singly in the clearings where the wood had lately been cut; but soon it was all merged in the clouds of snow. The coachman said he could see the forest; the examining magistrate could see nothing but the trace horse. The wind blew on their backs.

All at once the horses stopped.

"Well, what is it now?" asked Startchenko crossly.

The coachman got down from the box without a word and began running round the sledge, treading on his heels; he made larger and larger circles, getting further and further away from the sledge, and it looked as though he were dancing; at last he came back and began to turn off to the right.

"You've got off the road, eh?" asked Startchenko.

"It's all ri-ight. . . ."

Then there was a little village and not a single light in it. Again the forest and the fields. Again they lost the road, and again the coachman got down from the box and danced round the sledge. The sledge flew along a dark avenue, flew swiftly on. And the heated trace horse's hoofs knocked against the sledge. Here there was a fearful roaring sound from the trees, and nothing could be seen, as though they were flying on into space; and all at once the glaring light at the entrance and the windows flashed upon their eyes, and they heard the good-natured, drawn-out barking of dogs. They had arrived.

While they were taking off their fur coats and their felt boots below, "Un Petit Verre de Clicquot" was being played upon the piano overhead, and they could hear the children beating time with their feet. Immediately on going in they were aware of the snug warmth and special smell of the old apartments of a mansion where, whatever the weather outside, life is so warm and clean and comfortable.

"That's capital!" said Von Taunitz, a fat man with an incredibly thick neck and with whiskers, as he shook the examining magistrate's hand. "That's capital! You are very welcome, delighted to make your acquaintance. We are colleagues to some extent, you know. At one time I was deputy prosecutor; but not for long, only two years. I came here to look after the estate, and here I have grown old - an old fogey, in fact. You are very welcome," he went on, evidently restraining his voice so as not to speak too loud; he was going upstairs with his guests. "I have no wife, she's dead. But here, I will introduce my daughters," and turning round, he shouted down the stairs in a voice of thunder: "Tell Ignat to have the sledge ready at eight o'clock to-morrow morning."

His four daughters, young and pretty girls, all wearing gray dresses and with their hair done up in the same style, and their cousin, also young and attractive, with her children, were in the drawing-room. Startchenko, who knew them already, began at once begging them to sing something, and two of the young ladies spent a long time declaring they could not sing and that they had no music; then the cousin sat down to the piano, and with trembling voices, they sang a duet from

"The Queen of Spades." Again "Un Petit Verre de Clicquot" was played, and the children skipped about, beating time with their feet. And Startchenko pranced about too. Everybody laughed.

Then the children said good-night and went off to bed. The examining magistrate laughed, danced a quadrille, flirted, and kept wondering whether it was not all a dream? The kitchen of the Zemstvo hut, the heap of hay in the corner, the rustle of the beetles, the revolting poverty-stricken surroundings, the voices of the witnesses, the wind, the snow storm, the danger of being lost; and then all at once this splendid, brightly lighted room, the sounds of the piano, the lovely girls, the curly-headed children, the gay, happy laughter - such a transformation seemed to him like a fairy tale, and it seemed incredible that such transitions were possible at the distance of some two miles in the course of one hour. And dreary thoughts prevented him from enjoying himself, and he kept thinking this was not life here, but bits of life fragments, that everything here was accidental, that one could draw no conclusions from it; and he even felt sorry for these girls, who were living and would end their lives in the wilds, in a province far away from the center of culture, where nothing is accidental, but everything is in accordance with reason and law, and where, for instance, every suicide is intelligible, so that one can explain why it has happened and what is its significance in the general scheme of things. He imagined that if the life surrounding him here in the wilds were not intelligible to him, and if he did not see it, it meant that it did not exist at all.

At supper the conversation turned on Lesnitsky

"He left a wife and child," said Startchenko. "I would forbid neurasthenics and all people whose nervous system is out of order to marry, I would deprive them of the right and possibility of multiplying their kind. To bring into the world nervous, invalid children is a crime."

"He was an unfortunate young man," said Von Taunitz, sighing gently and shaking his head. "What a lot one must suffer and think about before one brings oneself to take one's own life, . . . a young life! Such a misfortune may happen in any family, and that is awful. It is hard to bear such a thing, insufferable. . . ."

And all the girls listened in silence with grave faces, looking at their father. Lyzhin felt that he, too, must say something, but he couldn't think of anything, and merely said:

"Yes, suicide is an undesirable phenomenon."

He slept in a warm room, in a soft bed covered with a quilt under which there were fine clean sheets, but for some reason did not feel comfortable: perhaps because the doctor and Von Taunitz were, for a long time, talking in the adjoining room, and overhead he heard, through the ceiling and in the stove, the wind roaring just as in the Zemstvo hut, and as plaintively howling: "Oo-oo-oo-oo!"

Von Taunitz's wife had died two years before, and he was still unable to resign himself to his loss and, whatever he was talking about, always mentioned his wife; and there was no trace of a prosecutor left about him now.

"Is it possible that I may some day come to such a condition?" thought Lyzhin, as he fell asleep, still hearing through the wall his host's subdued, as it were bereaved, voice.

The examining magistrate did not sleep soundly. He felt hot and uncomfortable, and it seemed to him in his sleep that he was not at Von Taunitz's, and not in a soft clean bed, but still in the hay at the Zemstvo hut, hearing the subdued voices of the witnesses; he fancied that Lesnitsky was close by, not fifteen paces away. In his dreams he remembered how the insurance agent, black-haired and pale, wearing dusty high boots, had come into the bookkeeper's office. "This is our insurance agent. . . ."

Then he dreamed that Lesnitsky and Loshadin the constable were walking through the open country in the snow, side by side, supporting each other; the snow was whirling about their heads, the wind was blowing on their backs, but they walked on, singing: We go on, and on, and on. . . ."

The old man was like a magician in an opera, and both of them were singing as though they were on the stage:

"We go on, and on, and on! . . . You are in the warmth, in the light and snugness, but we are walking in the frost and the storm, through the deep snow. . . . We know nothing of ease, we know nothing of joy. . . . We bear all the burden of this life, yours and ours. . . . Oo-oo-oo! We go on, and on, and on. . . ."

Lyzhin woke and sat up in bed. What a confused, bad dream! And why did he dream of the constable and the agent together? What nonsense! And now while Lyzhin's heart was throbbing violently and he was sitting on his bed, holding his head in his hands, it seemed to him that there really was something in common between the lives of the insurance agent and the constable. Don't they really go side by side holding each other up? Some tie unseen, but significant and essential, existed between them, and even between them and Von Taunitz and between all men - all men; in this life, even in the remotest desert, nothing is accidental, everything is full of one common idea, everything has one soul, one aim, and to understand it it is not enough to think, it is not enough to reason, one must have also, it seems, the gift of insight into life, a gift which is evidently not bestowed on all. And the unhappy man who had broken down, who had killed himself - the "neurasthenic," as the doctor called him - and the old peasant who spent every day of his life going from one man to another, were only accidental, were only fragments of life for one who thought of his own life as accidental, but were parts of one organism - marvelous and rational - for one who thought of his own life as part of that universal whole and understood it. So thought Lyzhin, and it was a thought that had long lain hidden in his soul, and only now it was unfolded broadly and clearly to his consciousness.

He lay down and began to drop asleep; and again they were going along together, singing: "We go on, and on, and on. . . . We take from life what is hardest and bitterest in it, and we leave you what is easy and joyful; and sitting at supper, you can coldly and sensibly discuss why we suffer and perish, and why we are not as sound and as satisfied as you."

What they were singing had occurred to his mind before, but the thought was somewhere in the background behind his other thoughts, and flickered timidly like a faraway light in foggy weather. And he felt that this suicide and the peasant's sufferings lay upon his conscience, too; to resign himself to the fact that these people, submissive to their fate, should take up the burden of what was hardest and gloomiest in life - how awful it was! To accept this, and to desire for himself a life full of light and movement among happy and contented people, and to be continually dreaming of such, means dreaming of fresh suicides of men crushed by toil and anxiety, or of men weak and outcast whom people only talk of sometimes at supper with annoyance or mockery, without going to their help. . . . And again:

"We go on, and on, and on . . ." as though someone were beating with a hammer on his temples.

He woke early in the morning with a headache, roused by a noise; in the next room Von Taunitz was saying loudly to the doctor:

"It's impossible for you to go now. Look what's going on outside. Don't argue, you had better ask the coachman; he won't take you in such weather for a million."

"But it's only two miles," said the doctor in an imploring voice.

"Well, if it were only half a mile. If you can't, then you can't. Directly you drive out of the gates it is perfect hell, you would be off the road in a minute. Nothing will induce me to let you go, you can say what you like."

"It's bound to be quieter towards evening," said the peasant who was heating the stove.

And in the next room the doctor began talking of the rigorous climate and its influence on the character of the Russian, of the long winters which, by preventing movement from place to place, hinder the intellectual development of the people; and Lyzhin listened with vexation to these observations and looked out of window at the snow drifts which were piled on the fence. He gazed at the white dust which covered the whole visible expanse, at the trees which bowed their heads despairingly to right and then to left, listened to the howling and the banging, and thought gloomily:

"Well, what moral can be drawn from it? It's a blizzard and that is all about it. . . ."

At midday they had lunch, then wandered aimlessly about the house; they went to the windows.

"And Lesnitsky is lying there," thought Lyzhin, watching the whirling snow, which raced furiously round and round upon the drifts. "Lesnitsky is lying there, the witnesses are waiting. . . ."

They talked of the weather, saying that the snowstorm usually lasted two days and nights, rarely longer. At six o'clock they had dinner, then they played cards, sang, danced; at last they had supper. The day was over, they went to bed.

In the night, towards morning, it all subsided. When they got up and looked out of window, the bare willows with their weakly drooping branches were standing perfectly motionless; it was dull and still, as though nature now were ashamed of its orgy, of its mad nights, and the license it had given to its passions. The horses, harnessed tandem, had been waiting at the front door since five o'clock in the morning. When it was fully daylight the doctor and the examining magistrate put on their fur coats and felt boots, and, saying good-by to their host, went out.

At the steps beside the coachman stood the familiar figure of the constable, Ilya Loshadin, with an old leather bag across his shoulder and no cap on his head, covered with snow all over, and his face was red and wet with perspiration. The footman who had come out to help the gentlemen and cover their legs looked at him sternly and said:

"What are you standing here for, you old devil? Get away!"

"Your honor, the people are anxious," said Loshadin, smiling naïvely all over his face, and evidently pleased at seeing at last the people he had waited for so long. "The people are very uneasy, the children are crying. . . . They thought, your honor, that you had gone back to the town again. Show us the heavenly mercy, our benefactors! . . ."

The doctor and the examining magistrate said nothing, got into the sledge, and drove to Syrnya.

THE LADY WITH THE DOG

I

It was said that a new person had appeared on the sea-front: a lady with a little dog. Dmitri Dmitritch Gurov, who had by then been a fortnight at Yalta, and so was fairly at home there, had begun to take an interest in new arrivals. Sitting in Verney's pavilion, he saw, walking on the sea-front, a fair-haired young lady of medium height, wearing a *béret;* a white Pomeranian dog was running behind her.

And afterwards he met her in the public gardens and in the square several times a day. She was walking alone, always wearing the same *béret,* and always with the same white dog; no one knew who she was, and everyone called her simply "the lady with the dog."

"If she is here alone without a husband or friends, it wouldn't be amiss to make her acquaintance," Gurov reflected.

He was under forty, but he had a daughter already twelve years old, and two sons at school. He had been married young, when he was a student in his second year, and by now his wife seemed half as old again as he. She was a tall, erect woman with dark eyebrows, staid and dignified, and, as she said of herself, intellectual. She read a great deal, used phonetic spelling, called her husband, not Dmitri, but Dimitri, and he secretly considered her unintelligent, narrow, inelegant, was afraid of her, and did not like to be at home. He had begun being unfaithful to her long ago - had been unfaithful to her often, and, probably on that account, almost always spoke ill of women, and when they were talked about in his presence, used to call them "the lower race."

It seemed to him that he had been so schooled by bitter experience that he might call them what he liked, and yet he could not get on for two days together without "the lower race." In the society of men he was bored and not himself, with them he was cold and uncommunicative; but when he was in the company of women he felt free, and knew what to say to them and how to behave; and he was at ease with them even when he was silent. In his appearance, in his character, in his whole nature, there was something attractive and elusive which allured women and disposed them in his favour; he knew that, and some force seemed to draw him, too, to them.

Experience often repeated, truly bitter experience, had taught him long ago that with decent people, especially Moscow people - always slow to move and irresolute - every intimacy, which at first so agreeably diversifies life and appears a light and charming adventure, inevitably grows into a regular problem of extreme intricacy, and in the long run the situation becomes unbearable. But at every fresh meeting with an interesting woman this experience seemed to slip out of his memory, and he was eager for life, and everything seemed simple and amusing.

One evening he was dining in the gardens, and the lady in the *béret* came up slowly to take the next table. Her expression, her gait, her dress, and the way she did her hair told him that she was a lady, that she was married, that she was in Yalta for the first time and alone, and that she was dull there. . . . The stories told of the immorality in such places as Yalta are to a great extent untrue; he despised them, and knew that such stories were for the most part made up by persons who would themselves have been glad to sin if they had been able; but when the lady sat down at the next table three paces from him, he remembered these tales of easy conquests, of trips to the mountains, and the tempting thought of a swift, fleeting love affair, a romance with an unknown woman, whose name he did not know, suddenly took possession of him.

He beckoned coaxingly to the Pomeranian, and when the dog came up to him he shook his finger at it. The Pomeranian growled: Gurov shook his finger at it again.

The lady looked at him and at once dropped her eyes.

"He doesn't bite," she said, and blushed.

"May I give him a bone?" he asked; and when she nodded he asked courteously, "Have you been long in Yalta?"

"Five days."

"And I have already dragged out a fortnight here."

There was a brief silence.

"Time goes fast, and yet it is so dull here!" she said, not looking at him.

"That's only the fashion to say it is dull here. A provincial will live in Belyov or Zhidra and not be dull, and when he comes here it's 'Oh, the dulness! Oh, the dust!' One would think he came from Grenada."

She laughed. Then both continued eating in silence, like strangers, but after dinner they walked side by side; and there sprang up between them the light jesting conversation of people who are free and satisfied, to whom it does not matter where they go or what they talk about. They walked and talked of the strange light on the sea: the water was of a soft warm lilac hue, and there was a golden streak from the moon upon it. They talked of how sultry it was after a hot day. Gurov told her that he came from Moscow, that he had taken his degree in Arts, but had a post in a bank; that he had trained as an opera-singer, but had given it up, that he owned two houses in Moscow. . . . And from her he learnt that she had grown up in Petersburg, but had lived in S-- since her marriage two years before, that she was staying another month in Yalta, and that her husband, who needed a holiday too, might perhaps come and fetch her. She was not sure whether her husband had a post in a Crown Department or under the Provincial Council - and was amused by her own ignorance. And Gurov learnt, too, that she was called Anna Sergeyevna.

Afterwards he thought about her in his room at the hotel - thought she would certainly meet him next day; it would be sure to happen. As he got into bed he thought how lately she had been a girl at school, doing lessons like his own daughter; he recalled the diffidence, the angularity, that was still manifest in her laugh and her manner of talking with a stranger. This must have been the first time in her life she had been alone in surroundings in which she was followed, looked at, and spoken to merely from a secret motive which she could hardly fail to guess. He recalled her slender, delicate neck, her lovely grey eyes.

"There's something pathetic about her, anyway," he thought, and fell asleep.

II

A week had passed since they had made acquaintance. It was a holiday. It was sultry indoors, while in the street the wind whirled the dust round and round, and blew people's hats off. It was a thirsty day, and Gurov often went into the pavilion, and pressed Anna Sergeyevna to have syrup and water or an ice. One did not know what to do with oneself.

In the evening when the wind had dropped a little, they went out on the groyne to see the steamer come in. There were a great many people walking about the harbour; they had gathered to welcome some one, bringing bouquets. And two peculiarities of a well-dressed Yalta crowd were very conspicuous: the elderly ladies were dressed like young ones, and there were great numbers of generals.

Owing to the roughness of the sea, the steamer arrived late, after the sun had set, and it was a long time turning about before it reached the groyne. Anna Sergeyevna looked through her lorgnette at the steamer and the passengers as though looking for acquaintances, and when she turned to Gurov her eyes were shining. She talked a great deal and asked disconnected questions, forgetting next moment what she had asked; then she dropped her lorgnette in the crush.

The festive crowd began to disperse; it was too dark to see people's faces. The wind had completely dropped, but Gurov and Anna Sergeyevna still stood as though waiting to see some one else come from the steamer. Anna Sergeyevna was silent now, and sniffed the flowers without looking at Gurov.

"The weather is better this evening," he said. "Where shall we go now? Shall we drive somewhere?"

She made no answer.

Then he looked at her intently, and all at once put his arm round her and kissed her on the lips, and breathed in the moisture and the fragrance of the flowers; and he immediately looked round him, anxiously wondering whether any one had seen them.

"Let us go to your hotel," he said softly. And both walked quickly.

The room was close and smelt of the scent she had bought at the Japanese shop. Gurov looked at her and thought: "What different people one meets in the world!" From the past he preserved memories of careless, good-natured women, who loved cheerfully and were grateful to him for the happiness he gave them, however brief it might be; and of women like his wife who loved without any genuine feeling, with superfluous phrases, affectedly, hysterically, with an expression that suggested that it was not love nor passion, but something more significant; and of two or three others, very beautiful, cold women, on whose faces he had caught a glimpse of a rapacious expression - an obstinate desire to snatch from life more than it could give, and these were capricious, unreflecting, domineering, unintelligent women not in their first youth, and when Gurov grew cold to them their beauty excited his hatred, and the lace on their linen seemed to him like scales.

But in this case there was still the diffidence, the angularity of inexperienced youth, an awkward feeling; and there was a sense of consternation as though some one had suddenly knocked at the door. The attitude of Anna Sergeyevna - "the lady with the dog" - to what had happened was somehow peculiar, very grave, as though it were her fall - so it seemed, and it was strange and inappropriate. Her face dropped and faded, and on both sides of it her long hair hung down mournfully; she mused in a dejected attitude like "the woman who was a sinner" in an old-fashioned picture.

"It's wrong," she said. "You will be the first to despise me now."

There was a water-melon on the table. Gurov cut himself a slice and began eating it without haste. There followed at least half an hour of silence.

Anna Sergeyevna was touching; there was about her the purity of a good, simple woman who had seen little of life. The solitary candle burning on the table threw a faint light on her face, yet it was clear that she was very unhappy.

"How could I despise you?" asked Gurov. "You don't know what you are saying."

"God forgive me," she said, and her eyes filled with tears. "It's awful."

"You seem to feel you need to be forgiven."

"Forgiven? No. I am a bad, low woman; I despise myself and don't attempt to justify myself. It's not my husband but myself I have deceived. And not only just now; I have been deceiving myself for a long time. My husband may be a good, honest man, but he is a flunkey! I don't know what he does there, what his work is, but I know he is a flunkey! I was twenty when I was married to him. I have been tormented by curiosity; I wanted something better. 'There must be a different sort of life,' I said to myself. I wanted to live! To live, to live! . . . I was fired by curiosity . . . you don't understand it, but, I swear to God, I could not control myself; something happened to me: I could not be restrained. I told my husband I was ill, and came here. . . . And here I have been walking about as though I were dazed, like a mad creature; . . . and now I have become a vulgar, contemptible woman whom any one may despise."

Gurov felt bored already, listening to her. He was irritated by the naïve tone, by this remorse, so unexpected and inopportune; but for the tears in her eyes, he might have thought she was jesting or playing a part.

"I don't understand," he said softly. "What is it you want?"

She hid her face on his breast and pressed close to him.

"Believe me, believe me, I beseech you . . ." she said. "I love a pure, honest life, and sin is loathsome to me. I don't know what I am doing. Simple people say: 'The Evil One has beguiled me.' And I may say of myself now that the Evil One has beguiled me."

"Hush, hush! . . ." he muttered.

He looked at her fixed, scared eyes, kissed her, talked softly and affectionately, and by degrees she was comforted, and her gaiety returned; they both began laughing.

Afterwards when they went out there was not a soul on the sea-front. The town with its cypresses had quite a deathlike air, but the sea still broke noisily on the shore; a single barge was rocking on the waves, and a lantern was blinking sleepily on it.

They found a cab and drove to Oreanda.

"I found out your surname in the hall just now: it was written on the board - Von Diderits," said Gurov. "Is your husband a German?"

"No; I believe his grandfather was a German, but he is an Orthodox Russian himself."

At Oreanda they sat on a seat not far from the church, looked down at the sea, and were silent. Yalta was hardly visible through the morning mist; white clouds stood motionless on the mountain-tops. The leaves did not stir on the trees, grasshoppers chirruped, and the monotonous hollow sound of the sea rising up from below, spoke of the peace, of the eternal sleep awaiting us. So it must have sounded when there was no Yalta, no Oreanda here; so it sounds now, and it will sound as indifferently and monotonously when we are all no more. And in this constancy, in this complete indifference to the life and death of each of us, there lies hid, perhaps, a pledge of our eternal salvation, of the unceasing movement of life upon earth, of unceasing progress towards perfection. Sitting beside a young woman who in the dawn seemed so lovely, soothed and spellbound in these magical surroundings - the sea, mountains, clouds, the open sky - Gurov thought how in reality everything is beautiful in this world when one reflects: everything except what we think or do ourselves when we forget our human dignity and the higher aims of our existence.

A man walked up to them - probably a keeper - looked at them and walked away. And this detail seemed mysterious and beautiful, too. They saw a steamer come from Theodosia, with its lights out in the glow of dawn.

"There is dew on the grass," said Anna Sergeyevna, after a silence.

"Yes. It's time to go home."

They went back to the town.

Then they met every day at twelve o'clock on the sea-front, lunched and dined together, went for walks, admired the sea. She complained that she slept badly, that her heart throbbed violently; asked the same questions, troubled now by jealousy and now by the fear that he did not respect her sufficiently. And often in the square or gardens, when there was no one near them, he suddenly drew her to him and kissed her passionately. Complete idleness, these kisses in broad daylight while he looked round in dread of some one's seeing them, the heat, the smell of the sea, and the continual passing to and fro before him of idle, well-dressed, well-fed people, made a new man of him; he told Anna Sergeyevna how beautiful she was, how fascinating. He was impatiently passionate, he would not move a step away from her, while she was often pensive and continually urged him to confess that he did not respect her, did not love her in the least, and thought of her as nothing but a common woman. Rather late almost every evening they drove somewhere out of town, to Oreanda or to the waterfall; and the expedition was always a success, the scenery invariably impressed them as grand and beautiful.

They were expecting her husband to come, but a letter came from him, saying that there was something wrong with his eyes, and he entreated his wife to come home as quickly as possible. Anna Sergeyevna made haste to go.

"It's a good thing I am going away," she said to Gurov. "It's the finger of destiny!"

She went by coach and he went with her. They were driving the whole day. When she had got into a compartment of the express, and when thesecond bell had rung, she said:

"Let me look at you once more . . . look at you once again. That's right."

She did not shed tears, but was so sad that she seemed ill, and her face was quivering.

"I shall remember you . . . think of you," she said. "God be with you; be happy. Don't remember evil against me. We are parting forever - it must be so, for we ought never to have met. Well, God be with you."

The train moved off rapidly, its lights soon vanished from sight, and a minute later there was no sound of it, as though everything had conspired together to end as quickly as possible that sweet delirium, that madness. Left alone on the platform, and gazing into the dark distance, Gurov listened to the chirrup of the grasshoppers and the hum of the telegraph wires, feeling as though he had only just waked up. And he thought, musing, that there had been another episode or adventure in his life, and it, too, was at an end, and nothing was left of it but a memory. . . . He was moved, sad, and conscious of a slight remorse. This young woman whom he would never meet again had not been happy with him; he was genuinely warm and affectionate with her, but yet in his manner, his tone, and his caresses there had been a shade of light irony, the coarse condescension of a happy man who was, besides, almost twice her age. All the time she had called him kind, exceptional, lofty; obviously he had seemed to her different from what he really was, so he had unintentionally deceived her. . . .

Here at the station was already a scent of autumn; it was a cold evening.

"It's time for me to go north," thought Gurov as he left the platform. "High time!"

III

At home in Moscow everything was in its winter routine; the stoves were heated, and in the morning it was still dark when the children were having breakfast and getting ready for school, and the nurse would light the lamp for a short time. The frosts had begun already. When the first snow has fallen, on the first day of sledge-driving it is pleasant to see the white earth, the white roofs, to draw soft, delicious breath, and the season brings back the days of one's youth. The old limes and birches, white with hoar-frost, have a good-natured expression; they are nearer to one's heart than cypresses and palms, and near them one doesn't want to be thinking of the sea and the mountains.

Gurov was Moscow born; he arrived in Moscow on a fine frosty day, and when he put on his fur coat and warm gloves, and walked along Petrovka, and when on Saturday evening he heard the ringing of the bells, his recent trip and the places he had seen lost all charm for him. Little by little he became absorbed in Moscow life, greedily read three newspapers a day, and declared he did not read the Moscow papers on principle! He already felt a longing to go to restaurants, clubs, dinner-parties, anniversary celebrations, and he felt flattered at entertaining distinguished lawyers and artists, and at playing cards with a professor at the doctors' club. He could already eat a whole plateful of salt fish and cabbage.

In another month, he fancied, the image of Anna Sergeyevna would be shrouded in a mist in his memory, and only from time to time would visit him in his dreams with a touching smile as others did. But more than a month passed, real winter had come, and everything was still clear in his memory as though he had parted with Anna Sergeyevna only the day before. And his memories glowed more and more vividly. When in the evening stillness he heard from his study the voices of his children, preparing their lessons, or when he listened to a song or the organ at the restaurant, or the storm howled in the chimney, suddenly everything would rise up in his memory: what had happened on the groyne, and the early morning with the mist on the mountains, and the steamer coming from Theodosia, and the kisses. He would pace a long time about his room, remembering it all and smiling; then his memories passed into dreams, and in his fancy the past was mingled with what was to come. Anna Sergeyevna did not visit him in dreams, but followed him about everywhere like a shadow and haunted him. When he shut his eyes he saw her as though she were living before him, and she seemed to him lovelier, younger, tenderer than she was; and he imagined himself finer than he had been in Yalta. In the evenings she peeped out at him from the bookcase, from the fireplace, from the corner - he heard her breathing, the caressing rustle of her dress. In the street he watched the women, looking for some one like her.

He was tormented by an intense desire to confide his memories to some one. But in his home it was impossible to talk of his love, and he had no one outside; he could not talk to his tenants nor to any one at the bank. And what had he to talk of? Had he been in love, then? Had there been anything beautiful, poetical, or edifying or simply interesting in his relations with Anna Sergeyevna? And there was nothing for him but to talk vaguely of love, of woman, and no one guessed what it meant; only his wife twitched her black eyebrows, and said:

"The part of a lady-killer does not suit you at all, Dimitri."

One evening, coming out of the doctors' club with an official with whom he had been playing cards, he could not resist saying:

"If only you knew what a fascinating woman I made the acquaintance of in Yalta!"

The official got into his sledge and was driving away, but turned suddenly and shouted:

"Dmitri Dmitritch!"

"What?"

"You were right this evening: the sturgeon was a bit too strong!"

These words, so ordinary, for some reason moved Gurov to indignation, and struck him as degrading and unclean. What savage manners, what people! What senseless nights, what uninteresting, uneventful days! The rage for card-playing, the gluttony, the drunkenness, the continual talk always about the same thing. Useless pursuits and conversations always about the same things absorb the better part of one's time, the better part of one's strength, and in the end there is left a life grovelling and curtailed, worthless and trivial, and there is no escaping or getting away from it - just as though one were in a madhouse or a prison.

Gurov did not sleep all night, and was filled with indignation. And he had a headache all next day. And the next night he slept badly; he sat up in bed, thinking, or paced up and down his room. He was sick of his children, sick of the bank; he had no desire to go anywhere or to talk of anything.

In the holidays in December he prepared for a journey, and told his wife he was going to Petersburg to do something in the interests of a young friend - and he set off for S--. What for? He did not very well know himself. He wanted to see Anna Sergeyevna and to talk with her - to arrange a meeting, if possible.

He reached S-- in the morning, and took the best room at the hotel, in which the floor was covered with grey army cloth, and on the table was an inkstand, grey with dust and adorned with a figure on horseback, with its hat in its hand and its head broken off. The hotel porter gave him the necessary information; Von Diderits lived in a house of his own in Old Gontcharny Street - it was not far from the hotel: he was rich and lived in good style, and had his own horses; everyone in the town knew him. The porter pronounced the name "Dridirits."

Gurov went without haste to Old Gontcharny Street and found the house. Just opposite the house stretched a long grey fence adorned with nails.

"One would run away from a fence like that," thought Gurov, looking from the fence to the windows of the house and back again.

He considered: to-day was a holiday, and the husband would probably be at home. And in any case it would be tactless to go into the house and upset her. If he were to send her a note it might fall into her husband's hands, and then it might ruin everything. The best thing was to trust to chance. And he kept walking up and down the street by the fence, waiting for the chance. He saw a beggar go in at the gate and dogs fly at him; then an hour later he heard a piano, and the sounds were faint and indistinct. Probably it was Anna Sergeyevna playing. The front door suddenly opened, and an old woman came out, followed by the familiar white Pomeranian. Gurov was on the point of calling to the dog, but his heart began beating violently, and in his excitement he could not remember the dog's name.

He walked up and down, and loathed the grey fence more and more, and by now he thought irritably that Anna Sergeyevna had forgotten him, and was perhaps already amusing herself with some one else, and that that was very natural in a young woman who had nothing to look at from morning till night but that confounded fence. He went back to his hotel room and sat for a long while on the sofa, not knowing what to do, then he had dinner and a long nap.

"How stupid and worrying it is!" he thought when he woke and looked at the dark windows: it was already evening. "Here I've had a good sleep for some reason. What shall I do in the night?"

He sat on the bed, which was covered by a cheap grey blanket, such as one sees in hospitals, and he taunted himself in his vexation:

"So much for the lady with the dog . . . so much for the adventure. . . . You're in a nice fix. . . ."

That morning at the station a poster in large letters had caught his eye. "The Geisha" was to be performed for the first time. He thought of this and went to the theatre.

"It's quite possible she may go to the first performance," he thought.

The theatre was full. As in all provincial theatres, there was a fog above the chandelier, the gallery was noisy and restless; in the front row the local dandies were standing up before the beginning of the performance, with their hands behind them; in the Governor's box the Governor's daughter, wearing a boa, was sitting in the front seat, while the Governor himself lurked modestly behind the curtain with only his hands visible; the orchestra was a long time tuning up; the stage curtain swayed. All the time the audience were coming in and taking their seats Gurov looked at them eagerly.

Anna Sergeyevna, too, came in. She sat down in the third row, and when Gurov looked at her his heart contracted, and he understood clearly that for him there was in the whole world no creature so near, so precious, and so important to him; she, this little woman, in no way remarkable, lost in a provincial crowd, with a vulgar lorgnette in her hand, filled his whole life now, was his sorrow and his joy, the one happiness that he now desired for himself, and to the sounds of the inferior orchestra, of the wretched provincial violins, he thought how lovely she was. He thought and dreamed.

A young man with small side-whiskers, tall and stooping, came in with Anna Sergeyevna and sat down beside her; he bent his head at every step and seemed to be continually bowing. Most likely this was the husband whom at Yalta, in a rush of bitter feeling, she had called a flunkey. And there really was in his long figure, his side-whiskers, and the small bald patch on his head, something of the flunkey's obsequiousness; his smile was sugary, and in his buttonhole there was some badge of distinction like the number on a waiter.

During the first interval the husband went away to smoke; she remained alone in her stall. Gurov, who was sitting in the stalls, too, went up to her and said in a trembling voice, with a forced smile:

"Good-evening."

She glanced at him and turned pale, then glanced again with horror, unable to believe her eyes, and tightly gripped the fan and the lorgnette in her hands, evidently struggling with herself not to faint. Both were silent. She was sitting, he was standing, frightened by her confusion and not venturing to sit down beside her. The violins and the flute began tuning up. He felt suddenly frightened; it seemed as though all the people in the boxes were looking at them. She got up and went quickly to the door; he followed her, and both walked senselessly along passages, and up and down stairs, and figures in legal, scholastic, and civil service uniforms, all wearing badges, flitted before their eyes. They caught glimpses of ladies, of fur coats hanging on pegs; the draughts blew on them, bringing a smell of stale tobacco. And Gurov, whose heart was beating violently, thought:

"Oh, heavens! Why are these people here and this orchestra! . . ."

And at that instant he recalled how when he had seen Anna Sergeyevna off at the station he had thought that everything was over and they would never meet again. But how far they were still from the end!

On the narrow, gloomy staircase over which was written "To the Amphitheatre," she stopped.

"How you have frightened me!" she said, breathing hard, still pale and overwhelmed. "Oh, how you have frightened me! I am half dead. Why have you come? Why?"

"But do understand, Anna, do understand . . ." he said hastily in a low voice. "I entreat you to understand. . . ."

She looked at him with dread, with entreaty, with love; she looked at him intently, to keep his features more distinctly in her memory.

"I am so unhappy," she went on, not heeding him. "I have thought of nothing but you all the time; I live only in the thought of you. And I wanted to forget, to forget you; but why, oh, why, have you come?"

On the landing above them two schoolboys were smoking and looking down, but that was nothing to Gurov; he drew Anna Sergeyevna to him, and began kissing her face, her cheeks, and her hands.

"What are you doing, what are you doing!" she cried in horror, pushing him away. "We are mad. Go away to-day; go away at once. . . . I beseech you by all that is sacred, I implore you. . . . There are people coming this way!"

Some one was coming up the stairs.

"You must go away," Anna Sergeyevna went on in a whisper. "Do you hear, Dmitri Dmitritch? I will come and see you in Moscow. I have never been happy; I am miserable now, and I never, never shall be happy, never! Don't make me suffer still more! I swear I'll come to Moscow. But now let us part. My precious, good, dear one, we must part!"

She pressed his hand and began rapidly going downstairs, looking round at him, and from her eyes he could see that she really was unhappy. Gurov stood for a little while, listened, then, when all sound had died away, he found his coat and left the theatre.

IV

And Anna Sergeyevna began coming to see him in Moscow. Once in two or three months she left S--, telling her husband that she was going to consult a doctor about an internal complaint - and her husband believed her, and did not believe her. In Moscow she stayed at the Slaviansky Bazaar hotel, and at once sent a man in a red cap to Gurov. Gurov went to see her, and no one in Moscow knew of it.

Once he was going to see her in this way on a winter morning (the messenger had come the evening before when he was out). With him walked his daughter, whom he wanted to take to school: it was on the way. Snow was falling in big wet flakes.

"It's three degrees above freezing-point, and yet it is snowing," said Gurov to his daughter. "The thaw is only on the surface of the earth; there is quite a different temperature at a greater height in the atmosphere."

"And why are there no thunderstorms in the winter, father?"

He explained that, too. He talked, thinking all the while that he was going to see her, and no living soul knew of it, and probably never would know. He had two lives: one, open, seen and known by all who cared to know, full of relative truth and of relative falsehood, exactly like the lives of his friends and acquaintances; and another life running its course in secret. And through some strange, perhaps accidental, conjunction of circumstances, everything that was essential, of interest and of value to him, everything in which he was sincere and did not deceive himself, everything that made the kernel of his life, was hidden from other people; and all that was false in him, the sheath in which he hid himself to conceal the truth - such, for instance, as his work in the bank, his discussions at the club, his "lower race," his presence with his wife at anniversary festivities - all that was open. And he judged of others by himself, not believing in what he saw, and always believing that every man had his real, most interesting life under the cover of secrecy and under the cover of night. All personal life rested on secrecy, and possibly it was partly on that account that civilised man was so nervously anxious that personal privacy should be respected.

After leaving his daughter at school, Gurov went on to the Slaviansky Bazaar. He took off his fur coat below, went upstairs, and softly knocked at the door. Anna Sergeyevna, wearing his favourite grey dress, exhausted by the journey and the suspense, had been expecting him since the evening before. She was pale; she looked at him, and did not smile, and he had hardly come in when she fell on his breast. Their kiss was slow and prolonged, as though they had not met for two years.

"Well, how are you getting on there?" he asked. "What news?"

"Wait; I'll tell you directly. . . . I can't talk."

She could not speak; she was crying. She turned away from him, and pressed her handkerchief to her eyes.

"Let her have her cry out. I'll sit down and wait," he thought, and he sat down in an arm-chair.

Then he rang and asked for tea to be brought him, and while he drank his tea she remained standing at the window with her back to him. She was crying from emotion, from the miserable consciousness that their life was so hard for them; they could only meet in secret, hiding themselves from people, like thieves! Was not their life shattered?

"Come, do stop!" he said.

It was evident to him that this love of theirs would not soon be over, that he could not see the end of it. Anna Sergeyevna grew more and more attached to him. She adored him, and it was unthinkable to say to her that it was bound to have an end some day; besides, she would not have believed it!

He went up to her and took her by the shoulders to say something affectionate and cheering, and at that moment he saw himself in the looking-glass.

His hair was already beginning to turn grey. And it seemed strange to him that he had grown so much older, so much plainer during the last few years. The shoulders on which his hands rested were warm and quivering. He felt compassion for this life, still so warm and lovely, but probably already not far from beginning to fade and wither like his own. Why did she love him so much? He always seemed to women different from what he was, and they loved in him not himself, but the man created by their imagination, whom they had been eagerly seeking all their lives; and afterwards, when they noticed their mistake, they loved him all the same. And not one of them had been happy with him. Time passed, he had made their acquaintance, got on with them, parted, but he had never once loved; it was anything you like, but not love.

And only now when his head was grey he had fallen properly, really in love - for the first time in his life.

Anna Sergeyevna and he loved each other like people very close and akin, like husband and wife, like tender friends; it seemed to them that fate itself had meant them for one another, and they could not understand why he had a wife and she a husband; and it was as though they were a pair of birds of passage, caught and forced to live in different cages. They forgave each other for what they were ashamed of in their past, they forgave everything in the present, and felt that this love of theirs had changed them both.

In moments of depression in the past he had comforted himself with any arguments that came into his mind, but now he no longer cared for arguments; he felt profound compassion, he wanted to be sincere and tender. . . .

"Don't cry, my darling," he said. "You've had your cry; that's enough. . . . Let us talk now, let us think of some plan."

Then they spent a long while taking counsel together, talked of how to avoid the necessity for secrecy, for deception, for living in different towns and not seeing each other for long at a time. How could they be free from this intolerable bondage?

"How? How?" he asked, clutching his head. "How?"

And it seemed as though in a little while the solution would be found, and then a new and splendid life would begin; and it was clear to both of them that they had still a long, long road before them, and that the most complicated and difficult part of it was only just beginning.

AT CHRISTMAS TIME

I

"What shall I write?" said Yegor, and he dipped his pen in the ink.

Vasilisa had not seen her daughter for four years. Her daughter Yefimya had gone after her wedding to Petersburg, had sent them two letters, and since then seemed to vanish out of their lives; there had been no sight nor sound of her. And whether the old woman were milking her cow at dawn, or heating her stove, or dozing at night, she was always thinking of one and the same thing - what was happening to Yefimya, whether she were alive out yonder. She ought to have sent a letter, but the old father could not write, and there was no one to write.

But now Christmas had come, and Vasilisa could not bear it any longer, and went to the tavern to Yegor, the brother of the innkeeper's wife, who had sat in the tavern doing nothing ever since he came back from the army; people said that he could write letters very well if he were properly paid. Vasilisa talked to the cook at the tavern, then to the mistress of the house, then to Yegor himself. They agreed upon fifteen kopecks.

And now - it happened on the second day of the holidays, in the tavern kitchen - Yegor was sitting at the table, holding the pen in his hand. Vasilisa was standing before him, pondering with an expression of anxiety and woe on her face. Pyotr, her husband, a very thin old man with a brownish bald patch, had come with her; he stood looking straight before him like a blind man. On the stove a piece of pork was being braised in a saucepan; it was spurting and hissing, and seemed to be actually saying: "Flu-flu-flu." It was stifling.

"What am I to write?" Yegor asked again.

"What?" asked Vasilisa, looking at him angrily and suspiciously. "Don't worry me! You are not writing for nothing; no fear, you'll be paid for it. Come, write: 'To our dear son-in-law, Andrey Hrisanfitch, and to our only beloved daughter, Yefimya Petrovna, with our love we send a low bow and our parental blessing abiding for ever.' "

"Written; fire away."

" 'And we wish them a happy Christmas; we are alive and well, and I wish you the same, please the Lord . . . the Heavenly King.' "

Vasilisa pondered and exchanged glances with the old man.

" 'And I wish you the same, please the Lord the Heavenly King,' " she repeated, beginning to cry.

She could say nothing more. And yet before, when she lay awake thinking at night, it had seemed to her that she could not get all she had to say into a dozen letters. Since the time when her daughter had gone away with her husband much water had flowed into the sea, the old people had lived feeling bereaved, and sighed heavily at night as though they had buried their daughter. And how many events had occurred in the village since then, how many marriages and deaths! How long the winters had been! How long the nights!

"It's hot," said Yegor, unbuttoning his waistcoat. "It must be seventy degrees. What more?" he asked.

The old people were silent.

"What does your son-in-law do in Petersburg?" asked Yegor.

"He was a soldier, my good friend," the old man answered in a weak voice. " He left the service at the same time as you did. He was a soldier, and now, to be sure, he is at Petersburg at a hydropathic establishment. The doctor treats the sick with water. So he, to be sure, is house-porter at the doctor's."

"Here it is written down," said the old woman, taking a letter out of her pocket. "We got it from Yefimya, goodness knows when. Maybe they are no longer in this world."

Yegor thought a little and began writing rapidly:

"At the present time"- he wrote - "since your destiny through your own doing allotted you to the Military Career, we counsel you to look into the Code of Disciplinary Offences and Fundamental Laws of the War Office, and you will see in that law the Civilization of the Officials of the War Office."

He wrote and kept reading aloud what was written, while Vasilisa considered what she ought to write: how great had been their want the year before, how their corn had not lasted even till Christmas, how they had to sell their cow. She ought to ask for money, ought to write that the old father was often ailing and would soon no doubt give up his soul to God . . . but how to express this in words? What must be said first and what afterwards?

"Take note," Yegor went on writing, "in volume five of the Army Regulations soldier is a common noun and a proper one, a soldier of the first rank is called a general, and of the last a private. . . ."

The old man stirred his lips and said softly:

"It would be all right to have a look at the grandchildren."

"What grandchildren?" asked the old woman, and she looked angrily at him; "perhaps there are none."

"Well, but perhaps there are. Who knows?"

"And thereby you can judge," Yegor hurried on, "what is the enemy without and what is the enemy within. The foremost of our enemies within isBacchus." The pen squeaked, executing upon the paper flourishes like fish-hooks. Yegor hastened and read over every line several times. He sat on a stool sprawling his broad feet under the table, well-fed, bursting with health, with a coarse animal face and a red bull neck. He was vulgarity itself: coarse, conceited, invincible, proud of having been born and bred in a pot-house; and Vasilisa quite understood the vulgarity, but could not express it in words, and could only look angrily and suspiciously at Yegor. Her head was beginning to ache, and her thoughts were in confusion from the sound of his voice and his unintelligible words, from the heat and the stuffiness, and she said nothing and thought nothing, but simply waited for him to finish scribbling. But the old man looked with full confidence. He believed in his old woman who had brought him there, and in Yegor; and when he had mentioned the hydropathic establishment it could be seen that he believed in the establishment and the healing efficacy of water.

Having finished the letter, Yegor got up and read the whole of it through from the beginning. The old man did not understand, but he nodded his head trustfully.

"That's all right; it is smooth . . ." he said. "God give you health. That's all right. . . ."

They laid on the table three five-kopeck pieces and went out of the tavern; the old man looked immovably straight before him as though he were blind, and perfect trustfulness was written on his face; but as Vasilisa came out of the tavern she waved angrily at the dog, and said angrily:

"Ugh, the plague."

The old woman did not sleep all night; she was disturbed by thoughts, and at daybreak she got up, said her prayers, and went to the station to send off the letter.

It was between eight and nine miles to the station.

II

Dr. B. O. Mozelweiser's hydropathic establishment worked on New Year's Day exactly as on ordinary days; the only difference was that the porter, Andrey Hrisanfitch, had on a uniform with new braiding, his boots had an extra polish, and he greeted every visitor with "A Happy New Year to you!"

It was the morning; Andrey Hrisanfitch was standing at the door, reading the newspaper. Just at ten o'clock there arrived a general, one of the habitual visitors, and directly after him the postman; Andrey Hrisanfitch helped the general off with his great-coat, and said:

"A Happy New Year to your Excellency!"

"Thank you, my good fellow; the same to you."

And at the top of the stairs the general asked, nodding towards the door (he asked the same question every day and always forgot the answer):

"And what is there in that room?"

"The massage room, your Excellency."

When the general's steps had died away Andrey Hrisanfitch looked at the post that had come, and found one addressed to himself. He tore it open, read several lines, then, looking at the newspaper, he walked without haste to his own room, which was downstairs close by at the end of the passage. His wife Yefimya was sitting on the bed, feeding her baby; another child, the eldest, was standing by, laying its curly head on her knee; a third was asleep on the bed.

Going into the room, Andrey gave his wife the letter and said:

"From the country, I suppose."

Then he walked out again without taking his eyes from the paper. He could hear Yefimya with a shaking voice reading the first lines. She read them and could read no more; these lines were enough for her. She burst into tears, and hugging her eldest child, kissing him, she began saying - and it was hard to say whether she were laughing or crying:

"It's from granny, from grandfather," she said. "From the country. . . . The Heavenly Mother, Saints and Martyrs! The snow lies heaped up under the roofs now . . . the trees are as white as white. The boys slide on little sledges . . . and dear old bald grandfather is on the stove . . . and there is a little yellow dog. . . . My own darlings!"

Andrey Hrisanfitch, hearing this, recalled that his wife had on three or four occasions given him letters and asked him to send them to the country, but some important business had always prevented him; he had not sent them, and the letters somehow got lost.

"And little hares run about in the fields," Yefimya went on chanting, kissing her boy and shedding tears. "Grandfather is kind and gentle; granny is good, too - kind-hearted. They are warm-hearted in the country, they are God-fearing . . . and there is a little church in the village; the peasants sing in the choir. Queen of Heaven, Holy Mother and Defender, take us away from here!"

Andrey Hrisanfitch returned to his room to smoke a little till there was another ring at the door, and Yefimya ceased speaking, subsided, and wiped her eyes, though her lips were still quivering. She was very much frightened of him - oh, how frightened of him! She trembled and was reduced to terror by the sound of his steps, by the look in his eyes, and dared not utter a word in his presence.

Andrey Hrisanfitch lighted a cigarette, but at that very moment there was a ring from upstairs. He put out his cigarette, and, assuming a very grave face, hastened to his front door.

The general was coming downstairs, fresh and rosy from his bath.

"And what is there in that room?" he asked, pointing to a door.

Andrey Hrisanfitch put his hands down swiftly to the seams of his trousers, and pronounced loudly:

"Charcot douche, your Excellency!"

IN THE RAVINE

I

The village of Ukleevo lay in a ravine so that only the belfry and the chimneys of the printed cottons factories could be seen from the high road and the railway-station. When visitors asked what village this was, they were told:

"That's the village where the deacon ate all the caviare at the funeral."

It had happened at the dinner at the funeral of Kostukov that the old deacon saw among the savouries some large-grained caviare and began eating it greedily; people nudged him, tugged at his arm, but he seemed petrified with enjoyment: felt nothing, and only went on eating. He ate up all the caviare, and there were four pounds in the jar. And years had passed since then, the deacon had long been dead, but the caviare was still remembered. Whether life was so poor here or people had not been clever enough to notice anything but that unimportant incident that had occurred ten years before, anyway the people had nothing else to tell about the village Ukleevo.

The village was never free from fever, and there was boggy mud there even in the summer, especially under the fences over which hung old willow-trees that gave deep shade. Here there was always a smell from the factory refuse and the acetic acid which was used in the finishing of the cotton print.

The three cotton factories and the tanyard were not in the village itself, but a little way off. They were small factories, and not more than four hundred workmen were employed in all of them. The tanyard often made the water in the little river stink; the refuse contaminated the meadows, the peasants' cattle suffered from Siberian plague, and orders were given that the factory should be closed. It was considered to be closed, but went on working in secret with the connivance of the local police officer and the district doctor, who was paid ten roubles a month by the owner. In the whole village there were only two decent houses built of brick with iron roofs; one of them was the local court, in the other, a two-storied house just opposite the church, there lived a shopkeeper from Epifan called Grigory Petrovitch Tsybukin.

Grigory kept a grocer's shop, but that was only for appearance' sake: in reality he sold vodka, cattle, hides, grain, and pigs; he traded in anything that came to hand, and when, for instance, magpies were wanted abroad for ladies' hats, he made some thirty kopecks on every pair of birds; he bought timber for felling, lent money at interest, and altogether was a sharp old man, full of resources.

He had two sons. The elder, Anisim, was in the police in the detective department and was rarely at home. The younger, Stepan, had gone in for trade and helped his father: but no great help was expected from him as he was weak in health and deaf; his wife Aksinya, a handsome woman with a good figure, who wore a hat and carried a parasol on holidays, got up early and went to bed late, and ran about all day long, picking up her skirts and jingling her keys, going from the granary to the cellar and from there to the shop, and old Tsybukin looked at her good-humouredly while his eyes glowed, and at such moments he regretted she had not been married to his elder son instead of to the younger one, who was deaf, and who evidently knew very little about female beauty.

The old man had always an inclination for family life, and he loved his family more than anything on earth, especially his elder son, the detective, and his daughter-in-law. Aksinya had no sooner married the deaf son than she began to display an extraordinary gift for business, and knew who could be allowed to run up a bill and who could not: she kept the keys and would not trust them even to her husband; she kept the accounts by means of the reckoning beads, looked at the horses' teeth like a peasant, and was always laughing or shouting; and whatever she did or said the old man was simply delighted and muttered:

"Well done, daughter-in-law! You are a smart wench!"

He was a widower, but a year after his son's marriage he could not resist getting married himself. A girl was found for him, living twenty miles from Ukleevo, called Varvara Nikolaevna, no longer quite young, but good-looking, comely, and belonging to a decent family. As soon as she was installed into the upper-storey room everything in the house seemed to brighten up as though new glass had been put into all the windows. The lamps gleamed before the ikons, the tables were covered with snow-white cloths, flowers with red buds made their appearance in the windows and in the front garden, and at dinner, instead of eating from a single bowl, each person had a separate plate set for him. Varvara Nikolaevna had a pleasant, friendly smile, and it seemed as though the whole house were smiling, too. Beggars and pilgrims, male and female, began to come into the yard, a thing which had never happened in the past; the plaintive sing-song voices of the Ukleevo peasant women and the apologetic coughs of weak, seedy-looking men, who had been dismissed from the factory for drunkenness were heard under the windows. Varvara helped them with money, with bread, with old clothes, and afterwards, when she felt more at home, began taking things out of the shop. One day the deaf man saw her take four ounces of tea and that disturbed him.

"Here, mother's taken four ounces of tea," he informed his father afterwards; "where is that to be entered?"

The old man made no reply but stood still and thought a moment, moving his eyebrows, and then went upstairs to his wife.

"Varvarushka, if you want anything out of the shop," he said affectionately, "take it, my dear. Take it and welcome; don't hesitate."

And the next day the deaf man, running across the yard, called to her:

"If there is anything you want, mother, take it."

There was something new, something gay and light-hearted in her giving of alms, just as there was in the lamps before the ikons and in the red flowers. When at Carnival or at the church festival, which lasted for three days, they sold the peasants tainted salt meat, smelling so strong it was hard to stand near the tub of it, and took scythes, caps, and their wives' kerchiefs in pledge from the drunken men; when the factory hands stupefied with bad vodka lay rolling in the mud, and sin seemed to hover thick like a fog in the air, then it was a relief to think that up there in the house there was a gentle, neatly dressed woman who had nothing to do with salt meat or vodka; her charity had in those burdensome, murky days the effect of a safety valve in a machine.

The days in Tsybukin's house were spent in business cares. Before the sun had risen in the morning Aksinya was panting and puffing as she washed in the outer room, and the samovar was boiling in the kitchen with a hum that boded no good. Old Grigory Petrovitch, dressed in a long black coat, cotton breeches and shiny top boots, looking a dapper little figure, walked about the rooms, tapping with his little heels like the father-in-law in a well-known song. The shop was opened. When it was daylight a racing droshky was brought up to the front door and the old man got jauntily on to it, pulling his big cap down to his ears; and, looking at him, no one would have said he was fifty-six. His wife and daughter-in-law saw him off, and at such times when he had on a good, clean coat, and had in the droshky a huge black horse that had cost three hundred roubles, the old man did not like the peasants to come up to him with their complaints and petitions; he hated the peasants and disdained them, and if he saw some peasants waiting at the gate, he would shout angrily:

"Why are you standing there? Go further off."

Or if it were a beggar, he would say:

"God will provide!"

He used to drive off on business; his wife, in a dark dress and a black apron, tidied the rooms or helped in the kitchen. Aksinya attended to the shop, and from the yard could be heard the clink of bottles and of money, her laughter and loud talk, and the anger of customers whom she had offended; and at the same time it could be seen that the secret sale of vodka was already going on in the shop. The deaf man sat in the shop, too, or walked about the street bare-headed, with his hands in his pockets looking absent-mindedly now at the huts, now at the sky overhead. Six times a day they had tea; four times a day they sat down to meals; and in the evening they counted over their takings, put them down, went to bed, and slept soundly.

All the three cotton factories in Ukleevo and the houses of the factory owners - Hrymin Seniors, Hrymin Juniors, and Kostukov - were on a telephone. The telephone was laid on in the local court, too, but it soon ceased to work as bugs and beetles bred there. The elder of the rural district had had little education and wrote every word in the official documents in capitals. But when the telephone was spoiled he said:

"Yes, now we shall be badly off without a telephone."

The Hrymin Seniors were continually at law with the Juniors, and sometimes the Juniors quarrelled among themselves and began going to law, and their factory did not work for a month or two till they were reconciled again, and this was an entertainment for the people of Ukleevo, as there was a great deal of talk and gossip on the occasion of each quarrel. On holidays Kostukov and the Juniors used to get up races, used to dash about Ukleevo and run over calves. Aksinya, rustling her starched petticoats, used to promenade in a low-necked dress up and down the street near her shop; the Juniors used to snatch her up and carry her off as though by force. Then old Tsybukin would drive out to show his new horse and take Varvara with him.

In the evening, after the races, when people were going to bed, an expensive concertina was played in the Juniors' yard and, if it were a moonlight night, those sounds sent a thrill of delight to the heart, and Ukleevo no longer seemed a wretched hole.

II

The elder son Anisim came home very rarely, only on great holidays, but he often sent by a returning villager presents and letters written in very good writing by some other hand, always on a sheet of foolscap in the form of a petition. The letters were full of expressions that Anisim never made use of in conversation: "Dear papa and mamma, I send you a pound of flower tea for the satisfaction of your physical needs."

At the bottom of every letter was scratched, as though with a broken pen: "Anisim Tsybukin," and again in the same excellent hand: "Agent."

The letters were read aloud several times, and the old father, touched, red with emotion, would say:

"Here he did not care to stay at home, he has gone in for an intellectual line. Well, let him! Every man to his own job!

It happened just before Carnival there was a heavy storm of rain mixed with hail; the old man and Varvara went to the window to look at it, and lo and behold! Anisim drove up in a sledge from the station. He was quite unexpected. He came indoors, looking anxious and troubled about something, and he remained the same all the time; there was something free and easy in his manner. He was in no haste to go away, it seemed, as though he had been dismissed from the service. Varvara was pleased at his arrival; she looked at him with a sly expression, sighed, and shook her head.

"How is this, my friends?" she said. "Tut, tut, the lad's in his twenty-eighth year, and he is still leading a gay bachelor life; tut, tut, tut. . . ."

From the other room her soft, even speech sounded like tut, tut, tut. She began whispering with her husband and Aksinya, and their faces wore the same sly and mysterious expression as though they were conspirators.

It was decided to marry Anisim.

"Oh, tut, tut . . . the younger brother has been married long ago," said Varvara, "and you are still without a helpmate like a cock at a fair. What is the meaning of it? Tut, tut, you will be married, please God, then as you choose - you will go into the service and your wife will remain here at home to help us. There is no order in your life, young man, and I see you have forgotten how to live properly. Tut, tut, it's the same trouble with all you townspeople."

When the Tsybukins married, the most handsome girls were chosen as brides for them as rich men. For Anisim, too, they found a handsome one. He was himself of an uninteresting and inconspicuous appearance; of a feeble, sickly build and short stature; he had full, puffy cheeks which looked as though he were blowing them out; his eyes looked with a keen, unblinking stare; his beard was red and scanty, and when he was thinking he always put it into his mouth and bit it; moreover he often drank too much, and that was noticeable from his face and his walk. But when he was informed that they had found a very beautiful bride for him, he said:

"Oh well, I am not a fright myself. All of us Tsybukins are handsome, I may say."

The village of Torguevo was near the town. Half of it had lately been incorporated into the town, the other half remained a village. In the first - the town half - there was a widow living in her own little house; she had a sister living with her who was quite poor and went out to work by the day, and this sister had a daughter called Lipa, a girl who went out to work, too. People in Torguevo were already talking about Lipa's good looks, but her terrible poverty put everyone off; people opined that some widower or elderly man would marry her regardless of her poverty, or would perhaps take her to himself without marriage, and that her mother would get enough to eat living with her. Varvara heard about Lipa from the matchmakers, and she drove over to Torguevo.

Then a visit of inspection was arranged at the aunt's, with lunch and wine all in due order, and Lipa wore a new pink dress made on purpose for this occasion, and a crimson ribbon like a flame gleamed in her hair. She was pale-faced, thin, and frail, with soft, delicate features sunburnt from working in the open air; a shy, mournful smile always hovered about her face, and there was a childlike look in her eyes, trustful and curious.

She was young, quite a little girl, her bosom still scarcely perceptible, but she could be married because she had reached the legal age. She really was beautiful, and the only thing that might be thought unattractive was her big masculine hands which hung idle now like two big claws.

"There is no dowry - and we don't think much of that," said Tsybukin to the aunt. "We took a wife from a poor family for our son Stepan, too, and now we can't say too much for her. In house and in business alike she has hands of gold."

Lipa stood in the doorway and looked as though she would say: "Do with me as you will, I trust you," while her mother Praskovya the work-woman hid herself in the kitchen numb with shyness. At one time in her youth a merchant whose floors she was scrubbing stamped at her in a rage; she went chill with terror and there always was a feeling of fear at the bottom of her heart. When she was frightened her arms and legs trembled and her cheeks twitched. Sitting in the kitchen she tried to hear what the visitors were saying, and she kept crossing herself, pressing her fingers to her forehead, and gazing at the ikons. Anisim, slightly drunk, opened the door into the kitchen and said in a free-and-easy way:

"Why are you sitting in here, precious mamma? We are dull without you."

And Praskovya, overcome with timidity, pressing her hands to her lean, wasted bosom, said:

"Oh, not at all. . . . It's very kind of you."

After the visit of inspection the wedding day was fixed. Then Anisim walked about the rooms at home whistling, or suddenly thinking of something, would fall to brooding and would look at the floor fixedly, silently, as though he would probe to the depths of the earth. He expressed neither pleasure that he was to be married, married so soon, on Low Sunday, nor a desire to see his bride, but simply went on whistling. And it was evident he was only getting married because his father and stepmother wished him to, and because it was the custom in the village to marry the son in order to have a woman to help in the house. When he went away he seemed in no haste, and behaved altogether not as he had done on previous visits - was particularly free and easy, and talked inappropriately.

III

In the village Shikalovo lived two dressmakers, sisters, belonging to the Flagellant sect. The new clothes for the wedding were ordered from them, and they often came to try them on, and stayed a long while drinking tea. They were making Varvara a brown dress with black lace and bugles on it, and Aksinya a light green dress with a yellow front, with a train. When the dressmakers had finished their work Tsybukin paid them not in money but in goods from the shop, and they went away depressed, carrying parcels of tallow candles and tins of sardines which they did not in the least need, and when they got out of the village into the open country they sat down on a hillock and cried.

Anisim arrived three days before the wedding, rigged out in new clothes from top to toe. He had dazzling india-rubber goloshes, and instead of a cravat wore a red cord with little balls on it, and over his shoulder he had hung an overcoat, also new, without putting his arms into the sleeves.

After crossing himself sedately before the ikon, he greeted his father and gave him ten silver roubles and ten half-roubles; to Varvara he gave as much, and to Aksinya twenty quarter-roubles. The chief charm of the present lay in the fact that all the coins, as though carefully matched, were new and glittered in the sun. Trying to seem grave and sedate he pursed up his face and puffed out his cheeks, and he smelt of spirits. Probably he had visited the refreshment bar at every station. And again there was a free-and-easiness about the man - something superfluous and out of place. Then Anisim had lunch and drank tea with the old man, and Varvara turned the new coins over in her hand and inquired about villagers who had gone to live in the town.

"They are all right, thank God, they get on quite well," said Anisim. "Only something has happened to Ivan Yegorov: his old wife Sofya Nikiforovna is dead. From consumption. They ordered the memorial dinner for the peace of her soul at the confectioner's at two and a half roubles a head. And there was real wine. Those who were peasants from our village - they paid two and a half roubles for them, too. They ate nothing, as though a peasant would understand sauce!"

"Two and a half," said his father, shaking his head.

"Well, it's not like the country there, you go into a restaurant to have a snack of something, you ask for one thing and another, others join till there is a party of us, one has a drink - and before you know where you are it is daylight and you've three or four roubles each to pay. And when one is with Samorodov he likes to have coffee with brandy in it after everything, and brandy is sixty kopecks for a little glass."

"And he is making it all up," said the old man enthusiastically; "he is making it all up, lying!"

"I am always with Samorodov now. It is Samorodov who writes my letters to you. He writes splendidly. And if I were to tell you, mamma," Anisim went on gaily, addressing Varvara, "the sort of fellow that Samorodov is, you would not believe me. We call him Muhtar, because he is black like an Armenian. I can see through him, I know all his affairs like the five fingers of my hand, and he feels that, and he always follows me about, we are regular inseparables. He seems not to like it in a way, but he can't get on without me. Where I go he goes. I have a correct, trustworthy eye, mamma. One sees a peasant selling a shirt in the market place. 'Stay, that shirt's stolen.' And really it turns out it is so: the shirt was a stolen one."

"What do you tell from?" asked Varvara.

"Not from anything, I have just an eye for it. I know nothing about the shirt, only for some reason I seem drawn to it: it's stolen, and that's all I can say. Among us detectives it's come to their saying, 'Oh, Anisim has gone to shoot snipe!' That means looking for stolen goods. Yes. . . . Anybody can steal, but it is another thing to keep! The earth is wide, but there is nowhere to hide stolen goods."

"In our village a ram and two ewes were carried off last week," said Varvara, and she heaved a sigh, and there is no one to try and find them. . . . Oh, tut, tut. ."

"Well, I might have a try. I don't mind."

The day of the wedding arrived. It was a cool but bright, cheerful April day. People were driving about Ukleevo from early morning with pairs or teams of three horses decked with many-coloured ribbons on their yokes and manes, with a jingle of bells. The rooks, disturbed by this activity, were cawing noisily in the willows, and the starlings sang their loudest unceasingly as though rejoicing that there was a wedding at the Tsybukins'.

Indoors the tables were already covered with long fish, smoked hams, stuffed fowls, boxes of sprats, pickled savouries of various sorts, and a number of bottles of vodka and wine; there was a smell of smoked sausage and of sour tinned lobster. Old Tsybukin walked about near the tables, tapping with his heels and sharpening the knives against each other. They kept calling Varvara and asking for things, and she was constantly with a distracted face running breathlessly into the kitchen, where the man cook from Kostukov's and the woman cook from Hrymin Juniors' had been at work since early morning. Aksinya, with her hair curled, in her stays without her dress on, in new creaky boots, flew about the yard like a whirlwind showing glimpses of her bare knees and bosom.

It was noisy, there was a sound of scolding and oaths; passers-by stopped at the wide-open gates, and in everything there was a feeling that something extraordinary was happening.

"They have gone for the bride!"

The bells began jingling and died away far beyond the village. . . . Between two and three o'clock people ran up: again there was a jingling of bells: they were bringing the bride! The church was full, the candelabra were lighted, the choir were singing from music books as old Tsybukin had wished it. The glare of the lights and the bright coloured dresses dazzled Lipa; she felt as though the singers with their loud voices were hitting her on the head with a hammer. Her boots and the stays, which she had put on for the first time in her life, pinched her, and her face looked as though she had only just come to herself after fainting; she gazed about without understanding. Anisim, in his black coat with a red cord instead of a tie, stared at the same spot lost in thought, and when the singers shouted loudly he hurriedly crossed himself. He felt touched and disposed to weep. This church was familiar to him from earliest childhood; at one time his dead mother used to bring him here to take the sacrament; at one time he used to sing in the choir; every ikon he remembered so well, every corner. Here he was being married, he had to take a wife for the sake of doing the proper thing, but he was not thinking of that now, he had forgotten his wedding completely. Tears dimmed his eyes so that he could not see the ikons, he felt heavy at heart; he prayed and besought God that the misfortunes that threatened him, that were ready to burst upon him to-morrow, if not to-day, might somehow pass him by as storm-clouds in time of drought pass over the village without yielding one drop of rain. And so many sins were heaped up in the past, so many sins, all getting away from them or setting them right was so beyond hope that it seemed incongruous even to ask forgiveness. But he did ask forgiveness, and even gave a loud sob, but no one took any notice of that, since they all supposed he had had a drop too much.

There was a sound of a fretful childish wail:

"Take me away, mamma darling!"

"Quiet there!" cried the priest.

When they returned from the church people ran after them; there were crowds, too, round the shop, round the gates, and in the yard under the windows. The peasant women came in to sing songs of congratulation to them. The young couple had scarcely crossed the threshold when the singers, who were already standing in the outer room with their music books, broke into a loud chant at the top of their voices; a band ordered expressly from the town began playing. Foaming Don wine was brought in tall wine-glasses, and Elizarov, a carpenter who did jobs by contract, a tall, gaunt old man with eyebrows so bushy that his eyes could scarcely be seen, said, addressing the happy pair:

"Anisim and you, my child, love one another, live in God's way, little children, and the Heavenly Mother will not abandon you."

He leaned his face on the old father's shoulder and gave a sob.

"Grigory Petrovitch, let us weep, let us weep with joy!" he said in a thin voice, and then at once burst out laughing in a loud bass guffaw. "Ho-ho-ho! This is a fine daughter-in-law for you too! Everything is in its place in her; all runs smoothly, no creaking, the mechanism works well, lots of screws in it."

He was a native of the Yegoryevsky district, but had worked in the factories in Ukleevo and the neighborhood from his youth up, and had made it his home. He had been a familiar figure for years as old and gaunt and lanky as now, and for years he had been nicknamed "Crutch." Perhaps because he had been for forty years occupied in repairing the factory machinery he judged everybody and everything by its soundness or its need of repair. And before sitting down to the table he tried several chairs to see whether they were solid, and he touched the smoked fish also.

After the Don wine, they all sat down to the table. The visitors talked, moving their chairs. The singers were singing in the outer room. The band was playing, and at the same time the peasant women in the yard were singing their songs all in chorus - and there was an awful, wild medley of sounds which made one giddy.

Crutch turned round in his chair and prodded his neighbours with his elbows, prevented people from talking, and laughed and cried alternately.

"Little children, little children, little children," he muttered rapidly. "Aksinya my dear, Varvara darling, we will live all in peace and harmony, my dear little axes. . . ."

He drank little and was now only drunk from one glass of English bitters. The revolting bitters, made from nobody knows what, intoxicated everyone who drank it as though it had stunned them. Their tongues began to falter.

The local clergy, the clerks from the factories with their wives, the tradesmen and tavern-keepers from the other villages were present. The clerk and the elder of the rural district who had served together for fourteen years, and who had during all that time never signed a single document for anybody nor let a single person out of the local court without deceiving or insulting him, were sitting now side by side, both fat and well-fed, and it seemed as though they were so saturated in injustice and falsehood that even the skin of their faces was somehow peculiar, fraudulent. The clerk's wife, a thin woman with a squint, had brought all her children with her, and like a bird of prey looked aslant at the plates and snatched anything she could get hold of to put in her own or her children's pockets.

Lipa sat as though turned to stone, still with the same expression as in church. Anisim had not said a single word to her since he had made her acquaintance, so that he did not yet know the sound of her voice; and now, sitting beside her, he remained mute and went on drinking bitters, and when he got drunk he began talking to the aunt who was sitting opposite:

"I have a friend called Samorodov. A peculiar man. He is by rank an honorary citizen, and he can talk. But I know him through and through, auntie, and he feels it. Pray join me in drinking to the health of Samorodov, auntie!"

Varvara, worn out and distracted, walked round the table pressing the guests to eat, and was evidently pleased that there were so many dishes and that everything was so lavish - no one could disparage them now. The sun set, but the dinner went on: the guests were beyond knowing what they were eating or drinking, it was impossible to distinguish what was said, and only from time to time when the band subsided some peasant woman could be heard shouting:

"They have sucked the blood out of us, the Herods; a pest on them!"

In the evening they danced to the band. The Hrymin Juniors came, bringing their wine, and one of them, when dancing a quadrille, held a bottle in each hand and a wineglass in his mouth, and that made everyone laugh. In the middle of the quadrille they suddenly crooked their knees and danced in a squatting position; Aksinya in green flew by like a flash, stirring up a wind with her train. Someone trod on her flounce and Crutch shouted:

"Aie, they have torn off the panel! Children!"

Aksinya had naïve grey eyes which rarely blinked, and a naïve smile played continually on her face. And in those unblinking eyes, and in that little head on the long neck, and in her slenderness there was something snake-like; all in green but for the yellow on her bosom, she looked with a smile on her face as a viper looks out of the young rye in the spring at the passers-by, stretching itself and lifting its head. The Hrymins were free in their behaviour to her, and it was very noticeable that she was on intimate terms with the elder of them. But her deaf husband saw nothing, he did not look at her; he sat with his legs crossed and ate nuts, cracking them so loudly that it sounded like pistol shots.

But, behold, old Tsybukin himself walked into the middle of the room and waved his handkerchief as a sign that he, too, wanted to dance the Russian dance, and all over the house and from the crowd in the yard rose a roar of approbation:

"*He's* going to dance! *He* himself!"

Varvara danced, but the old man only waved his handkerchief and kicked up his heels, but the people in the yard, propped against one another, peeping in at the windows, were in raptures, and for the moment forgave him everything - his wealth and the wrongs he had done them.

"Well done, Grigory Petrovitch!" was heard in the crowd. "That's right, do your best! You can still play your part! Ha-ha!"

It was kept up till late, till two o'clock in the morning. Anisim, staggering, went to take leave of the singers and bandsmen, and gave each of them a new half-rouble. His father, who was not staggering but still seemed to be standing on one leg, saw his guests off, and said to each of them:

"The wedding has cost two thousand."

As the party was breaking up, someone took the Shikalovo innkeeper's good coat instead of his own old one, and Anisim suddenly flew into a rage and began shouting:

"Stop, I'll find it at once; I know who stole it, stop."

He ran out into the street and pursued someone. He was caught, brought back home and shoved, drunken, red with anger, and wet, into the room where the aunt was undressing Lipa, and was locked in.

IV

Five days had passed. Anisim, who was preparing to go, went upstairs to say good-bye to Varvara. All the lamps were burning before the ikons, there was a smell of incense, while she sat at the window knitting a stocking of red wool.

"You have not stayed with us long," she said. "You've been dull, I dare say. Oh, tut, tut. We live comfortably; we have plenty of everything. We celebrated your wedding properly, in good style; your father says it came to two thousand. In fact we live like merchants, only it's dreary. We treat the people very badly. My heart aches, my dear; how we treat them, my goodness! Whether we exchange a horse or buy something or hire a labourer - it's cheating in everything. Cheating and cheating. The Lenten oil in the shop is bitter, rancid, the people have pitch that is better. But surely, tell me pray, couldn't we sell good oil?"

"Every man to his job, mamma."

"But you know we all have to die? Oy, oy, really you ought to talk to your father . . . !"

"Why, you should talk to him yourself."

"Well, well, I did put in my word, but he said just what you do: 'Every man to his own job.' Do you suppose in the next world they'll consider what job you have been put to? God's judgment is just."

"Of course no one will consider," said Anisim, and he heaved a sigh. "There is no God, anyway, you know, mamma, so what considering can there be?"

Varvara looked at him with surprise, burst out laughing, and clasped her hands. Perhaps because she was so genuinely surprised at his words and looked at him as though he were a queer person, he was confused.

"Perhaps there is a God, only there is no faith. When I was being married I was not myself. Just as you may take an egg from under a hen and there is a chicken chirping in it, so my conscience was beginning to chirp in me, and while I was being married I thought all the time there was a God! But when I left the church it was nothing. And indeed, how can I tell whether there is a God or not? We are not taught right from childhood, and while the babe is still at his mother's breast he is only taught 'every man to his own job.' Father does not believe in God, either. You were saying that Guntorev had some sheep stolen. . . . I have found them; it was a peasant at Shikalovo stole them; he stole them, but father's got the fleeces . . . so that's all his faith amounts to."

Anisim winked and wagged his head.

"The elder does not believe in God, either," he went on. "And the clerk and the deacon, too. And as for their going to church and keeping the fasts, that is simply to prevent people talking ill of them, and in case it really may be true that there will be a Day of Judgment. Nowadays people say that the end of the world has come because people have grown weaker, do not honour their parents, and so on. All that is nonsense. My idea, mamma, is that all our trouble is because there is so little conscience in people. I see through things, mamma, and I understand. If a man has a stolen shirt I see it. A man sits in a tavern and you fancy he is drinking tea and no more, but to me the tea is neither here nor there; I see further, he has no conscience. You can go about the whole day and not meet one man with a conscience. And the whole reason is that they don't know whether there is a God or not. . . .

Well, good-bye, mamma, keep alive and well, don't remember evil against me."

Anisim bowed down at Varvara's feet.

"I thank you for everything, mamma," he said. "You are a great gain to our family. You are a very ladylike woman, and I am very pleased with you."

Much moved, Anisim went out, but returned again and said:

"Samorodov has got me mixed up in something: I shall either make my fortune or come to grief. If anything happens, then you must comfort my father, mamma."

"Oh, nonsense, don't you worry, tut, tut, tut. . . God is merciful. And, Anisim, you should be affectionate to your wife, instead of giving each other sulky looks as you do; you might smile at least."

"Yes, she is rather a queer one," said Anisim, and he gave a sigh. "She does not understand anything, she never speaks. She is very young, let her grow up."

A tall, sleek white stallion was already standing at the front door, harnessed to the chaise.

Old Tsybukin jumped in jauntily with a run and took the reins. Anisim kissed Varvara, Aksinya, and his brother. On the steps Lipa, too, was standing; she was standing motionless, looking away, and it seemed as though she had not come to see him off but just by chance for some unknown reason. Anisim went up to her and just touched her cheek with his lips.

"Good-bye," he said.

And without looking at him she gave a strange smile; her face began to quiver, and everyone for some reason felt sorry for her. Anisim, too, leaped into the chaise with a bound and put his arms jauntily akimbo, for he considered himself a good-looking fellow.

When they drove up out of the ravine Anisim kept looking back towards the village. It was a warm, bright day. The cattle were being driven out for the first time, and the peasant girls and women were walking by the herd in their holiday dresses. The dun-coloured bull bellowed, glad to be free, and pawed the ground with his forefeet. On all sides, above and below, the larks were singing. Anisim looked round at the elegant white church - it had only lately been whitewashed - and he thought how he had been praying in it five days before; he looked round at the school with its green roof, at the little river in which he used once to bathe and catch fish, and there was a stir of joy in his heart, and he wished that walls might rise up from the ground and prevent him from going further, and that he might be left with nothing but the past.

At the station they went to the refreshment room and drank a glass of sherry each. His father felt in his pocket for his purse to pay.

"I will stand treat," said Anisim. The old man, touched and delighted, slapped him on the shoulder, and winked to the waiter as much as to say, "See what a fine son I have got."

"You ought to stay at home in the business, Anisim," he said; "you would be worth any price to me! I would shower gold on you from head to foot, my son."

"It can't be done, papa."

The sherry was sour and smelt of sealing-wax, but they had another glass.

When old Tsybukin returned home from the station, for the first moment he did not recognize his younger daughter-in-law. As soon as her husband had driven out of the yard, Lipa was transformed and suddenly brightened up. Wearing a threadbare old petticoat, with her feet bare and her sleeves tucked up to the shoulders, she was scrubbing the stairs in the entry and singing in a silvery little voice, and when she brought out a big tub of dirty water and looked up at the sun with her childlike smile it seemed as though she, too, were a lark.

An old labourer who was passing by the door shook his head and cleared his throat.

"Yes, indeed, your daughters-in-law, Grigory Petrovitch, are a blessing from God," he said. "Not women, but treasures!"

V

On Friday the 8th of July, Elizarov, nicknamed Crutch, and Lipa were returning from the village of Kazanskoe, where they had been to a service on the occasion of a church holiday in the honour of the Holy Mother of Kazan. A good distance after them walked Lipa's mother Praskovya, who always fell behind, as she was ill and short of breath. It was drawing towards evening.

"A-a-a . . ." said Crutch, wondering as he listened to Lipa. "A-a! . . . We-ell!

"I am very fond of jam, Ilya Makaritch," said Lipa. "I sit down in my little corner and drink tea and eat jam. Or I drink it with Varvara Nikolaevna, and she tells some story full of feeling. We have a lot of jam - four jars. 'Have some, Lipa; eat as much as you like.' "

"A-a-a, four jars!"

"They live very well. We have white bread with our tea; and meat, too, as much as one wants. They live very well, only I am frightened with them, Ilya Makaritch. Oh, oh, how frightened I am!"

"Why are you frightened, child?" asked Crutch, and he looked back to see how far Praskovya was behind.

"To begin with, when the wedding had been celebrated I was afraid of Anisim Grigoritch. Anisim Grigoritch did nothing, he didn't ill-treat me, only when he comes near me a cold shiver runs all over me, through all my bones. And I did not sleep one night, I trembled all over and kept praying to God. And now I am afraid of Aksinya, Ilya Makaritch. It's not that she does anything, she is always laughing, but sometimes she glances at the window, and her eyes are so fierce and there is a gleam of green in them - like the eyes of the sheep in the shed. The Hrymin Juniors are leading her astray: 'Your old man,' they tell her, 'has a bit of land at Butyokino, a hundred and twenty acres,' they say, 'and there is sand and water there, so you, Aksinya,' they say, 'build a brickyard there and we will go shares in it.' Bricks now are twenty roubles the thousand, it's a profitable business. Yesterday at dinner Aksinya said to my father-in-law: 'I want to build a brickyard at Butyokino; I'm going into business on my own account.' She laughed as she said it. And Grigory Petrovitch's face darkened, one could see he did not like it. 'As long as I live,' he said, 'the family must not break up, we must go on altogether.' She gave a look and gritted her teeth. . . . Fritters were served, she would not eat them."

"A-a-a! . . ." Crutch was surprised.

"And tell me, if you please, when does she sleep?" said Lipa. "She sleeps for half an hour, then jumps up and keeps walking and walking about to see whether the peasants have not set fire to something, have not stolen something. . . . I am frightened with her, Ilya Makaritch. And the Hrymin Juniors did not go to bed after the wedding, but drove to the town to go to law with each other; and folks do say it is all on account of Aksinya. Two of the brothers have promised to build her a brickyard, but the third is offended, and the factory has been at a standstill for a month, and my uncle Prohor is without work and goes about from house to house getting crusts. 'Hadn't you better go working on the land or sawing up wood, meanwhile, uncle?' I tell him; 'why disgrace yourself?' 'I've got out of the way of it,' he says; 'I don't know how to do any sort of peasant's work now, Lipinka.' . . ."

They stopped to rest and wait for Praskovya near a copse of young aspen-trees. Elizarov had long been a contractor in a small way, but he kept no horses, going on foot all over the district with nothing but a little bag in which there was bread and onions, and stalking along with big strides, swinging his arms. And it was difficult to walk with him.

At the entrance to the copse stood a milestone. Elizarov touched it; read it. Praskovya reached them out of breath. Her wrinkled and always scared-looking face was beaming with happiness; she had been at church to-day like anyone else, then she had been to the fair and there had drunk pear cider. For her this was unusual, and it even seemed to her now that she had lived for her own pleasure that day for the first time in her life. After resting they all three walked on side by side. The sun had already set, and its beams filtered through the copse, casting a light on the trunks of the trees. There was a faint sound of voices ahead. The Ukleevo girls had long before pushed on ahead but had lingered in the copse, probably gathering mushrooms.

"Hey, wenches!" cried Elizarov. "Hey, my beauties!"

There was a sound of laughter in response.

"Crutch is coming! Crutch! The old horseradish."

And the echo laughed, too. And then the copse was left behind. The tops of the factory chimneys came into view. The cross on the belfry glittered: this was the village: "the one at which the deacon ate all the caviare at the funeral." Now they were almost home; they only had to go down into the big ravine. Lipa and Praskovya, who had been walking barefooted, sat down on the grass to put on their boots; Elizar sat down with them. If they looked down from above Ukleevo looked beautiful and peaceful with its willow-trees, its white church, and its little river, and the only blot on the picture was the roof of the factories, painted for the sake of cheapness a gloomy ashen grey. On the slope on the further side they could see the rye - some in stacks and sheaves here and there as though strewn about by the storm, and some freshly cut lying in swathes; the oats, too, were ripe and glistened now in the sun like mother-of-pearl. It was harvest-time. To-day was a holiday, to-morrow they would harvest the rye and carry the hay, and then Sunday a holiday again; every day there were mutterings of distant thunder. It was misty and looked like rain, and, gazing now at the fields, everyone thought, God grant we get the harvest in in time; and everyone felt gay and joyful and anxious at heart.

"Mowers ask a high price nowadays," said Praskovya. "One rouble and forty kopecks a day."

People kept coming and coming from the fair at Kazanskoe: peasant women, factory workers in new caps, beggars, children. . . . Here a cart would drive by stirring up the dust and behind it would run an unsold horse, and it seemed glad it had not been sold; then a cow was led along by the horns, resisting stubbornly; then a cart again, and in it drunken peasants swinging their legs. An old woman led a little boy in a big cap and big boots; the boy was tired out with the heat and the heavy boots which prevented his bending his legs at the knees, but yet blew unceasingly with all his might at a tin trumpet. They had gone down the slope and turned into the street, but the trumpet could still be heard.

"Our factory owners don't seem quite themselves . . ." said Elizarov. "There's trouble. Kostukov is angry with me. 'Too many boards have gone on the cornices.' 'Too many? As many have gone on it as were needed, Vassily Danilitch; I don't eat them with my porridge.' 'How can you speak to me like that?' said he, 'you good-for-nothing blockhead! Don't forget yourself! It was I made you a contractor.' 'That's nothing so wonderful,' said I. 'Even before I was a contractor I used to have tea every day.' 'You are a rascal . . .' he said. I said nothing. 'We are rascals in this world,' thought I, 'and you will be rascals in the next. . . .' Ha-ha-ha! The next day he was softer. 'Don't you bear malice against me for my words, Makaritch,' he said. 'If I said too much,' says he, 'what of it? I am a merchant of the first guild, your superior - you ought to hold your tongue.' 'You,' said I, 'are a merchant of the first guild and I am a carpenter, that's correct. And Saint Joseph was a carpenter, too. Ours is a righteous calling and pleasing to God, and if you are pleased to be my superior you are very welcome to it, Vassily Danilitch.' And later on, after that conversation I mean, I thought: 'Which was the superior? A merchant of the first guild or a carpenter?' The carpenter must be, my child!"

Crutch thought a minute and added:

"Yes, that's how it is, child. He who works, he who is patient is the superior."

By now the sun had set and a thick mist as white as milk was rising over the river, in the church enclosure, and in the open spaces round the factories. Now when the darkness was coming on rapidly, when lights were twinkling below, and when it seemed as though the mists were hiding a fathomless abyss, Lipa and her mother who were born in poverty and prepared to live so till the end, giving up to others everything except their frightened, gentle souls, may have fancied for a minute perhaps that in the vast, mysterious world, among the endless series of lives, they, too, counted for something, and they, too, were superior to someone; they liked sitting here at the top, they smiled happily and forgot that they must go down below again all the same.

At last they went home again. The mowers were sitting on the ground at the gates near the shop. As a rule the Ukleevo peasants did not go to Tsybukin's to work, and they had to hire strangers, and now in the darkness it seemed as though there were men sitting there with long black beards. The shop was open, and through the doorway they could see the deaf man playing draughts with a boy. The mowers were singing softly, scarcely audibly, or loudly demanding their wages for the previous day, but they were not paid for fear they should go away before to-morrow. Old Tsybukin, with his coat off, was sitting in his waistcoat with Aksinya under the birch-tree, drinking tea; a lamp was burning on the table.

"I say, grandfather," a mower called from outside the gates, as though taunting him, "pay us half anyway! Hey, grandfather."

And at once there was the sound of laughter, and then again they sang hardly audibly. . . . Crutch, too, sat down to have some tea.

"We have been at the fair, you know," he began telling them. "We have had a walk, a very nice walk, my children, praise the Lord. But an unfortunate thing happened: Sashka the blacksmith bought some tobacco and gave the shopman half a rouble to be sure. And the half rouble was a false one" -Crutch went on, and he meant to speak in a whisper, but he spoke in a smothered husky voice which was audible to everyone. "The half-rouble turned out to be a bad one. He was asked where he got it. 'Anisim Tsybukin gave it me,' he said. 'When I went to his wedding,' he said. They called the police inspector, took the man away. . . . Look out, Grigory Petrovitch, that nothing comes of it, no talk. . . ."

"Gra-ndfather!" the same voice called tauntingly outside the gates. "Gra-andfather!"

A silence followed.

"Ah, little children, little children, little children . . ." Crutch muttered rapidly, and he got up. He was overcome with drowsiness. "Well, thank you for the tea, for the sugar, little children. It is time to sleep. I am like a bit of rotten timber nowadays, my beams are crumbling under me. Ho-ho-ho! I suppose it's time I was dead."

And he gave a gulp. Old Tsybukin did not finish his tea but sat on a little, pondering; and his face looked as though he were listening to the footsteps of Crutch, who was far away down the street.

"Sashka the blacksmith told a lie, I expect," said Aksinya, guessing his thoughts.

He went into the house and came back a little later with a parcel; he opened it, and there was the gleam of roubles - perfectly new coins. He took one, tried it with his teeth, flung it on the tray; then flung down another.

"The roubles really are false . . ." he said, looking at Aksinya and seeming perplexed. "These are those Anisim brought, his present. Take them, daughter," he whispered, and thrust the parcel into her hands. "Take them and throw them into the well . . . confound them! And mind there is no talk about it. Harm might come of it. . . . Take away the samovar, put out the light."

Lipa and her mother sitting in the barn saw the lights go out one after the other; only overhead in Varvara's room there were blue and red lamps gleaming, and a feeling of peace, content, and happy ignorance seemed to float down from there. Praskovya could never get used to her daughter's being married to a rich man, and when she came she huddled timidly in the outer room with a deprecating smile on her face, and tea and sugar were sent out to her. And Lipa, too, could not get used to it either, and after her husband had gone away she did not sleep in her bed, but lay down anywhere to sleep, in the kitchen or the barn, and every day she scrubbed the floor or washed the clothes, and felt as though she were hired by the day. And now, on coming back from the service, they drank tea in the kitchen with the cook, then they went into the barn and lay down on the ground between the sledge and the wall. It was dark here and smelt of harness. The lights went out about the house, then they could hear the deaf man shutting up the shop, the mowers settling themselves about the yard to sleep. In the distance at the Hrymin Juniors' they were playing on the expensive concertina. . . . Praskovya and Lipa began to go to sleep.

And when they were awakened by somebody's steps it was bright moonlight; at the entrance of the barn stood Aksinya with her bedding in her arms.

"Maybe it's a bit cooler here," she said; then she came in and lay down almost in the doorway so that the moonlight fell full upon her.

She did not sleep, but breathed heavily, tossing from side to side with the heat, throwing off almost all the bedclothes. And in the magic moonlight what a beautiful, what a proud animal she was! A little time passed, and then steps were heard again: the old father, white all over, appeared in the doorway.

"Aksinya," he called, " are you here?"

"Well?" she responded angrily.

"I told you just now to throw the money into the well, have you done so?"

"What next, throwing property into the water! I gave them to the mowers. . . ."

"Oh my God!" cried the old man, dumbfounded and alarmed. "Oh my God! you wicked woman. . . ."

He flung up his hands and went out, and he kept saying something as he went away. And a little later Aksinya sat up and sighed heavily with annoyance, then got up and, gathering up her bedclothes in her arms, went out.

"Why did you marry me into this family, mother?" said Lipa.

"One has to be married, daughter. It was not us who ordained it."

And a feeling of inconsolable woe was ready to take possession of them. But it seemed to them that someone was looking down from the height of the heavens, out of the blue from where the stars were seeing everything that was going on in Ukleevo, watching over them. And however great was wickedness, still the night was calm and beautiful, and still in God's world there is and will be truth and justice as calm and beautiful, and everything on earth is only waiting to be made one with truth and justice, even as the moonlight is blended with the night.

And both, huddling close to one another, fell asleep comforted.

VI

News had come long before that Anisim had been put in prison for coining and passing bad money. Months passed, more than half a year passed, the long winter was over, spring had begun, and everyone in the house and the village had grown used to the fact that Anisim was in prison. And when anyone passed by the house or the shop at night he would remember that Anisim was in prison; and when they rang at the churchyard for some reason, that, too, reminded them that he was in prison awaiting trial.

It seemed as though a shadow had fallen upon the house. The house looked darker, the roof was rustier, the heavy, iron-bound door into the shop, which was painted green, was covered with cracks, or, as the deaf man expressed it, "blisters"; and old Tsybukin seemed to have grown dingy, too. He had given up cutting his hair and beard, and looked shaggy. He no longer sprang jauntily into his chaise, nor shouted to beggars: "God will provide!" His strength was on the wane, and that was evident in everything. People were less afraid of him now, and the police officer drew up a formal charge against him in the shop though he received his regular bribe as before; and three times the old man was called up to the town to be tried for illicit dealing in spirits, and the case was continually adjourned owing to the non-appearance of witnesses, and old Tsybukin was worn out with worry.

He often went to see his son, hired somebody, handed in a petition to somebody else, presented a holy banner to some church. He presented the governor of the prison in which Anisim was confined with a silver glass stand with a long spoon and the inscription: "The soul knows its right measure."

"There is no one to look after things for us," said Varvara. "Tut, tut. . . . You ought to ask someone of the gentlefolks, they would write to the head officials. . . . At least they might let him out on bail! Why wear the poor fellow out?"

She, too, was grieved, but had grown stouter and whiter; she lighted the lamps before the ikons as before, and saw that everything in the house was clean, and regaled the guests with jam and apple cheese. The deaf man and Aksinya looked after the shop. A new project was in progress - a brickyard in Butyokino - and Aksinya went there almost every day in the chaise. She drove herself, and when she met acquaintances she stretched out her neck like a snake out of the young rye, and smiled naïvely and enigmatically. Lipa spent her time playing with the baby which had been born to her before Lent. It was a tiny, thin, pitiful little baby, and it was strange that it should cry and gaze about and be considered a human being, and even be called Nikifor. He lay in his swinging cradle, and Lipa would walk away towards the door and say, bowing to him:

"Good-day, Nikifor Anisimitch!"

And she would rush at him and kiss him. Then she would walk away to the door, bow again, and say:

'Good-day, Nikifor Anisimitch!

And he kicked up his little red legs, and his crying was mixed with laughter like the carpenter Elizarov's.

At last the day of the trial was fixed. Tsybukin went away five days before. Then they heard that the peasants called as witnesses had been fetched; their old workman who had received a notice to appear went too.

The trial was on a Thursday. But Sunday had passed, and Tsybukin was still not back, and there was no news. Towards the evening on Tuesday Varvara was sitting at the open window, listening for her husband to come. In the next room Lipa was playing with her baby. She was tossing him up in her arms and saying enthusiastically:

"You will grow up ever so big, ever so big. You will be a peasant, we shall go out to work together! We shall go out to work together!"

"Come, come," said Varvara, offended. "Go out to work, what an idea, you silly girl! He will be a merchant . . .!"

Lipa sang softly, but a minute later she forgot and again:

"You will grow ever so big, ever so big. You will be a peasant, we'll go out to work together."

"There she is at it again!"

Lipa, with Nikifor in her arms, stood still in the doorway and asked:

"Why do I love him so much, mamma? Why do I feel so sorry for him?" she went on in a quivering voice, and her eyes glistened with tears. "Who is he? What is he like? As light as a little feather, as a little crumb, but I love him; I love him like a real person. Here he can do nothing, he can't talk, and yet I know what he wants with his little eyes."

Varvara was listening; the sound of the evening train coming in to the station reached her. Had her husband come? She did not hear and she did not heed what Lipa was saying, she had no idea how the time passed, but only trembled all over - not from dread, but intense curiosity. She saw a cart full of peasants roll quickly by with a rattle. It was the witnesses coming back from the station. When the cart passed the shop the old workman jumped out and walked into the yard. She could hear him being greeted in the yard and being asked some questions. . . .

"Deprivation of rights and all his property," he said loudly, "and six years' penal servitude in Siberia."

She could see Aksinya come out of the shop by the back way; she had just been selling kerosene, and in one hand held a bottle and in the other a can, and in her mouth she had some silver coins.

"Where is father?" she asked, lisping.

"At the station," answered the labourer. " 'When it gets a little darker,' he said, 'then I shall come.' "

And when it became known all through the household that Anisim was sentenced to penal servitude, the cook in the kitchen suddenly broke into a wail as though at a funeral, imagining that this was demanded by the proprieties:

"There is no one to care for us now you have gone, Anisim Grigoritch, our bright falcon. . . ."

The dogs began barking in alarm. Varvara ran to the window, and rushing about in distress, shouted to the cook with all her might, straining her voice:

"Sto-op, Stepanida, sto-op! Don't harrow us, for Christ's sake!"

They forgot to set the samovar, they could think of nothing. Only Lipa could not make out what it was all about and went on playing with her baby.

When the old father arrived from the station they asked him no questions. He greeted them and walked through all the rooms in silence; he had no supper.

"There was no one to see about things . . ." Varvara began when they were alone. "I said you should have asked some of the gentry, you would not heed me at the time. . . . A petition would . . ."

"I saw to things," said her husband with a wave of his hand. "When Anisim was condemned I went to the gentleman who was defending him. 'It's no use now,' he said, 'it's too late'; and Anisim said the same; it's too late. But all the same as I came out of the court I made an agreement with a lawyer, I paid him something in advance. I'll wait a week and then I will go again. It is as God wills."

Again the old man walked through all the rooms, and when he went back to Varvara he said:

"I must be ill. My head's in a sort of . . . fog. My thoughts are in a maze."

He closed the door that Lipa might not hear, and went on softly:

"I am unhappy about my money. Do you remember on Low Sunday before his wedding Anisim's bringing me some new roubles and half-roubles? One parcel I put away at the time, but the others I mixed with my own money. When my uncle Dmitri Filatitch - the kingdom of heaven be his - was alive, he used constantly to go journeys to Moscow and to the Crimea to buy goods. He had a wife, and this same wife, when he was away buying goods, used to take up with other men. She had half a dozen children. And when uncle was in his cups he would laugh and say: 'I never can make out,' he used to say, 'which are my children and which are other people's.' An easy-going disposition, to be sure; and so I now can't distinguish which are genuine roubles and which are false ones. And it seems to me that they are all false."

"Nonsense, God bless you."

"I take a ticket at the station, I give the man three roubles, and I keep fancying they are false. And I am frightened. I must be ill."

"There's no denying it, we are all in God's hands. . . . Oh dear, dear . . ." said Varvara, and she shook her head. "You ought to think about this, Grigory Petrovitch: you never know, anything may happen, you are not a young man. See they don't wrong your grandchild when you are dead and gone. Oy, I am afraid they will be unfair to Nikifor! He has as good as no father, his mother's young and foolish . . . you ought to secure something for him, poor little boy, at least the land, Butyokino, Grigory Petrovitch, really! Think it over!" Varvara went on persuading him. "The pretty boy, one is sorry for him! You go to-morrow and make out a deed; why put it off?"

"I'd forgotten about my grandson," said Tsybukin. "I must go and have a look at him. So you say the boy is all right? Well, let him grow up, please God."

He opened the door and, crooking his finger, beckoned to Lipa. She went up to him with the baby in her arms.

"If there is anything you want, Lipinka, you ask for it," he said. "And eat anything you like, we don't grudge it, so long as it does you good. . . ." He made the sign of the cross over the baby. "And take care of my grandchild. My son is gone, but my grandson is left."

Tears rolled down his cheeks; he gave a sob and went away. Soon afterwards he went to bed and slept soundly after seven sleepless nights.

VII

Old Tsybukin went to the town for a short time. Someone told Aksinya that he had gone to the notary to make his will and that he was leaving Butyokino, the very place where she had set up a brickyard, to Nikifor, his grandson. She was informed of this in the morning when old Tsybukin and Varvara were sitting near the steps under the birch-tree, drinking their tea. She closed the shop in the front and at the back, gathered together all the keys she had, and flung them at her father-in-law's feet.

"I am not going on working for you," she began in a loud voice, and suddenly broke into sobs. "It seems I am not your daughter-in-law, but a servant! Everybody's jeering and saying, 'See what a servant the Tsybukins have got hold of!' I did not come to you for wages! I am not a beggar, I am not a slave, I have a father and mother."

She did not wipe away her tears, she fixed upon her father-in-law eyes full of tears, vindictive, squinting with wrath; her face and neck were red and tense, and she was shouting at the top of her voice.

"I don't mean to go on being a slave!" she went on. "I am worn out. When it is work, when it is sitting in the shop day in and day out, scurrying out at night for vodka - then it is my share, but when it is giving away the land then it is for that convict's wife and her imp. She is mistress here, and I am her servant. Give her everything, the convict's wife, and may it choke her! I am going home! Find yourselves some other fool, you damned Herods!"

Tsybukin had never in his life scolded or punished his children, and had never dreamed that one of his family could speak to him rudely or behave disrespectfully; and now he was very much frightened; he ran into the house and there hid behind the cupboard. And Varvara was so much flustered that she could not get up from her seat, and only waved her hands before her as though she were warding off a bee.

"Oh, Holy Saints! what's the meaning of it?" she muttered in horror. "What is she shouting? Oh, dear, dear! . . . People will hear! Hush. Oh, hush!"

"He has given Butyokino to the convict's wife," Aksinya went on bawling. "Give her everything now, I don't want anything from you! Let me alone! You are all a gang of thieves here! I have seen my fill of it, I have had enough! You have robbed folks coming in and going out; you have robbed old and young alike, you brigands! And who has been selling vodka without a licence? And false money? You've filled boxes full of false coins, and now I am no more use!"

A crowd had by now collected at the open gate and was staring into the yard.

"Let the people look," bawled Aksinya. "I will shame you all! You shall burn with shame! You shall grovel at my feet. Hey! Stepan," she called to the deaf man, "let us go home this minute! Let us go to my father and mother; I don't want to live with convicts. Get ready!"

Clothes were hanging on lines stretched across the yard; she snatched off her petticoats and blouses still wet and flung them into the deaf man's arms. Then in her fury she dashed about the yard by the linen, tore down all of it, and what was not hers she threw on the ground and trampled upon.

"Holy Saints, take her away," moaned Varvara. "What a woman! Give her Butyokino! Give it her, for the Lord's sake!

"Well! Wha-at a woman!" people were saying at the gate. "She's a wo-oman! She's going it - something like!"

Aksinya ran into the kitchen where washing was going on. Lipa was washing alone, the cook had gone to the river to rinse the clothes. Steam was rising from the trough and from the caldron on the side of the stove, and the kitchen was thick and stifling from the steam. On the floor was a heap of unwashed clothes, and Nikifor, kicking up his little red legs, had been put down on a bench near them, so that if he fell he should not hurt himself. Just as Aksinya went in Lipa took the former's chemise out of the heap and put it in the trough, and was just stretching out her hand to a big ladle of boiling water which was standing on the table.

"Give it here," said Aksinya, looking at her with hatred, and snatching the chemise out of the trough; "it is not your business to touch my linen! You are a convict's wife, and ought to know your place and who you are."

Lipa gazed at her, taken aback, and did not understand, but suddenly she caught the look Aksinya turned upon the child, and at once she understood and went numb all over.

"You've taken my land, so here you are!" Saying this Aksinya snatched up the ladle with the boiling water and flung it over Nikifor.

After this there was heard a scream such as had never been heard before in Ukleevo, and no one would have believed that a little weak creature like Lipa could scream like that. And it was suddenly silent in the yard.

Aksinya walked into the house with her old naïve smile. . . . The deaf man kept moving about the yard with his arms full of linen, then he began hanging it up again, in silence, without haste. And until the cook came back from the river no one ventured to go into the kitchen and see what was there.

VIII

Nikifor was taken to the district hospital, and towards evening he died there. Lipa did not wait for them to come for her, but wrapped the dead baby in its little quilt and carried it home.

The hospital, a new one recently built, with big windows, stood high up on a hill; it was glittering from the setting sun and looked as though it were on fire from inside. There was a little village below. Lipa went down along the road, and before reaching the village sat down by a pond. A woman brought a horse down to drink and the horse did not drink.

"What more do you want?" said the woman to it softly. "What do you want?"

A boy in a red shirt, sitting at the water's edge, was washing his father's boots. And not another soul was in sight either in the village or on the hill.

"It's not drinking," said Lipa, looking at the horse.

Then the woman with the horse and the boy with the boots walked away, and there was no one left at all. The sun went to bed wrapped in cloth of gold and purple, and long clouds, red and lilac, stretched across the sky, guarded its slumbers. Somewhere far away a bittern cried, a hollow, melancholy sound like a cow shut up in a barn. The cry of that mysterious bird was heard every spring, but no one knew what it was like or where it lived. At the top of the hill by the hospital, in the bushes close to the pond, and in the fields the nightingales were trilling. The cuckoo kept reckoning someone's years and losing count and beginning again. In the pond the frogs called angrily to one another, straining themselves to bursting, and one could even make out the words: "That's what you are! That's what you are! " What a noise there was! It seemed as though all these creatures were singing and shouting so that no one might sleep on that spring night, so that all, even the angry frogs, might appreciate and enjoy every minute: life is given only once.

A silver half-moon was shining in the sky; there were many stars. Lipa had no idea how long she sat by the pond, but when she got up and walked on everybody was asleep in the little village, and there was not a single light. It was probably about nine miles' walk home, but she had not the strength, she had not the power to think how to go: the moon gleamed now in front, now on the right, and the same cuckoo kept calling in a voice grown husky, with a chuckle as though gibing at her: "Oy, look out, you'll lose your way!" Lipa walked rapidly; she lost the kerchief from her head . . . she looked at the sky and wondered where her baby's soul was now: was it following her, or floating aloft yonder among the stars and thinking nothing now of his mother? Oh, how lonely it was in the open country at night, in the midst of that singing when one cannot sing oneself; in the midst of the incessant cries of joy when one cannot oneself be joyful, when the moon, which cares not whether it is spring or winter, whether men are alive or dead, looks down as lonely, too. . . . When there is grief in the heart it is hard to be without people. If only her mother, Praskovya, had been with her, or Crutch, or the cook, or some peasant!

"Boo-oo!" cried the bittern. "Boo-oo!"

And suddenly she heard clearly the sound of human speech: "Put the horses in, Vavila!"

By the wayside a camp fire was burning ahead of her: the flames had died down, there were only red embers. She could hear the horses munching. In the darkness she could see the outlines of two carts, one with a barrel, the other, a lower one with sacks in it, and the figures of two men; one was leading a horse to put it into the shafts, the other was standing motionless by the fire with his hands behind his back. A dog growled by the carts. The one who was leading the horse stopped and said:

"It seems as though someone were coming along the road."

"Sharik, be quiet!" the other called to the dog.

And from the voice one could tell that the second was an old man. Lipa stopped and said:

"God help you."

The old man went up to her and answered not immediately:

"Good-evening!"

"Your dog does not bite, grandfather?"

"No, come along, he won't touch you."

"I have been at the hospital," said Lipa after a pause. "My little son died there. Here I am carrying him home."

It must have been unpleasant for the old man to hear this, for he moved away and said hurriedly:

"Never mind, my dear. It's God's will. You are very slow, lad," he added, addressing his companion; "look alive!

"Your yoke's nowhere," said the young man; "it is not to be seen."

"You are a regular Vavila."

The old man picked up an ember, blew on it - only his eyes and nose were lighted up - then, when they had found the yoke, he went with the light to Lipa and looked at her, and his look expressed compassion and tenderness.

"You are a mother," he said; "every mother grieves for her child."

And he sighed and shook his head as he said it. Vavila threw something on the fire, stamped on it - and at once it was very dark; the vision vanished, and as before there were only the fields, the sky with the stars, and the noise of the birds hindering each other from sleep. And the landrail called, it seemed, in the very place where the fire had been.

But a minute passed, and again she could see the two carts and the old man and lanky Vavila. The carts creaked as they went out on the road.

"Are you holy men?" Lipa asked the old man.

"No. We are from Firsanovo."

"You looked at me just now and my heart was softened. And the young man is so gentle. I thought you must be holy men."

"Are you going far?"

"To Ukleevo."

"Get in, we will give you a lift as far as Kuzmenki, then you go straight on and we turn off to the left."

Vavila got into the cart with the barrel and the old man and Lipa got into the other. They moved at a walking pace, Vavila in front.

"My baby was in torment all day," said Lipa. "He looked at me with his little eyes and said nothing; he wanted to speak and could not. Holy Father, Queen of Heaven! In my grief I kept falling down on the floor. I stood up and fell down by the bedside. And tell me, grandfather, why a little thing should be tormented before his death? When a grown-up person, a man or woman, are in torment their sins are forgiven, but why a little thing, when he has no sins? Why?"

"Who can tell?" answered the old man.

They drove on for half an hour in silence.

"We can't know everything, how and wherefore," said the old man. "It is ordained for the bird to have not four wings but two because it is able to fly with two; and so it is ordained for man not to know everything but only a half or a quarter. As much as he needs to know so as to live, so much he knows."

"It is better for me to go on foot, grandfather. Now my heart is all of a tremble."

"Never mind, sit still."

The old man yawned and made the sign of the cross over his mouth.

"Never mind," he repeated. "Yours is not the worst of sorrows. Life is long, there will be good and bad to come, there will be everything. Great is mother Russia," he said, and looked round on each side of him. "I have been all over Russia, and I have seen everything in her, and you may believe my words, my dear. There will be good and there will be bad. I went as a delegate from my village to Siberia, and I have been to the Amur River and the Altai Mountains and I settled in Siberia; I worked the land there, then I was homesick for mother Russia and I came back to my native village. We came back to Russia on foot; and I remember we went on a steamer, and I was thin as thin, all in rags, barefoot, freezing with cold, and gnawing a crust, and a gentleman who was on the steamer - the kingdom of heaven be his if he is dead - looked at me pitifully, and the tears came into his eyes. 'Ah,' he said, 'your bread is black, your days are black. . . .' And when I got home, as the saying is, there was neither stick nor stall; I had a wife, but I left her behind in Siberia, she was buried there. So I am living as a day labourer. And yet I tell you: since then I have had good as well as bad. Here I do not want to die, my dear, I would be glad to live another twenty years; so there has been more of the good. And great is our mother Russia!" and again he gazed to each side and looked round.

"Grandfather," Lipa asked, "when anyone dies, how many days does his soul walk the earth?"

"Who can tell! Ask Vavila here, he has been to school. Now they teach them everything. Vavila!" the old man called to him.

"Yes!"

"Vavila, when anyone dies how long does his soul walk the earth?

Vavila stopped the horse and only then answered:

"Nine days. My uncle Kirilla died and his soul lived in our hut thirteen days after."

"How do you know?"

"For thirteen days there was a knocking in the stove."

"Well, that's all right. Go on," said the old man, and it could be seen that he did not believe a word of all that.

Near Kuzmenki the cart turned into the high road while Lipa went straight on. It was by now getting light. As she went down into the ravine the Ukleevo huts and the church were hidden in fog. It was cold, and it seemed to her that the same cuckoo was calling still.

When Lipa reached home the cattle had not yet been driven out; everyone was asleep. She sat down on the steps and waited. The old man was the first to come out; he understood all that had happened from the first glance at her, and for a long time he could not articulate a word, but only moved his lips without a sound.

"Ech, Lipa," he said, "you did not take care of my grandchild. . . ."

Varvara was awakened. She clasped her hands and broke into sobs, and immediately began laying out the baby.

"And he was a pretty child . . ." she said. "Oh, dear, dear. . . . You only had the one child, and you did not take care enough of him, you silly girl. . . ."

There was a requiem service in the morning and the evening. The funeral took place the next day, and after it the guests and the priests ate a great deal, and with such greed that one might have thought that they had not tasted food for a long time. Lipa waited at table, and the priest, lifting his fork on which there was a salted mushroom, said to her:

"Don't grieve for the babe. For of such is the kingdom of heaven."

And only when they had all separated Lipa realized fully that there was no Nikifor and never would be, she realized it and broke into sobs. And she did not know what room to go into to sob, for she felt that now that her child was dead there was no place for her in the house, that she had no reason to be here, that she was in the way; and the others felt it, too.

"Now what are you bellowing for?" Aksinya shouted, suddenly appearing in the doorway; in honour of the funeral she was dressed all in new clothes and had powdered her face. "Shut up!"

Lipa tried to stop but could not, and sobbed louder than ever.

"Do you hear?" shouted Aksinya, and she stamped her foot in violent anger. "Who is it I am speaking to? Go out of the yard and don't set foot here again, you convict s wife. Get away."

"There, there, there," the old man put in fussily. "Aksinya, don't make such an outcry, my girl. . . . She is crying, it is only natural . . . her child is dead. . . ."

" 'It's only natural,' " Aksinya mimicked him. "Let her stay the night here, and don't let me see a trace of her here to-morrow! 'It's only natural!' . . ." she mimicked him again, and, laughing, she went into the shop.

Early the next morning Lipa went off to her mother at Torguevo.

IX

At the present time the steps and the front door of the shop have been repainted and are as bright as though they were new, there are gay geraniums in the windows as of old, and what happened in Tsybukin's house and yard three years ago is almost forgotten.

Grigory Petrovitch is looked upon as the master as he was in old days, but in reality everything has passed into Aksinya's hands; she buys and sells, and nothing can be done without her consent. The brickyard is working well; and as bricks are wanted for the railway the price has gone up to twenty-four roubles a thousand; peasant women and girls cart the bricks to the station and load them up in the trucks and earn a quarter-rouble a day for the work.

Aksinya has gone into partnership with the Hrymin Juniors, and their factory is now called Hrymin Juniors and Co. They have opened a tavern near the station, and now the expensive concertina is played not at the factory but at the tavern, and the head of the post office often goes there, and he, too, is engaged in some sort of traffic, and the stationmaster, too. Hrymin Juniors have presented the deaf man Stepan with a gold watch, and he is constantly taking it out of his pocket and putting it to his ear.

People say of Aksinya that she has become a person of power; and it is true that when she drives in the morning to her brickyard, handsome and happy, with the naïve smile on her face, and afterwards when she is giving orders there, one is aware of great power in her. Everyone is afraid of her in the house and in the village and in the brickyard. When she goes to the post the head of the postal department jumps up and says to her:

"I humbly beg you to be seated, Aksinya Abramovna!"

A certain landowner, middle-aged but foppish, in a tunic of fine cloth and patent leather high boots, sold her a horse, and was so carried away by talking to her that he knocked down the price to meet her wishes. He held her hand a long time and, looking into her merry, sly, naïve eyes, said:

"For a woman like you, Aksinya Abramovna, I should be ready to do anything you please. Only say when we can meet where no one will interfere with us?"

"Why, when you please."

And since then the elderly fop drives up to the shop almost every day to drink beer. And the beer is horrid, bitter as wormwood. The landowner shakes his head, but he drinks it.

Old Tsybukin does not have anything to do with the business now at all. He does not keep any money because he cannot distinguish between the good and the false, but he is silent, he says nothing of this weakness. He has become forgetful, and if they don't give him food he does not ask for it. They have grown used to having dinner without him, and Varvara often says:

"He went to bed again yesterday without any supper."

And she says it unconcernedly because she is used to it. For some reason, summer and winter alike, he wears a fur coat, and only in very hot weather he does not go out but sits at home. As a rule putting on his fur coat, wrapping it round him and turning up his collar, he walks about the village, along the road to the station, or sits from morning till night on the seat near the church gates. He sits there without stirring. Passers-by bow to him, but he does not respond, for as of old he dislikes the peasants. If he is asked a question he answers quite rationally and politely, but briefly.

There is a rumour going about in the village that his daughter-in-law turns him out of the house and gives him nothing to eat, and that he is fed by charity; some are glad, others are sorry for him.

Varvara has grown even fatter and whiter, and as before she is active in good works, and Aksinya does not interfere with her.

There is so much jam now that they have not time to eat it before the fresh fruit comes in; it goes sugary, and Varvara almost sheds tears, not knowing what to do with it.

They have begun to forget about Anisim. A letter has come from him written in verse on a big sheet of paper as though it were a petition, all in the same splendid handwriting. Evidently his friend Samorodov was sharing his punishment. Under the verses in an ugly, scarcely legible handwriting there was a single line: "I am ill here all the time; I am wretched, for Christ's sake help me!"

Towards evening - it was a fine autumn day - old Tsybukin was sitting near the church gates, with the collar of his fur coat turned up and nothing of him could be seen but his nose and the peak of his cap. At the other end of the long seat was sitting Elizarov the contractor, and beside him Yakov the school watchman, a toothless old man of seventy. Crutch and the watchman were talking.

"Children ought to give food and drink to the old. . . . Honour thy father and mother . . ." Yakov was saying with irritation, "while she, this daughter-in-law, has turned her father-in-law out of his own house; the old man has neither food nor drink, where is he to go? He has not had a morsel for these three days."

"Three days!" said Crutch, amazed.

"Here he sits and does not say a word. He has grown feeble. And why be silent? He ought to prosecute her, they wouldn't flatter her in the police court."

"Wouldn't flatter whom?" asked Crutch, not hearing.

"What?"

"The woman's all right, she does her best. In their line of business they can't get on without that . . . without sin, I mean. . . ."

"From his own house," Yakov went on with irritation. "Save up and buy your own house, then turn people out of it! She is a nice one, to be sure! A pla-ague!"

Tsybukin listened and did not stir.

"Whether it is your own house or others' it makes no difference so long as it is warm and the women don't scold . . ." said Crutch, and he laughed. "When I was young I was very fond of my Nastasya. She was a quiet woman. And she used to be always at it: 'Buy a house, Makaritch! Buy a house, Makaritch! Buy a house, Makaritch!' She was dying and yet she kept on saying, 'Buy yourself a racing droshky, Makaritch, that you may not have to walk.' And I bought her nothing but gingerbread."

"Her husband's deaf and stupid," Yakov went on, not hearing Crutch; "a regular fool, just like a goose. He can't understand anything. Hit a goose on the head with a stick and even then it does not understand."

Crutch got up to go home to the factory. Yakov also got up, and both of them went off together, still talking. When they had gone fifty paces old Tsybukin got up, too, and walked after them, stepping uncertainly as though on slippery ice.

The village was already plunged in the dusk of evening and the sun only gleamed on the upper part of the road which ran wriggling like a snake up the slope. Old women were coming back from the woods and children with them; they were bringing baskets of mushrooms. Peasant women and girls came in a crowd from the station where they had been loading the trucks with bricks, and their noses and their cheeks under their eyes were covered with red brick-dust. They were singing. Ahead of them all was Lipa singing in a high voice, with her eyes turned upwards to the sky, breaking into trills as though triumphant and ecstatic that at last the day was over and she could rest. In the crowd was her mother Praskovya, who was walking with a bundle in her arms and breathless as usual.

"Good-evening, Makaritch! " cried Lipa, seeing Crutch. "Good-evening, darling!"

"Good-evening, Lipinka," cried Crutch delighted. "Dear girls and women, love the rich carpenter! Ho-ho! My little children, my little children. (Crutch gave a gulp.) My dear little axes!"

Crutch and Yakov went on further and could still be heard talking. Then after them the crowd was met by old Tsybukin and there was a sudden hush. Lipa and Praskovya had dropped a little behind, and when the old man was on a level with them Lipa bowed down low and said:

"Good-evening, Grigory Petrovitch."

Her mother, too, bowed down. The old man stopped and, saying nothing, looked at the two in silence; his lips were quivering and his eyes full of tears. Lipa took out of her mother's bundle a piece of savoury turnover and gave it him. He took it and began eating.

The sun had by now set: its glow died away on the road above. It grew dark and cool. Lipa and Praskovya walked on and for some time they kept crossing themselves.

THE BISHOP

I

The evening service was being celebrated on the eve of Palm Sunday in the Old Petrovsky Convent. When they began distributing the palm it was close upon ten o'clock, the candles were burning dimly, the wicks wanted snuffing; it was all in a sort of mist. In the twilight of the church the crowd seemed heaving like the sea, and to Bishop Pyotr, who had been unwell for the last three days, it seemed that all the faces - old and young, men's and women's - were alike, that everyone who came up for the palm had the same expression in his eyes. In the mist he could not see the doors; the crowd kept moving and looked as though there were no end to it. The female choir was singing, a nun was reading the prayers for the day.

How stifling, how hot it was! How long the service went on! Bishop Pyotr was tired. His breathing was laboured and rapid, his throat was parched, his shoulders ached with weariness, his legs were trembling. And it disturbed him unpleasantly when a religious maniac uttered occasional shrieks in the gallery. And then all of a sudden, as though in a dream or delirium, it seemed to the bishop as though his own mother Marya Timofyevna, whom he had not seen for nine years, or some old woman just like his mother, came up to him out of the crowd, and, after taking a palm branch from him, walked away looking at him all the while good-humouredly with a kind, joyful smile until she was lost in the crowd. And for some reason tears flowed down his face. There was peace in his heart, everything was well, yet he kept gazing fixedly towards the left choir, where the prayers were being read, where in the dusk of evening you could not recognize anyone, and - wept. Tears glistened on his face and on his beard. Here someone close at hand was weeping, then someone else farther away, then others and still others, and little by little the church was filled with soft weeping. And a little later, within five minutes, the nuns' choir was singing; no one was weeping and everything was as before.

Soon the service was over. When the bishop got into his carriage to drive home, the gay, melodious chime of the heavy, costly bells was filling the whole garden in the moonlight. The white walls, the white crosses on the tombs, the white birch-trees and black shadows, and the far-away moon in the sky exactly over the convent, seemed now living their own life, apart and incomprehensible, yet very near to man. It was the beginning of April, and after the warm spring day it turned cool; there was a faint touch of frost, and the breath of spring could be felt in the soft, chilly air. The road from the convent to the town was sandy, the horses had to go at a walking pace, and on both sides of the carriage in the brilliant, peaceful moonlight there were people trudging along home from church through the sand. And all was silent, sunk in thought; everything around seemed kindly, youthful, akin, everything - trees and sky and even the moon, and one longed to think that so it would be always.

At last the carriage drove into the town and rumbled along the principal street. The shops were already shut, but at Erakin's, the millionaire shopkeeper's, they were trying the new electric lights, which flickered brightly, and a crowd of people were gathered round. Then came wide, dark, deserted streets, one after another; then the highroad, the open country, the fragrance of pines. And suddenly there rose up before the bishop's eyes a white turreted wall, and behind it a tall belfry in the full moonlight, and beside it five shining, golden cupolas: this was the Pankratievsky Monastery, in which Bishop Pyotr lived. And here, too, high above the monastery, was the silent, dreamy moon. The carriage drove in at the gate, crunching over the sand; here and there in the moonlight there were glimpses of dark monastic figures, and there was the sound of footsteps on the flag-stones. . . .

"You know, your holiness, your mamma arrived while you were away," the lay brother informed the bishop as he went into his cell.

"My mother? When did she come?"

"Before the evening service. She asked first where you were and then she went to the convent."

"Then it was her I saw in the church, just now! Oh, Lord!"

And the bishop laughed with joy.

"She bade me tell your holiness," the lay brother went on, "that she would come to-morrow. She had a little girl with her - her grandchild, I suppose. They are staying at Ovsyannikov's inn."

"What time is it now?"

"A little after eleven."

"Oh, how vexing!"

The bishop sat for a little while in the parlour, hesitating, and as it were refusing to believe it was so late. His arms and legs were stiff, his head ached. He was hot and uncomfortable. After resting a little he went into his bedroom, and there, too, he sat a little, still thinking of his mother; he could hear the lay brother going away, and Father Sisoy coughing the other side of the wall. The monastery clock struck a quarter.

The bishop changed his clothes and began reading the prayers before sleep. He read attentively those old, long familiar prayers, and at the same time thought about his mother. She had nine children and about forty grandchildren. At one time, she had lived with her husband, the deacon, in a poor village; she had lived there a very long time from the age of seventeen to sixty. The bishop remembered her from early childhood, almost from the age of three, and - how he had loved her! Sweet, precious childhood, always fondly remembered! Why did it, that long-past time that could never return, why did it seem brighter, fuller, and more festive than it had really been? When in his childhood or youth he had been ill, how tender and sympathetic his mother had been! And now his prayers mingled with the memories, which gleamed more and more brightly like a flame, and the prayers did not hinder his thinking of his mother.

When he had finished his prayers he undressed and lay down, and at once, as soon as it was dark, there rose before his mind his dead father, his mother, his native village Lesopolye . . . the creak of wheels, the bleat of sheep, the church bells on bright summer mornings, the gypsies under the window - oh, how sweet to think of it! He remembered the priest of Lesopolye, Father Simeon - mild, gentle, kindly; he was a lean little man, while his son, a divinity student, was a huge fellow and talked in a roaring bass voice. The priest's son had flown into a rage with the cook and abused her: "Ah, you Jehud's ass!" and Father Simeon overhearing it, said not a word, and was only ashamed because he could not remember where such an ass was mentioned in the Bible. After him the priest at Lesopolye had been Father Demyan, who used to drink heavily, and at times drank till he saw green snakes, and was even nicknamed Demyan Snakeseer. The schoolmaster at Lesopolye was Matvey Nikolaitch, who had been a divinity student, a kind and intelligent man, but he, too, was a drunkard; he never beat the schoolchildren, but for some reason he always had hanging on his wall a bunch of birch-twigs, and below it an utterly meaningless inscription in Latin: "Betula kinderbalsamica secuta." He had a shaggy black dog whom he called Syntax.

And his holiness laughed. Six miles from Lesopolye was the village Obnino with a wonder-working ikon. In the summer they used to carry the ikon in procession about the neighbouring villages and ring the bells the whole day long; first in one village and then in another, and it used to seem to the bishop then that joy was quivering in the air, and he (in those days his name was Pavlusha) used to follow the ikon, bareheaded and barefoot, with naïve faith, with a naïve smile, infinitely happy. In Obnino, he remembered now, there were always a lot of people, and the priest there, Father Alexey, to save time during mass, used to make his deaf nephew Ilarion read the names of those for whose health or whose souls' peace prayers were asked. Ilarion used to read them, now and then getting a five or ten kopeck piece for the service, and only when he was grey and bald, when life was nearly over, he suddenly saw written on one of the pieces of paper: "What a fool you are, Ilarion." Up to fifteen at least Pavlusha was undeveloped and idle at his lessons, so much so that they thought of taking him away from the clerical school and putting him into a shop; one day, going to the post at Obnino for letters, he had stared a long time at the post-office clerks and asked: "Allow me to ask, how do you get your salary, every month or every day?"

His holiness crossed himself and turned over on the other side, trying to stop thinking and go to sleep.

"My mother has come," he remembered and laughed.

The moon peeped in at the window, the floor was lighted up, and there were shadows on it. A cricket was chirping. Through the wall Father Sisoy was snoring in the next room, and his aged snore had a sound that suggested loneliness, forlornness, even vagrancy. Sisoy had once been housekeeper to the bishop of the diocese, and was called now "the former Father Housekeeper"; he was seventy years old, he lived in a monastery twelve miles from the town and stayed sometimes in the town, too. He had come to the Pankratievsky Monastery three days before, and the bishop had kept him that he might talk to him at his leisure about matters of business, about the arrangements here. . . .

At half-past one they began ringing for matins. Father Sisoy could be heard coughing, muttering something in a discontented voice, then he got up and walked barefoot about the rooms.

"Father Sisoy," the bishop called.

Sisoy went back to his room and a little later made his appearance in his boots, with a candle; he had on his cassock over his underclothes and on his head was an old faded skull-cap.

"I can't sleep," said the bishop, sitting up. "I must be unwell. And what it is I don't know. Fever!"

"You must have caught cold, your holiness. You must be rubbed with tallow." Sisoy stood a little and yawned. "O Lord, forgive me, a sinner."

"They had the electric lights on at Erakin's today," he said; "I don't like it!"

Father Sisoy was old, lean, bent, always dissatisfied with something, and his eyes were angry-looking and prominent as a crab's.

"I don't like it," he said, going away. "I don't like it. Bother it!"

II

Next day, Palm Sunday, the bishop took the service in the cathedral in the town, then he visited the bishop of the diocese, then visited a very sick old lady, the widow of a general, and at last drove home. Between one and two o'clock he had welcome visitors dining with him - his mother and his niece Katya, a child of eight years old. All dinner-time the spring sunshine was streaming in at the windows, throwing bright light on the white tablecloth and on Katya's red hair. Through the double windows they could hear the noise of the rooks and the notes of the starlings in the garden.

"It is nine years since we have met," said the old lady. "And when I looked at you in the monastery yesterday, good Lord! you've not changed a bit, except maybe you are thinner and your beard is a little longer. Holy Mother, Queen of Heaven! Yesterday at the evening service no one could help crying. I, too, as I looked at you, suddenly began crying, though I couldn't say why. His Holy Will!"

And in spite of the affectionate tone in which she said this, he could see she was constrained as though she were uncertain whether to address him formally or familiarly, to laugh or not, and that she felt herself more a deacon's widow than his mother. And Katya gazed without blinking at her uncle, his holiness, as though trying to discover what sort of a person he was. Her hair sprang up from under the comb and the velvet ribbon and stood out like a halo; she had a turned-up nose and sly eyes. The child had broken a glass before sitting down to dinner, and now her grandmother, as she talked, moved away from Katya first a wineglass and then a tumbler. The bishop listened to his mother and remembered how many, many years ago she used to take him and his brothers and sisters to relations whom she considered rich; in those days she was taken up with the care of her children, now with her grandchildren, and she had brought Katya. . . .

"Your sister, Varenka, has four children," she told him; "Katya, here, is the eldest. And your brother-in-law Father Ivan fell sick, God knows of what, and died three days before the Assumption; and my poor Varenka is left a beggar."

"And how is Nikanor getting on?" the bishop asked about his eldest brother.

"He is all right, thank God. Though he has nothing much, yet he can live. Only there is one thing: his son, my grandson Nikolasha, did not want to go into the Church; he has gone to the university to be a doctor. He thinks it is better; but who knows! His Holy Will!"

"Nikolasha cuts up dead people," said Katya, spilling water over her knees.

"Sit still, child," her grandmother observed calmly, and took the glass out of her hand. "Say a prayer, and go on eating."

"How long it is since we have seen each other!" said the bishop, and he tenderly stroked his mother's hand and shoulder; "and I missed you abroad, mother, I missed you dreadfully."

"Thank you."

"I used to sit in the evenings at the open window, lonely and alone; often there was music playing, and all at once I used to be overcome with homesickness and felt as though I would give everything only to be at home and see you."

His mother smiled, beamed, but at once she made a grave face and said:

"Thank you."

His mood suddenly changed. He looked at his mother and could not understand how she had come by that respectfulness, that timid expression of face: what was it for? And he did not recognize her. He felt sad and vexed. And then his head ached just as it had the day before; his legs felt fearfully tired, and the fish seemed to him stale and tasteless; he felt thirsty all the time. . . .

After dinner two rich ladies, landowners, arrived and sat for an hour and a half in silence with rigid countenances; the archimandrite, a silent, rather deaf man, came to see him about business. Then they began ringing for vespers; the sun was setting behind the wood and the day was over. When he returned from church, he hurriedly said his prayers, got into bed, and wrapped himself up as warm as possible.

It was disagreeable to remember the fish he had eaten at dinner. The moonlight worried him, and then he heard talking. In an adjoining room, probably in the parlour, Father Sisoy was talking politics:

"There's war among the Japanese now. They are fighting. The Japanese, my good soul, are the same as the Montenegrins; they are the same race. They were under the Turkish yoke together."

And then he heard the voice of Marya Timofyevna:

"So, having said our prayers and drunk tea, we went, you know, to Father Yegor at Novokatnoye, so. . ."

And she kept on saying, "having had tea" or "having drunk tea," and it seemed as though the only thing she had done in her life was to drink tea.

The bishop slowly, languidly, recalled the seminary, the academy. For three years he had been Greek teacher in the seminary: by that time he could not read without spectacles. Then he had become a monk; he had been made a school inspector. Then he had defended his thesis for his degree. When he was thirty-two he had been made rector of the seminary, and consecrated archimandrite: and then his life had been so easy, so pleasant; it seemed so long, so long, no end was in sight. Then he had begun to be ill, had grown very thin and almost blind, and by the advice of the doctors had to give up everything and go abroad.

"And what then?" asked Sisoy in the next room.

"Then we drank tea . . ." answered Marya Timofyevna.

"Good gracious, you've got a green beard," said Katya suddenly in surprise, and she laughed.

The bishop remembered that the grey-headed Father Sisoy's beard really had a shade of green in it, and he laughed.

"God have mercy upon us, what we have to put up with with this girl!" said Sisoy, aloud, getting angry. " Spoilt child! Sit quiet!"

The bishop remembered the perfectly new white church in which he had conducted the services while living abroad, he remembered the sound of the warm sea. In his flat he had five lofty light rooms; in his study he had a new writing-table, lots of books. He had read a great deal and often written. And he remembered how he had pined for his native land, how a blind beggar woman had played the guitar under his window every day and sung of love, and how, as he listened, he had always for some reason thought of the past. But eight years had passed and he had been called back to Russia, and now he was a suffragan bishop, and all the past had retreated far away into the mist as though it were a dream. . . .

Father Sisoy came into the bedroom with a candle.

"I say!" he said, wondering, "are you asleep already, your holiness?"

"What is it?"

"Why, it's still early, ten o'clock or less. I bought a candle to-day; I wanted to rub you with tallow."

"I am in a fever . . ." said the bishop, and he sat up. "I really ought to have something. My head is bad. . . ."

Sisoy took off the bishop's shirt and began rubbing his chest and back with tallow.

"That's the way . . . that's the way . . ." he said. "Lord Jesus Christ . . . that's the way. I walked to the town to-day; I was at what's-his-name's - the chief priest Sidonsky's. . . . I had tea with him. I don't like him. Lord Jesus Christ. . . . That's the way. I don't like him."

III

The bishop of the diocese, a very fat old man, was ill with rheumatism or gout, and had been in bed for over a month. Bishop Pyotr went to see him almost every day, and saw all who came to ask his help. And now that he was unwell he was struck by the emptiness, the triviality of everything which they asked and for which they wept; he was vexed at their ignorance, their timidity; and all this useless, petty business oppressed him by the mass of it, and it seemed to him that now he understood the diocesan bishop, who had once in his young days written on "The Doctrines of the Freedom of the Will," and now seemed to be all lost in trivialities, to have forgotten everything, and to have no thoughts of religion. The bishop must have lost touch with Russian life while he was abroad; he did not find it easy; the peasants seemed to him coarse, the women who sought his help dull and stupid, the seminarists and their teachers uncultivated and at times savage. And the documents coming in and going out were reckoned by tens of thousands; and what documents they were! The higher clergy in the whole diocese gave the priests, young and old, and even their wives and children, marks for their behaviour - a five, a four, and sometimes even a three; and about this he had to talk and to read and write serious reports. And there was positively not one minute to spare; his soul was troubled all day long, and the bishop was only at peace when he was in church.

He could not get used, either, to the awe which, through no wish of his own, he inspired in people in spite of his quiet, modest disposition. All the people in the province seemed to him little, scared, and guilty when he looked at them. Everyone was timid in his presence, even the old chief priests; everyone "flopped" at his feet, and not long previously an old lady, a village priest's wife who had come to consult him, was so overcome by awe that she could not utter a single word, and went empty away. And he, who could never in his sermons bring himself to speak ill of people, never reproached anyone because he was so sorry for them, was moved to fury with the people who came to consult him, lost his temper and flung their petitions on the floor. The whole time he had been here, not one person had spoken to him genuinely, simply, as to a human being; even his old mother seemed now not the same! And why, he wondered, did she chatter away to Sisoy and laugh so much; while with him, her son, she was grave and usually silent and constrained, which did not suit her at all. The only person who behaved freely with him and said what he meant was old Sisoy, who had spent his whole life in the presence of bishops and had outlived eleven of them. And so the bishop was at ease with him, although, of course, he was a tedious and nonsensical man.

After the service on Tuesday, his holiness Pyotr was in the diocesan bishop's house receiving petitions there; he got excited and angry, and then drove home. He was as unwell as before; he longed to be in bed, but he had hardly reached home when he was informed that a young merchant called Erakin, who subscribed liberally to charities, had come to see him about a very important matter. The bishop had to see him. Erakin stayed about an hour, talked very loud, almost shouted, and it was difficult to understand what he said.

"God grant it may," he said as he went away. "Most essential! According to circumstances, your holiness! I trust it may!"

After him came the Mother Superior from a distant convent. And when she had gone they began ringing for vespers. He had to go to church.

In the evening the monks sang harmoniously, with inspiration. A young priest with a black beard conducted the service; and the bishop, hearing of theBridegroom who comes at midnight and of the Heavenly Mansion adorned for the festival, felt no repentance for his sins, no tribulation, but peace at heart and tranquillity. And he was carried back in thought to the distant past, to his childhood and youth, when, too, they used to sing of the Bridegroom and of the Heavenly Mansion; and now that past rose up before him - living, fair, and joyful as in all likelihood it never had been. And perhaps in the other world, in the life to come, we shall think of the distant past, of our life here, with the same feeling. Who knows? The bishop was sitting near the altar. It was dark; tears flowed down his face. He thought that here he had attained everything a man in his position could attain; he had faith and yet everything was not clear, something was lacking still. He did not want to die; and he still felt that he had missed what was most important, something of which he had dimly dreamed in the past; and he was troubled by the same hopes for the future as he had felt in childhood, at the academy and abroad.

"How well they sing to-day!" he thought, listening to the singing. "How nice it is!"

IV

On Thursday he celebrated mass in the cathedral; it was the Washing of Feet. When the service was over and the people were going home, it was sunny, warm; the water gurgled in the gutters, and the unceasing trilling of the larks, tender, telling of peace, rose from the fields outside the town. The trees were already awakening and smiling a welcome, while above them the infinite, fathomless blue sky stretched into the distance, God knows whither.

On reaching home his holiness drank some tea, then changed his clothes, lay down on his bed, and told the lay brother to close the shutters on the windows. The bedroom was darkened. But what weariness, what pain in his legs and his back, a chill heavy pain, what a noise in his ears! He had not slept for a long time - for a very long time, as it seemed to him now, and some trifling detail which haunted his brain as soon as his eyes were closed prevented him from sleeping. As on the day before, sounds reached him from the adjoining rooms through the walls, voices, the jingle of glasses and teaspoons. . . . Marya Timofyevna was gaily telling Father Sisoy some story with quaint turns of speech, while the latter answered in a grumpy, ill-humoured voice: "Bother them! Not likely! What next!" And the bishop again felt vexed and then hurt that with other people his old mother behaved in a simple, ordinary way, while with him, her son, she was shy, spoke little, and did not say what she meant, and even, as he fancied, had during all those three days kept trying in his presence to find an excuse for standing up, because she was embarrassed at sitting before him. And his father? He, too, probably, if he had been living, would not have been able to utter a word in the bishop's presence. . . .

Something fell down on the floor in the adjoining room and was broken; Katya must have dropped a cup or a saucer, for Father Sisoy suddenly spat and said angrily:

"What a regular nuisance the child is! Lord forgive my transgressions! One can't provide enough for her."

Then all was quiet, the only sounds came from outside. And when the bishop opened his eyes he saw Katya in his room, standing motionless, staring at him. Her red hair, as usual, stood up from under the comb like a halo.

"Is that you, Katya?" he asked. "Who is it downstairs who keeps opening and shutting a door?"

"I don't hear it," answered Katya; and she listened.

"There, someone has just passed by."

"But that was a noise in your stomach, uncle."

He laughed and stroked her on the head.

"So you say Cousin Nikolasha cuts up dead people?" he asked after a pause.

"Yes, he is studying."

"And is he kind?"

"Oh, yes, he's kind. But he drinks vodka awfully."

"And what was it your father died of?"

"Papa was weak and very, very thin, and all at once his throat was bad. I was ill then, too, and brother Fedya; we all had bad throats. Papa died, uncle, and we got well."

Her chin began quivering, and tears gleamed in her eyes and trickled down her cheeks.

"Your holiness," she said in a shrill voice, by now weeping bitterly, "uncle, mother and all of us are left very wretched. . . . Give us a little money . . . do be kind . . . uncle darling. . . ."

He, too, was moved to tears, and for a long time was too much touched to speak. Then he stroked her on the head, patted her on the shoulder and said:

"Very good, very good, my child. When the holy Easter comes, we will talk it over. . . . I will help you. . . . I will help you. . . ."

His mother came in quietly, timidly, and prayed before the ikon. Noticing that he was not sleeping, she said:

"Won't you have a drop of soup?"

"No, thank you," he answered, "I am not hungry."

"You seem to be unwell, now I look at you. I should think so; you may well be ill! The whole day on your legs, the whole day. . . . And, my goodness, it makes one's heart ache even to look at you! Well, Easter is not far off; you will rest then, please God. Then we will have a talk, too, but now I'm not going to disturb you with my chatter. Come along, Katya; let his holiness sleep a little."

And he remembered how once very long ago, when he was a boy, she had spoken exactly like that, in the same jestingly respectful tone, with a Church dignitary. . . . Only from her extraordinarily kind eyes and the timid, anxious glance she stole at him as she went out of the room could one have guessed that this was his mother. He shut his eyes and seemed to sleep, but twice heard the clock strike and Father Sisoy coughing the other side of the wall. And once more his mother came in and looked timidly at him for a minute. Someone drove up to the steps, as he could hear, in a coach or in a chaise. Suddenly a knock, the door slammed, the lay brother came into the bedroom.

"Your holiness," he called.

"Well?"

"The horses are here; it's time for the evening service."

"What o'clock is it?"

"A quarter past seven."

He dressed and drove to the cathedral. During all the "Twelve Gospels" he had to stand in the middle of the church without moving, and the first gospel, the longest and the most beautiful, he read himself. A mood of confidence and courage came over him. That first gospel, "Now is the Son of Man glorified," he knew by heart; and as he read he raised his eyes from time to time, and saw on both sides a perfect sea of lights and heard the splutter of candles, but, as in past years, he could not see the people, and it seemed as though these were all the same people as had been round him in those days, in his childhood and his youth; that they would always be the same every year and till such time as God only knew.

His father had been a deacon, his grandfather a priest, his great-grandfather a deacon, and his whole family, perhaps from the days when Christianity had been accepted in Russia, had belonged to the priesthood; and his love for the Church services, for the priesthood, for the peal of the bells, was deep in him, ineradicable, innate. In church, particularly when he took part in the service, he felt vigorous, of good cheer, happy. So it was now. Only when the eighth gospel had been read, he felt that his voice had grown weak, even his cough was inaudible. His head had begun to ache intensely, and he was troubled by a fear that he might fall down. And his legs were indeed quite numb, so that by degrees he ceased to feel them and could not understand how or on what he was standing, and why he did not fall. . . .

It was a quarter to twelve when the service was over. When he reached home, the bishop undressed and went to bed at once without even saying his prayers. He could not speak and felt that he could not have stood up. When he had covered his head with the quilt he felt a sudden longing to be abroad, an insufferable longing! He felt that he would give his life not to see those pitiful cheap shutters, those low ceilings, not to smell that heavy monastery smell. If only there were one person to whom he could have talked, have opened his heart!

For a long while he heard footsteps in the next room and could not tell whose they were. At last the door opened, and Sisoy came in with a candle and a tea-cup in his hand.

"You are in bed already, your holiness?" he asked. "Here I have come to rub you with spirit and vinegar. A thorough rubbing does a great deal of good. Lord Jesus Christ! . . . That's the way . . . that's the way. . . . I've just been in our monastery. . . . I don't like it. I'm going away from here to-morrow, your holiness; I don't want to stay longer. Lord Jesus Christ. . . . That's the way. . . ."

Sisoy could never stay long in the same place, and he felt as though he had been a whole year in the Pankratievsky Monastery. Above all, listening to him it was difficult to understand where his home was, whether he cared for anyone or anything, whether he believed in God. . . . He did not know himself why he was a monk, and, indeed, he did not think about it, and the time when he had become a monk had long passed out of his memory; it seemed as though he had been born a monk.

"I'm going away to-morrow; God be with them all."

"I should like to talk to you. . . . I can't find the time," said the bishop softly with an effort. "I don't know anything or anybody here. . . ."

"I'll stay till Sunday if you like; so be it, but I don't want to stay longer. I am sick of them!"

"I ought not to be a bishop," said the bishop softly. "I ought to have been a village priest, a deacon . . . or simply a monk. . . . All this oppresses me . . . oppresses me."

"What? Lord Jesus Christ. . . . That's the way. Come, sleep well, your holiness! . . . What's the good of talking? It's no use. Good-night!"

The bishop did not sleep all night. And at eight o'clock in the morning he began to have hemorrhage from the bowels. The lay brother was alarmed, and ran first to the archimandrite, then for the monastery doctor, Ivan Andreyitch, who lived in the town. The doctor, a stout old man with a long grey beard, made a prolonged examination of the bishop, and kept shaking his head and frowning, then said:

"Do you know, your holiness, you have got typhoid?"

After an hour or so of hemorrhage the bishop looked much thinner, paler, and wasted; his face looked wrinkled, his eyes looked bigger, and he seemed older, shorter, and it seemed to him that he was thinner, weaker, more insignificant than any one, that everything that had been had retreated far, far away and would never go on again or be repeated.

"How good," he thought, "how good!"

His old mother came. Seeing his wrinkled face and his big eyes, she was frightened, she fell on her knees by the bed and began kissing his face, his shoulders, his hands. And to her, too, it seemed that he was thinner, weaker, and more insignificant than anyone, and now she forgot that he was a bishop, and kissed him as though he were a child very near and very dear to her.

"Pavlusha, darling," she said; "my own, my darling son! . . . Why are you like this? Pavlusha, answer me!"

Katya, pale and severe, stood beside her, unable to understand what was the matter with her uncle, why there was such a look of suffering on her grandmother's face, why she was saying such sad and touching things. By now he could not utter a word, he could understand nothing, and he imagined he was a simple ordinary man, that he was walking quickly, cheerfully through the fields, tapping with his stick, while above him was the open sky bathed in sunshine, and that he was free now as a bird and could go where he liked!

"Pavlusha, my darling son, answer me," the old woman was saying. "What is it? My own!"

"Don't disturb his holiness," Sisoy said angrily, walking about the room. "Let him sleep . . . what's the use . . . it's no good. . . ."

Three doctors arrived, consulted together, and went away again. The day was long, incredibly long, then the night came on and passed slowly, slowly, and towards morning on Saturday the lay brother went in to the old mother who was lying on the sofa in the parlour, and asked her to go into the bedroom: the bishop had just breathed his last.

Next day was Easter Sunday. There were forty-two churches and six monasteries in the town; the sonorous, joyful clang of the bells hung over the town from morning till night unceasingly, setting the spring air aquiver; the birds were singing, the sun was shining brightly. The big market square was noisy, swings were going, barrel organs were playing, accordions were squeaking, drunken voices were shouting. After midday people began driving up and down the principal street.

In short, all was merriment, everything was satisfactory, just as it had been the year before, and as it will be in all likelihood next year.

A month later a new suffragan bishop was appointed, and no one thought anything more of Bishop Pyotr, and afterwards he was completely forgotten. And only the dead man's old mother, who is living to-day with her son-in-law the deacon in a remote little district town, when she goes out at night to bring her cow in and meets other women at the pasture, begins talking of her children and her grandchildren, and says that she had a son a bishop, and this she says timidly, afraid that she may not be believed. . . .

And, indeed, there are some who do not believe her.

BETROTHED

I

It was ten o'clock in the evening and the full moon was shining over the garden. In the Shumins' house an evening service celebrated at the request of the grandmother, Marfa Mihalovna, was just over, and now Nadya - she had gone into the garden for a minute - could see the table being laid for supper in the dining-room, and her grandmother bustling about in her gorgeous silk dress; Father Andrey, a chief priest of the cathedral, was talking to Nadya's mother, Nina Ivanovna, and now in the evening light through the window her mother for some reason looked very young; Andrey Andreitch, Father Andrey's son, was standing by listening attentively.

It was still and cool in the garden, and dark peaceful shadows lay on the ground. There was a sound of frogs croaking, far, far away beyond the town. There was a feeling of May, sweet May! One drew deep breaths and longed to fancy that not here but far away under the sky, above the trees, far away in the open country, in the fields and the woods, the life of spring was unfolding now, mysterious, lovely, rich and holy beyond the understanding of weak, sinful man. And for some reason one wanted to cry.

She, Nadya, was already twenty-three. Ever since she was sixteen she had been passionately dreaming of marriage and at last she was engaged to Andrey Andreitch, the young man who was standing on the other side of the window; she liked him, the wedding was already fixed for July 7, and yet there was no joy in her heart, she was sleeping badly, her spirits drooped. . . . She could hear from the open windows of the basement where the kitchen was the hurrying servants, the clatter of knives, the banging of the swing door; there was a smell of roast turkey and pickled cherries, and for some reason it seemed to her that it would be like that all her life, with no change, no end to it.

Some one came out of the house and stood on the steps; it was Alexandr Timofeitch, or, as he was always called, Sasha, who had come from Moscow ten days before and was staying with them. Years ago a distant relation of the grandmother, a gentleman's widow called Marya Petrovna, a thin, sickly little woman who had sunk into poverty, used to come to the house to ask for assistance. She had a son Sasha. It used for some reason to be said that he had talent as an artist, and when his mother died Nadya's grandmother had, for the salvation of her soul, sent him to the Komissarovsky school in Moscow; two years later he went into the school of painting, spent nearly fifteen years there, and only just managed to scrape through the leaving examination in the section of architecture. He did not set up as an architect, however, but took a job at a lithographer's. He used to come almost every year, usually very ill, to stay with Nadya's grandmother to rest and recover.

He was wearing now a frock-coat buttoned up, and shabby canvas trousers, crumpled into creases at the bottom. And his shirt had not been ironed and he had somehow all over a look of not being fresh. He was very thin, with big eyes, long thin fingers and a swarthy bearded face, and all the same he was handsome. With the Shumins he was like one of the family, and in their house felt he was at home. And the room in which he lived when he was there had for years been called Sasha's room. Standing on the steps he saw Nadya, and went up to her.

"It's nice here," he said.

"Of course it's nice, you ought to stay here till the autumn."

"Yes, I expect it will come to that. I dare say I shall stay with you till September."

He laughed for no reason, and sat down beside her.

"I'm sitting gazing at mother," said Nadya. "She looks so young from here! My mother has her weaknesses, of course," she added, after a pause, "but still she is an exceptional woman."

"Yes, she is very nice . . ." Sasha agreed. "Your mother, in her own way of course, is a very good and sweet woman, but . . . how shall I say? I went early this morning into your kitchen and there I found four servants sleeping on the floor, no bedsteads, and rags for bedding, stench, bugs, beetles . . . it is just as it was twenty years ago, no change at all. Well, Granny, God bless her, what else can you expect of Granny? But your mother speaks French, you know, and acts in private theatricals. One would think she might understand."

As Sasha talked, he used to stretch out two long wasted fingers before the listener's face.

"It all seems somehow strange to me here, now I am out of the habit of it," he went on. "There is no making it out. Nobody ever does anything. Your mother spends the whole day walking about like a duchess, Granny does nothing either, nor you either. And your Andrey Andreitch never does anything either."

Nadya had heard this the year before and, she fancied, the year before that too, and she knew that Sasha could not make any other criticism, and in old days this had amused her, but now for some reason she felt annoyed.

"That's all stale, and I have been sick of it for ages," she said and got up. "You should think of something a little newer."

He laughed and got up too, and they went together toward the house. She, tall, handsome, and well-made, beside him looked very healthy and smartly dressed; she was conscious of this and felt sorry for him and for some reason awkward.

"And you say a great deal you should not," she said. "You've just been talking about my Andrey, but you see you don't know him."

"My Andrey. . . . Bother him, your Andrey. I am sorry for your youth."

They were already sitting down to supper as the young people went into the dining-room. The grandmother, or Granny as she was called in the household, a very stout, plain old lady with bushy eyebrows and a little moustache, was talking loudly, and from her voice and manner of speaking it could be seen that she was the person of most importance in the house. She owned rows of shops in the market, and the old-fashioned house with columns and the garden, yet she prayed every morning that God might save her from ruin and shed tears as she did so. Her daughter-in-law, Nadya's mother, Nina Ivanovna, a fair-haired woman tightly laced in, with a pince-nez, and diamonds on every finger, Father Andrey, a lean, toothless old man whose face always looked as though he were just going to say something amusing, and his son, Andrey Andreitch, a stout and handsome young man with curly hair looking like an artist or an actor, were all talking of hypnotism.

"You will get well in a week here," said Granny, addressing Sasha. "Only you must eat more. What do you look like!" she sighed. "You are really dreadful! You are a regular prodigal son, that is what you are."

"After wasting his father's substance in riotous living," said Father Andrey slowly, with laughing eyes. "He fed with senseless beasts."

"I like my dad," said Andrey Andreitch, touching his father on the shoulder. "He is a splendid old fellow, a dear old fellow."

Everyone was silent for a space. Sasha suddenly burst out laughing and put his dinner napkin to his mouth.

"So you believe in hypnotism?" said Father Andrey to Nina Ivanovna.

"I cannot, of course, assert that I believe," answered Nina Ivanovna, assuming a very serious, even severe, expression; "but I must own that there is much that is mysterious and incomprehensible in nature."

"I quite agree with you, though I must add that religion distinctly curtails for us the domain of the mysterious."

A big and very fat turkey was served. Father Andrey and Nina Ivanovna went on with their conversation. Nina Ivanovna's diamonds glittered on her fingers, then tears began to glitter in her eyes, she grew excited.

"Though I cannot venture to argue with you," she said, "you must admit there are so many insoluble riddles in life!"

"Not one, I assure you."

After supper Andrey Andreitch played the fiddle and Nina Ivanovna accompanied him on the piano. Ten years before he had taken his degree at the university in the Faculty of Arts, but had never held any post, had no definite work, and only from time to time took part in concerts for charitable objects; and in the town he was regarded as a musician.

Andrey Andreitch played; they all listened in silence. The samovar was boiling quietly on the table and no one but Sasha was drinking tea.

Then when it struck twelve a violin string suddenly broke; everyone laughed, bustled about, and began saying good-bye.

After seeing her fiancé out, Nadya went upstairs where she and her mother had their rooms (the lower storey was occupied by the grandmother). They began putting the lights out below in the dining-room, while Sasha still sat on drinking tea. He always spent a long time over tea in the Moscow style, drinking as much as seven glasses at a time. For a long time after Nadya had undressed and gone to bed she could hear the servants clearing away downstairs and Granny talking angrily. At last everything was hushed, and nothing could be heard but Sasha from time to time coughing on a bass note in his room below.

II

When Nadya woke up it must have been two o'clock, it was beginning to get light. A watchman was tapping somewhere far away. She was not sleepy, and her bed felt very soft and uncomfortable. Nadya sat up in her bed and fell to thinking as she had done every night in May. Her thoughts were the same as they had been the night before, useless, persistent thoughts, always alike, of how Andrey Andreitch had begun courting her and had made her an offer, how she had accepted him and then little by little had come to appreciate the kindly, intelligent man. But for some reason now when there was hardly a month left before the wedding, she began to feel dread and uneasiness as though something vague and oppressive were before her.

"Tick-tock, tick-tock . . ." the watchman tapped lazily. ". . . Tick-tock."

Through the big old-fashioned window she could see the garden and at a little distance bushes of lilac in full flower, drowsy and lifeless from the cold; and the thick white mist was floating softly up to the lilac, trying to cover it. Drowsy rooks were cawing in the far-away trees.

"My God, why is my heart so heavy?"

Perhaps every girl felt the same before her wedding. There was no knowing! Or was it Sasha's influence? But for several years past Sasha had been repeating the same thing, like a copybook, and when he talked he seemed naïve and queer. But why was it she could not get Sasha out of her head? Why was it?

The watchman left off tapping for a long while. The birds were twittering under the windows and the mist had disappeared from the garden. Everything was lighted up by the spring sunshine as by a smile. Soon the whole garden, warm and caressed by the sun, returned to life, and dewdrops like diamonds glittered on the leaves and the old neglected garden on that morning looked young and gaily decked.

Granny was already awake. Sasha's husky cough began. Nadya could hear them below, setting the samovar and moving the chairs. The hours passed slowly, Nadya had been up and walking about the garden for a long while and still the morning dragged on.

At last Nina Ivanovna appeared with a tear-stained face, carrying a glass of mineral water. She was interested in spiritualism and homeopathy, read a great deal, was fond of talking of the doubts to which she was subject, and to Nadya it seemed as though there were a deep mysterious significance in all that.

Now Nadya kissed her mother and walked beside her.

"What have you been crying about, mother?" she asked.

"Last night I was reading a story in which there is an old man and his daughter. The old man is in some office and his chief falls in love with his daughter. I have not finished it, but there was a passage which made it hard to keep from tears," said Nina Ivanovna and she sipped at her glass. "I thought of it this morning and shed tears again."

"I have been so depressed all these days," said Nadya after a pause. "Why is it I don't sleep at night!"

"I don't know, dear. When I can't sleep I shut my eyes very tightly, like this, and picture to myself Anna Karenin moving about and talking, or something historical from the ancient world. . . ."

Nadya felt that her mother did not understand her and was incapable of understanding. She felt this for the first time in her life, and it positively frightened her and made her want to hide herself; and she went away to her own room.

At two o'clock they sat down to dinner. It was Wednesday, a fast day, and so vegetable soup and bream with boiled grain were set before Granny.

To tease Granny Sasha ate his meat soup as well as the vegetable soup. He was making jokes all through dinner-time, but his jests were laboured and invariably with a moral bearing, and the effect was not at all amusing when before making some witty remark he raised his very long, thin, deathly-looking fingers; and when one remembered that he was very ill and would probably not be much longer in this world, one felt sorry for him and ready to weep.

After dinner Granny went off to her own room to lie down. Nina Ivanovna played on the piano for a little, and then she too went away.

"Oh, dear Nadya!" Sasha began his usual afternoon conversation, "if only you would listen to me! If only you would!"

She was sitting far back in an old-fashioned armchair, with her eyes shut, while he paced slowly about the room from corner to corner.

"If only you would go to the university," he said. "Only enlightened and holy people are interesting, it's only they who are wanted. The more of such people there are, the sooner the Kingdom of God will come on earth. Of your town then not one stone will be left, everything will he blown up from the foundations, everything will be changed as though by magic. And then there will be immense, magnificent houses here, wonderful gardens, marvellous fountains, remarkable people. . . . But that's not what matters most. What matters most is that the crowd, in our sense of the word, in the sense in which it exists now - that evil will not exist then, because every man will believe and every man will know what he is living for and no one will seek moral support in the crowd. Dear Nadya, darling girl, go away! Show them all that you are sick of this stagnant, grey, sinful life. Prove it to yourself at least!"

"I can't, Sasha, I'm going to be married."

"Oh nonsense! What's it for!"

They went out into the garden and walked up and down a little.

"And however that may be, my dear girl, you must think, you must realize how unclean, how immoral this idle life of yours is," Sasha went on. "Do understand that if, for instance, you and your mother and your grandmother do nothing, it means that someone else is working for you, you are eating up someone else's life, and is that clean, isn't it filthy?"

Nadya wanted to say "Yes, that is true"; she wanted to say that she understood, but tears came into her eyes, her spirits drooped, and shrinking into herself she went off to her room.

Towards evening Andrey Andreitch arrived and as usual played the fiddle for a long time. He was not given to much talk as a rule, and was fond of the fiddle, perhaps because one could be silent while playing. At eleven o'clock when he was about to go home and had put on his greatcoat, he embraced Nadya and began greedily kissing her face, her shoulders, and her hands.

"My dear, my sweet, my charmer," he muttered. "Oh how happy I am! I am beside myself with rapture!"

And it seemed to her as though she had heard that long, long ago, or had read it somewhere . . . in some old tattered novel thrown away long ago. In the dining-room Sasha was sitting at the table drinking tea with the saucer poised on his five long fingers; Granny was laying out patience; Nina Ivanovna was reading. The flame crackled in the ikon lamp and everything, it seemed, was quiet and going well. Nadya said good-night, went upstairs to her room, got into bed and fell asleep at once. But just as on the night before, almost before it was light, she woke up. She was not sleepy, there was an uneasy, oppressive feeling in her heart. She sat up with her head on her knees and thought of her fiancé and her marriage. . . . She for some reason remembered that her mother had not loved her father and now had nothing and lived in complete dependence on her mother-in-law, Granny. And however much Nadya pondered she could not imagine why she had hitherto seen in her mother something special and exceptional, how it was she had not noticed that she was a simple, ordinary, unhappy woman.

And Sasha downstairs was not asleep, she could hear him coughing. He is a queer, naïve man, thought Nadya, and in all his dreams, in all those marvellous gardens and wonderful fountains one felt there was something absurd. But for some reason in his naïveté, in this very absurdity there was something so beautiful that as soon as she thought of the possibility of going to the university, it sent a cold thrill through her heart and her bosom and flooded them with joy and rapture.

"But better not think, better not think . . ." she whispered. "I must not think of it."

"Tick-tock," tapped the watchman somewhere far away. "Tick-tock . . . tick-tock. . . ."

III

In the middle of June Sasha suddenly felt bored and made up his mind to return to Moscow.

"I can't exist in this town," he said gloomily. "No water supply, no drains! It disgusts me to eat at dinner; the filth in the kitchen is incredible. . . ."

"Wait a little, prodigal son!" Granny tried to persuade him, speaking for some reason in a whisper, "the wedding is to be on the seventh."

"I don't want to."

"You meant to stay with us until September!"

"But now, you see, I don't want to. I must get to work."

The summer was grey and cold, the trees were wet, everything in the garden looked dejected and uninviting, it certainly did make one long to get to work. The sound of unfamiliar women's voices was heard downstairs and upstairs, there was the rattle of a sewing machine in Granny's room, they were working hard at the trousseau. Of fur coats alone, six were provided for Nadya, and the cheapest of them, in Granny's words, had cost three hundred roubles! The fuss irritated Sasha; he stayed in his own room and was cross, but everyone persuaded him to remain, and he promised not to go before the first of July.

Time passed quickly. On St. Peter's day Andrey Andreitch went with Nadya after dinner to Moscow Street to look once more at the house which had been taken and made ready for the young couple some time before. It was a house of two storeys, but so far only the upper floor had been furnished. There was in the hall a shining floor painted and parqueted, there were Viennese chairs, a piano, a violin stand; there was a smell of paint. On the wall hung a big oil painting in a gold frame - a naked lady and beside her a purple vase with a broken handle.

"An exquisite picture," said Andrey Andreitch, and he gave a respectful sigh. "It's the work of the artist Shismatchevsky."

Then there was the drawing-room with the round table, and a sofa and easy chairs upholstered in bright blue. Above the sofa was a big photograph of Father Andrey wearing a priest's velvet cap and decorations. Then they went into the dining-room in which there was a sideboard; then into the bedroom; here in the half dusk stood two bedsteads side by side, and it looked as though the bedroom had been decorated with the idea that it would always be very agreeable there and could not possibly be anything else. Andrey Andreitch led Nadya about the rooms, all the while keeping his arm round her waist; and she felt weak and conscience-stricken. She hated all the rooms, the beds, the easy chairs; she was nauseated by the naked lady. It was clear to her now that she had ceased to love Andrey Andreitch or perhaps had never loved him at all; but how to say this and to whom to say it and with what object she did not understand, and could not understand, though she was thinking about it all day and all night. . . . He held her round the waist, talked so affectionately, so modestly, was so happy, walking about this house of his; while she saw nothing in it all but vulgarity, stupid, naïve, unbearable vulgarity, and his arm round her waist felt as hard and cold as an iron hoop. And every minute she was on the point of running away, bursting into sobs, throwing herself out of a window. Andrey Andreitch led her into the bathroom and here he touched a tap fixed in the wall and at once water flowed.

"What do you say to that?" he said, and laughed. "I had a tank holding two hundred gallons put in the loft, and so now we shall have water."

They walked across the yard and went out into the street and took a cab. Thick clouds of dust were blowing, and it seemed as though it were just going to rain.

"You are not cold?" said Andrey Andreitch, screwing up his eyes at the dust.

She did not answer.

"Yesterday, you remember, Sasha blamed me for doing nothing," he said, after a brief silence. "Well, he is right, absolutely right! I do nothing and can do nothing. My precious, why is it? Why is it that the very thought that I may some day fix a cockade on my cap and go into the government service is so hateful to me? Why do I feel so uncomfortable when I see a lawyer or a Latin master or a member of the Zemstvo? O Mother Russia! O Mother Russia! What a burden of idle and useless people you still carry! How many like me are upon you, long-suffering Mother!"

And from the fact that he did nothing he drew generalizations, seeing in it a sign of the times.

"When we are married let us go together into the country, my precious; there we will work! We will buy ourselves a little piece of land with a garden and a river, we will labour and watch life. Oh, how splendid that will be!"

He took off his hat, and his hair floated in the wind, while she listened to him and thought: "Good God, I wish I were home!"

When they were quite near the house they overtook Father Andrey.

"Ah, here's father coming," cried Andrey Andreitch, delighted, and he waved his hat. "I love my dad really," he said as he paid the cabman. "He's a splendid old fellow, a dear old fellow."

Nadya went into the house, feeling cross and unwell, thinking that there would be visitors all the evening, that she would have to entertain them, to smile, to listen to the fiddle, to listen to all sorts of nonsense, and to talk of nothing but the wedding.

Granny, dignified, gorgeous in her silk dress, and haughty as she always seemed before visitors, was sitting before the samovar. Father Andrey came in with his sly smile.

"I have the pleasure and blessed consolation of seeing you in health," he said to Granny, and it was hard to tell whether he was joking or speaking seriously.

IV

The wind was beating on the window and on the roof; there was a whistling sound, and in the stove the house spirit was plaintively and sullenly droning his song. It was past midnight; everyone in the house had gone to bed, but no one was asleep, and it seemed all the while to Nadya as though they were playing the fiddle below. There was a sharp bang; a shutter must have been torn off. A minute later Nina Ivanovna came in in her nightgown, with a candle.

"What was the bang, Nadya?" she asked.

Her mother, with her hair in a single plait and a timid smile on her face, looked older, plainer, smaller on that stormy night. Nadya remembered that quite a little time ago she had thought her mother an exceptional woman and had listened with pride to the things she said; and now she could not remember those things, everything that came into her mind was so feeble and useless.

In the stove was the sound of several bass voices in chorus, and she even heard "O-o-o my G-o-od!" Nadya sat on her bed, and suddenly she clutched at her hair and burst into sobs.

"Mother, mother, my own," she said. "If only you knew what is happening to me! I beg you, I beseech you, let me go away! I beseech you!"

"Where?" asked Nina Ivanovna, not understanding, and she sat down on the bedstead. "Go where?"

For a long while Nadya cried and could not utter a word.

"Let me go away from the town," she said at last. "There must not and will not be a wedding, understand that! I don't love that man . . . I can't even speak about him."

"No, my own, no!" Nina Ivanovna said quickly, terribly alarmed. "Calm yourself - it's just because you are in low spirits. It will pass, it often happens. Most likely you have had a tiff with Andrey; but lovers' quarrels always end in kisses!"

"Oh, go away, mother, oh, go away," sobbed Nadya.

"Yes," said Nina Ivanovna after a pause, "it's not long since you were a baby, a little girl, and now you are engaged to be married. In nature there is a continual transmutation of substances. Before you know where you are you will be a mother yourself and an old woman, and will have as rebellious a daughter as I have."

"My darling, my sweet, you are clever you know, you are unhappy," said Nadya. "You are very unhappy; why do you say such very dull, commonplace things? For God's sake, why?"

Nina Ivanovna tried to say something, but could not utter a word; she gave a sob and went away to her own room. The bass voices began droning in the stove again, and Nadya felt suddenly frightened. She jumped out of bed and went quickly to her mother. Nina Ivanovna, with tear-stained face, was lying in bed wrapped in a pale blue quilt and holding a book in her hands.

"Mother, listen to me!" said Nadya. "I implore you, do understand! If you would only understand how petty and degrading our life is. My eyes have been opened, and I see it all now. And what is your Andrey Andreitch? Why, he is not intelligent, mother! Merciful heavens, do understand, mother, he is stupid!"

Nina Ivanovna abruptly sat up.

"You and your grandmother torment me," she said with a sob. "I want to live! to live," she repeated, and twice she beat her little fist upon her bosom. "Let me be free! I am still young, I want to live, and you have made me an old woman between you!"

She broke into bitter tears, lay down and curled up under the quilt, and looked so small, so pitiful, so foolish. Nadya went to her room, dressed, and sitting at the window fell to waiting for the morning. She sat all night thinking, while someone seemed to be tapping on the shutters and whistling in the yard.

In the morning Granny complained that the wind had blown down all the apples in the garden, and broken down an old plum tree. It was grey, murky, cheerless, dark enough for candles; everyone complained of the cold, and the rain lashed on the windows. After tea Nadya went into Sasha's room and without saying a word knelt down before an armchair in the corner and hid her face in her hands.

"What is it?" asked Sasha.

"I can't . . ." she said. "How I could go on living here before, I can't understand, I can't conceive! I despise the man I am engaged to, I despise myself, I despise all this idle, senseless existence."

"Well, well," said Sasha, not yet grasping what was meant. "That's all right . . . that's good."

"I am sick of this life," Nadya went on. "I can't endure another day here. To-morrow I am going away. Take me with you for God's sake!"

For a minute Sasha looked at her in astonishment; at last he understood and was delighted as a child. He waved his arms and began pattering with his slippers as though he were dancing with delight.

"Splendid," he said, rubbing his hands. "My goodness, how fine that is!"

And she stared at him without blinking, with adoring eyes, as though spellbound, expecting every minute that he would say something important, something infinitely significant; he had told her nothing yet, but already it seemed to her that something new and great was opening before her which she had not known till then, and already she gazed at him full of expectation, ready to face anything, even death.

"I am going to-morrow," he said after a moment's thought. "You come to the station to see me off. . . . I'll take your things in my portmanteau, and I'll get your ticket, and when the third bell rings you get into the carriage, and we'll go off. You'll see me as far as Moscow and then go on to Petersburg alone. Have you a passport?"

"Yes."

"I can promise you, you won't regret it," said Sasha, with conviction. "You will go, you will study, and then go where fate takes you. When you turn your life upside down everything will be changed. The great thing is to turn your life upside down, and all the rest is unimportant. And so we will set off to-morrow?"

"Oh yes, for God's sake!"

It seemed to Nadya that she was very much excited, that her heart was heavier than ever before, that she would spend all the time till she went away in misery and agonizing thought; but she had hardly gone upstairs and lain down on her bed when she fell asleep at once, with traces of tears and a smile on her face, and slept soundly till evening.

V

A cab had been sent for. Nadya in her hat and overcoat went upstairs to take one more look at her mother, at all her belongings. She stood in her own room beside her still warm bed, looked about her, then went slowly in to her mother. Nina Ivanovna was asleep; it was quite still in her room. Nadya kissed her mother, smoothed her hair, stood still for a couple of minutes . . . then walked slowly downstairs.

It was raining heavily. The cabman with the hood pulled down was standing at the entrance, drenched with rain.

"There is not room for you, Nadya," said Granny, as the servants began putting in the luggage. "What an idea to see him off in such weather! You had better stop at home. Goodness, how it rains!"

Nadya tried to say something, but could not. Then Sasha helped Nadya in and covered her feet with a rug. Then he sat down beside her.

"Good luck to you! God bless you!" Granny cried from the steps. "Mind you write to us from Moscow, Sasha!"

"Right. Good-bye, Granny."

"The Queen of Heaven keep you!"

"Oh, what weather!" said Sasha.

It was only now that Nadya began to cry. Now it was clear to her that she certainly was going, which she had not really believed when she was saying good-bye to Granny, and when she was looking at her mother. Good-bye, town! And she suddenly thought of it all: Andrey, and his father and the new house and the naked lady with the vase; and it all no longer frightened her, nor weighed upon her, but was naïve and trivial and continually retreated further away. And when they got into the railway carriage and the train began to move, all that past which had been so big and serious shrank up into something tiny, and a vast wide future which till then had scarcely been noticed began unfolding before her. The rain pattered on the carriage windows, nothing could be seen but the green fields, telegraph posts with birds sitting on the wires flitted by, and joy made her hold her breath; she thought that she was going to freedom, going to study, and this was just like what used, ages ago, to be called going off to be a free Cossack.

She laughed and cried and prayed all at once.

"It's a-all right," said Sasha, smiling. "It's a-all right."

VI

Autumn had passed and winter, too, had gone. Nadya had begun to be very homesick and thought every day of her mother and her grandmother; she thought of Sasha too. The letters that came from home were kind and gentle, and it seemed as though everything by now were forgiven and forgotten. In May after the examinations she set off for home in good health and high spirits, and stopped on the way at Moscow to see Sasha. He was just the same as the year before, with the same beard and unkempt hair, with the same large beautiful eyes, and he still wore the same coat and canvas trousers; but he looked unwell and worried, he seemed both older and thinner, and kept coughing, and for some reason he struck Nadya as grey and provincial.

"My God, Nadya has come!" he said, and laughed gaily. "My darling girl!"

They sat in the printing room, which was full of tobacco smoke, and smelt strongly, stiflingly of Indian ink and paint; then they went to his room, which also smelt of tobacco and was full of the traces of spitting; near a cold samovar stood a broken plate with dark paper on it, and there were masses of dead flies on the table and on the floor. And everything showed that Sasha ordered his personal life in a slovenly way and lived anyhow, with utter contempt for comfort, and if anyone began talking to him of his personal happiness, of his personal life, of affection for him, he would not have understood and would have only laughed.

"It is all right, everything has gone well," said Nadya hurriedly. "Mother came to see me in Petersburg in the autumn; she said that Granny is not angry, and only keeps going into my room and making the sign of the cross over the walls."

Sasha looked cheerful, but he kept coughing, and talked in a cracked voice, and Nadya kept looking at him, unable to decide whether he really were seriously ill or whether it were only her fancy.

"Dear Sasha," she said, "you are ill."

"No, it's nothing, I am ill, but not very . . ."

"Oh, dear!" cried Nadya, in agitation. "Why don't you go to a doctor? Why don't you take care of your health? My dear, darling Sasha," she said, and tears gushed from her eyes and for some reason there rose before her imagination Andrey Andreitch and the naked lady with the vase, and all her past which seemed now as far away as her childhood; and she began crying because Sasha no longer seemed to her so novel, so cultured, and so interesting as the year before. "Dear Sasha, you are very, very ill . . . I would do anything to make you not so pale and thin. I am so indebted to you! You can't imagine how much you have done for me, my good Sasha! In reality you are now the person nearest and dearest to me."

They sat on and talked, and now, after Nadya had spent a winter in Petersburg, Sasha, his works, his smile, his whole figure had for her a suggestion of something out of date, old-fashioned, done with long ago and perhaps already dead and buried.

"I am going down the Volga the day after tomorrow," said Sasha, "and then to drink koumiss. I mean to drink koumiss. A friend and his wife are going with me. His wife is a wonderful woman; I am always at her, trying to persuade her to go to the university. I want her to turn her life upside down."

After having talked they drove to the station. Sasha got her tea and apples; and when the train began moving and he waved his handkerchief at her, smiling, it could be seen even from his legs that he was very ill and would not live long.

Nadya reached her native town at midday. As she drove home from the station the streets struck her as very wide and the houses very small and squat; there were no people about, she met no one but the German piano-tuner in a rusty greatcoat. And all the houses looked as though they were covered with dust. Granny, who seemed to have grown quite old, but was as fat and plain as ever, flung her arms round Nadya and cried for a long time with her face on Nadya's shoulder, unable to tear herself away. Nina Ivanovna looked much older and plainer and seemed shrivelled up, but was still tightly laced, and still had diamonds flashing on her fingers.

"My darling," she said, trembling all over, "my darling!"

Then they sat down and cried without speaking. It was evident that both mother and grandmother realized that the past was lost and gone, never to return; they had now no position in society, no prestige as before, no right to invite visitors; so it is when in the midst of an easy careless life the police suddenly burst in at night and made a search, and it turns out that the head of the family has embezzled money or committed forgery - and goodbye then to the easy careless life for ever!

Nadya went upstairs and saw the same bed, the same windows with naïve white curtains, and outside the windows the same garden, gay and noisy, bathed in sunshine. She touched the table, sat down and sank into thought. And she had a good dinner and drank tea with delicious rich cream; but something was missing, there was a sense of emptiness in the rooms and the ceilings were so low. In the evening she went to bed, covered herself up and for some reason it seemed to her to be funny lying in this snug, very soft bed.

Nina Ivanovna came in for a minute; she sat down as people who feel guilty sit down, timidly, and looking about her.

"Well, tell me, Nadya," she enquired after a brief pause, "are you contented? Quite contented?"

"Yes, mother."

Nina Ivanovna got up, made the sign of the cross over Nadya and the windows.

"I have become religious, as you see," she said. "You know I am studying philosophy now, and I am always thinking and thinking. . . . And many things have become as clear as daylight to me. It seems to me that what is above all necessary is that life should pass as it were through a prism."

"Tell me, mother, how is Granny in health?"

"She seems all right. When you went away that time with Sasha and the telegram came from you, Granny fell on the floor as she read it; for three days she lay without moving. After that she was always praying and crying. But now she is all right again."

She got up and walked about the room.

"Tick-tock," tapped the watchman. "Tick-tock, tick-tock. . . ."

"What is above all necessary is that life should pass as it were through a prism," she said; "in other words, that life in consciousness should be analyzed into its simplest elements as into the seven primary colours, and each element must be studied separately."

What Nina Ivanovna said further and when she went away, Nadya did not hear, as she quickly fell asleep.

May passed; June came. Nadya had grown used to being at home. Granny busied herself about the samovar, heaving deep sighs. Nina Ivanovna talked in the evenings about her philosophy; she still lived in the house like a poor relation, and had to go to Granny for every farthing. There were lots of flies in the house, and the ceilings seemed to become lower and lower. Granny and Nina Ivanovna did not go out in the streets for fear of meeting Father Andrey and Andrey Andreitch. Nadya walked about the garden and the streets, looked at the grey fences, and it seemed to her that everything in the town had grown old, was out of date and was only waiting either for the end, or for the beginning of something young and fresh. Oh, if only that new, bright life would come more quickly - that life in which one will be able to face one's fate boldly and directly, to know that one is right, to be light-hearted and free! And sooner or later such a life will come. The time will come when of Granny's house, where things are so arranged that the four servants can only live in one room in filth in the basement - the time will come when of that house not a trace will remain, and it will be forgotten, no one will remember it. And Nadya's only entertainment was from the boys next door; when she walked about the garden they knocked on the fence and shouted in mockery: "Betrothed! Betrothed!"

A letter from Sasha arrived from Saratov. In his gay dancing handwriting he told them that his journey on the Volga had been a complete success, but that he had been taken rather ill in Saratov, had lost his voice, and had been for the last fortnight in the hospital. She knew what that meant, and she was overwhelmed with a foreboding that was like a conviction. And it vexed her that this foreboding and the thought of Sasha did not distress her so much as before. She had a passionate desire for life, longed to be in Petersburg, and her friendship with Sasha seemed now sweet but something far, far away! She did not sleep all night, and in the morning sat at the window, listening. And she did in fact hear voices below; Granny, greatly agitated, was asking questions rapidly. Then some one began crying. . . . When Nadya went downstairs Granny was standing in the corner, praying before the ikon and her face was tearful. A telegram lay on the table.

For some time Nadya walked up and down the room, listening to Granny's weeping; then she picked up the telegram and read it.

It announced that the previous morning Alexandr Timofeitch, or more simply, Sasha, had died at Saratov of consumption.

Granny and Nina Ivanovna went to the church to order a memorial service, while Nadya went on walking about the rooms and thinking. She recognized clearly that her life had been turned upside down as Sasha wished; that here she was, alien, isolated, useless and that everything here was useless to her; that all the past had been torn away from her and vanished as though it had been burnt up and the ashes scattered to the winds. She went into Sasha's room and stood there for a while.

"Good-bye, dear Sasha," she thought, and before her mind rose the vista of a new, wide, spacious life, and that life, still obscure and full of mysteries, beckoned her and attracted her.

She went upstairs to her own room to pack, and next morning said good-bye to her family, and full of life and high spirits left the town - as she supposed for ever.